THE
CUTTHROAT
COUNTESS

Also by Minerva Spencer

Dangerous

Barbarous

Scandalous

Notorious

Outrageous

Infamous

The Boxing Baroness

The Dueling Duchess

And read more Minerva Spencer in

The Arrangement

THE CUTTHROAT COUNTESS

MINERVA SPENCER

KENSINGTON
PUBLISHING CORP.

www.kensingtonbooks.com

KENSINGTON BOOKS are published by

Kensington Publishing Corp.
119 West 40th Street
New York, NY 10018

Special book excerpts or customized printings can also be created to fit specific needs. For details, write or phone the office of the Kensington Sales Manager: Kensington Publishing Corp., 119 West 40th Street, New York, NY 10018. Attn. Sales Department. Phone: 1-800-221-2647.

The K with book logo Reg US Pat. & TM Off.

ISBN: 978-1-4967-3814-1 (ebook)

ISBN: 978-1-4967-3813-4

First Kensington Trade Paperback Printing: November 2023

10 9 8 7 6 5 4 3 2 1

Printed in the United States of America

For Brantly, my favorite person in the world

Part I

France

Chapter 1

France
March 1815

Elliot lost count of the number of times the three men hit him.

Whenever he slipped into unconsciousness, one of them threw a bucket of freezing water on him and shook him until he awakened.

And then they started hitting him all over again and asking the same question:

À qui rapportez-vous?

Who do you report to?

Elliot always gave one of three answers, always in impeccably accented French:

I don't know what you mean.

I report to nobody.

You must have mistaken me for somebody else.

It had been going on for days. Today, for some reason, the men seemed angrier.

"We are running out of patience, you English bastard!" A fist connected with Elliot's jaw and slammed him to the side, turning everything gray and hazy.

Rough hands shook his shoulders until his teeth rattled. "Wake up, you pig!"

Elliot's eyelids felt weighted down with lead, a fact he was grateful for; he didn't want to see what the men did to him next.

A voice pushed through the thick fog: "Should I hit him again?"

"Too much more hitting and he won't talk at all," a different voice said, the words followed by loud, raucous laughter and yet another jaw-cracking punch.

White, agonizing explosions blossomed inside his skull like lethal chrysanthemums.

And then darkness . . .

"Smithy?"

The voice—low, calm, and feminine—insinuated itself through the fog as gently as the weak light of dawn breached the darkness.

It was the first voice in days that hadn't been accompanied by pain.

"*Smithy*. You need to wake up."

Elliot could only force one eye to open.

The sight that met his gaze was a filthy face fringed with ragged strands of gray hair. A stranger's face.

He squinted and then gasped at the ache the action caused, his head throbbing and his eye watering as he stared.

"It's me—Jo," the stranger hissed.

Jo?

Only the eyes gave her away, because that was something she couldn't hide: pale, opalescent eyes that he would have known any-where.

"Why, if it isn't Josephine Brown," Elliot teased, or at least tried to. But his voice came out a cracked wheeze, his jaw too swollen to form the words correctly.

"Can you walk?" Jo asked, her face and voice expressionless.

Elliot gave a rusty laugh. "I'll bloody well walk out of here."

Jo—or Blade, as she was known by just about everyone at Farn-ham's Fantastical Female Fayre, the circus where they both worked—helped Elliot into a sitting position and then draped his arm over her shoulder and kept hold of his wrist. "On three we're going to stand," she murmured. "One . . . two . . . three."

They pushed up together, although Elliot had to admit it was more Jo's effort than his own that propelled him to his feet.

His head felt like a bowl full of liquid that had been set spinning, sloshing, and pitching so violently that he was surprised nothing leaked out his ears.

"Can you stay upright?" she whispered.

Barely.

"Yes, I'm good," he lied.

She shifted her shoulder and tightened her grip on his wrist. "Ready?"

No.

"Yes," he lied again. "But you'll have to guide me, as I seem to have some trouble seeing."

Rather than answer, she took a step.

Elliot's stomach joined his head, both pitching and sloshing now, but in different directions. It reminded him of his unpleasant journey across the Channel on the way to France—a memory he could easily do without.

The first step was the worst, but the next one wasn't much better. After ten steps, he was shivering, rivulets of sweat running down his skin, his muscles were spasming so badly it was impossible to control his legs. He staggered against her, almost knocking her off her feet.

Shame joined nausea as she struggled to keep them both upright and moving. "I'm sorry," he muttered. "You should just leave me, Jo. I'll only slow you down."

She didn't answer or even acknowledge that she'd heard him. Instead, she kept walking, her slim, strong body bearing more of his weight with each step.

Just five more steps, he ordered his body.

After four more steps, they paused so she could open a door.

A body lay on the ground. Elliot noticed the worn bottom of boots first, and then the man they were connected to. It was one of his captors, the one who'd always smiled while beating him. He wasn't smiling now—at least not his mouth. Instead, he looked surprised, eyes wide and unseeing, the slash across his throat a gruesome red grin.

Jo guided him over the man's body, saying only, "Lift your feet."

He obeyed, eager to put the corpse behind them. He'd hated his tormentor but couldn't bring himself to rejoice at the sight of his mutilated body.

"Almost there," Jo said.

Elliot ordered his limbs to cooperate, to help her, but the next time he tried to pick up his foot, his opposite knee buckled.

Jo gave a muffled grunt and sagged under his weight, but she didn't fall. "Just a little bit more, Elliot."

He blinked at the sound of his Christian name on her tongue. How did she know it? He'd never told her his real name; he'd told everyone at the Fayre to call him *Smithy*.

Elliot was so intrigued by the mystery that he took a few steps without even realizing he was moving.

"Fifteen more steps to the door," she said. "You can do it. Just fifteen."

Elliot closed his eyes and counted in his head. *One, two, three, four—*

Somewhere between five and nine, he must have lost consciousness; her voice jolted him awake. "You have to hold on to me, Elliot. Only four more."

One, two, three, four.

He forced his eyes open when he noticed they were still walking. "That's four. Why are we—?"

"I lied," Jo said. "Keep going. You can do it."

Elliot snorted weakly and kept walking, but he was no longer lifting his feet.

"Take his other arm," Jo said.

Elliot's eyelids lifted slightly at her low, sharp command. "I don't know what you—"

A hand—far bigger than Jo's—took his free arm, and a second set of shoulders slid beneath, somebody taller and far broader than Jo.

Elliot was just conscious enough to feel mortified that he'd not even heard the newcomer's approach.

"We've got steps now, Elliot, so you'll need to lift your feet."

Steps?

Elliot blinked rapidly, struggling to keep the darkness at bay, and lifted one foot; this time both his legs gave out.

A male voice cursed in French and said, "Let him go and I'll carry him, Blade."

Burly arms shifted him, positioning Elliot's body as if he were a doll. He gave a hoarse yelp when his feet abruptly left the ground, and up suddenly became down. An arm clamped around his thighs, and a hard shoulder pressed against his midriff.

This time, when the blackness came for him, Elliot welcomed it.

Chapter 2

Josephine Brown—or at least that was the name she'd been using for the last eight months—stared down at the Honorable Elliot Wingate, foreign and unnerving emotions churning inside her as she studied his handsome but badly abused face.

Jo had already deviated from her very well-paid job by stopping to rescue him. Instead of staring at his sleeping face, she should be hundreds of miles away.

Leave him, hen, Mungo's voice hectored. *Ye've already done more than enough for him. Ye cannae allow anythin' to get between you and your mission.*

Jo couldn't argue that Elliot had interfered with her current *mission*—as Mungo had grandiosely called their services—but it hadn't sat right with her to leave him in the hands of his brutal captors.

It had been foolish, reckless, and dangerous to steal Elliot away from the Red Cats—a militia that flourished in the war-torn French landscape, preying on terrified provincials.

While the men who'd been torturing and questioning Elliot were not part of the army, the French government often paid coin for the information the Red Cats stumbled on while they were raping and pillaging their way across the unprotected French countryside.

Regardless of what Elliot was really doing in France, a British

Home Office agent would likely fetch a handsome price. Elliot's future would have been beyond bleak—and probably very brief—if Jo and her small cadre of ruffians hadn't liberated him. Not that it had taken much skill or stealth, thanks to the fact that the Red Cats were too fond of spirits and whores to set more than one guard over the cell where Elliot had been held.

They'd been working on the slim, wiry Englishman for five days, and he'd not broken yet, a fact which had impressed Jo as much as it horrified her. But she knew far too much about torture and how effective it was; Elliot would have eventually given the men all the information they wanted, no matter how good an agent he was.

And once the Red Cats had established his identity, it would have been one short step to linking Elliot to Farnham's Fantastical Female Fayre and then to the woman Jo was supposed to be protecting: Marianne Simpson.

So, Jo could claim that by rescuing Elliot, she had taken care of a small problem before it could blossom into a much larger one that would threaten her mission.

Ye ken that yer interest in the man cannae come to anything, lass, Mungo's voice persisted, just as he would have persisted if he'd still been alive. Not that Jo had been idiotic enough to develop such a *tendre* in the years she'd been with Mungo.

I think the word yer lookin' for is obsession, *hen.*

Jo rolled her eyes. *Fine,* obsession.

Mungo had made sure they'd never lived in any one place long enough.

We must keep moving.

It had been his mantra, and the two of them had lived by it for most of Jo's twenty-eight years. Or at least as long as she could remember.

She was still living by it, even though Mungo was now gone.

He'd been dead almost six months, and the pain of loss was still as sharp as the edge of any of the six knives currently secreted on her person.

Elliot groaned and shifted on the bed, his eyes fluttering open.

His gaze flicked around the room, his forehead furrowing. Finally, his eyes settled on Jo. The tension seemed to drain from his body, and his face—taut only seconds before—softened slightly; although features that were as sharp and angular as Elliot Wingate's could never look soft.

"I thought I dreamed you," he said in a raspy voice.

Jo's heart sped at his words. And then her face heated when she realized he didn't mean that the way it had sounded—not that he'd *dreamed* of *her*. But that he'd dreamed his escape.

"How long?" he asked when she remained silent.

"Three days."

His eyes widened, and he winced. Although the black eye had lost a great deal of its prior swelling, Jo knew it must hurt.

"Where are we?"

"Not far from Charleville."

The tension returned in an instant. "The men who had me were based—"

"They won't find you," she assured him quietly. "I sent my people out to lead them on a wild goose chase. We're safe here for the moment."

He sighed. "Thank you."

Jo nodded, using the tail of her shirt to wipe the oil from the blade she'd been sharpening.

Elliot's gaze dropped to the knife, the flicker of emotion in his eyes so quick and subtle that she almost didn't catch it: he was recalling the body of the Red Cat she'd dispatched when she'd rescued him.

He was remembering that she'd committed murder to free him.

"Don't worry," she said. "He's not dead because of you."

He looked away from the knife and met her eyes.

"I could have knocked him out, but I didn't. I wanted to kill him, and I'd do the same thing again given the chance." Not just for what he'd done to Elliot, but also for the trail of innocent victims all the Red Cats had left behind them over the years.

Elliot inhaled deeply, as if he need a lot of air for what he had to say.

But before he could speak, there was a tapping at the room's tiny window. Her raven, Angus, was standing on the sill. Jo lifted the sash, and he hopped inside.

"There's a good fellow," she crooned, taking a small lump of sugar from her pocket and offering it to him. Jo rarely gave the bird sweets, but he'd done a great deal of flying over the past three days and deserved a treat.

Angus made a soft *quork, quork* and fluffed his feathers—his polite way of demanding petting—while delicately taking the sugar from her fingers.

Jo scratched his neck ruff and turned back to Elliot, waiting for whatever he'd been working himself up to say—judgment, condemnation? Or—unlikely—gratitude?

But the tension had leaked out of him, and he was merely watching her and Angus with interest.

It worried Jo how glad she was that he'd decided to let the matter of the murdered Red Cat be, but she was skilled at shoving such concerns aside. Instead, she said, "Marianne and the others are only about four or five days ahead of us."

"How do you know that?"

"Angus just told me."

Elliot snorted softly.

Jo dug around in her boiled leather satchel and removed an apple, a heel of bread, and a chunk of cured ham. When she placed the food on the rickety table, Angus wasted no time helping himself to the meal.

Jo turned back to Elliot. "Angus left early this morning, and it's now almost nightfall. His instruction was to follow the road, and I can make a close guess about how far he went based on how long he was gone and how hungry he is. It's not precise, but the time of his return tells me where they are within a day."

"What does his appetite have to do with measuring the distance?"

"He's hungry, which means he didn't stop to feed anywhere.

Sometimes it can take him hours to find something to eat. Again, it's not an exact science."

"It's Marianne you are protecting, isn't it? Somebody has hired you."

Jo didn't bother asking how he knew that; it was his job to know such things. Elliot Wingate was one of His Majesty's spies, working in one of those secretive departments in the Home Office that most people had never heard of.

"I'm not doing such a grand job protecting her right now," Jo pointed out wryly.

"You've fallen behind because you helped me."

"I had some other matters to attend to that took me out of the way." Not as much out of the way as rescuing Elliot, but there was no point in making him feel guilty.

"I should get up and"—he pushed back the covers and then yanked them up again. "Er, or perhaps not. It appears I'm naked."

"Your clothes stank and weren't worth saving." Jo could see by his expression that he took her meaning. His cheeks darkened, although—in her opinion—there was no shame in soiling oneself when one had undergone days of excruciating torture.

"Who undressed me?" he asked, twin bright spots of color staining his high, blade-sharp cheekbones and standing out on his pale skin even though there were so many bruises and cuts.

"I did." Jo turned away to give him a moment to collect his shattered pride. She dug another apple from her bag and slipped a knife from her boot, quickly peeling, coring, and quartering the apple before re-sheathing her knife.

When she turned, Elliot was still flushed, but no longer discomposed.

She offered him the peeled fruit.

"Thank you," he said, taking one piece.

"I peeled it for you; take it all."

Jo wiped her hands on her breeches and gestured to his left hand. "Can you manage a sandwich if I make one?"

He stared silently at the two smallest fingers, which Jo and Etienne had straightened and splinted while he'd been unconscious. He'd screamed during the horrible procedure but, thankfully, he hadn't woken up.

"I suppose you did this, too?"

She nodded.

"Thank you again," he murmured, flexing his three free digits and only wincing slightly. "Yes, I can hold food."

Jo busied herself making a sandwich rather than gazing at the object of her fascination, something she'd done far too much of over the past few days. She should have been guilty about how much she'd enjoyed undressing him. After all, he'd been bruised, lacerated, and filthy—like an Old Master painting that had been defiled by vandals. But even all that abuse hadn't been enough to hide his magnificent physique. Elliot Wingate wasn't big or brawny, but elegant sleekness and toned efficiency. He was, in Jo's opinion, masculine perfection.

Not that her opinion mattered, of course.

"I must be holding you back," he said.

Jo shrugged.

"I know you're following Marianne and the three wagons that are traveling with her," he continued, "but I don't know *why*."

Jo smirked faintly at his pained tone. For a man whose duty it was to gather information, such an admission must rankle.

He snorted softly. "You aren't going to tell me."

It wasn't a question, so she didn't answer. Instead, she gave Angus a chunk of cheese before rewrapping the rest.

Once she'd poured a glass of buttermilk from an earthenware jug, she turned and carried both it and the sandwich to Elliot.

"I hope you like buttermilk," she said.

"I do, although I've not had any since I was a boy." He took the sandwich. "Thank you. I seem to be saying that a great deal."

Jo ignored his thanks. "I'm leaving tomorrow morning. I'll pay for the room for the next week and give you enough money to make your way back home."

He lowered the sandwich without taking a bite. "I'll be going with you."

Rather than argue, Jo just allowed her eyes to roam down his supine body and then back up. By the time she reached his face, it was flaming, and his lips were compressed in a thin, stern line.

"You needn't worry that I'll slow you down," he assured her.

"I'm not worried. I just don't want you with us." That was both a lie and the truth; Jo wanted him to come with her, but it wasn't something that she *should* want.

"Don't sugarcoat it for me," he said wryly. "You might not want me along, but you can either take me with you or I can trail behind you. We're heading in the same direction with the same goal in mind."

Jo doubted that but didn't argue. Instead, she shrugged and said, "Fine."

Once again, he appeared nonplussed, this time by her easy acquiescence.

"Unfortunately, I'll need to borrow money from you. The Red Cats took everything I had—including my horse, obviously. But I've got more money stashed in our caravan."

He meant the caravan that he and two of his friends—both aristocrats—had been using while pretending to be workers in Farnham's Fantastical Female Fayre.

Elliot had managed to blend in as an employee, but his two aristocratic companions—the Duke of Staunton and the Marquess of Carlisle—had been as conspicuous as tropical parrots among a flock of pigeons.

Jo knew the men had come to France to rescue the duke's brother. She also knew that Elliot was likely acting without the approval of his employer, the Home Office, jeopardizing his job to help out his two friends.

Angus suddenly flew the short distance across the room to Elliot's bed, landing on the blankets near his hip.

Elliot made a surprised sound but otherwise didn't move.

It was Jo's turn to be startled; Angus rarely showed any interest in people.

"He must want some of your sandwich," she said.

But when Elliot broke off a piece and handed it to the bird, Angus ignored the food. Instead, he fluffed up his feathers.

Jo gave a snort of disbelief.

Elliot cut her a questioning glance. "What should I do?"

"I think he wants you to pet him," Jo admitted grudgingly.

Elliot lifted one eyebrow in surprise and then tentatively reached for the bird. His split, swollen lips curved into a smile when Angus began to purr just like a cat, a noise he'd learned to mimic from the two mousers who lived in the London theater that housed the all-female circus.

Jo narrowed her eyes at her bird, but Angus refused to meet her gaze.

Angus and Jo had been together almost eight years, and not once had Angus showed any interest in another person. Not even Mungo, whom he'd tolerated, but had never begged for attention.

Just why was her reserved raven suddenly showing affection to the very same man Jo was trying—and failing miserably—to resist?

Chapter 3

Jo was impressed.

In the ten days since they'd left Charleville, not only had Elliot managed to keep up with her small cadre, but he'd earned a place in the hierarchy when he'd demonstrated his superlative intelligence-gathering skills. He was shockingly good at ferreting out information, and he somehow managed to do so without anyone noticing.

"It's as if the man can blend right into whatever chair he sits in," Jean-Louis had told Jo upon returning from a reconnaissance expedition to an inn in the tiny village of Mouzon. "I thought he'd left the tap room entirely, and yet there he was, sitting among a group of six or seven locals, as if he were one of them." His expression had been one of awe and respect.

After that, Jo had sent Elliot off on his own to comb the area and ensure that Baron Strickland's private army wasn't any larger than her initial information had suggested.

The men who'd held Elliot captive—a militia called the Red Cats led by a man named Broussard—were the very same ones that Strickland, Jo's quarry, was using.

Elliot had discovered Broussard had been paid to capture him, although whoever had paid Broussard hadn't given the brutal militia leader his real identity.

Jo was almost certain that Broussard's employer was Baron Dominic Strickland, the man responsible for not only luring Marianne on this journey, but also the three aristocratic men who'd traveled with the circus.

Elliot and his two friends had traveled to Europe in response to a ransom demand from Strickland—who claimed to be holding the Duke of Staunton's brother captive.

Privately, Jo didn't think that Strickland had the duke's brother, a man who'd gone missing while gathering intelligence for Wellington, himself. She believed Staunton's brother had died over a year ago in an undercover military engagement that had gone awry. Jo could have told the duke why she suspected that and perhaps saved him and his two friends the journey to France, but that wasn't part of her job.

Neither is taking Mr. Wingate along, is it, hen?

Jo rolled her eyes at phantom Mungo. She'd made peace with herself when it came to Elliot Wingate. Rescuing him from Broussard's men hadn't required much time or effort, and it hadn't knocked her schedule off course, either. She'd still get to Strickland in plenty of time to make sure Marianne was safe. She'd also collect the incriminating documents and other articles her employer had paid her to retrieve.

Everything was fine.

Everything was going according to plan.

Arriving on Strickland's doorstep any earlier than she'd planned would just mean there would be more opportunities for exposure. Baron Strickland wasn't a fool; he'd have people monitoring activity around Himmelhaus Castle and the tiny Prussian village that serviced it. If Jo and her crew showed up too soon and lingered in the area, they would immediately draw attention.

She finished sharpening her favorite knife, tested the balance, and then slid it into one of the sheaths in her boots.

"Hungry?"

Jo looked up to find Monique, one of her group's four operatives—five, now, counting Elliot—standing in front of her, holding out a bowl of steaming soup.

"*Merci*," Jo murmured.

She ate her supper, idly watching the others but not joining in with their conversation, which was—not surprisingly—about Napoleon Bonaparte's recent escape from Elba.

The four French nationals and Elliot were engaged in a lively debate about the recent Treaty of Alliance against Napoleon that the Coalition Powers had ratified only days before. War was imminent, that much was clear. When and where the powder keg would explode—and who would be victorious—was a matter of dispute.

Jo was surprised that two of her four French employees were royalists while two were sympathetic to Bonaparte's cause, if not his chances of defeating the allied powers. She had worked with all four of them for years and had never known their political alignment. Elliot had been with them only days and already was more closely acquainted than she'd ever be.

Friends are for other people, hen.

Jo sighed at her father's voice. *Yes, Mungo, I know.*

Just because she wasn't allowed friends didn't mean she couldn't listen in and enjoy the spirited debate.

"Bah!" Jean-Louis snorted, deriding Arlette's support for Napoleon's promises of constitutional reform. "His back is to the wall; so of course he will promise anything and everything to gather support."

Monique nodded her head in support of her colleague and lover while topping up everyone's tin cups with more wine.

"The fifth and seventh follow him—even Ney, who once said Bonaparte should be paraded through Paris in a cage—not because of what he promises them, but because we've all had a taste of life beneath the Bourbon coward." This from Arlette, who handed her unfinished bowl of stew to her husband, Etienne, a mountain of a man who seemed to eat constantly and yet never get full.

"What do you think, Smithy?" Etienne asked Elliot, who was

methodically polishing off his second bowl of stew. He, too, ate a prodigious amount, although it never seemed to accumulate anywhere on his whipcord-lean body. "Will Bonaparte deliver on his promises?"

Elliot wiped his mouth with his cuff before answering. "It's possible, but there are other concerns on people's minds right now. All his efforts will necessarily be focused in another direction before any great changes can be made at home."

Jean-Louis nodded. "The Bourbon coward left him very little army to work with. He'll have his hands full raising troops. Promises of reform are nothing but a sop."

Etienne, Jean-Louis, Arlette, and Monique were not the only operatives Jo had worked with over the years. Jo and Mungo's jobs had taken them as far west as Lisbon and—one time—all the way to Moscow. Her father had built networks of efficient and skilled associates from one end of Europe to the other, and Jo had, for the most part, inherited those connections.

Of course, things had changed as the war dragged on. People disappeared, died, or joined one army or another—often without wishing to do so—and many of her former associates were no longer available. She'd been relieved to discover that these four, who'd been favorites, were still alive, well, and at liberty.

Jo lifted the last spoonful of stew to her mouth and was considering having a second bowl when Elliot sat down on the log beside her.

She gave him a questioning look.

"Could we take a stroll? I need to talk to you about something," he said in a voice so quiet she could barely hear it. She glanced at the others, but their calm discussion had heated, and they didn't appear to be paying Jo or Elliot any mind.

Jo nodded and stood. Angus, who'd been dozing on a dead tree nearby, sat up, his black eyes glinting in the light of the fire, waiting for Jo's signal that he should follow. When she didn't call him, he tucked his head back beneath his wing and resumed his slumber.

By nature, ravens were diurnal, but Angus had gradually adapted his sleeping pattern to Jo's, especially since she'd been working at the Fayre, and he often stayed up far later than a raven in the wild would do. But even wild ravens could be alert for short periods of time at night when necessary.

Of course, the things that Angus deemed *necessary* weren't always what Jo considered important. Like the time a cat had wandered into a tree where he was sleeping. Angus had woken, alerted by some sixth sense that a predator was nearby. A sleeping bird was easy prey for the average housecat, but a roused raven—at close to two pounds in weight—was a nightmare for a feline even four times Angus's weight.

The unfortunate tabby had spent probably the longest, most miserable, night of its life trapped in the tree while Angus had relentlessly toyed with it, chasing it up and down the tree and from one branch to another, refusing to allow it to escape.

Jo could have stopped him, of course, but far be it from her to interfere when Angus was teaching a lesson.

She followed Elliot away from the campfire and toward the horses, which were picketed near a tiny stream that would better be called a rill.

"Do you mind if I smoke?" he asked, lifting a small, dark cigar.

"No," she said, taking a seat on a nearby stump and watching while he took a flint and strike plate from his pocket and lit his cigar.

Mungo, too, had enjoyed *blowing a cloud*, as he called it. A habit he'd picked up while serving in the Americas.

Elliot tilted his head back, his eyes briefly closed and an expression of near bliss on his face before he slowly exhaled a ghostly silver stream of smoke.

He gave her a slightly embarrassed smile. "Sorry, it has been some time since I've enjoyed one of these."

"My uncle used to love them," she said, more than a little surprised by her uncharacteristic volunteering of information.

Yer chatty because ye want him to linger.

Jo wanted to argue with the accusation but knew it was true.

"Oh?" he asked, leaning against a tree, only half of his face illu-minated by the moon, which was waxing gibbous and bathing every-thing in a silvery-blue light. "Was your uncle a military man?"

"Why do you ask?"

"Just a guess. Is he the one who raised you?"

Jo knew that Elliot would have investigated her background every bit as much as she'd investigated his when they'd been in Lon-don. Because he was employed by the Home Office—although she wasn't exactly sure which agency—his resources would be much bet-ter than hers.

"I think you know who raised me," she countered. A ribbon of smoke drifted toward her, and she inhaled it deeply, the smell re-minding her of Mungo.

Elliot's teeth flashed. "I know the official story—the one in your file."

Jo pondered his disclosure for a moment. What was he trying to do by admitting that he knew who she was and that their govern-ment had investigated her actions in the past? Gain her trust? Warn her? To what purpose?

"What makes you think there is an unofficial story?"

"Just a hunch."

"Out of curiosity, what is the official story?" she asked.

"Why don't you tell me?"

Jo couldn't help smiling at his caginess. "The only story I know is the real one," she lied. "I was born and raised on a farm in York-shire until I was twelve. The farm burned to the ground and killed my parents and brothers and sisters—everyone but me. I escaped death because I'd sneaked out to look at the new foal that had been born that day. My uncle Mungo Brown—my only relative other than my aged grandparents—had recently been discharged from the army, and he took charge of me. He worked doing odd jobs, which meant we traveled from place to place."

He nodded slowly, taking another deep draw from his cigar. "Yes, that is what the official version says."

"But?" she prodded.

"But it leaves me wondering where you learned all your, er, blade skills."

Jo wasn't surprised that Elliot knew the story—he was a government agent, after all. She also wasn't surprised that he'd seen through the flimsy tale, which was one that Mungo—who was actually her father, not her uncle—had concocted years ago, for reasons of his own.

Jo had always believed her father's caution had been excessive and unnecessary. But then, a few months before Mungo's death and right after they'd moved to England, both of them had been brought in for questioning by some men working for an agency that fell under the aegis of the Home Office. The reason for the interrogation was a job they'd done for the British Navy three years earlier. It had amazed Jo that the men who'd questioned her had no clue that Jo and Mungo had been working for a British admiral at the time. Mungo had often mentioned how greedy—and frustrating—the government could be about sharing information, but not until that interrogation—which had become quite ugly and lasted over two weeks—had she fully understood just how little the left hand knew what the right hand was doing.

Thankfully the investigation had withered on the vine for lack of information or proof. Jo had known that if things became serious—meaning if the government had decided to actually charge her and Mungo, rather than detain them—there would have been no appealing for help to the admiral they'd worked for. They'd known when they'd taken the job that the admiral would disavow any knowledge of them or their mission. If they had been charged, there would have been nobody to intervene on their behalf.

Although it bothered Jo that Elliot believed she was the same sort of self-serving mercenary as the man they were heading toward—Dominic Strickland—she had no way to prove to him that she wasn't a traitor and that they were working for the same side.

But then, Jo was accustomed to having her actions viewed in the harshest of lights.

Elliot traced a pattern in the dirt with the toe of one boot before turning to her and saying, "The official story also leaves me wondering how you and your . . . uncle . . . managed to meet associates like those by the fire if you spent your formative years in Britain."

Jo wasn't surprised that he was skeptical of her flimsy story.

"Is there a point to this conversation?" she asked.

"You mean other than finding out the truth about you?"

"Why does that matter?"

"Because I like to know who I've thrown my lot in with."

"You're free to leave at any time."

"I don't want to leave. And I'm sorry if what I'm saying sounds . . . suspicious."

"Aren't you suspicious?" she asked, allowing her exasperation to show. "We risked our lives to get you out of Broussard's hands. Shouldn't that tell you I'm not the villain your associates at the Home Office seem to think I am?"

It wasn't light enough for her to see whether he was blushing at her words, but she recognized the expression of regret that flickered across his normally impassive face.

"I read your file, Jo. I know the evidence they had about your activities in Paris in 1812. It was—"

"Damning."

"Very. I don't want to believe what that evidence points to."

"You mean treason?" She snorted and went on before he could answer. "Would my word suffice to convince you, Elliot?"

"Yes."

His lack of hesitation was both reassuring and startling. "Really? You'd take my word that I'm not a traitor?"

"I would."

"I can't tell you that I haven't sold information to French government officials."

His face went hard and taut.

"But I *can* tell you that none of it was harmful to any of our soldiers."

His brow furrowed in perplexity, and Jo didn't blame him. Unfortunately, she wasn't at liberty to clear up his confusion.

"Why are you asking me this right now?" she asked.

"I have my reasons."

"I take it the main *reason* is that you have some information you'd like to pass along but are worried I'll interfere. You doubt I can be trusted?"

"Something like that."

She tried not to let his words sting, but they did. "If you are looking for a courier, there is somebody in Metz I can recommend."

His lips parted slightly, and he stared, his pupils huge in the low light. Finally, he nodded. "Thank you. I'll take you up on that."

"Anything else?" she asked, getting to her feet.

"As a matter of fact, there is."

Elliot had never stared into the eyes of another human being and understood that person less than he did at that moment. Josephine Brown—or whatever her name might really be—was the opaquest person he'd ever met.

That should have made him extremely suspicious of her.

Instead, he inexplicably trusted her. Of course, that might be the result of his cock leading his brain, because he'd trusted her even before she'd given him her word and even before she'd rescued him from certain torture and death.

For whatever reason, he simply could not believe that she was betraying her country, regardless of the government file he'd read that contained evidence to the contrary.

Elliot trusted her, and he desperately wanted some trust in return.

"I want to know what the plan is," he said.

"Plan?" she repeated.

He recognized this particular response she often employed—looking befuddled and repeating words, which usually made the person talking to her either give up in frustration or volunteer information they'd had no intention of sharing.

Elliot knew that because he'd watched it happen time after time, people underestimating Jo and thinking she was slow-witted or too much of a bother to try and understand.

"Yes, the plan involving Marianne?" he explained, even though he knew that *she* knew what he'd meant. "What are we doing hanging back several days behind the rest of the group? I know we could have caught up ages ago. If you're protecting her, then why aren't you with her? If you know Broussard is after Marianne, then why not warn her and the others? Sin and Guy could help us catch Broussard and stop him."

Her lips curled into a smile so faint and fleeting that Elliot doubted he'd really seen it.

"I guess I can tell you the *plan*," she said. "At least the part that pertains to you and your two friends. Perhaps you'd like to tell me about them?"

Elliot snorted. "I suspect you already know everything there is to know."

"I know Staunton is going to meet up with Dominic Strickland because he believes the baron is holding his brother captive."

"Yes, that about sums it up," Elliot said. "Did Marianne tell you that?"

"No."

Elliot wanted to ask her how the hell she knew about Staunton's brother, but it didn't really matter at this point. Instead, he asked, "Since you appear to know so much, do you know if Strickland really has Benjamin?"

Her mocking expression was replaced by something that looked like regret. "Staunton's brother died in that skirmish last year—regardless of the fact that nobody found his body—just as the authorities reported."

He made a noise of disbelief. "How long have you known about that, Jo?"

"A while," she admitted.

"And you didn't think it was worth telling Sin that his brother isn't really alive?"

She shrugged. "I have no proof of what I know. Or do you think he would have just taken a strange woman's word on the matter?"

"Perhaps he might have, if you were compelling enough. And then he wouldn't have needed to come on this journey at all, and Marianne wouldn't be forced to confront her former lover."

"That second point is debatable—Strickland would have used whatever tool he needed to get Marianne in his grasp. As it happened, the tool he chose to use was your friend."

"Which brings me back to my first point," he persisted. "That you should have spared Sin the mental anguish and a dangerous journey."

"I'm sorry, but that's not what I'm being paid to do."

"It would have been the humane thing to do."

She stared for a long moment, and just when he thought she was going to ignore his comment, she said, "If it wouldn't have interfered with my job, I would have told Staunton about his brother. But I couldn't tell him; my first loyalty is to my employer. I couldn't interfere or Baron Strickland might have known that somebody was aware of what he was up to. The person who is paying me wants to recover incriminating documents from Strickland. If he gets wind that I know what he is doing, he might go to ground, and the information I want will go with him."

"What sort of documents?"

"Don't worry, none of it relates to spying or selling secrets." She paused and then said, "You work for the government in sensitive situations. You know that sometimes you must do things you don't like in order to reach your objective."

"The end justifies the means."

"Just so," she said. "Now, as to why I'm hanging back? Strickland didn't just hire Broussard and his gang to capture you; he paid Broussard to bring a quarter of his militia—which is somewhere around twenty-five men—with him. The baron, for some reason, wants a private army. He must be paying well, because Broussard isn't just taking any riffraff, he's collecting the most skilled men he can find—not to mention the most brutal and conscienceless."

"So why don't we stop him *now*, before he has assembled his vicious little army."

"We'll stop him—don't worry about that—but if I am too hasty *now* word will reach Strickland, and then he will—"

"Go to ground and take whatever information you want with him," Elliot finished.

"Yes."

He flicked the butt of his cigar into the stream, sending sparks arcing through the air. "So we're watching and waiting while a dangerous man like Broussard gathers other dangerous men and converges on our friends."

"Yes."

He gave a bitter laugh. "Need I mention this is a *dangerous* game you are playing, Jo?"

"No, you don't need to mention that." She pushed off the tree she'd been leaning against and closed the distance between them before saying, "One, this isn't a game to me; it's what I do for a living. And two"—she gave him a smile that showed more than a few teeth—"I'm more dangerous than Broussard and Strickland put together."

Chapter 4

Elliot watched as the young woman dressed in boys' clothing scampered away from the grove of trees where Jo had brought him to meet the girl.

"She's a child," he said, unable to take his gaze off the girl, Fabian, who'd arrived bare-footed and dressed in rags.

"She's twenty," Jo said with a hint of amusement in her voice.

"She has no *shoes*."

Jo laughed, and Elliot turned to stare at her.

"What?" she said.

"I've never heard you laugh before."

"Well, you won't be able to say that again, will you?" she shot back.

He snorted and fell into step beside her as she started walking the short distance back to the village. They'd left Jean-Louis at the only inn the area boasted while the other three went off for several days, doing God knows what. Elliot had learned not to ask what activities Jo's employees were engaged in. Or at least he'd learned not to expect an answer.

"So," he said, "are we headed to Metz in the morning?" The date of the meeting—the one between Dominic Strickland and Marianne and Elliot's friend Sin—had crept up on them and was only a few days away.

"I'm going to Metz in the morning, but you'll head out with Jean-Louis and join Etienne, Arlette, and Monique along the way."

"Along the way to where?"

"Strickland's base of operations is a castle called Himmelhaus, and it's about a day and a half away from the meeting place."

"You've known where he is all this time?" he asked, allowing his annoyance to show.

"No, not *all* this time. That was what Etienne found out on his last foray—when he intercepted a messenger Broussard sent to Strickland."

"Won't Dominic notice if there is no message or response?"

"Don't worry, Strickland received a message; it just wasn't the same one that Broussard sent. Nor was it the same messenger."

Elliot didn't want to ask what had happened to the man after Etienne was finished with him. He'd already seen evidence of Jo's ruthlessness the night she rescued him.

"You said that *I* would go meet up with the others. You're coming with us, right?" he asked.

"No, I've got to take care of Broussard first, and after that I'm going to where Marianne and Sin will meet up with Dominic."

"Wait, you're going *alone*? And what do you mean *take care of*?"

She gave a huff of exasperation. "Just do what I tell you and go with Jean-Louis."

Elliot reached out for her shoulder, only intending to stop her so they could conduct this conversation face-to-face.

One minute she was striding along, and the next she was holding the blade of a knife beneath his chin, the tip barely touching him.

"Stand down!" he hissed through clenched teeth, not wanting to open his jaw and risk impalement. He raised his hands in the universal gesture of surrender.

Jo stared at him, her gaze strangely flat. As he watched, she came back from wherever she'd been, seeming to realize what had happened.

Irritation flashed across her face as she lowered the hand holding the knife. "Don't ever surprise me like that again."

Elliot realized his own hands were still raised and lowered them—slowly.

"What did you want?" she asked, ramming her knife so hard into one of the reinforced sheathes sewn into her breeches that he was surprised it didn't tear through the leather.

"I wanted to ask you why you're heading off alone?"

"Because."

"Because," he repeated flatly.

"Yes, because. I am the employer, and I decide who goes where and when. You are the employee, and you do what I tell you."

"But you don't pay me."

Her brow furrowed at that.

Elliot struck while she was pondering her response. "You're going to go and *take care of* Broussard and his band of ruffians and then go to where Strickland—a known traitor and suspected murderer—will be meeting the others, alone."

"Yes."

"No." Elliot crossed his arms.

Her pale eyebrows, the color of goose down, arched high. "I beg your pardon?"

"I said *no*. I'm not employed by you, and I don't have to obey your orders. I will accompany you because, believe it or not, you might just need a bit of help while you set out to dispense with upwards of thirty French mercenaries."

"There won't be thirty men—just a few at most."

"*Just a few*," he repeated, shaking his head and briefly casting his gaze skyward. "I'm going with you."

She inhaled deeply, the very image of a woman who was pushed to the limit of her patience by male stupidity. And then she exhaled in a rush and said, "Fine."

Elliot blinked. "Er, what?"

"I said *fine*."

"Fine what?"

"Fine, you can come along. Now, are we done here?"

"Ye—"

He didn't even get the one-syllable word out before she turned and resumed her determined striding.

"I let you come along, but *you* wait *here*," Jo whispered, her eyes not on Elliot but flickering over the cottage where Broussard and three of his men—along with several working women—had holed up for the night.

They were the first words she'd spoken to him in hours, and when Elliot didn't answer, she turned to him, eyebrow raised.

Jaws gritted and mouth pressed into a thin line, Elliot looked like a man who wanted to argue, but he just nodded.

Jo left him shielded by a big olive tree and crept toward the back of the cottage, where a privy stood near a shed in which the mercenaries had stabled their nags.

Jo and Mungo had briefly seen—from a safe distance—Luc Broussard a half dozen times over the years, and she'd heard stories of the devastation he and his men had wrought on those who'd had the misfortune to find themselves in his path.

This was the first paying job Jo had taken that actually involved Broussard—a bonus, in her opinion—and she'd been keeping an eye on him for weeks, waiting for her chance to cut the head off the snake.

Not only were Broussard and his men greedy, vicious, and cruel, but they were remarkably poorly mounted. Indeed, for men whose lives and livelihood relied on horseflesh, she was disgusted by how little money and effort they put into maintaining healthy, sturdy mounts. Nor did any of them ever practice their marksmanship skills, and most of them were either too corpulent to walk more than a quarter of a mile without being winded or—like Broussard—skinny to the point of emaciation, thanks to a life of dissipation.

Jo and her small band could probably have successfully ambushed Broussard's entire army when they converged on Himmelhaus, but taking care of matters before they even got underway would be far less messy and would also keep the bulk of the mercenaries far away from Marianne.

She only had to wait a quarter of an hour before one of the men came outside. Like the pigs they were, he didn't bother using the privy for its purpose. Instead, he opened his breeches and pissed against the wall of the cottage.

Jo was almost on top of him when a twig snapped—she'd been hasty and clumsy and cursed herself for it. If the man had just turned around rather than fumbling with his breeches, he might have put up a struggle. As it was, his hesitation gave her plenty of time to slip her hands around him—one over his mouth, the other drawing a quick, deep slash across his throat—before he could utter so much as a grunt of surprise, although he did thrash a great deal.

He was far too heavy and violent for her to keep upright, so she released him and let him fall to the ground, staring down into his wide, frantic gaze as the life left his eyes. He opened his mouth, but the wound across his throat ensured no words or sounds came out. Jo waited until his movements were sluggish, and then she slid her hands beneath his upper arms and started dragging him.

She'd only gone a few feet when Elliot appeared and, without being asked, took the man's bootheels and lifted, halving her burden.

"Where to?" he whispered.

She jerked her head toward the nearby woodshed rather than behind the stable. It was her experience that horses often became restless if they scented blood.

Once they'd laid the body behind the haphazardly stacked firewood, Jo returned to her post behind the privy, Elliot following noiselessly on her heels.

She was tempted to tell him to get back in the woods, but the truth was, he might come in handy.

Don't let yer pride get in yer way, hen.

Indeed, no.

They leaned against the small stone structure and waited.

"Do you plan on killing all of them—even the women?" he asked after a few moments, his voice tense.

"No, I'll send the women back to the village on foot—it's only two miles, and the night is fair. But the men? Yes. I'm going to kill every last one of them. If you have a problem with that, you should leave. Now."

He opened his mouth and then shut it.

The moon was almost full, and she could see him clearly. His judgmental expression sent a spike of rage through her body.

"These same men set six houses on fire in a village not far from Cambray, all because the people there refused to pay them for *protection*—from *them*. When the occupants tried to escape the fire, the Red Cats drove the husbands and children back inside with bullets, allowing only the women to escape. By the time the women realized that their loved ones were trapped and tried to run back inside, it was too late. I'm sure you can imagine the night those women endured in the company of their three dozen captors. After raping them all night long, they killed them. Six women, two men—the other husbands were off fighting for the glory of France—and *seventeen* children died that night. So, yes, Elliot—I will kill as many of Broussard's men as I can. My only regret is that I can't take longer and make them suffer more."

Elliot was just returning from escorting one of the women toward the road—she'd come outside after a second man had stumbled out to search for the first—when the back door opened yet again and Broussard himself stepped out of the house.

Elliot could see from the Frenchman's unsteady stance that he'd been drinking heavily.

"Have you two idiots fallen down the hole?" Broussard called out with a rude laugh and then took a few more unsteady steps and peered into the shadows. "Oliver? Gulli—"

Only the faint hiss of air and flicker of silver announced the blade that sank with a quiet *thud* into Broussard's chest. He made a sound remarkably like a chicken's squawk and reflexively grabbed at his heart, yelping when his hand jostled the knife.

A second and third blade followed in rapid succession, the final knife actually pinning Broussard's hand to his chest.

The light from the open doorway wavered as the last man ran outside, drawn by his leader's cry, shirtless and clutching his breeches with one hand, a pistol in the other.

"Broussard!" he shouted, running to his commander, his head swiveling to and fro, the gun in his hand whipping wildly from side to side.

Broussard collapsed against him, and the pistol discharged as another knife flew from the shadow behind the privy. This blade struck the newcomer with enough force that it knocked him back a step.

Some part of Elliot's brain pointed out that he was just standing there while Jo Brown systematically executed two more men.

Another far more clinical part pointed out that he would only get in the way if he tried to do anything. The woman was a killing machine, an angel of retribution, and she didn't need any help from him.

The second man fell to the ground, and the air was full of gurgling, gasping, and muttering for a long moment.

Two more women in dishabille ran from the house, and screams split the night.

Elliot strode toward the thrashing men and kicked aside the pistol before turning to the women.

"Get back inside," he said, softly but firmly, in French.

The woman who wasn't screaming recovered her wits first, grabbed her friend's arm, and yanked her so hard she almost pulled her off her feet.

Elliot closed the door behind them and turned.

Jo was kneeling beside Broussard and calmly removing her knives, wiping them clean using his shirt before sheathing them.

Broussard reached for her hands, but his movements were not only drunken now, but those of a man who couldn't see clearly, and he grabbed weakly at air.

Jo ignored his pitiful grasping and moved to the second man.

He was losing a great deal of blood but might have survived with treatment.

Jo pulled out the knife in his chest and flicked the blade across his neck, the movement so quick Elliot only knew what she'd done when the gaping smile opened in the man's throat.

She cleaned the blade, stood, and turned to him.

Elliot closed his mouth.

"Without Broussard or his two lieutenants, the others won't know where to go or what to do—he never trusted any of his men enough to share such details. He was too concerned they'd kill him and take the job for themselves," she explained. "Now we don't have to worry about Strickland's private army dogging us every step of the way."

Elliot couldn't argue with that assessment.

Jo headed toward the road, striding back the way they'd come.

"You don't want to bury the bodies?"

"No. Let them be a message to anyone who sees them."

Elliot blinked at that. "What about the women?" he called after her.

"They'll be fine. You'd better leave them in the house. Unless you want them to get another look at your face."

Elliot hesitated, but decided she was right. The two whores would have a tense evening, but they'd be safe inside and could leave when it was light.

He had to jog to catch up to Jo as they made their way back to where they'd tied their horses. His mind raced even faster than their feet as he reflected on the events of the past hour. She'd killed four men, quickly, efficiently, and without hesitation. Aside from the dubious morality of her actions—something Elliot simply couldn't bring himself to think about right then—he had to admit that she truly hadn't needed help from him.

Elliot could have gone on ahead with the others and he would never have known what happened. Right now he would be blissfully ignorant of what she was capable of.

He was ashamed to admit that he wished he'd done exactly that.

You knew she had killed at least one man when she freed you from Broussard's torturers.

That was true. But knowing something and watching it happen were two *very* different matters.

"Have you ever killed a man?"

His head whipped around at the quiet words. Jo was staring straight ahead, her profile distant and perfect and starkly beautiful in the moonlight.

"No," he admitted. He'd always considered himself fortunate that he'd not had to kill in the furtherance of his duties.

"You think what I did back there was wrong—that I'm a monster."

Elliot gave her question the consideration it deserved before answering. "In a way, it is justice—of a Biblical sort."

"But *you* think what I did was wrong."

"I think we could have resolved the matter with fewer bodies."

She snorted. "You think we should just let rapists and murderers go free to continue their path of destruction?"

"No, of course I don't. But I think we might have turned them over to what passes for authority in this area."

This time she didn't merely snort, she laughed, but there was no amusement in the sound.

Elliot deserved her derision; France was a country ravaged by decades of war, and it was currently staggering toward yet another conflict.

"Broussard and his men are the only *authority* in this area," she said, quite correctly. "Or at least. they were."

"Another man will rise up and take Broussard's place."

"Undoubtedly. But he will be somebody else's problem to manage."

They trudged in silence until they reached the small outbuilding where they'd left their horses and few possessions. Although the weather had been pleasant the last few weeks, they usually tried to find covered shelter, even if it was only a shack.

This barn was well-maintained and housed two oxen, a milk cow, a few goats, and a horse stall that was a home to a dozen laying hens. It was filled with fresh, sweet hay—pitchforked into place by Elliot's own hands—and was obviously cleaned regularly.

The farmer had been willing to give them a place to bed down in exchange for a few sous and the aforementioned pitchforking. The house was far enough away from the barn that they'd been able to come and go without too much oversight.

Elliot lit the lantern that hung outside and then opened the door. Once they were inside, he hung the light on the post farthest from the hay.

Jo reached for the buttons on her coat and scowled when her hand came away bloody.

"If you want to wash, I brought in water before we left." Elliot gestured to the large wooden bucket not far from their bedrolls.

She shrugged out of the ragged, patched garment and tossed it aside before examining the rest of her clothing.

Jo, like the other two women, preferred dressing as a man. Elliot couldn't blame them. The work they did was difficult and dangerous enough for a man; doing their jobs in skirts wouldn't just be inconvenient, it would be madness.

Jo suddenly turned to him. "Are you going to turn me in when we return home? Report me for murder?"

His mouth opened in surprise, both at her words and her hostile expression. "No, I'm not."

"That makes you complicit in murder."

"I can live with that."

"I might do some things you *can't* live with when we reach Himmelhaus."

"What are you trying to say, Jo?"

"That you should go home and let me finish this. You don't need to worry about Sin and Guy; I promise I will make sure your friends return to England safe and sound."

Her tone wasn't dismissive so much as weary; so weary.

Elliot took a step toward her. The light was behind him and allowed him to see her eyes clearly. Her pupils had shrunk down to pinpricks in the lanternlight, exposing her unusual irises. From a distance, they were a uniform gray, but up close, they ran the spectrum from slate to the silver of newly minted coins—hundreds of shades of gray, the outer edge the darkest shade of all.

"I think I'll just tag along, if you don't mind," Elliot said, his gaze dropping to her mouth when she released a sigh, her pale pink lips parting slightly.

"What are you doing, Elliot?" she asked, her voice softer than he'd ever heard it, almost breathless.

That's when Elliot realized he'd leaned even closer. He could feel the *thud, thud, thud* of his heart and the blood rushing through his veins.

He wrenched his gaze from her mouth.

Tendrils of her shockingly pale hair danced in the moonlight, as if celebrating their success in escaping the ugly knitted cap she wore to conceal her crowning glory.

She reached up and brushed the hair away, her fingers tapered and elegant despite the ragged nails and myriad cuts and scars.

Elliot gorged on the sight of her, feasting on her cool beauty and the perfection of her narrow, aquiline nose, high, sharp cheekbones, and skin so pale he could see a faint tracery of blue veins at her temples.

"I like the way you say my name," he said, his voice harsh—like a man who was dying of thirst. And he *was* thirsty; there was only one thing that could slake his thirst.

"What do you want from me?" she asked, her voice even lower than usual. She swallowed, the gulping sound loud in the heavy silence of the night.

Elliot didn't know what time it was, but it was late—that time of the night when bad ideas somehow seemed like good ones.

"You, Jo," he said. "I want you."

Maybe Elliot moved closer; maybe Jo did.

Either way, the result was the same.

Chapter 5

Jo had imagined what Elliot would feel like dozens upon dozens of times: muscle and bone and sinew; lithe, hard, and coiled.

He was all that and more as his body pressed against hers, his heat and strength almost shocking in the cool night air.

"Jo," he murmured against her lips, and then his mouth covered hers, and her restraint snapped.

She slid her hands around his neck, molding her body against his as she opened to him.

Jo had been kissed before—she'd done that and more—but never like this. Never with both heat and skill and reverence, his lips soft but firm, his heart pounding against hers, fast and hard. His mouth was hot and sweet, and he tasted slightly botanical, like rosemary, sprigs of which she'd seen him chewing on more than one occasion.

His hands framed her face as he pulled away, his eyes twin pools of black, his lips parted, his expression wondrous. "You have ensorcelled me."

More than his words, it was his tone and hungry gaze that affected her, robbing her of speech—what did a person respond to such a comment? Jo had always favored actions above words, and so she claimed his mouth.

He opened to her without prodding, his tongue hot and slick.

His clothing and hair smelled of campfires and horse, leather and crisp night air—how was it that she'd never noticed the night smelled so much different from the day?

Jo was vaguely aware of labored breaths snatched between kisses, as if neither of them could bear to part long enough to properly fill their lungs.

As though they might come to their senses if they came up for air.

Their hands met between their bodies as they toed off their boots. Again, it wasn't clear who opened the first button, shrugged off the first coat, waistcoat, or shirt.

Elliot drew back and sank to his knees on one of the bedrolls they'd used the night before. His? Hers? What did it matter?

He stared up at her as his hands went to the catches on her breeches, his own already puddled on the floor. His body was so lean and hard, it looked carved from marble as he knelt before her, his arousal jutting up thick and stiff from a nest of dark curls.

Elliot pulled down both her breeches and small clothes, lifting her feet one after the other to liberate the tangle of garments, nudging her legs wider in the process.

Their eyes locked for one long, charged moment as he slid his hands slowly, deliberately, up her thighs, until his fingers delved into her private curls.

His eyes lowered, and they both watched as he spread her lips with his thumbs, opening her to his gaze.

"My God, you're beautiful," he muttered, and then lowered his hot wet mouth over her sex.

It was Jo's turn to groan as his tongue explored and caressed, light and teasing, until she slid her fingers into his hair and pulled him closer, positioning him the way she wanted and sliding her legs wider to give him better access.

His eyes flickered up to meet hers, and he gave her a quick, smug smirk before he took her aching bud in his mouth.

Jo's body shook with desire as soft lips closed on that most sensitive part of her and he tongued and nibbled and sucked her toward bliss.

Elliot caught her when her knees turned to water and laid her out on the blanket, one hand lightly stroking her belly in soothing circles.

Jo opened her eyes to find him watching her, a slight smile on his swollen lips.

"Did I fall asleep?"

"Just for a minute." He was on his side, his head propped in his hand, his other hand still resting low on her stomach, the smallest finger resting over her mound like a promise.

"I wanted you from the moment I first saw you," he said.

Heat bloomed low in her abdomen, and his hand firmed over the thin skin, as if he could feel the tumult his words had caused inside her.

"I wanted *this*." He slid a finger between her sensitive, swollen folds, his nostrils flaring as he stroked, careful not to touch her too-sensitive bud. "You're so perfect."

Jo swallowed hard, her own breathing turning jerky and uneven at the hunger in his gaze. Her eyelids lowered as he breeched her, his entry eased by her body's slickness, but the invasion still stretching her channel. It had been a long time—not since that hellish time in Paris almost four years before—since she'd had a man inside her.

He hummed with pleasure as he pumped her, slowly but deeply, baring his teeth as he hissed out a breath. "You're so tight; I want to feel you."

Jo spread her thighs wider in silent invitation.

He withdrew his hand, his gaze pinning her as he took his slick finger into his mouth and licked it clean, his lean cheeks hollowing as he sucked.

Jo vibrated with want, her empty sheath clenching on nothing, the contractions sending teasing ripples of desire to every part of her.

"Please," she whispered, lifting her hips toward him like an offering. "I want you."

She didn't have to ask twice.

Moving with the effortless grace that defined him, Elliot positioned himself at her entrance and pressed against her, his slick flesh feverishly hot as he penetrated her with one long thrust.

Jo whimpered at the almost painful stretching sensation but hooked her feet around his thighs and tilted her pelvis to take him that last bit deeper.

He held her, full and pinned, for a long moment, his soft, adoring gaze at odds with the primitive, dominating act.

"You feel so good, Jo," he murmured, his hips beginning to pulse, gently at first, filling her completely with each thrust, their eyes locked as he stroked into her body.

Jo squeezed and relaxed, finding a rhythm.

"Yes," he groaned, propping himself on one arm so he could push his hand between them, his thumb caressing the source of her pleasure, his touch like magic. "Will you come for me again, Jo?"

Such erotic words coming from a man as reserved as Elliot were an astounding aphrodisiac, and Jo cried out and exploded, her climax catching her by surprise.

Elliot's hips drummed faster and faster, working her with a savage rhythm, and then—suddenly—he withdrew, leaving her shockingly empty.

Jo was vaguely aware of his grunt of surrender and hot, wet splashes on her belly, her inner muscles contracting around nothing. Even as the sentient part of her regretted his loss, she couldn't help being grateful that he'd thought of her even as *la petite mort* claimed them both.

Jo fell asleep again.

Elliot couldn't help smiling; he'd never had a lover who dropped off right after coitus. He felt a sense of pride, although he suspected her ease in sleeping was a result of exhaustion and the strain of leadership rather than his astounding sexual skills.

He sat back on his heels to admire her for a moment before he got up. His mouth watered at the sight of her small, plump breasts and their tight pink nipples, both of which he'd done no more than caress before plunging into her like a man crazed by lust.

Well, it had been a while—almost a year—since his last lover, so he'd brought considerable hunger to the table, but then so had she.

He'd been relieved to discover she wasn't a maiden. Indeed, their lovemaking would have ended at kissing if she'd given any indication of inexperience. Elliot might be starving for her—obsessed by her, to own the truth—but he drew the line at deflowering virgins.

In sleep, she looked even younger than her twenty-eight years. During most of their journey, she'd disguised her striking hair color and beautiful face with generous lashings of dirt and ash, which she rubbed into her hair, turning it a flat grayish shade. Elliot knew from experience how few people wanted to get close to a truly filthy individual, and he'd used the technique himself more than a few times over the years.

Yesterday, after they'd arrived at the barn, she had disappeared for an hour and then returned so clean and sparkling and beautiful that he'd gawked like a yokel.

Her cheeks had darkened the longer he'd stared. "The stream isn't so cold right now," she'd said, wincing as she attempted to yank a comb through her hair.

He'd taken her words as a hint. Indeed, he'd smelled more than a bit ripe and had been grateful to bathe away the accumulated grime and grit of weeks on the road.

Elliot suspected that they'd both resume their dirt disguises again tomorrow, so he refused to feel guilty about gorging on the sight of her passion-flushed body and silky blond hair tonight.

She was not voluptuous, but sleek and firm, her delicate bone structure held together with streamlined, elegant muscles. As pale as her hands and face were, they'd been darkened by the sun; the rest of her body was the color of fresh cream.

Jo Brown's beauty was an understated, elegant sort. If she'd been born in another life and time, she might have graced the canvases of painters like Watteau or Reynolds, although she lacked the theatrical playfulness of the former's models or the coy helplessness of the latter's.

She was an intriguing contradiction—sylphlike yet strong, fragile yet fierce.

She shifted restlessly and her eyes opened, a flash of abject terror flickering across her face like sunlight glancing off water.

"Is something wrong?" she demanded, sitting bolt upright.

"Shh," he soothed. "Nothing is amiss. I'll be right back," Elliot murmured, giving her a moment to collect herself while he fetched yesterday's drying cloth and dipped it into the bucket of cool water.

When he returned, she'd propped herself up on her elbows and was gazing at her stomach, where evidence of his lust had pooled.

Elliot's ears and face heated as he knelt beside her. "I would have cleaned you earlier, but I didn't want to wake you. This might be a little chilly," he warned, lowering the damp towel to her belly, pleased that she was allowing him to tend to her.

She watched him through inscrutable eyes as he cleaned and then dried her. Once he'd finished, he tossed the cloth away and lifted the corner of the blanket.

"Come here," he said.

She hesitated a second but then moved beneath the covering and made no comment when Elliot joined her, even though they had a second set of blankets already laid out from the night before.

Once again, he rested on his side and reached for her slowly. He laid a hand on her waist, pleased and surprised when she didn't pull away.

"Jo? Are you—"

"I'm fine," she said, her voice toneless. "This didn't mean anything."

Her curt dismissal should have hurt, but the bluntness of it was strangely amusing. He laughed softly. "Duly noted."

She turned to him, her expression as flat as her tone had been. "I mean it."

"I know you do." Elliot was either fearless or brainless or both, because he risked stroking her smooth, flat belly, feeling as if he were petting a dangerous jungle cat. "Just relax and let's enjoy the moment, shall we? Tomorrow—and the days that follow—won't leave much time for pleasure of any sort."

Her body tensed beneath his caressing, but she didn't pull away. Or pull a knife on him.

Finally, after what felt like ten minutes but was probably only ten seconds, she gave a slight nod, her taut muscles relaxing.

Emboldened, Elliot continued his circular stroking, increasing the circumference until his fingers brushed not only her mound, but the silky undersides of breasts.

Instead of gutting him, she arched her back slightly, thrusting against his palm.

"I won't ask who you really are or where you really come from," he promised softly. "But I want to know how long you've been doing this sort of work alone."

Her jaw flexed and her belly tightened as she stared at him. "Is this for you? Or your employers?"

Elliot considered her question. "You're right to ask. I have no intention of sharing any information about you, but if my superiors asked—"

"You would answer them," she finished but didn't sound angry about it.

"Yes."

Her brow furrowed slightly, and her gaze went vague, as if she were consulting somebody or something that wasn't in the room with them. He thought a struggle of sorts was taking place inside her and honestly expected nothing from her when she opened her mouth and said, "It's been six months since my uncle died."

Jo was astounded to hear the words come out of her mouth. Not only that, but she felt physically exhausted from the effort of speaking them—as if she'd been caught in some sort of invisible grasp and had suddenly broken free. The sensation was a wrenching one, as if the moon had suddenly escaped the earth's gravitational pull.

She couldn't help smiling at the dramatic analogy, although it was true that the words she'd just spoken were among the first she'd ever shared about her life.

More than two decades of living with Mungo had bent her into a fixed position, like a tree defined by the direction of the wind.

To go against the wind wasn't easy.

So why had she suddenly cast off the training of a lifetime now? Was it merely because of their physical proximity? Something as basic as human contact, his hand on her abdomen, the warmth of his body alongside her? The pleasing recollection of his body filling and stretching hers?

Jo refused to believe it was that simple. She'd had lovers before— more than a few—and had never shared so much as her name with any of them. Mungo had never said anything about what she'd done, but she knew he'd guessed at the furtive encounters she'd engaged in over the years.

But Elliot Wingate was different from those other men.

He'd said earlier that he'd wanted her from the very first time they'd met. She knew exactly what he was talking about, because she'd felt it, too—a powerful, instant attraction that had left her dizzy and confused and worried by its intensity. She could only think the feeling was extremely rare. At least *she'd* never experienced anything like it before.

Objectively Jo knew Elliot wasn't the handsomest man she'd ever seen or the richest or most powerful, but he epitomized every-thing that she respected and liked about the masculine sex: he was in-telligent, competent, controlled, and humane. He was kind, but not weak. He was practical, but not emotionless.

"What happened to your uncle?" he asked, his hand stilling, the tip of his thumb resting against the underside of her breast.

Once again, everything inside her rebelled against telling him anything—certainly not the truth—but what difference did it make at this point?

"It was an accident—the sort of freak occurrence that couldn't happen again even if a person tried to engineer it," Jo said, for once speaking the entire truth.

All her life, Mungo had feared a violent death at the hands of his enemies. In the end, his death had been the result of an unlucky twist of fate.

"He was walking down a street when a wagon passed by and its gate broke, allowing a half dozen barrels to escape. One of them rolled over the wreckage and onto the walkway. The barrel itself wouldn't have done more than deliver a few bruises and scrapes—perhaps a broken toe—but it missed my uncle and struck a man holding a rope that was lifting a pallet of lead roof tiles. He lost his grip and the pallet fell; my uncle died instantly, his head crushed."

Elliot's arm slid around her waist, and he pulled her close. "I'm sorry," he murmured into her hair, his lips pressing against her scalp. "That is dreadful."

It would be dreadful for anyone, but it was especially horrific for a man who'd lived for over thirty years always looking over his shoulder.

Jo swallowed and blinked her burning eyes. "It's my turn to ask a question."

Elliot kissed her again and then released her, leaning on his elbow. "Go ahead," he said, and then chuckled. "But I somehow suspect there isn't much you don't know about me."

"Tell me about your family."

"My family?"

"You look so surprised. Did you think I was going to try to winkle His Majesty's secrets out of you?" Humor glinted in her pale, silvery eyes, and the faint smile on her lips was devastatingly attractive; at that moment, Elliot would have told her whatever she wanted to know.

"What about my family?"

"I know you have an older brother—the Earl of Norriton. Do you have other siblings?"

"Yes, I'm the youngest of four."

"Sisters? Brothers?"

"Just four boys, much to my mother's abiding disappointment."

"Do any of the others work?"

"Not as such," he said. "Although they'd tell you otherwise. My second oldest brother was in the army but sold his commission after—well, after we all believed the war was over. My next oldest brother, Nigel, was to have entered the church but doesn't have the temperament for it, so he has assumed the management of one of my oldest brother's secondary estates." He hesitated and then added, "My parents had wanted me to take Nigel's place and join the Church, but I thwarted them by choosing government service over service to God. Why are you smirking?" he asked warily.

"Just visualizing you in a pulpit, preaching a sermon."

Elliot laughed. "You have a better imagination than I do because I never could imagine it. Now, it's my turn," he said. "Where and when did you and Angus meet?"

She cut a fond look up to the rafters, where Elliot suddenly noticed the bird roosting.

"Do you think he watched us while we, er . . . well, you know?" Elliot asked, only partly in jest.

"No, Angus has better manners than that."

He chuckled. "I see."

"Besides, he's more interested in sleeping than watching human folly."

Elliot squinted up at the black lump, sure he saw the telltale glint of a glossy black eye.

"He wasn't fully fledged when I found him, not far from a downed nest and evidence that he'd had at least one other sibling. He'd wedged himself under a haycock to hide from two magpies who were attacking him, and he was making the most piteous noise. Mungo said he'd never survive, but—well, here he is, years later, hearty and hale."

"Mungo?"

"No, you already had your question, it's my turn."

Elliot was amused by her enthusiasm. "Go on, then," he said, resuming his stroking of her stomach.

"Dominic Strickland used to be your friend. What happened?"

His smile slid away at her question. The last thing he wanted to do was talk about Dominic—ever—but it wasn't as if the topic was politically or militarily sensitive, so he had no reason to avoid answering it.

"We were close—me, Sin, Guy, Dominic, and another friend of ours, a man named Daniel Norris, who was in the army and died during the same attack as Sin's brother Benjamin. We were in the same year at school." He snorted. "Our classmates called us the Brotherhood to mock us for being such close friends."

"Strickland doesn't seem like the sort of man that you would have liked. Or Staunton. Not even Guy, for all that the newspapers refer to him as an unrepentant rake."

When Jo said *Guy*, she was referring to Elliot's friend Gauis Darlington, whom the newspapers called the Darling of the *Ton*.

"Guy might be a rake, but at least he has standards," Elliot said dryly, and then sighed as his thoughts went back to his erstwhile friend Dominic. "You'd have to know Dom to understand his rather magnetic appeal." Elliot tried to think of a fair way to describe Dominic Strickland, the reason that he, Jo, and all their friends were currently risking their lives to travel through a war-torn country. "He is the sort of person who oozes charisma." He cut her a quick look. "I'm sure you know about Dominic's connection to Marianne?"

"I know they were briefly lovers and that he's the reason people call her the Boxing Baroness—and I know that he lied to her." Jo hesitated and then added, "I'll admit it surprises me that a smart woman like Marianne would be taken in by a man like that."

"Dom is the sort who can charm the birds from the trees—but only so long as he *needs* something from them. As the member of our little *brotherhood* with the least money and status, I was treated to glimpses of Dom's true nature long before he exposed himself to Sin or Guy or Daniel." He shrugged. "We all of us pulled away from him even before we left Eton. Although Sin—with his tendency to want to save people—gave him chance after chance, even long after it was apparent that Dominic was beyond redemption."

"What was the act that made that clear?"

"No, it's my turn. How did you become so proficient with bladed weapons?"

Her body tensed beneath his hand, and he thought this might be the end of their post-coital sharing.

But then she said, "My uncle taught me. It was . . . well, not exactly a game, but a pastime, I suppose. It was soon apparent I had an aptitude for it." Elliot laughed at that understatement. " If I wanted him to take me with him, I had to become proficient and learn how to defend myself."

"Why would he take a young girl on such dangerous missions?"

She blinked, as if he'd said something confusing, but quickly masked the look. "There was nobody else to look after me. He never put me in any danger," she added, sounding faintly belligerent.

Elliot didn't believe that for a moment.

"My turn," she said, turning onto her side and mirroring his pose.

He rested his hand on her hip, unwilling to break contact with her just yet. When she didn't shrug him away, he smiled and taunted, "Well, what is your question?"

"I need a moment to think," she said, chewing her lower lip.

A bolt of emotion—something more complex than simple desire—struck him hard enough to make his heart ache painfully.

Elliot wasn't stupid. He recognized at least part of what he was feeling: he wanted her—and not just her body. For the first time in his life, he wanted something—some*one* badly. Viscerally. And she just so happened to be the most elusive woman he'd ever met.

How his friend Guy would laugh and laugh if he were privy to Elliot's thoughts. Thank God, the mischievous man would never find out the truth . . .

"You could have gone into diplomacy or the army or navy," Jo said, shaking him out of his musing. "But you chose a way to serve that is generally despised by your sort. Why?"

He snorted, "My sort?"

But she merely stared at him, unwilling to be diverted.

Elliot sighed. "It is true that gathering information—or *spying*—is not considered a gentlemanly pastime. Fortunately for me, I don't really care what most other men believe. Especially when what they believe is asinine." He shrugged. "My friends know what I do and respect me, and that is good enough for me. My turn."

She shook her head and placed her hand on his chest, her cool, work-roughened fingers grazing his nipples. "No more questions."

"No?" He arched his eyebrows, his pulse quickening at the way her pupils flared.

"No." Her hand slid down his chest, over his abdomen, and closed around his cock, which had been hard the entire time he'd lain beside her.

Elliot swallowed and let his own hand trail lower.

Her breathing hitched and she propped up one knee, the invitation unmistakable.

He slid a finger between the slick petals of her sex, filling her to his knuckles and then crooking his finger.

A soft moan slipped from between her parted lips, and she stroked his cock from tip to root and then back again.

Elliot's lips curved into a hungry smile as they pleasured each other, their exploratory touches settling into a rhythm once they learned what the other liked.

Jo moaned again when he added another finger, her hips meeting his thrusts. Elliot gritted his teeth and hissed when the rough skin of her thumb grazed the sensitive slit in his crown.

The greater his pleasure, the more of a challenge it was to maintain his erotic caressing, to up the ante, to not lose track of her needs in pursuit of his climax.

Finally, it was simply too much, and Elliot carefully withdrew from her before rolling onto his back and lifting her hand from his cock.

"I want you to ride me, Jo."

Her eyelids lowered and her cheeks flushed, but she straddled his hips, holding his gaze while positioning him at her entrance.

Elliot stared up at her, enrapt, his hips lifting off the blankets to meet her when she slammed down on him. "My God!" he groaned, reaching up to cup her breasts.

She leaned lower to oblige him, holding herself up on both arms as she kept him deep inside her body, her already snug passage squeezing him almost painfully tight.

He took a pebbled nipple in his mouth and sucked hard.

Jo shivered, her eyes turning glassy with bliss as he alternated between breasts, sucking and nipping and licking, until her body began to rock, her slim hips working every inch of him.

"Yesss," he hissed, sliding a hand between them and caressing her responsive body toward one orgasm and then a second, even stronger climax right on the heels of the first.

Her contractions were fierce and drove him toward his own pleasure with lamentable haste; he desperately wanted to finish inside her, the primitive urge to fill her with his seed, to mark her as *his* almost overwhelming. It was all Elliot could do to recall himself—and her—and withdraw from her body before he spent.

This time, it was he who sank into oblivion.

Chapter 6

Jo and Elliot met up with the rest of their small band two days after the carnage at Broussard's cottage.

Of course, that wasn't the only carnage that had occurred that night. Jo was still kicking herself for her reckless—and yes, damaging—behavior with Elliot.

Damaging to her because she liked him far more than was good for her. She had watched in horror as Marianne had capitulated to her attraction for the Duke of Staunton and Cecile had lowered her defenses to the Marquess of Carlisle over the past weeks.

And now she'd gone and done the exact same thing.

Although Jo didn't know either woman very well, they were the closest things she'd had to friends in her life, and she had grieved for the heartbreak they would both face when they returned from this brief time-out-of-world experience in France.

Because they *would* face heartbreak. And now she had joined her two friends in their reckless idiocy.

Jo might be completely ignorant of society, but peers of the realm—and their children—did not marry circus performers.

Especially not murderers and suspected traitors, hen, Mungo helpfully added.

Yes, especially not murderers and suspected traitors.

Jo told herself she didn't care if Elliot was disgusted by her—if he thought she was an inhuman monster. He hadn't seen the smoking ruins of those houses in that village or heard the wailing of their neighbors as they'd tried to come to terms with the nightmare Broussard's men had visited upon them.

At the time, she and Mungo hadn't been in a position to do anything to help the villagers, but he'd insisted they stay and bear witness to their deaths.

"One day we might get the chance to avenge them," he'd promised her, tears running freely down his cheeks as he'd spoken.

People decried brutality and cruelty, but most would draw the line at murdering to stop more of it. Jo could live with herself and suffered no guilt over any of the men she'd killed. It was better than thinking about what those men would have done if left unchecked.

She heard hooves as a horse moved up beside her and knew who it was before she turned.

Jo had avoided Elliot like the proverbial plague since leaving that farmer's barn three mornings ago. She'd woken up before first light and crawled from their shared blankets like a burglar slinking from the scene of her last crime.

It had been a relief to join up with the others, all four of whom were accustomed to her lack of social skills and simply left her to herself, pulling Elliot into their orbit and keeping him away from her.

He cleared his throat, and she turned to face him, annoyed by the way her pulse was already speeding. "Yes?"

"We are approaching the meeting place—the Iron Helm Inn, are we not?"

"Yes."

"I can't help noticing that we have few pistols and very little extra in the way of ammunition."

"I am aware of that."

They rode in silence.

He broke it with a heavy sigh. "Can you share your plan with me, Jo?"

"We will take the weapons that you, Guy, and Sin stored in the false floor of your caravan."

He gave a startled laugh. "I suppose I shouldn't be surprised that you not only know about those weapons but also feel entitled to simply take them, even though they don't belong to you."

"No, I suppose you shouldn't."

His eyes narrowed. "Are you angry with me?"

"No."

"Because you seem angry."

Jo twisted in her saddle; the others were far behind them, Jean-Louis and Arlette engaged in a discussion that involved a lot of laughter and gesticulation.

"Don't worry; they can't hear us," Elliot said.

"I'm angry at myself," Jo said, staring straight ahead.

"Ah."

Her head whipped around. "What does that mean?"

"Nothing in particular, just *ah*."

"That night was the only time."

"So you've already said." He spoke with a mildness that made her even more irritable.

Jo ground her teeth; why was she acting like such a missish schoolgirl?

Because ye've caught feelings for him, hen.

Oh, bugger off, Mungo.

"Has it occurred to you that Guy and Sin might have plans for the weapons they brought all this way?" Elliot asked.

"It's safer for them—and everyone else—if they don't meet up with Dominic Strickland armed."

Elliot opened his mouth, as if to argue, and then surprised her by saying, "I happen to agree with you. But what if they've already taken the weapons out by the time we get there?"

"Then we'll steal guns from somewhere else."

He laughed.

"What is so amusing?"

"Just the fact that you are so certain there will be weapons to be stolen—not to mention your lack of guilt at doing the stealing."

"After two decades of constant war, Europe is awash in weapons. If a person can't find a gun at this point, they have no right using one."

"That's true," he admitted, "but they are expensive, and people usually keep close watch over them."

"Drunken soldiers are the same the world over—careless about everything when women or wine are involved."

"What do you mean?"

"What do you think I mean?"

His thin, shapely lips pulled down at the corners. "Let's hope the weapons are still in the caravan and you don't need to *persuade* any drunken soldiers to relinquish their weapons."

"Why?"

"Because *seducing* drunken soldiers is dangerous," he retorted, looking a little dangerous himself.

"Well, that is my business, not yours."

His eyebrows pulled down over his high-bridged nose, until they formed a menacing V. "If you think—" He broke off, and his eyes widened. And then he laughed. "Oh, I see."

"What do you see?"

"You're spoiling for an argument."

"*What?*"

"You are."

"I am not."

"Yes, you are." He gave her a smug smirk that made her want to smack it off his face.

Nae, hen. Ye want to kiss it off his face.

Ugh. *Go away, Mungo.*

Elliot chortled as Jo gave Angus a tiny knife to hold in his talons and sent him off to their friends. Not surprisingly, Dominic had betrayed Marianne, Sin, and the rest of them. Instead of merely talking to Marianne—as Dom had promised in his letter—he'd captured the entire group and they were being held in the dungeon of the world's smallest castle.

"I wish I could be there to see Guy's reaction when he gets that knife," Elliot said.

A rare smile flickered across Jo's face. "If I sent them anything bigger, I'm afraid they'd use it to fight their way out."

Elliot knew she was right. The small knife and Angus's appearance were only meant to give their friends a sign that they weren't alone. According to Jo, everything was going to plan—not that she'd shared the details of that plan with *him*, of course.

Jean-Louis emerged noiselessly from the trees and joined them behind their collection of boulders.

He dropped into a crouch beside Jo. "You were right about Strickland counting on Broussard and his men. The young boy we captured said they'd been told their services wouldn't be needed for much longer, that the *real* soldiers would arrive shortly, and *they* would guard Strickland as he travels to wherever he is going after he leaves here." He cleared his throat, flicked a look at Elliot, and said, "The lad also said the soldiers would *see to* the others who are locked in the dungeon."

Jo met Elliot's gaze.

"*See to.* I don't like those words. You don't think Dominic is planning to release Sin, Marianne, and the others, do you?" Elliot asked after a moment of pregnant silence.

"No, I don't."

"What do you think?" Elliot asked Jean-Louis.

The Frenchman shook his head. "I think Strickland is planning to have Broussard kill them all when he arrives. The people guarding your friends right now are just simple villagers, most of them employed as servants, not mercenaries. They are not the sort who would kill in cold blood, nor would they approve of such actions."

Elliot's stomach churned with worry and revulsion, sickened by what Dominic had become. And weak with relief that Jo was involved in this affair. Without her intervention—well, he didn't like to think what would have happened to him, his friends, and Marianne. As much as he hated to admit it, if Jo hadn't intervened Elliot would be locked in that dungeon, awaiting death, with his friends right now.

"I'd better get ready," Jo said, going off to change into the disguise she would be using.

Once she'd gone Elliot turned to look at the castle perched hundreds of feet up on the face of a cliff. It was the smallest castle he'd ever seen—no bigger than a cottage, but with turrets.

Amazingly, it was occupied by a king. Well, a king of sorts, although this particular king's kingdom was limited to this castle and the fifteen or so servants he currently employed.

Elliot had felt as if he'd entered the pages of a gothic novel when he'd learned the occupant of the miniature castle was none other than the deposed King of Sweden, Gustav IV Adolph.

He'd asked Jo what the hell that meant, but of course she hadn't been willing to explain what the former King of Sweden and Dominic Strickland wanted with Marianne Simpson, a circus entertainer.

"It's not my story to share with you," was all she would say.

As Jo had predicted, the weapons that he, Sin, and Guy had cached in a false floor of their circus caravan had been exactly where they were supposed to be. Also, as Jo had predicted, it had been a damned good thing they'd taken the guns, because Dominic had got the jump on Elliot's friends, and it would have been painful to allow the weapons to fall into his hands.

Elliot and Jo had arrived in Metz to find Dominic already there, watching Sin and Marianne. It was a bit farcical: Dominic was spying on Marianne and the others, and Elliot and Jo were spying on Dominic.

In any case, the baron had baited and set his trap before showing himself. Instead of only capturing Marianne, he'd taken her entire group—at gunpoint.

Jo and Elliot had trailed behind them to this tiny fortress in the forest.

And tonight—one way or another—it would all end.

When Jo returned a few minutes later, Elliot would never have recognized her. She'd donned the clean but simple garments of a kitchen servant, her hair a dull gray, her shoulders rounded and stooped, her body thickened by several layers of clothing. The only thing that was recognizable was the giant bird on her shoulder.

Angus hopped onto the rock where Jean-Louis was eating stew. The Frenchman laughed and set down the bowl in front of him. "Here you go, you beggar."

Angus gave a polite *quork* and set to work cleaning the Frenchman's almost empty bowl.

"It's time, Jean-Louis," Jo said.

Jean-Louis nodded and stood, holding out his hand.

They clasped each other's forearms, and Jo said, "Remember, we don't want—"

"—to hurt anyone," Jean-Louis finished with a grin. "You forget that we've worked for you and your uncle for years, *mon amie*. We know how you feel about civilian casualties. We will take care."

Jo nodded and Jean-Louis loped off to inform the others that it was time to make their move.

Elliot had already loaded two pistols and a rifle, and he offered one to Jo.

"No, thank you, I'll stick with knives."

He couldn't argue with that, even though he would have felt better if she'd at least carried a pistol. But then he'd watched her take out four men with nothing but a few knives.

"What is Angus's part in the plan?" he teased as he shoved one pistol into his coat, one into the back of his breeches, and slung the rifle strap over his shoulder.

Angus looked up from his stew at the sound of his name, his big black beak coated with thick gravy.

"Angus will stay here," Jo said, giving the bird a firm look.

Angus made a snapping sound with his beak and then turned back to his stew.

Jo gave Elliot a speculative look. "I don't suppose you would consider—"

"Staying here with Angus?" Elliot said, giving her a look of amused exasperation. "No, I will not stay behind with your pet bird. I will come and help, but don't worry, I promise to keep out of the way. You've already given me my orders, Jo. I won't do anything stupid."

"Or heroic."

"Or, God forbid, heroic."

She gave a noncommittal grunt, then opened the spyglass and turned back to the castle.

"See anything?" he asked.

"There's movement and lights in the windows on the top floors," she said. "But I can't see who is up there."

"If I know Dominic, he'll want to indulge in a little bit of theater with his captive audience. I'm guessing they'll be dressing for dinner right about now. Well, maybe not all of them, but certainly Sin and Marianne."

Elliot didn't know how relations were between Marianne Simpson and Strickland—who'd once been her lover—but he knew for a fact that Dominic hated Sin with a passion. Whatever else Dom did, he wouldn't miss this opportunity to lord his triumph over his erstwhile friend.

Elliot felt a pang when he realized that Sin would now know that his brother Ben—the reason for their journey to France—really *had* died in the ambush a year ago. It had to be agonizing to lose a person you loved not once, but twice. Dominic should be flogged for that cruelty alone.

"Jean-Louis and Etienne are leading the servants across the bridge to the castle," Jo said in a low voice, closing the spyglass and slipping it into a pocket in her gown. She turned and looked at Elliot. "Are you ready to do this?"

"As ready as I'll ever be."

*   *   *

The elderly armed guard who'd been standing at the front door ever since Strickland and the others had arrived was nowhere in sight when they approached the castle.

Elliot followed in Jo's wake, keeping a lookout for any stragglers as they walked through the miniature foyer and entry hall, which was almost laughably grand considering how small it was.

Behind the sweeping staircase was a narrow door that led down to the dungeon.

They didn't pass a soul as they descended two flights of stairs that had been cut into the stone forming the bottom level of the castle.

The distinctive voice of Jo's friend Cecile Tremblay floated up to them as they reached the landing outside the single cell that made up the dungeon.

"Just shove him in there, Guy!"

"Good Lord, Cecile—this was never meant to hold even *three* bodies, not to mention seven."

"Will you two quit bickering and just get it done!" Barnabas Farnham snapped. The owner of Farnham's Fantastical Femail Fayre was never exactly a calm man, but her erstwhile employer's tone was shriller than Jo had ever heard it before.

"If you want to do it, *Barney*, perhaps you should come over here and—"

Jo opened the door, cutting off the rest of what Cecile had been about to say.

"Elliot!" Guy bellowed, elbowing aside the others to throw his arms around his friend.

"Shh!" Jo, Elliot, Cecile, and Barnabas all hissed.

"Thank God you're alive!" Guy said, his whisper barely any quieter than his shouting had been.

"Can't breathe," Elliot gasped, squirming out of the much larger man's grasp.

Guy laughed and released him, turning to Jo. He looked as if he were contemplating subjecting her to the same treatment.

"I wouldn't," Elliot said quickly and quietly.

"Ah, no, of course." Guy raised his hands palm out, as if to demonstrate he wouldn't be crushing her. "Thanks for sending your bird to rescue us." He reached into his pocket and withdrew the small knife. "I believe this is yours?"

Jo took it without comment and slid it into one of the sheathes sewn into her ugly heavy wool coat. "You were just supposed to use it to open any manacles, not to escape."

He grinned. "It was too hard to resist when our guard fell asleep."

Jo grunted.

Cecile slammed the door with a clang, dusted off her hands, and turned to Jo, giving her a wry smile. "I knew you would come." Before Jo could stop her, she caught her up in a crushing embrace. "Thank you, my friend," Cecile whispered in her ear before kissing each cheek and releasing Jo's flaming face.

"Er, alright then," Jo muttered, glaring at both Guy and Elliot, who were sniggering like schoolboys.

Arlette appeared silently in the doorway, giving a sharp bark of laughter at the cell full of men before turning to Jo. "That's it, Jo— everyone is secured. The duke, Marianne, Strickland, and the king are the only ones still at liberty inside the building. They are on the third floor in the dining room—it's the only room with double doors. The serving girl said there were at least two pistols in the room. One is on the mantlepiece and the other was on the table in front of the king, but she's not sure where it is now. She did mention there's a minstrel gallery overlooking the dining room."

Jo turned to Cecile. "That sounds like a good place for you to be. But only if you believe you could shoot to kill if necessary," she added, not wanting to put the other woman in an uncomfortable position.

Cecile snorted. "What? you mean would I feel bad if I accidentally shot Strickland or the fool conspiring with him—both of whom were likely planning to kill us?"

Jo nodded.

Cecile smiled grimly. "I just need a gun."

Elliot gestured to the rifle hanging crossways across his torso. "Would this do? Or this?" He held up his two pistols.

"I think the rifle would be best."

"I'm going with you," Guy said when Elliot gave her the rifle and she checked it. When Cecile didn't respond, Guy turned to Jo and said, "I'm going with Cecile."

"Fine, just stay out of her way," Jo said, ignoring his affronted huff and turning to Arlette. "Stay down here with these gentlemen just to make sure they don't get into any trouble."

Arlette smiled, removed a pistol from somewhere in her petticoat, and turned to the seven men crammed into the tiny cell. "I'll see they behave."

Etienne came down the narrow stairs, pushing Sonia—Barnabas Farnham's longtime lover—in front of him. "We found this one hiding in the pantry, Jo."

"She's the one who sold us all to Strickland," Cecile said, lowering the barrel of the rifle in a distinctly threatening manner.

"I know," Jo said.

Cecile, Guy, and Barnabas turned and gawked at her.

"You *knew* the bitch was working for Strickland and never said anything?" Guy demanded.

Jo opened her mouth, but Elliot beat her to it.

"Guy," he said, his expression cool and tone even cooler. "You should wait until you know everything before you speak."

Guy scowled but shut his mouth.

"What should we do with her?" Etienne asked, gesturing to Sonia. He jerked his thumb at the cell. "There's no more room in there."

"Bring her with us," Jo said after a moment's thought, and then turned to Sonia—a woman who was a bully *and* a traitor—and said, "You open your mouth and make so much as one peep or in any way jeopardize Marianne's life, and I'll cut your throat. Understood?"

Sonia's mouth sagged open, and her red-rimmed eyes went wide. She nodded.

Jo realized Cecile and Guy were staring at her with similarly shocked looks. Fortunately—before either of them could say something or ask any uncomfortable questions—Monique joined them, her face flushed as if she'd been running.

"His majesty is yanking the servant cord—he wants his dessert. You'd better go now before he or Strickland realizes something is wrong."

Jo nodded, took a deep breath, and turned to Elliot. "Ready?"

He nodded. "Let's go."

"Just wait for my signal," Elliot repeated to himself, pacing back and forth in front of the gold-leaf-covered double doors. That's all Jo had said to him before entering the dining room a moment earlier.

She didn't bother to say anything else—such as what that sign might *be*, she'd just—

"We should go in there," Barnabas said, taking a step toward the door.

Etienne yanked him back. "You shut your mouth and do as you're told," he hissed, his normally friendly face utterly terrifying.

Sonia laid a hand on Barnabas's arm. "Marianne will be fine. Come and stand with—"

Barnabas shook her hand off his arm and cut her a killing look. "Don't ever touch me again, you—you—"

A scream—a masculine one—cut off whatever he'd been about to say, and all of them took a step toward the door, but nobody made a move to open it.

"Was that the sign?" Elliot asked Monique.

She shrugged. "How in the world would Jo know some man would scream? Surely that—"

"Hands up!" Guy's familiar voice rang out so loudly that it was audible through the door.

"That's signal enough for me," Elliot muttered, opening the door a crack and peering inside before barging in.

He probably could have flung both doors wide and broken into an operatic aria and the occupants of the room wouldn't have noticed.

Everyone inside the dining room was staring at something else on the far side of the room.

"You . . . bitch!" Dominic's face was puckered in pain, and he was squeezing his bleeding arm.

"Blade!" Marianne shouted.

"Hello, Marianne," Jo said, as cool and calm as ever.

Bodies pushed against Elliot's back, shoving him into the room. Nobody noticed him or the four people crowding in behind him.

"You just about cut off my bloody arm," Dominic whined, glaring at Jo, whose back was to Elliot.

"Does it hurt, Dom?" Marianne taunted as she strode toward Strickland, her voice brimming with loathing.

"What the hell do you thi—"

Marianne's fist struck Dom with enough force to knock him onto his arse.

"You should have kept my hands tied up, Dominic," Marianne said, shaking out her hand.

Elliot grinned and strode deeper into the room. "I can personally vouch that she has an excellent right cross, Dominic."

Sin smiled at him from the far side of the table. "It's good to see your face, old man!"

"It's good to be seen. I'll admit it was touch-and-go for a while, thanks to our friend Dominic, here."

Dominic pushed himself up until he was sitting on the floor, still cradling his bleeding arm. "How in the name of all that is unholy did you get away from Broussard? The man has thirty-five armed men!"

"I had some excellent help." Elliot cut a look at Blade, who was stripping off her disguise and exposing her now-familiar battered breeches, old coat, and boots.

Dominic scoffed. "One bloody woman?"

"She took you down quickly enough," Elliot pointed out.

Dominic glared up at him and struggled to his feet, clutching his arm. "I don't suppose you'll—"

"You lying, cheating son of a whore!" Barnabas shoved past Elliot and Jo and barreled right into Dominic, knocking him to the floor yet again. He straddled the other man's much larger body, grabbed his lapels, and banged his head on the floor. "We had a bargain—I helped you plan your death and got you out of Britain, and you were supposed to give me back that goddamned book. You always—"

Elliot and Jo marched up on either side of Barnabas and lifted the squirming, thrashing older man off Dominic's body and set him on his feet.

Dominic struggled to his feet, glaring at Barnabas with open loathing. "How dare you lay hands on me, you—" He lunged at Barnabas, as if he were going to strike him, but at the last moment he slid his hand around the older man's neck, the elbow of his bleeding arm locking tight, while his other hand clutched a knife that seemed to appear from nowhere.

"Get back!" Dominic snarled, dragging Barnabas along with him as he backed up to the fireplace, where a slender, brown-haired stranger—the deposed king of Sweden, Elliot surmised—stood gawking.

"I want His Royal Highness's post chaise harnessed, with Staunton's trunk of money in it," Dominic barked in a breathless voice.

"Or what?" Guy shouted from up on the balcony.

"Or I'll kill Barnabas."

At least three people laughed at the threat.

A look of surprise flickered over Dominic's face, but then he, too, saw the humor in his threat and he gave a lopsided smile. "He's not much of a hostage, I'll admit—but I know there aren't any murderers among you beacons of morality willing to—"

"I'm sorry for everything, Marianne," Barnabas said as he looked across at his niece, his voice strangely calm as his hand slid into his opposite sleeve and he pulled out a knife.

"Uncle—no!" Marianne shouted as Barnabas reached back and drove the blade into Dominic's side.

Dominic screamed, and his arm jerked in such a way that he jammed the knife into Barnabas's throat just as an ear-shattering bang filled the room and Dominic's head disappeared into a pink mist.

"Nooooo!" Sonia cried as both she and Marianne ran to where Barnabas had fallen, blood gushing from a huge wound in his throat.

Barnabas fumbled for Marianne's hand, his mouth moving, but Elliot couldn't hear what he said over Sonia's loud weeping.

He realized he'd been holding his breath and released it. "It's over," he said to Jo.

"Not quite yet," she murmured.

Chapter 7

It was almost midnight by the time they'd buried Dominic and Barnabas in the small cemetery just outside the village that served Himmelhaus Castle.

Elliot had helped Jean-Louis and Etienne load the two bodies into the castle wagon and they rode into the village with Sonia to give burial information to the local priest.

He'd discussed the matter with Sin and Guy, and they'd decided to lie about Dominic Strickland's identity. Not out of courtesy to his memory, but for his widow and child, both of whom he'd abandoned in England after he'd faked his own death.

Once he'd finished with the burials Elliot had walked back to their campsite, leaving the wagon for Sonia. He had never warmed to Barnabas Farnham's lover during the weeks he'd worked with the circus, and he now found her company unbearable, especially her loud, hypocritical weeping for Farnham, a man she'd been betraying for years.

He'd planned to collect his clothing and horse and stay the night at Himmelhaus, but when he approached the campsite, he discovered it wasn't abandoned.

Jo looked up slowly, her gaze so hazy he thought for a moment she'd been sleeping upright, until he saw the bottle sitting on the ground between her feet.

Only by a slight slackening in her features did he realize that Josephine Blade was, in street cant, cup-shot.

"What are you doing here?" she asked, her words faintly slurred.

"I just came back from the village," he said, which didn't exactly answer her question.

"Hmmph." She lifted the bottle—a fine brandy that must have come from His Majesty's cellar. "Want some?"

"Thank you," Elliot said, glancing around for one of the tin cups they carried with them. Which was when he noticed the packs that usually held their food and other items were gone. "Where are all the others?"

"They're going to stay at the inn tonight."

"Do you want to come to Himmelhaus? Cecile told me there were a few empty rooms."

"No."

Elliot frowned and dropped to his haunches. "Jo, what's wrong?"

"Nothing." She reached for the bottle.

Elliot held onto it for a moment but then released it when her hand tightened.

She took a deep pull and then wiped her mouth with the back of her hand.

Elliot carefully extracted the bottle—half-full—from her hands and sat down on one of the chunks of wood they'd been using as seats. He placed the bottle on his far side before saying, "You seem a trifle out of sorts."

She shrugged.

Had Elliot ever met a person who was harder to talk to? If so, he couldn't recall when.

"Guy and I made sure both the caravans will be ready to leave first thing tomorrow. Marianne said she wants Sonia to have Barnabas's caravan." Elliot frowned at that. Instead of rewarding Sonia, Elliot thought they should drag the woman back to England to stand trial for decades of gathering secrets for the French while living on English soil. But Sin had wanted to leave the decision to Marianne.

"I was thinking I could—"

Jo turned, grabbed his collar, and yanked him close before crushing his mouth with hers.

The following moments—it might have been five or ten, but surely no longer—were a blur of kissing, grabbing, and tearing of cloth and popping of buttons.

"I want—" Jo muttered, lurching to her feet and pulling Elliot up with her.

"What do you want, Jo?" he asked, following her to a nearby tree, where she shoved him back against the trunk. She yanked open the catches on his breeches and then ripped open the buttons before shoving both them and his drawers down his thighs. And then she grabbed his erection.

Elliot gasped, pulling at her placket and fumbling with the buttons as if he had two left hands.

Her breeches slid down to her booted ankles and she shuffled one foot free and then wrapped her leg around his hip, bringing his crown to her entrance. Elliot spun her around, until she was leaning against the tree, and entered her with a thrust that was hard enough to lift her to her toes.

Jo grabbed a fistful of his short hair and held his head steady, her gaze dark and intense. "Only tonight. Understand?"

He didn't. He didn't understand at all, but now hardly seemed like the time to have a debate, so he said, "Fine. Only tonight. Er, wouldn't you like to lie down on a bedroll or—"

She slammed down on him hard, like a breaker pounding a beach.

Elliot groaned and held her still, his cock hilted, her body so hot and tight around him that he knew this wasn't going to last long.

"Elliot," she whispered in his ear, tightening her leg and pulling their hips together so tightly that he gasped. She sucked his earlobe into her mouth and nibbled and tugged, flexing her hips in a gesture that left him with no doubt as to what she wanted.

He firmed up his grip on her bottom and began to roll his hips.

She bit the lobe of his ear. "Yes," she muttered. "Hard."

The harsh demand caused something inside him to break loose, the last restraint of civilized behavior, and he rode her with a passionate lack of control that he knew would shame him.

But that would be later.

Elliot pushed aside every thought except the desire to make her come.

Jo was no passive passenger. She met him thrust for thrust, her heel digging into his arse and fingers grasping his shoulders in a bruising grip. It was fast, furious, and elemental.

Only after she'd cried out her release and he'd thrust himself deep inside her did he remember that he'd forgotten to withdraw.

Even in his befogged ecstasy he knew what that meant. It only took one time to create a child.

Jo hadn't been entirely sober when Elliot had wandered up, but now—after flinging herself at him and screaming like a wanton—she was painfully clearheaded.

What have I done?

After their passion had ebbed, Elliot had picked her up like a baby and carried her to her blankets, lying down alongside her.

His voice was soft in the darkness. "I know you're awake, Jo. I can practically *hear* you regretting what just happened."

"What's done is done."

He laughed. "Hastily done, I'll admit, but not so bad for all that."

No, it hadn't been bad at all. It had been far too good. Frighteningly good. Elliot was, in her opinion, the most perfect man she'd ever met.

The only thing that wasn't perfect about him was his heritage. There was no future for an earl's son and a murderous mercenary.

He sighed. "Why does this only have to be for tonight, Jo? Why couldn't we—"

"Don't say it. I'm no man's whore." She turned her head and glared at the fire, her eyes stinging. Probably from smoke, or perhaps a speck of dust or dirt or—

"Jo." He took her chin firmly and turned her. "Look at me," he said when she resisted.

She whipped her head around. "What?" she demanded, scowling at him, grateful the fire had died to a low glow and he wouldn't be able to see her face clearly.

"You know that's not what I meant," he said, hurt simmering just beneath his anger.

Jo inhaled deeply and expelled the air slowly, doing the same thing several times, until she felt calmer. "I'm sorry, I know you weren't saying that."

"Are you saying we have no future because you believe our social differences are too great?"

Jo could only stare.

A look of mortification flickered over his handsome face. "Lord, I guess that is assuming you feel anything at all for me, isn't it? You must think me an arrogant, insufferable—"

"I think you're perfect."

Elliot's jaw sagged.

Good God, she *must* be drunk. "I—I just mean that I like you," Jo stammered when he stared at her, lips parted and eyes wide. And then, because that sounded so much like adolescent infatuation, she blundered onward. "What I mean is that you are a good man. A decent man."

He cocked his head, his brow furrowing.

"You don't blather too much, and you don't fuss about things, and we travel well together without a great deal of—*argh*," she groaned, only after she'd said the words realizing how strange they sounded. "I sound like an idiot."

Elliot laughed. "You sound adorable."

"Adorable. Now there is one thing I've never been called."

"A gross oversight."

Her face heated at the warm, sincere look in his gaze. Oh, the man wouldn't be satisfied until he'd reduced her to a blubbering mess. Jo stared at anything other than his uncomfortably piercing blue eyes.

"You looked at me with disbelief when I mentioned our differing status. But I think you will find that matters are not so dire as you might think. It is true that I'm the fourth son of an earl, but my family does not rely on me for anything—I don't need to make a magnificent match to save the earldom—nor do I rely on my family. I don't even take an allowance. If they disapprove of who I choose to be with, all they can do is show their disapproval. They did exactly that when it came to my choice of careers, and we weathered the storm and are still close. Things might be difficult at first—or at least awkward—but when they came to know you—"

"What? You think they'd accept me once they knew what I did to earn my crust? That I was raised by a disgraced army sergeant? That I have consorted with criminals all my life? That I am currently employed in a circus?" Jo paused, and then added, "That I'm a murderer?"

He frowned. "Disgraced how?"

She couldn't help laughing, although it was bitter. "That is all you take from what I've said?"

He took her hand and held it in his. "Please. Won't you tell me what you are running from?"

"I'm not running from anything," she lied, pulling her hand away and sitting up, yanking the blanket to her chest.

"I don't care if your uncle was disgraced. As for consorting with criminals, who do you think I've dealt with over and over again in my work?" He leaned close. "And if by *murderer* you mean killing men like Broussard and his ilk, well, you've performed a public service."

Jo blinked at that.

He took advantage of her surprise and moved closer. "There is nothing about your past we cannot manage, Jo."

"You don't understand what you are saying." Jo's voice shook, from fear more than anything—fear at how tempted she was to throw caution to the wind and snatch at happiness, even though it could only end in misery.

Elliot grabbed her hands and pulled her close. "Then *make* me understand."

The compulsion to confide in someone—to unburden herself—was overwhelming. Besides, what could it hurt now? Everyone who would be damaged by her confession was dead and gone. Nobody could do anything to her—she'd committed no crimes. At least not in Britain, or against it. Who would be harmed if she spoke the truth?

Ye mean other than you, hen? Do you think he'll look at you with anything but disgust if you tell him the truth? Mungo's voice was so loud, it was as if he were right there, whispering in her ear.

"Please, Jo. Trust me. I swear I would never do anything to harm you," Elliot said.

Jo squeezed her eyes shut briefly. *I have to, Mungo. I can't stand carrying this alone anymore—it's too lonely with you gone.*

There was no response, because Mungo wasn't there.

Jo opened her eyes and met Elliot's gaze. "I'll tell you the truth about me, but you have to give me your word that you will tell nobody else. No one."

His brow furrowed, but he nodded. "I promise that what you tell me stays only with me."

"Even if your employers were to ask?"

"Yes, even then," he said without hesitation.

Jo took a deep breath and then said, "Have you ever heard of Major John Townshend?"

She knew the instant that he recognized the name because a look of intense loathing flickered across his face. "The Traitor of Yorktown."

Jo nodded, even though hearing the term was like a lash across her back. "What do you know?"

"Just what anyone in government service knows. He's the man who sold secrets to the colonists during the rebellion—what the Americans call their Revolutionary War. He was going to be executed for his actions, but then one of his men—his sergeant, who authorities believe was spying along with him—helped him escape. The traitors ran but were killed by a tribe of natives who were working with the British—I believe they are called Creeks—to collect a bounty."

Her throat was so dry she couldn't force out any words.

His eyes narrowed. "What are you saying, Jo?"

"I'm saying that Mungo Brown wasn't my uncle, he was my father. And his name wasn't Mungo Brown, it was Callum Mungo Brown, the same Callum Brown who was batman to Lord Major John Townshend, one of the two men widely believed to be the reason Britain lost the war with the American Colonies."

Chapter 8

The hair on the back of Elliot's neck stood up at Jo's words, as if a bolt of lightning had struck too close.

She nodded, even though he'd said nothing, her eyes once again opaque. "You see, don't you?"

"But—I don't understand. The men were apprehended and executed shortly after they escaped—that's over thirty years ago, and you're only twenty-eight."

"The story you know is not what really happened. My father had made friends with some of the Creek warriors over the course of the war. Many of the tribes sided with the British, but from expediency rather than any true loyalty to the king. Both Major Townshend and my father had been well-liked, so the Creek chief let them go free. He kept their uniforms as proof that they'd died in a skirmish. The British army accepted that, eager to close the book on a nasty, shameful episode."

"So, you're saying that the men are still *alive*?" he asked, the sickness in his belly spreading outward like a disease. God. He'd promised her that he would keep the matter between them. But if Townshend or Brown was still alive, then—

"No, they are both dead."

Relief swamped him, and then he saw the pain in her eyes and felt like a monster. Whoever and whatever those men had done, Brown had still been her father.

"I understand what you are feeling," Jo said, reading him far too clearly for his comfort. "You would have needed to break your word to me if either of them were still alive—I know that."

Elliot didn't deny it. Instead, he asked, "You grew up in America, then?"

"Only for the first few years. The men settled in the interior of the state called Georgia." Her lips twisted into a bitter smile. "A bit of irony there as it began as a penal colony, so it was the perfect place for two criminals on the run. Apparently, it wasn't difficult to find work—employers didn't care about people's pasts; they just needed able hands and strong backs to pick cotton or tobacco. Townshend died in 1787 when a sickness swept the plantation where they'd been living and working. It was the same fever that took my mother's life when I wasn't quite a year old. My father scraped together enough money to buy passage to France. He used the name Mungo—his middle name—rather than Callum, just to be on the safe side. Unfortunately, things deteriorated in Paris not long after we arrived, so we moved again. And he kept moving from place to place. Once war broke out, he had to avoid anywhere British troops were stationed, for fear he might be recognized."

"Good Lord—you were only a child. How was he able to raise you in such circumstances?"

"There were always women who would take care of me, earning a little extra money for their labors. When I turned twelve, Mungo started taking me with him."

Elliot sucked in a breath. "That must have been dangerous."

"He didn't really have much choice."

"What do you mean?"

"I mean that I followed him rather than be left behind." She chuckled. "I told him I'd follow him the next time, too—no matter whether he gave me a spanking, or not. Besides," she added, "he'd been teaching me how to be comfortable with guns and knives all along. He'd told me the truth—or at least some of it, that we were hiding from men who would take him away from me if they caught us—so it wasn't as if I'd had an ordinary childhood."

Elliot's heart ached for her, but he could see by the fierce glint in her pale gray eyes that the last thing she wanted was his pity. "How did you end up back in England?"

"We hadn't planned to go back, but he'd received several job offers through his various connections, and all of them seemed to be in England." She shrugged. "So we went to London, and he investigated the various options. The job involving Marianne paid so much that my father couldn't resist. We'd saved a great deal over the years, living cheaply, and he hoped this would be enough that we'd no longer need to keep moving or live this sort of life. It was our plan to return to America and buy some land where we could farm and stop running. He believed he could return without fear of capture. After all, he was so much older—the last time he'd seen anyone who might recognize him had been over twenty years before. His hair had gone white and was no longer the distinctive red. He grew a beard." She shrugged. "He did everything he could to disguise himself and felt safe returning to England for one last job. And he was right that he no longer looked the same; he once ran into a man he'd served with for years, and he never recognized my father." Jo snorted softly. "And then—right before we could begin our new life—he was killed by a rogue barrel of ale."

Elliot kept his mouth shut, because he knew he couldn't say anything that wouldn't either insult or hurt her.

She looked up from her thoughts, her vague gaze sharpening. "I know you're thinking that was more mercy than a traitor like him deserved."

His face heated, but he didn't deny it.

She nodded, her expression suddenly bitter. "He told me nobody would ever believe the truth."

"What truth?" he asked, although he could guess what she was going to say.

"They were both innocent."

He struggled to suppress his feelings, but judging by her scowl, he wasn't successful.

"You think I'm a fool to believe that, don't you?"

Elliot ignored the question and asked—as kindly as he could—"What else would he tell his daughter, Jo? That he was a traitor who was guilty of selling out his own country?"

"Yes, exactly." She rolled off the blanket and sprang to her feet, moving to where their clothes were scattered.

"Jo."

She ignored him, bending to yank a shirt off the ground and pull it down over her head so hard, he heard fabric tearing.

"*Jo.*"

She whirled on him. "What do you want from me, Elliot? I told you there was a good reason everything began and ended tonight, and now you know I'm right. If you think I will listen to you denigrate my father, you are sorely—"

"Tell me the rest."

"What *rest?*"

"Your father must have explained what happened? Surely he didn't just say *we're innocent* without any further explanation?"

She glared down at him. "What do you care? You've already made up your mind that they were guilty. Don't lie."

"I won't deny that is what I believe—only because of the evidence I've heard. But that doesn't mean I'm not willing to listen."

Her jaw worked, and he could see the desire to exonerate her father warring with her anger at Elliot.

"There was a man—a handler, somebody at the Home Office, and he was using Major Townshend to feed information to the Colonists."

"You mean Townshend was a double agent?" Elliot asked, pushing himself up and reaching for his breeches.

She nodded, her eyes moving over him as he stood and dressed.

"Why didn't his handler come forward when Townshend was accused of spying?"

"Because he *died*."

Elliot shook his head. "That wouldn't have mattered—there would have been some record of the arrangement, some proof that—"

"The whole point of what he was doing was to ferret out a *real* spy inside the Home Office. The man who arranged for Townshend and my father to infiltrate the colonists couldn't trust anyone else because he knew somebody on his staff was disloyal, but he didn't know who it was."

"Who was it—this handler? What was his name?"

She frowned.

"What can it hurt to tell me?"

"It was Sir David Patton. Have you heard of him?"

"Yes." Patton *had* been the head of the Secret Office—Elliot's own department—during most of the decade the British had fought the colonials. The man's reputation was spotless. Elliot didn't know exactly when he'd died, but it was sometime before the war ended. Elliot had never heard rumors of any traitor inside the Home Office, but if Patton had feared that somebody in his ranks was disloyal, it was possible—although highly unlikely—that he might have used Townshend in such an extremely covert operation.

"Did your father ever say if Townshend figured out who was selling information?"

She shook her head. "He said the Major believed it was more than just one person. He thought there was somebody in the colonies and somebody in London. Maybe even more than two people involved. Exiled as he was to the American hinterlands after the war was over, Townshend couldn't easily gather any information, but there were still a few people who remained loyal to him"—she shook her head when he opened his mouth—"and no, I don't know who those people are, so you can't get their names from me and charge *them* with conspiracy to commit treason."

Elliot kept his mouth shut, because he couldn't deny that was exactly what he would have done. Anyone who'd aided and abetted Brown or Townshend would be guilty of treason, as well.

"So Townshend had no proof, then?" he asked, instead.

"My father said Townshend had several people in mind before his cover was exposed, but he simply had no evidence."

"A spy *network* within the Secret Office," Elliot said, not bothering to hide his skepticism.

She glared. "You're the one who wanted to know," she shot back, stomping off to find the rest of her clothing.

Elliot felt like an arse. He went toward her and set his hands on her shoulders as she buttoned up her waistcoat.

"Jo."

She whirled around, jerking out of his grasp. "Just leave me be."

When she tried to push past him, he stepped in front of her and lightly set his hands on her shoulders again. "Please—I'm sorry I sounded like I didn't believe you—"

"Because you don't."

"I'm willing to suspend my disbelief. When we return to London, I can do some poking about and—"

"No."

He frowned. "I can look into the matter without any—"

"*No!* You promised me you would leave it be."

He gave an exasperated huff. "Surely you can't expect me to just—"

"What? Are you going back on your word so readily?" she taunted, pulling back until he dropped his hands.

"Why wouldn't you want me to investigate? If what you're saying is true—"

"Then there might be more than one real spy—still *alive*—who would like nothing more than to find me and shut me up."

Elliot's jaw sagged.

"Yes, clearly you didn't think of *that* possibility since you believe I'm so deluded."

"But you don't have any proof, so how could you be any danger to anyone?"

"Do you think people facing hanging would stop to worry about that?"

Elliot opened his mouth and then closed it.

She nodded, even though he'd said nothing. "The men involved already hounded Major Townshend and my father into exile. If they're still alive, I daresay they wouldn't look kindly on my appearing in England and going about trumpeting Townshend's innocence. I've been running all my life, Elliot, and I'd like to stop. Perhaps even stay in London and continue working at Farnham's. If you start *poking about,* then I'll need to run again. So please, don't make me regret that I confided in you." She pushed past him, and this time he didn't stop her.

"So, that's it, then?" he asked.

"That's it," she said, jerking on a stocking and then ramming her foot into her boot. "Don't expect this"—she gestured to the rumpled bedroll—"to happen again. Tomorrow we leave here and head to Reims. You will drive one caravan, and I will drive the other. All we need to do is get through the next few weeks, and then we never need to see each other again." She put on her second boot, snatched up her coat, and headed off into the darkness.

"Where are you going?" he called after her, scrambling for his own stockings.

"Somewhere else," she shouted over her shoulder.

"Jo! Don't leave. You can sleep here. I won't bother you."

But there was no reply, not even the rustle of leaves.

When he looked overhead to where Angus had been roosting, he discovered the bird was no longer there.

Part II

London

Chapter 9

Jo was watching him.

Again.

Was it only yesterday that she'd promised herself she wouldn't do this anymore?

Yes, it had been just yesterday. And the day before that. And before that. And so on.

Well, why should her continued mania for Elliot Wingate surprise her? Jo had lived for almost thirty years without feeling anything for a man; now it appeared all that unused yearning and interest had decided to manifest itself all at once. So here she was, utterly, profoundly, and annoyingly captivated by a man. If not the last man she could have, certainly among that number.

Yer obsessed, hen—nae doubt about it.

Jo sighed. *Leave me alone, Mungo.*

Quork, quork.

She looked up to see Angus in the big oak tree overhead. She made a soft *quork* back at the huge bird to acknowledge his presence but kept her gaze on the object of her obsession.

Elliot was walking with a young woman. Strolling, really. This was the third time this month Jo had watched the two of them together in the park.

She told herself she didn't care, but clearly that was a lie, or she wouldn't be stalking him during every free moment.

Lately that had meant a lot of moments. Although she still performed her knife routine six nights of the week at Farnham's Fantastical Female Fayre, Jo hadn't taken any new extra work since returning from France last year. She told herself she had no business going back to France while the Continent was still reeling from Bonaparte's return, but that was a lie. She simply didn't want to leave the city where she had the best chance of setting eyes on Elliot Wingate.

As she watched Elliot smile and converse with the pretty, feminine woman—whose name was Lady Elizabeth Dryer—she couldn't help wishing that Mungo had lived long enough to meet him. She thought the two men would have gotten on well together.

That makes no difference to anything, hen. You should keep moving, Jo. Settlin' down isn't for the likes of us.

Yes, he certainly would have chided her for deciding to settle in London. And he would have been furious that she'd stayed with Farnham's.

But she was tired of moving. Tired of looking over her shoulder. In the eighteen months since Mungo's death, Jo had only moved once—and that had just been across London. She was done running.

Not only did she like her job in the circus, but she liked the people she worked with. Other than Mungo, she'd never worked closely with anyone before, and she was tired of feeling isolated and alone.

After Barnabas Farnham's death at Himmelhaus last year, his niece, Marianne Simpson, had assumed operation of the circus—but then she'd surprised all of Britain by marrying the Duke of Staunton at the beginning of the year.

When Marianne decided to marry, she sold her interest in the Fayre to Cecile Tremblay, and life at the circus had become even better under the Frenchwoman's vigilant, more hands-on management.

Cecile had immediately raised everyone's wages, hired more employees, and reinvested some of the profits into the old building, which Barnabas had neglected for years, preferring to spend his money at the gaming tables. The theater was a cleaner, safer, and far more lucrative place to work.

When Jo had returned from France, she'd told herself that she'd only stay with the Fayre until Marianne had found her feet and no longer needed Jo's act. But then Marianne had left, so she'd told herself she'd only stay until Cecile was able to replace her. Yet here she was—almost four months after Cecile had taken over—still showing up six nights a week to perform.

And stalking Elliot in your spare moments, mooning over him and hoping he'll do . . . something.

That voice wasn't Mungo's but Jo's own better angel trying to talk some sense into her.

Go back to France. You can find plenty of work there—you can choose only the jobs you like. You don't need money, so you can please yourself. Why stay here and drown in your own misery? Elliot has forgotten you. He has moved on to one of his own kind. And so should you.

Jo scowled, wishing the voice would shut up and leave her in peace.

Not only was the voice annoying, but it was also wrong. Elliot *hadn't* forgotten all about her. He remembered who she was just fine. In fact, he'd sought Jo out only a few weeks ago.

Not to talk to you about you. *He wanted to give you a job.*

Well, that was true. He'd asked her to investigate a matter for Guy Darlington, who was no longer the Marquess of Darlington, or even a peer at all.

Poor Guy had come down in the world, suffering something of a shock when his cousin had returned to England to claim the dukedom that Guy had been groomed to assume.

Now Guy was plain old Mr. Darlington.

Astoundingly enough, Guy had actually come to work at the Fayre, hoping to win back Cecile Tremblay's heart after the two had been lovers last year in France. Jo knew that they had parted acrimoniously—at least on Cecile's side—when Guy had offered Cecile a carte blanche.

In any event, Guy needed somebody to do a bit of investigatory work—some of which had involved looking into Cecile's past. He'd first gone to his friend Elliot to help him, but Elliot had been spending too much time shuttling between London and Paris to take the job, so Elliot had brought the job offer to Jo.

Seeing him again had been a shock, but not an unpleasant one.

Elliot had caught up with Jo when she'd been leaving the theater one night after a performance. Amusingly, he'd been lurking in the alley where all the hopeful swains loitered every night, hoping to catch one of the female performers and ply them with flowers, jewels, or offers of varying respectability.

"Let me get this straight," Jo had said, after she'd forced her stupidly palpitating heart back into line. "You want me to spy on Cecile—my friend and employer?"

"I'm not asking you to do anything," he'd protested, falling into step beside her, as if he were intending to follow her home, where she'd been headed.

Jo had changed her direction and had gone toward the pub where she and the other theater people often congregated. The last thing she wanted to do was bring the son of an earl to see her meager lodgings, although she suspected that he probably already knew where she lived.

"So, then what do you want with me?" she'd demanded rudely.

"I'm just telling you that Guy is looking for somebody to find out some things about Cecile's past. If you don't help him, he'll probably blunder around and make a mull of everything. He's not looking for anything to use against her, Jo," he'd added when she didn't answer. "He wants to help her."

"Then why doesn't he go to Cecile directly?"

Elliot had laughed at that, as well he should. Guy and Cecile's relationship was characterized by loud and emotional exchanges on both sides.

While Cecile had agreed to hire Guy at the Fayre when he'd lost his title, home, and money, she'd only done so to humiliate him and extract her pound of flesh. Her current favorite entertainment was making Guy grovel as much as possible.

To give Guy credit, he was doing a great deal of groveling, most of it with a smile on his face. It was obvious to anyone with eyes that he was head over heels in love with Cecile. But he'd hurt her badly, and Cecile—whom Jo was pretty sure loved Guy in return—was either too angry, too scared, or too proud to give him a second opportunity to break her badly bruised heart.

So, Elliot had been right to laugh when Jo had suggested Guy and Cecile deal with one another like mature adults. That might happen eventually, but not anytime soon.

"Just talk to Guy and see what he wants before you make up your mind," Elliot had urged. "What can it hurt?"

"Fine, I'll go and talk to Guy," Jo had agreed. When Elliot had continued to walk beside her, she'd asked, "Was there something else?"

"How have you been?"

"Fine."

"Are you going to Marianne and Sin's ball?"

"*What?*" She'd stopped and turned to him.

"They're having a ball—Marianne's first as the new Duchess of Staunton."

"What's that to me? They're hardly going to invite a circus performer."

"That's not what Sin told me."

Jo hadn't felt comfortable with the warm sensation that had spread in her belly at his words. Could Marianne really want *her* to attend what was probably the most important event of the other woman's new life as a duchess?

Rather than argue with Elliot about how improbable an invitation was, Jo had resumed walking, the mist rapidly turning to rain.

"Will you go if you're invited?" Elliot had persisted, keeping pace with her easily.

"No."

"Why not?"

"Do you think it would do either Sin or Marianne any good to have *me* in their house?"

"Why not? Nobody knows who you are. You wear a mask on stage."

"Was that all you wanted to ask me? About Guy and this ball?"

"Well, er, yes. But won't you—"

"I'll talk to Guy, and I'm not going to the ball. There. Now, goodbye, Mr. Wingate."

And that had been the last time Jo had spoken to him. Although she'd spied on him plenty.

As things turned out, Jo *had* decided to talk to Guy and—yes, against her better judgment—she had agreed to investigate the matter he'd asked about. Mostly because what Elliot had said was right— Guy would bumble into Cecile's business if neither she nor Elliot put a stop to it. Considering what she'd discovered during her investigation, Jo was glad that she'd taken the work.

In any event, that investigation—which hadn't been difficult and hadn't taken her long—was over, and now she was at loose ends again.

Which meant she had more time to stalk Elliot.

Like right now, for instance.

Not that stalking him was bringing her anything but pain; a pain that worsened every time she watched him with Lady Elizabeth.

Because Elliot was courting Lady Elizabeth. Jo could see it as plain as day, even though nobody had ever courted *her*.

He tried to court ye, lass. He did his best.

Now *that* was something Mungo would never have said in real life, because he *never* encouraged her to get close to anyone. No, that was just her treacherous mind making up thoughts in Mungo's voice to convince her to run after Elliot and fling herself at his feet and beg him to forgive her shrewish behavior and take her back—even if it was just as a lover.

Thank God Jo was too smart to listen to the voice.

Whenever she felt herself begin to weaken, she just had to remember how Elliot had looked when she'd murdered Broussard and his men, or when she'd told him that Mungo was her father.

Ye'll need to hide your special skills from the average punter, hen, because men just won't understand a woman who can do the things ye can do.

Jo wished she'd taken that advice when it came to Elliot. Maybe if he'd only known her as a circus performer, then things would never have progressed as far as they had. But once she'd liberated him from Broussard, he'd been far too curious about her and far too close at hand to resist. She should have freed him and then left him at the inn to recover. She should have—

Jo sighed. Should have, could have. What difference did any of that make now?

She leaned against the trunk of the tree and stared at Elliot and Lady Elizabeth. They looked good together, right—as if they were made for each other—two handsome, dark-haired, slim people from the same social class.

From what Jo had seen of Lady Elizabeth, she was gentle and kind—always pleasant to the servants who assisted her in and out of her fancy carriage and generous to beggars, street sweepers, and those less fortunate.

You'd never see Lady Elizabeth cutting men's throats or impaling them with knives. You'd never see Lady Elizabeth so filthy that good, decent folk crossed the street to avoid her.

And you'd never see Lady Elizabeth crawling up Elliot's body like a monkey scaling a tree and begging him to fuck her.

Elliot deserved somebody just like her, somebody pretty, gentle, and kind.

Jo had behaved like a shrew with him that last night they'd been together. As if he were a monster not to believe her vague utterings about Townshend and Mungo's innocence. She'd been angry not because he hadn't believed her, but because she couldn't really blame him.

Though she believed in Mungo's innocence, she couldn't expect anyone else to do so.

There was no proof of any network of spies, and there'd probably been nobody chasing after Mungo, regardless of the fact that he'd looked over his shoulder for the last thirty years of his life. It wasn't that she thought he'd lied to her. No, he'd believed with all his being that Major John Townshend had been innocent—a man who'd been serving his country and had paid for his service with his reputation, family, and ultimately, his life.

The sound of familiar male laughter pulled Jo from her thoughts, and she blinked away the past.

Elliot was chuckling at something Lady Elizabeth had said, and the sound did strange things to Jo's chest. It was both fascinating and painful to watch him socialize with a beautiful woman. Fascinating because she simply couldn't imagine being so free and natural with anyone. And painful because she would have liked to make him laugh that way.

The pair walked back to the fancy carriage they'd arrived in; it belonged to Elliot's older brother, the Earl of Norriton. Elliot didn't own any carriages himself, nor did he keep any horses. He was not the sort of man who was flamboyant or extravagant. Indeed, he never tried to pretend to be something he wasn't. He never pretended, at all. When he'd looked at her that last night, she'd seen genuine affection in his gaze—he'd not tried to hide it from her.

Earning the regard of such a man had made Jo feel proud. It had been devastating to throw it away.

It amazed her that he could look just as much at home sitting in a scruffy little pub in rural France as he did garbed in expensive clothing walking in Hyde Park. He fit in anywhere. *That* ability was Elliot Wingate's special talent: to look at home no matter where he was; to avoid drawing attention to himself.

Anyone could be fooled by his façade. Indeed, he was quite the most remarkable man she'd ever met. True, he wasn't as handsome as his two closest friends—Sin and Guy—both of whom were physically imposing men, but he was striking, clever, and vibrant, and so . . . *textured*, yes, that was the word for him. He was composed of layer after layer after layer. What would be at the core of all those layers? Jo burned to know.

Unfortunately, thanks to her own actions, she would never find out.

Chapter 10

After Elliot had dropped Lady Elizabeth at her family's house on Berkeley Square, he hopped into his brother's carriage and headed back to his own, far humbler lodgings.

His mind wasn't on the woman he'd just left—although Lady Elizabeth was clever, charming, and lovely—but on the woman who'd spied on him in Hyde Park.

Or at least Elliot assumed Jo Brown was somewhere nearby if Angus was flying about.

His lips curved into a slight smile. Although Jo could blend into the woodwork—or anywhere else, actually—her giant black familiar was more difficult to disguise in London than he'd been in the forests of France and Prussia.

Elliot had not seen her for weeks, not since he'd leapt at the excuse to talk to her on Guy's behalf.

Guy had been pleased with her work, so Elliot knew she'd done the job creditably, ferreting out as much, if not more, information than he could have found.

As hard as he'd tried to root Jo Brown from his mind—and his heart—Elliot thought about her every day. And every day, he tried to conceive of a reason to go talk to her.

It had been a relief to be in France for two weeks. Not because he didn't think of her—he thought of her as much, if not more, than ever—but because he was in no danger of traveling across London to see her and make a fool of himself.

When he'd returned to town a few days ago, he'd been so tempted to catch her act at the Fayre that night—just to *see* her—that he'd immediately fled to the countryside to keep from behaving like an idiot.

Besides, it had been past time that he'd paid a visit to his grandmother—the Dowager Countess Norriton. She was a very old lady, and although she seemed healthy enough, she was fragile and would not live forever.

Elliot had always been her favorite among all her grandchildren for the simple reason that he, more than any of his uncles, brothers, or cousins, resembled his grandfather the most. His grandparents' marriage had been one of the few great love stories of their age. They'd grown up on adjacent properties and had known each other in swaddling clothes. They'd married their very first Season and had defied convention by flaunting their love in a society that seemed to favor spousal infidelity over devotion. It was the sort of marriage Elliot had always hoped to have but had given up on until meeting Jo. Oh, they had missed out on each other's childhoods, but he'd never before met a person—man or woman—with whom he felt so at ease.

In any case, it had been good to go see his grandmother at her country estate, Foxglove, for several reasons. Not only because it gave her pleasure, but because it had brought home to him the duty Elliot owed to his family.

It didn't matter how obsessed—fine, how much in love—he was with Jo Brown. They could never be together, not without damaging both his family's reputation and his relationship with them. Because while he might be able to get away with marrying a former circus performer, his family would never forgive him for marrying a notorious traitor's daughter.

Elliot needed to forget Jo. He also needed to stop stalking her—yes, she wasn't the only one sneaking around in the shadows—although it was truly the only way he could ever get any time with the elusive, guarded, mysterious woman who'd captured his imagination and refused to relinquish it.

Going to Foxglove hadn't just kept him from haunting Jo in London, it had also forced him to consider his grandmother's request.

Elliot smiled at the word *request*. Really, his grandmother had made a demand: if Elliot wanted to inherit Foxglove—which was truly a lovely property where he could live in comfortable luxury as his own master—he needed to marry a woman from his grand-mother's approved list.

"You'd be a fool not to do it, Elliot," his older brother, Charles, the Earl of Norriton, had said the last time they'd had dinner at the earl's London residence. "Foxglove is a damned beautiful estate and worth a pretty penny. This would set you up for life. At thirty-four, you are no cockerel; it is well past the time you should marry."

Elliot agreed that he was no cockerel. And he didn't even have any objection to the thought of marriage.

But the women his grandmother approved of were not the sort who made his heart pound. Indeed, there was only one woman who did that, and Josephine Brown, knife thrower extraordinaire, was *not* the sort of woman his grandmother would approve of, even if Jo would consent to marry him and even if she wasn't the daughter of a traitor.

Elliot gave a soft snort of laughter. Jo would barely consent to speak to him, so marriage was not even within the realm of possibility.

It was unlike him to become infatuated—fine, *in love*, he conceded yet again, irritably. Indeed, he'd never been quite this fascinated by anyone before. He suspected part of his fascination could be attributed to the fact that she was a conundrum. And if there was one thing Elliot loved in life, it was mysteries or puzzles and figuring them out.

That was a terrible reason for a man to pursue a woman—because she was a puzzle.

Wasn't it?

But was it really any worse than courting Lady Elizabeth because she was the daughter of an earl and the sister of an earl and could trace her bloodlines back to The Conquest?

Elliot scowled at his tangled thoughts, relieved when the carriage rolled to a smooth, well-sprung stop.

He hopped out before either of the footmen came around to put down the steps. "Thank you, Edward, Thomas," he said, nodding up at the two liveried servants before turning to the coachman, whom Elliot had known since he'd been in short pants. "This is for you to share as you see fit, John."

"Thank you, Master Elliot," the coachman said.

Elliot always gave his brother's servants handsome vails for the extra services they rendered him. As the only working member of the House of Norriton—much to his family's chagrin—he sympathized with laboring folk.

His lodgings were on the second floor of a newish building that housed only bachelors, a generous suite of rooms that he had shared with his friend Guy up until a few months ago. He probably should have moved to smaller chambers when Guy left, but he found that he could afford the lease on his own and that he liked the extra bed-chamber rather than taking in another lodger.

As ever, his valet, Bevil Crisp, somehow knew he was coming home and opened the door before Elliot could slide his key into the lock.

"Good afternoon, sir," Crisp said, running an assessing look over Elliot's person—as if he hadn't *really* believed him when he'd said he was going walking with a lady in Hyde Park. As if he believed Elliot would return torn, bloody, and bedraggled.

Well, Elliot could hardly blame the poor man, as he'd done that more than a few times in their long association.

Crisp took his hat, gloves, and cane and then helped him off with his overcoat.

"Anything of interest happen while I was out?" Elliot asked.

Crisp handed him an envelope of expensive white paper with a bloodred seal. "An invitation arrived from the Duke of Staunton, sir."

"Ah, I've been expecting this. It will be the duchess's first official function since they married."

"I'm sure it will be a grand affair, sir. I trust this is one event you will attend?" Crisp took it personally that Elliot didn't accept more invitations to ton parties or have a reason to wear fine clothing more often.

"Yes, I will certainly be attending."

What about Jo? Would she be there?

Lady Elizabeth will be there.

Elliot grimaced. Lord. He'd forgotten all about the woman he was supposed to be courting. These past weeks in France hadn't helped him to forget about Jo; they'd only made him want her worse than ever.

Jo stared down at the expensive rectangle of parchment that Cecile had thrust into her hands the moment she'd entered the other woman's cramped business office. "What's this?" she asked, although she had a sinking feeling in her belly when she noticed the ducal crest.

"It's an invitation for you."

She glanced up. "Are you sure?"

Cecile snorted. "Your name is on it."

Yes, *Josephine Brown* was written across the front in exquisite copperplate.

"Marianne hand-delivered it for you. It is an invitation to her first big *ton* party."

So, Elliot had been right about the ball and Marianne's intention. The woman must be addled to invite a circus employee, and her husband far too infatuated with his new wife to have the sense to stop her. Jo should take the difficult decision out of their hands by rejecting the kind, but misguided, offer.

"Don't let that bird eat it," Cecile said.

"No, Angus isn't fond of paper," Jo mumbled, her forehead furrowed. "But . . . why would she invite me?"

Cecile sighed. "Because she likes you, Jo. And I'm sure she is grateful for all the help you gave her in France last year." She chuck-led. "I know *I'm* grateful to you for saving our hides."

"I was only doing my job—what I was paid to do."

Cecile sighed again, this one far more exasperated. "Whatever Marianne's reasons, she told me she'd appreciate your being there. It is the first event she will hostess as the Duchess of Staunton. I daresay she wants her friends around her."

"*Friends*," Angus echoed, rubbing his head against Jo's cheek.

Jo couldn't help smiling at the comforting gesture; her raven always knew when she needed a bit of moral support.

She gave him an affectionate scratch beneath his beak and said to Cecile, "I don't know how to dance."

Cecile grinned, the mischievous expression striking on her beautiful face. "It just so happens I have one of the best dancers in Britain living under my roof and working for me."

Jo snorted. "Guy?"

"Who else?"

"You think he is going to the ball, even after . . . everything?" Jo couldn't imagine the poor man wanted to face the same people who came to mock him on stage night after night.

Cecile shrugged. "I haven't asked him—I've been so busy train-ing Helen that I seem to have no time. But I can't imagine why not."

Helen Keeble was the woman Cecile had hired as her assistant and also as governess to Cat, the little girl whom Cecile and Guy had rescued from living on the street.

Cat was the only name she'd shared with anyone. Jo thought she was probably hiding information about her background—she recog-nized the cagey look in the waif's eyes—but it wasn't her place to pry. Besides, Cat and her dog George were onto a good thing now. Cecile and Guy, for all their differences with each other, were taking excellent care of the her. Indeed, taking in Cat had drawn the con-stantly bickering pair closer together.

"Sin and Guy are very close. Why do you think Guy wouldn't attend his best friend's ball?" Cecile asked, interrupting her thoughts.

"Don't you think it will be embarrassing for him to go and so-cialize with all the people who used to know him as a duke?"

"I don't know. But even if he doesn't go, he can still teach us to dance."

Jo lifted one eyebrow. "Us?"

Cecile shrugged, but her cheeks turned a rosy pink.

"You don't know how, either?" Jo asked, unable to keep the dis-belief from her voice.

"Where would I have learned to dance?" Cecile snapped.

Jo smothered her grin. Who would have guessed that Cecile Tremblay—with her obsession for everything *ton* and balls and par-ties—wouldn't know how to dance? It would have been fun to tease her a little, but she could see the other woman was mortified by the admission.

"Do you think there is enough time to learn?" Jo asked.

"Two weeks? I should think so."

Jo turned the invitation over in her hands and rubbed her thumb over the bloodred wax seal.

"Will you go with me, Jo?" Cecile asked after a moment.

It took Jo a moment to identify the bubble of emotion that seemed to be growing inside her: it was anticipation. She could learn to dance, and maybe . . . just maybe . . . she would dance with Elliot.

She looked up at Angus, who was watching her so intently that Jo swore he could understand the conversation. "What do you think, Angus? Want to learn how to dance?"

Jo's knife hit the playing card dead-center and pinned it to the board behind her assistant. The audience went wild—as it always did whenever Jo got to the part of the act with the blindfold—and she pulled off the black scarf covering her eyes, turned to the boisterous crowd, and took a bow.

She could tell by the laughter that Angus had just completed his part of the routine, which was to peck her assistant—Guy, this evening—in the arse when he bent over to retrieve his hat.

Angus flew over to her shoulder and then bobbed up and down in a way that looked as if he were bowing, to the delight of the noisy punters.

Jo made her exit while the audience was still laughing and calling for encores—a good half the men yelling Guy's name.

Hers was the last act of the evening, so the number of employees backstage had thinned considerably. She was halfway to the dressing room when Guy called her name.

Jo stopped and turned.

"Can you make him stop *pecking* my arse so damned hard?" Guy demanded, glaring at Angus.

The raven snapped his beak at the towering man.

Guy jabbed a finger at the bird. "Will you look at that? Just look at his expression . . . He *knows* what we're talking about! I swear he does." Raven and man engaged in a brief, but intense, glare.

Jo resisted the urge to smile. "I'll see what I can do."

"The beast almost took a chunk out of my hide," Guy muttered, absently rubbing said hide, which was currently garbed in green velvet livery, causing the former duke to resemble a very large and gorgeous footman—no doubt Cecile's humiliating objective in insisting on the clothing.

"Anything else?" Jo asked.

"Er, actually, Cecile says you'll be taking dancing lessons, too." Guy laughed at the expression that spread across Jo's face before she could check it. "I can see how happy that makes you."

"Perhaps you might talk some sense into her," Jo blurted.

"What do you mean?"

"I mean that my presence at Sin and Marianne's ball can hardly do either of them any good."

"Nobody will recognize you, because you wear that mask for your performances. Besides," he said with a snort, "it would be very hard to be more notorious than me or Cecile, and we are both going. So, no—I don't think that excuse will serve to get you out of this ball."

Jo scowled, angry—at herself—more at the surge of joy she felt than at Guy's words.

"If I'm to whip you two into shape, we'll need to practice every day before the ball." He smirked evilly. "Every. Single. Day."

"Every day?" Jo knew she was whining but couldn't stop herself.

"It's scarcely two weeks away, Blade. It will take that long just to get you up to snuff about ball etiquette, so we'll have to be diligent."

"Perhaps you should have become a dance master rather than a circus employee," she taunted.

He narrowed his eyes at her. "Perhaps you are correct. Perhaps I should be *charging* you for these services rather than offering to do such work for *free*."

"Er, no. Sorry," she said hastily. She didn't want to take dancing lessons, and she certainly didn't want to pay for something she'd never use more than this once. "*Thank you*, Guy. I am most grateful."

"*Grateful*," Angus echoed, proving what a clever bird he was.

Guy frowned at the raven, as if he suspected Angus might be mocking him. "I'll teach you, but I'm not teaching that bird."

His words surprised a laugh out of her. "Sorry, Angus—no dance lessons for you," she said, and then winked, which was the bird's signal to squawk.

Guy jolted at the loud, aggressive sound and then scowled when he realized how he'd reacted. "Very droll, you two. Keep that up and you'll be paying, after all."

"I'm sorry," she lied. "So, when shall we meet?"

"Cecile says midday is best. Helen will provide the music."

"Ah." That was all Jo felt safe to say on *that* subject.

Even so, Guy snorted. "Yes, quite a farce, isn't it?" He glanced around to make sure nobody was nearby. "My former betrothed helping me to teach the love of my life how to dance."

Jo couldn't help grinning; it *was* rather amusing that Guy's former fiancée—who'd jilted him—had come to work at the Fayre under an assumed name. Apparently Helen didn't like the way her fa-

ther moved her around like a chess piece, so she had run away to escape marrying Guy's cousin, who was the new Duke of Fairhurst.

"Oh, by the way—Cecile wanted me to remind you that the two
of you are going shopping for ball gowns tomorrow, right after your
first dancing lesson."

"*What?*"

Guy snickered. "Yes, you heard right: dress shopping."

That was enough to wipe the smile from Jo's face.

Chapter 11

Jo glanced around the magnificent entry hall and tried to keep from looking like a slack-jawed yokel. She'd known that the Duke of Staunton was one of the wealthiest peers in Britain, but the opulence of his townhouse was stupefying.

"Doesn't Marianne look magnificent?" Cecile whispered.

Jo looked to the head of the receiving line, where Marianne stood beside her husband and an elegant older woman who must be the Duke of Staunton's aunt, Lady Julia Powell, Marianne's mentor in her first Season as the Duchess of Staunton. Marianne wore a gown of antique gold, and the color was indeed lovely on her. Although she was smiling, it was a tight smile, and Jo thought she appeared more nervous than she'd ever looked before a boxing match.

"She looks just like a duchess," Cecile gushed when Jo didn't answer.

"She *is* a duchess," Jo said.

Guy—who was standing beside Cecile—chuckled. "She has you there, darling."

"Don't call me that," Cecile said, the words more involuntary than heated, her dark eyes darting about, as if she didn't want to miss a thing.

Guy and Jo exchanged an amused look. Watching Cecile's reaction was proving more entertaining than the actual function.

Although Cecile was thirty-six years old, this was her first ball, and she was exhibiting far more excitement than the jaded eighteen-year-old debutantes in the receiving line.

For years, Cecile had followed the society pages of half a dozen newspapers; Jo knew this night—a grand ball at a duke's house!—was a fantasy come true for the other woman. And although Cecile would never admit it, arriving at the exclusive Staunton ball with none other than Gaius Darlington—better known as the Darling of the *Ton*—on her arm made an already spectacular night perfect. Even though Guy was no longer a wealthy duke, there was no denying the man had been blessed with both looks and charm in abundance.

"I talked to Elliot today," Guy murmured in Jo's ear as Cecile continued to gawk.

Jo didn't care for the way her heart sped at the sound of that particular name, so she ignored Guy's comment while silently praying that he would keep talking.

"He just returned from France," Guy went on, answering her prayers.

"Oh?" she offered when it seemed that Guy was finished.

"He said he was looking forward to tonight, and he wanted me to tell you to save him a dance—two, actually."

Jo lifted her head and met Guy's smirking look.

"What?" he demanded when she merely glared at him.

The line inched forward.

"He returned a few days early just so he could attend this ball," Guy added when Jo went back to ignoring him.

"I'm sure he didn't wish to offend Sin or Marianne," Jo said.

"No, he wouldn't want to do that."

Her head whipped around again at his smug tone. Yes, he had a smug smile to go with it.

Jo refused to encourage him when it came to his hopes for her and his friend, Elliot. Already she'd had to listen to Cecile's opinion about what Jo should do with Elliot Wingate. Over and over again, month after month. Apparently enduring unsolicited romantic advice was part and parcel of having friends.

Thankfully, before Guy could continue with his prodding and taunting, the three of them reached the head of the line.

"I'm so glad you could come," the Duke of Staunton said, his striking green eyes warm as he greeted her.

The people surrounding them were deadly silent, and Jo knew all the listeners were on tenterhooks and dying of curiosity to hear what was exchanged. Not just because of Guy—who had certainly caused a flutter when he'd entered the house—but also because a goodly number of the men would recognize Cecile, who was something of a celebrity because of her markswoman performances at the Fayre.

Thanks to the mask that Jo wore onstage, nobody would connect her to the blade expert at Farnham's Fayre. She was just plain old Josephine Brown.

Marianne, who stood beside her magnificent husband, looked every bit as grand as the duke, the sparkling stones around her neck— diamonds, Jo surmised—the largest she had ever seen.

Jo's hand went to her throat and the pearls she wore for the first time in her life. Her mother's pearls—or so Mungo had told her when he'd given them to her on her eighteenth birthday. Jo recalled wondering, as she'd stared at the earbobs and necklace, where in the world she would wear such things. Her younger self would never have believed that she'd attend a ball—certainly not a *duke's* ball.

Jo wished Mungo could see her tonight, dressed like a lady and wearing her mother's jewels. She even knew how to dance, thanks to Guy's diligence and skill. And if she didn't feel exactly secure in her ability to stun the assemblage with her grace on the dance floor, at least she wouldn't embarrass herself.

The duke took Jo's hand and bowed over it. "You look lovely this evening, Miss Brown."

Jo faltered under his kind gaze. Although she'd traveled with him for months—and had often thrown knives at him on stage—he had looked nothing like he did tonight, which was every inch a duke.

"Thank you, Your Grace. It is a pleasure to see you again."

A lightning-fast grin flashed across his handsome face. "I hope you enjoy yourself."

Marianne took one of her hands and one of Cecile's and gave them an almost painful squeeze. "I'm *so* pleased you two could come tonight!"

Jo couldn't help feeling warmed by her friend's joy at seeing them. Well, at least at seeing Cecile and Guy. She still wasn't positive that Cecile hadn't badgered Marianne to invite Jo along tonight, no matter how many times Cecile had denied it.

Although Jo had spent a large part of last year protecting Marianne, the two of them weren't close. They were friendly, but not—she thought—friends. Jo had never wanted to become too close to the other woman, as it had always been important to her to maintain a degree of reserve with her clients, even when those clients weren't aware that she was protecting them.

Marianne leaned forward slightly and said in a softer voice, "Elliot arrived a few minutes before you."

Before Jo could respond—although she didn't know what to say—Marianne lightly touched Cecile's necklace, which Jo knew Guy had given her. "My, what a lovely setting that is. So beautiful and unusual."

Cecile turned a fetching pink. "Thank you."

In a whisper, Marianne added, "Sin and I will save a table for the six of us for supper." And then she released Jo's hand and smiled, her cool mask firmly in place. "I do hope you enjoy yourselves tonight."

Jo and Cecile took the subtle hint and moved away from the head of the line.

Guy insinuated his large body between them and offered each an arm. "Shall we, ladies."

"I don't think that will be necessary," said a familiar voice.

"Elliot!" Guy grinned at his friend, who seemed to have appeared from nowhere. "What were you doing? Hiding behind that potted palm, old man?" He chuckled. "I'm glad you're here. Perhaps you might escort Miss Tremblay? Bl—er, Miss Brown has promised her first set to me."

Elliot gave his friend an unreadable look before turning to Cecile. "Would you honor me with the first set?" he asked her, his gaze only wandering to Jo for an instant.

"It would be my pleasure," Cecile said, and then—for some inexplicable reason—turned and winked at Jo.

Just what were Guy and Cecile up to?

Elliot escorted Cecile up the stairs to the ballroom. "What is Guy up to this evening?"

"Is he up to something?" Cecile asked, her expression far too innocent to be convincing.

"He had a certain gleam in his eyes when he looked at me."

"Well, I'm glad he is fixated on you rather than me," she said tartly, and then leaned close enough to whisper in his ear, "Is it my imagination, or are people staring?"

"It is not your imagination."

"Do you think they know who I am?" she asked, sounding both resigned and nervous.

"Perhaps, but it is more likely that most of them are staring because you and Jo are exceedingly beautiful women. And of course, everyone always stares at Guy."

Cecile laughed, her gaze darting around the grand ballroom, her excitement a trifle obvious, but charming, nonetheless. "I am new to this."

"Balls?"

"And dancing."

"Ah. Do you wish to sit this one out?"

"Not at all. Guy taught us a good many figures."

Elliot laughed. "He made himself useful for a change, did he? Well, you couldn't have had a better teacher. I'm afraid I won't compare to his graceful gliding; he was quite the best dancer at school." He guided her toward the far side of the ballroom. "It will be less of a crush away from the entrance," he said. "This first set should be an easy one for you—'Drops of Brandy,' it is called. Do you need—"

Cecile unfurled her fan and showed it to him.

Elliot smiled when he saw that the paper fan was printed with the instructions for the most common dance steps. "Good thinking."

"It was Guy's idea."

Elliot saw that Guy and Jo were also taking positions on the dance floor. He tried not to be annoyed with his friend for taking her first set; after all, there would be more dances tonight.

Cecile leaned close to him. "Guy asked Jo for the first dance because he didn't want her to feel left out. He knew that I would enjoy myself whether anyone asked me or not. But Jo?" She shrugged. "It wasn't easy to convince her to come tonight. Ballroom dancing is not something I think she ever imagined for herself."

"She told me she wouldn't come."

Cecile lifted an eyebrow, her expression sly. "Did she."

For some reason, the way she was looking at Elliot made his face scald.

"I took her shopping for her ball gown," Cecile said. "Doesn't she look lovely?"

Elliot's eyes slid to where Jo and Guy were chatting. Lovely? The word wasn't quite enough to describe her. She looked bloody amazing—just like an angel—in a simple yet elegant gown of white, silver threaded muslin. Her hair looked shorter, more fashionable, and the gorgeous pearls around her neck were nothing to the healthy glow on her pale skin.

She was heavenly.

"Yes?" Cecile prodded.

"Er, yes. She does—look lovely, very lovely." Elliot's voice broke, something that hadn't happened since he'd been an adolescent. He cleared his throat, his face no doubt flaming.

Cecile chuckled, making Elliot realize that he was staring at another woman while ignoring his dance partner.

Lord! Where were his manners?

He turned to the beautiful woman across from him. "You look ravishing this evening, Miss Tremblay."

Cecile laughed and tapped him on the arm with her fan, her eyes sparkling. "Thank you, kind sir."

The orchestra began playing and stopped him from making an even greater fool of himself.

Luckily for Elliot's scattered wits, Cecile was too busy concentrating on the dance to require much conversation, which left him free to snatch glances at Jo.

Guy—the suave bastard—could flirt, dance, and probably conjugate Latin verbs, albeit poorly, all at the same time.

As for Jo, Elliot was both surprised and pleased to see how relaxed she looked, able to talk with Guy even as she moved through the steps of the dance.

She was bloody gorgeous, and he simply could not stop looking at her, no matter that he was doubtless making an absolute cake of himself. He knew as well as anyone that staring across a ballroom was a sure way to find one's name linked with someone else's in the gossip columns. Good God. If his grandmother heard of this . . .

Elliot forced himself to look at his own partner, something he had to remember to do again and again over the course of the set. By the time they could leave the dance floor, Elliot was more than a little bit concerned over the jealousy that was roiling in his belly. He'd never felt so possessive about a woman, not even when he'd been a very young man.

It was not a comfortable sensation.

"That was quite nice," Cecile said happily, blithely unaware of Elliot's suffering. "Although it's much harder to converse than I thought it would be—at least not without colliding with other dancers. And it's so *loud*."

It was indeed a crush. Marianne and Sin could take pride in a ball that everyone in London was dying to attend.

"You did excellently," Elliot murmured as he led her off the floor.

"How would you know? Your eyes were somewhere else the entire time," she teased.

"I'm sorry. I don't—"

"Oh, hush. I'm thrilled you are as wild about her as she is about you."

He stumbled slightly—on nothing. "Er, is she?" he asked, aiming for sophisticated and falling far short of the mark.

Cecile just laughed.

"How was it?" Guy asked as they approached. "Did Elliot knock you over or tear your frock?"

"He dances exquisitely," said Cecile, far kinder than Elliot deserved.

Felix Lorimer, a handsome blond buck who was heir to the Marquess of Dorsey, appeared at Guy's elbow, his admiring gaze on Jo. "I say, Darlington—could you introduce—"

Guy growled at the much younger man. "Ask our hostess if you want an introduction, you impudent pup."

Cecile gave a low laugh and even Jo smiled as the youngster beat a hasty retreat, scurrying away like a rodent.

Guy looked thunderous—as well he should. It was a serious breach of etiquette to request an introduction in such a casual way.

"Good show, Guy," Elliot said. "Best to nip that sort of behavior in the bud." He turned to Jo. "May I have the first waltz and the supper set if you've not already thrown it away on this rogue?" He jerked his chin toward Guy.

Jo gave him an arch look. "You may."

Elliot felt a stupid grin spread across his face. "And may I also say that you look quite stunning this evening, Miss Brown?"

Jo's cheeks flushed, but her expression remained cool. "I believe you just did, Mr. Wingate."

Guy threw his head back and laughed.

Elliot smiled like the lovesick fool he was.

Jo's heart hadn't pounded nearly as fast when she'd learned the steps of the waltz with Guy. Nor had her breathing become so uneven. And it had been far easier to stare at Guy's cravat than into Elliot's cool blue eyes.

Jo was reserved, but she'd never been *shy*. And yet the way Elliot stared at her—into her—made her feel like an adolescent schoolgirl.

Not that she'd ever actually gone to school, or even dressed like a girl when she'd been one.

"So," Elliot said after they'd spent the first few minutes dancing in silence. "How is your investigation for Guy progressing?"

She perked up at that question, relieved he'd not asked any uncomfortable ones such as: Do you ever think about that night in the woods outside Himmelhaus Castle? Do you ever imagine doing it again? Do you ever—

"I've already turned over my findings to Guy."

One of Elliot's eyebrows arched.

"What?" she asked rudely.

"You're very quick."

She shrugged, unwilling to admit that she had nothing else in her life to fill her time other than work. Especially when Elliot was out of town, and she couldn't humiliate herself by stalking him.

"What do you mean by *most* of your findings?" Elliot asked.

"I mean that some of the information I found is private, and if Guy wants to know about it, he can ask Cecile directly." Jo still felt a bit traitorous taking the job, but Guy had assured her that he loved Cecile and that he simply wanted to help her out of a financial bind. Jo had only turned over information that wouldn't have offended *her* if some man who loved her had learned about it.

Though it was a stretch to imagine a man in love with her.

Elliot deftly avoided a very young couple whose dancing was more enthusiastic than skilled.

"You are a very good dancer," Jo said, deciding it was her turn to make conversation.

Elliot flashed her a grin, the rare expression beyond charming. "Thank you. You are quite good, yourself."

Jo snorted.

"What? You are."

"I'm adequate."

"I understand you only learned recently."

"I suppose two weeks counts as recent."

"You dance as though you've been doing it for years."

Jo rolled her eyes at his blatant untruth.

"I mean it. I wouldn't have wanted to make a public appearance after a mere two weeks."

Jo didn't tell him that she felt a bit mortified at not learning how to dance until she was almost thirty. But then it was hardly a skill she was likely to use ever again.

"I daresay you had a lot more fun learning with Guy than I did learning at school," Elliot said. "Our dance master at Eton used to smack us with a cane when we missed a step. Guy was the class pet, by the way."

Jo snickered. "I can believe that." She lowered her voice slightly. "Guy said you just got back from France. How are things there?"

The smile slid from Elliot's face. "Grim, chaotic, and they probably will be for a while. Oh," he said, his expression lightening, "you'll never believe who I saw when I was paying a visit to Versailles—" When Jo shook her head, he said, "Etienne and Jean-Louis."

"Good Lord! What were the two of them doing *there*, of all places? Robbing the palace? Their faces are on so many crime bills, they shouldn't go within a hundred miles of the capital. They shouldn't even be in France."

While Jo respected her colleagues' abilities, she couldn't deny that most of their skills had been honed while operating outside the law.

"I shared a few bottles of wine with them—and Arlette and Monique—and Etienne told me that their records have been, er, expunged, and they are currently working for the king, if you can believe it."

Jo gave a snort of laughter. "I *can't* believe it, but I'm glad to hear they've landed on their feet."

"They told me to pass along their gratitude for dropping a word in the ear of your former employer." He paused and added. "They said that without your help, they would still be working in the shadows."

Jo shrugged, her face warming at the unwanted praise. "It didn't cost me anything to help them." Indeed, it had given her former employer—the new Queen of Sweden—something to do to fill her long days. The older woman had met the two rogues once, and because she had a soft spot for handsome young men, she'd been happy to mention them to the Bourbon king, a man who was in dire need of trustworthy retainers.

"How are matters between Guy and Cecile progressing?" Elliot asked.

Jo smirked at his question; really, all three men—the Duke, Guy, and Elliot—were worse than gossiping old ladies when it came to each other's love lives.

"Oh, come now," he cajoled, cutting her the faint smile that caused only the hint of a dimple in his left cheek. Jo never would have guessed that a dimple could be more persuasive than a good, sharp knife.

"I think Cecile is softening toward him." Jo admitted, and then added with a smirk of her own, "But having Guy on stage six nights a week is making so much money for her that I'm not sure she can find it in herself to close the breach between them."

Elliot laughed, and the sound was almost as dangerous as his dimple. "Yes, I'd heard the shows quickly sell out these days." He lowered his voice. "I understand Cecile has a new employee—a woman named Helen Keeble—whom she engaged as governess for the little girl she recently adopted?"

Jo gave him a mocking look. "Are you sure you really went to France, Elliot? You seem remarkably well-informed about what is going on at the Fayre."

"Guy keeps me up to date," he admitted with a faint smile. "He mentioned that you knew about Miss Keeble's real identity before he told you."

Jo shrugged. It had just been coincidence that she'd known the real identity of Cecile's new governess—Helen Keeble, who was actually the heiress Helen Carter. Jo had once met Helen when she and

Mungo had gone to meet with Jacob Carter, Helen's father, shortly after they'd moved to London and were looking for work.

Mr. Carter had wanted to hire them to do some spying on his competitors, but Mungo had taken an instant dislike to the arrogant industrialist, so they'd never taken the job. Not long after that meeting, Mungo had received the offer to guard Marianne. If they'd taken the job with Carter, Jo would never have met Marianne or Cecile . . . or Elliot.

If they'd taken the job with Carter, then maybe Mungo wouldn't have walked down that particular street that day—maybe he'd still be alive. Maybe—

"Jo?"

A wave of emotion—that seemed to have come out of thin air—threatened to choke her.

"Jo?"

She blinked and wrenched her thoughts from the dreadful day when the constables had come to the lodgings she'd shared with Mungo and had asked her to come and identify his body.

Jo's gaze slowly focused on the man in front of her.

Only then did she realize the music had stopped.

"The dance is over, Jo," he said, frowning. "Is something wrong?"

"It's hot in here," she said, her voice rough with poorly suppressed emotion. "Could we—"

"Yes." Elliot took her arm and guided her off the dance floor. "There is a terrace out back. Let's get some air."

Chapter 12

Elliot glanced worriedly at Jo as he led her toward the French doors. What had happened to her? She'd seemed fine, and then suddenly she'd gone pale. He would have sworn she was on the verge of weeping. But Jo weeping? It was inconceivable.

One of the doors had been propped open, and a dozen couples milled about on the broad terrace.

Elliot led Jo down the steps and deeper into Sin's garden, which was one of the grandest in the city.

Paper lanterns marked the paths, but he'd been to the house hundreds of times and knew the way well without any extra lights. He led her off the illuminated walkway toward a rose arbor that sheltered a miniature pagoda.

Elliot used his handkerchief to dust off the bench. "Here, sit."

She sat without speaking.

"What is wrong, Jo?" he asked, dropping down beside her.

"Nothing—I'm fine. I don't know what came over me. Perhaps it was just the heat."

Elliot clucked his tongue and repeated, "What's wrong?"

She held her breath for a long moment, and then slowly let it out. "I was just thinking about why I knew Helen's identity."

"How *did* you know who she was?"

"Before my father died, he had an interview with Jacob Carter, who wanted us to do some work for him. Mungo took an immediate dislike to him."

Elliot thought it strange that she called her father by his Christian name but kept that to himself. Instead, he said, "What didn't he like about the fellow?"

"Carter is a cold, arrogant man, and he looked at me as if I were an insect, asking why Mungo had brought a *girl* along to the meeting. I could tell Mungo was furious and thought Carter was a fool. We took our leave not long afterward and encountered Helen, who was just returning home. Even that brief interaction was enough to see that she was kind, personable, and pleasant-faced—not at all like her father."

Elliot didn't say what he was thinking—that he had wondered how a man who sold secrets to the enemy and betrayed his country could have raised such an honorable daughter as Jo.

Jo went on. "Not long after that meeting, we took the job protecting Marianne. I was just thinking that if we had done differently, perhaps Mungo would still be alive."

"That sort of thinking could drive a person mad," Elliot said.

She nodded.

"So . . . are you still taking work? I mean outside the Fayre?"

"I took Guy's job."

"Right. But I meant—"

"Are you prying, Elliot?"

He laughed. "Maybe a little."

"No, I've not taken any other work." She sighed. "But I should."

"Why? I thought Cecile paid better than Barnabas."

She gave him a pointed look.

"What?"

"Have you been spying on me?"

"No, not at all," he lied. "I think Guy must have mentioned it."

"Hmm."

"Why do you say that you should take extra work?" he asked, deeming it prudent to move the conversation along.

She shrugged, staring at a moth fluttering around a nearby lantern.

"I'll be in town for a while—won't that keep you busy?" he teased.

Jo turned to him slowly, not just her face, but her body. "I beg your pardon?"

"I know you've been following me."

It might have been the first time he'd ever seen her completely taken by surprise. "Er, I don't know what you are talking about."

"Hmm, don't you?" Elliot tugged off one of his gloves and took a tempting ash blond curl between his fingers. It looked like coiled silver in the moonlight but was as soft as spun silk.

"You are so beautiful, Jo."

Her lips parted, and Elliot could no longer resist.

Jo met him halfway, her familiar scent and taste sending a shock wave of yearning through him.

They clashed like starving people. Elliot was vaguely aware that he'd clamped his arms around her in a too-tight hold—as if he could keep her there, as if they could stay on this bench forever.

Jo opened to him and probed him, giving and taking, conquering and submitting. He knew it was a cliché, but he honestly felt like a man who'd been deprived of water for months and could finally quench his thirst.

Elliot groaned when Jo wriggled away, but it was only so that she could slip her arms free and twine them around his neck, her gloved fingers clutching at his hair, which he'd allowed to grow back over the course of the last year.

"It's so much longer," she murmured when they came up for air. "And it is curly. I never would have guessed."

He smiled as he trailed kisses across to her ear and nibbled on her lobe. "I've always hated it," he confessed. "I was going to have my valet cut it tonight, but I didn't have time."

"I like it."

"Then I shall keep it long just for you."

"Is it private back here?" she murmured, leaving her own trail of kisses down his neck before pushing off his lap and standing before him.

"I think we're out of the way enough." Elliot stared up at her, not caring that his heart was probably in his eyes. "What do you have in mind? Something naughty, I hope?"

"Is this naughty?" she asked, her eyes almost black as she lifted her skirt and raised a stocking-clad knee to the bench by his hip, straddling him.

Elliot groaned. "God. Tell me I'm not dreaming this, Jo. Tell me I won't wake up in my bed, alone."

"You're not dreaming," she whispered, her hands going to the placket of his satin breeches.

Elliot left her to her work and pulled off his other glove before sliding his hands beneath the skirt of her gown.

"Bloody hell," he cursed as his fingers encountered hot satin flesh. "You feel so good," he whispered, stroking from the edge of her stockings up and up, until he encountered curls and then slippery, soft skin.

They both hissed in a breath when she closed her hand around his hard length.

"I've missed you," he murmured, breaching her tight entrance with one finger, pumping her slowly.

She rolled her hips to take him deeper, working his cock with tight, firm strokes. "I want you inside me," she said, lifting off his hand and then positioning him at her entrance.

"Good God, Jo," he groaned as she sank down on him slowly, taking him into her body inch by torturous inch, until he was seated deep within her.

He had to bite his tongue when she began to move, posting on him hard and fast.

She took his face in her hands and stared into his eyes. "Have you thought about me? About this?" she asked in a raspy voice.

"I've thought of little else," he admitted, not caring if that made him sound desperate for her. He *was* desperate. Not just to touch her and make love to her, but to wake up to her in the mornings and be with her for at least some part of every day.

Elliot groaned as she took him toward the brink far too fast. He had only enough wits remaining to slide a hand beneath her gown and locate the source of her pleasure.

"Elliot!" she hissed as he caressed her, riding him with a single-mindedness that had him coming far too quickly.

Once again, he forgot himself in his pleasure and spent inside her.

"Ah, Jo," he muttered dazedly as she gave in to her own climax.

They rested in a tangle of limbs, their breathing louder than the distant sounds from the house.

Elliot slid his arms around her body and held her tight. "I can't let you go. This can't be the last time. I love you, Jo."

Her body stiffened at his declaration, but he couldn't bring himself to regret it. She needed to know how he felt.

He needed her to know.

Jo's mind rang with his words as the two of them straightened their clothing.

I love you, Jo.

She'd never heard sweeter words.

Or sadder ones.

"Jo?"

She made herself meet his gaze.

He took her hand. "I meant what I said—it wasn't just the heat of passion." His lips curled up at the corners in a way that was unexpectedly boyish and charming. "Although I certainly felt moved by that. But it is true—I love you. Foolishly I'd hoped the feeling would fade—like some sort of influenza that would run its course. But it has been a year, and I am more . . . afflicted, than ever." He smoothed his thumb over her hand, which was—laughably—still properly gloved, even after what they'd just done. "I know you've seen me with Lady Elizabeth."

Jealousy twisted inside her at the name. Jo forced herself to nod.

"Courting her was my effort to move forward with my life. But it wasn't fair—not to her, you, or me. I shan't pursue her. Or anyone else. I just want you."

"We can never marry, Elliot. You *know* that. Please don't pretend that it wouldn't matter to your family. To you. You'd have to leave the Home Office. You would all be disgraced by association."

"It would not be easy. But there are ways we could—"

Jo grabbed his hands and squeezed hard enough to make him wince. "No, Elliot. *No.*"

"I don't want to be without you. I would rather—"

"I will be your lover—that is all I will agree to. But only if you promise me one thing."

His lips parted, and she saw hope warring with fear in his eyes. "What?"

"You must never pressure me to marry you. Please. It is a fairytale. Not a future for the likes of me. I will be your lover; that is my offer. Take it and we can find some happiness. If you can't accept that, then I will leave London and—"

"I accept, Jo," he said with flattering haste. "Some of you is far better than none of you. But I, too, have a promise I must ask for."

"What?" she asked, frowning.

"You are too good at leaving and too quick to do so. You can't just disappear without telling me. You must promise that. It's been one of my biggest fears. I know you moved from your last lodgings, and my heart just about stopped when I realized that you very well might have gone for good." He gave a weak laugh. "I still don't know where you're living."

Jo couldn't help smiling. "I'll take that as something of an accomplishment."

Elliot pulled her close and kissed her hard. "Don't ever disappear on me. Promise it."

She hesitated, but then nodded. "I will always tell you before I leave."

"And you'll tell me where you go?"

Jo chewed her lip, but then nodded.

"Good." He seemed to shake himself. "I suppose we should return to the ball."

"I don't want to go back in there."

Elliot laughed. "You've only danced twice."

"Twice was plenty."

He took her face in his hands, his skin warm and rough against her cheeks. "I'll admit I don't like to think of you dancing with another man. I wanted to kill Guy."

Jo gave a surprised bark of laughter. "You were jealous of *Guy*?"

"I've never felt so selfish about somebody in my life. I want you all to myself." He kissed her—deeply and lingeringly.

Jo never wanted it to end, but Elliot eventually broke their embrace. "I feel as if I'm dreaming."

"Me, too," she admitted.

Elliot took out his watch and grimaced. "We've been out here quite a while. It might be better to linger a little bit longer and then go back in during supper—that way, fewer people will notice."

"Do you think people were watching *us*?"

"Oh, there are always people watching at balls."

"Who?"

"Chaperones, for one. And then there is one of my grandmother's dearest, oldest friends in there—Lady Trentham. She will be watching me to report back to my grandmother."

"Will you be in trouble?"

He gave a rueful laugh. "Let's just say I shall need to endure an inquisition not so different from the infamous Spanish one."

"She will be unhappy to hear you disappeared with an unknown female."

He shrugged.

"What about Lady Elizabeth? Isn't she here tonight?"

He nodded.

"Weren't you engaged to dance with her?" she asked, even though she didn't want to hear the answer.

"She hadn't arrived yet when I saw you and the others. I am not committed for any other dances—which means I can slip away without hurting anyone's feelings." He hesitated. "Although we'll certainly face questions from Guy and Cecile."

Jo groaned. "They will be insufferable."

"We'll just tell them we got caught up in the cardroom."

Jo perked up at that.

Elliot smiled. "Do you like cards?"

"Better than dancing," she admitted.

"We could slip into the cardroom until supper, and that way we'd not be telling falsehoods."

"Let's do that—it might keep the two of them from letting their imaginations run wild."

Elliot stood and held out his hand. "Shall we?"

Jo let him help her to her feet. "I never asked you—how did you know I was watching you in the park?" she asked as they strolled back toward the house.

"I saw Angus."

She snorted. "Wait until I have a talk with him."

"I think he wanted me to see him."

So did Jo. Angus had taken a definite liking to Elliot.

"I'll bring you through this side door, and then we can sneak into the cardroom with nobody the wiser," Elliot said, leading her down a different path, rather than back to the terrace.

"You seem to know this house well."

"I spent a great deal of time here when I was a lad," he said, opening a door into a room that was dark. "This is the music room." His voice echoed eerily as he guided her quickly and surely through what felt like a huge room.

He opened the door just a crack and looked out. "Nobody around."

"Do we really have to be this concerned?" Jo asked, amused by his theatrics.

"It can damage a lady's reputation beyond repair to loiter with a gentleman," he said as he led her out into the corridor.

"I think you are just afraid of what your grandmother will do if she hears you've been sneaking around with a strange woman."

He laughed. "That, too." He opened a door and gestured her inside. Tables had been set up, most of them peopled with men, but there were women, too, although most were older.

Elliot led her to a table where there were two empty chairs.

One of the men looked up from the cards he was shuffling and smiled. "Hello, Wingate. Back from your travels, I see." The man's inquisitive gaze slid over Jo and then back to Elliot.

"Good to see you, Markham," Elliot said, nodding to the other two men at the table. "Edwards, Fisk."

Jo relaxed when she realized that nobody would demand to know her name or ask what she was doing there.

Over the course of the next hour, they played hand after hand of *vingt et un*. The amount they were allowed to wager was appropriately termed *chicken* stakes, and the play was commensurately casual, with lots of lazy banter between players.

Jo enjoyed listening far more than talking—what did she have to say to these people?—and Elliot seemed to understand her preference and protected her from any prying.

The deal passed around the table, and even she had a turn. Elliot, not surprisingly, was an excellent player. The other men were too impulsive and overbid more often than not.

Players came and went, and by the time supper rolled around, the room had mostly emptied out. When the other two card players at their table excused themselves, Elliot turned to Jo.

"Are you ready to—"

"Ah, Wingate." They looked up to find an older gentleman with piercing blue eyes and salt-and-pepper hair smiling down at them.

Elliot cocked his head and stood. "I'm sorry, do I—"

"No, we are not acquainted—not yet, at least. I'm Stanley Gray."

Only because she was watching Elliot so closely did she notice the slight stiffening of his posture. "A pleasure to meet you, Sir Stanley."

The older man nodded and smiled, and then his gaze settled on Jo. He frowned, his eyes widening as he stared at her. The silence dragged on. And on. It was clear he was waiting for an introduction, and just as clear that Elliot had no intention of providing one.

Sir Stanley finally broke the awkward moment. "I heard there was an unbeatable duo in here," he said in a teasing voice, settling into the chair across from them. "I thought I'd come try my luck. Unless you are going to supper?"

Elliot cut her a quick, speaking look.

Jo gave a slight shrug. They'd already ignored the man's request for an introduction; they could hardly just run off and leave him without inviting comment. Even Jo knew that much.

Elliot sat down and waved to a servant for a new pack. Another servant came to the table with a tray of champagne.

"Sir?" Elliot gestured to the older man.

"Why yes, I'll have one."

By the time Elliot had distributed the champagne, the new cards had arrived.

"It's your deal," he said, sliding the pack toward Jo.

It wasn't, but she appreciated his giving her something to do while the two men chatted about mutual acquaintances.

Whenever Jo looked up from the table, she caught Sir Stanley giving her a quizzical look.

"I'm sorry," he said the third time she caught him. "But you look so familiar." His eyes narrowed as he studied her. "I feel sure we've met before?"

"I don't think so," she said, shuffling the cards. "I only recently moved to London," she added to soften her somewhat harsh retort.

"Oh? From where, if you don't mind my asking?"

Jo did mind, but she could hardly say so. "Brussels." That was safe enough—half of England had traveled to the city when the war had ended the first time.

"Ah."

Gray was an excellent card player, and the next few hands went quickly, Jo losing three of the five hands.

By the time Elliot's deal was over, more players were returning from supper, and they had a full table.

Elliot gave her a querying look, and Jo nodded.

"If you'll excuse us, Sir Stanley," Elliot said, sliding the cards over to the other man. "We shall leave you in charge of the table."

He smiled up at them. "It was nice to meet you both."

They left the way they'd come in, rather than through the door that connected to the ballroom.

"Do you want to come with me to take our leave of Sin and Marianne?" Elliot asked once they were out in the corridor. "Or shall I just pop back inside and take care of it for us?"

"Would you mind?"

"Not at all. Why don't you go and fetch your things and send one of the servants for a carriage? I'll meet you in the foyer."

Jo was relieved that she wouldn't need to get tangled in awkward goodbyes. She knew she would already face enough questions tomorrow at work when Cecile interrogated her about where she'd disappeared to.

A servant was helping her with her cloak when Elliot came hurrying down the stairs.

"That was fast," she murmured as the servant went to fetch his coat.

"I didn't bother trying to get close to Sin or Marianne—they were being mobbed—so I told Guy; he said that he'd pass along the message—after he scolded me for sneaking off with you."

Jo groaned.

"Yes, you'd better prepare for a grilling tomorrow. From both of them."

The door opened, and a noisy group of young men poured into the foyer. Elliot glared them down when they ogled Jo.

She smirked up at him when they were outside the house. "Protecting me?"

"Somebody needs to teach these young jackanapes manners," he grumbled.

"You weren't like that at their age?"

"No. Maybe." He snorted. "Probably."

A hackney waited for them, wedged between the dozens of grand carriages and coaches.

Jo let Elliot pull down the steps, even though she was perfectly capable of hopping inside without them. Why not be a lady for one night?

"Where to?" he asked, standing beside the door.

"This is your way of finding out where I live, isn't it?"

"I promise to keep it a secret."

She cocked her head at him.

Elliot sighed, and said, "You take this cab. I'll get another. Good night, Jo."

"Get in, Elliot."

"Are you—"

"Get in before I come to my senses."

Elliot hopped in with such haste that she couldn't help smiling.

The vent opened. "Where to?" the driver asked.

When Jo gave the man her address, Elliot's jaw sagged.

"Why? You don't think I can afford rooms in that part of the city?"

"Er—"

Jo laughed. "Don't worry about offending me. The truth is that I couldn't afford it if I hadn't done a favor for the owner of the building. He graciously offered me a room in his attic—I suspect because it was too small for anyone else to want it."

"It wasn't so much the address as the fact that—"

"That it's only a few streets behind yours?" she suggested.

Elliot laughed. "I'm not much of a spy, am I? I searched all over the place looking for you, and you were only a few hundred feet away the entire time."

"Don't worry, I won't tell anyone," she promised, unable to resist smirking.

Chapter 13

Elliot followed Jo up four flights of stairs and was gasping by the time he reached the top floor, which contained two doors on the landing, but only one with a tiny lantern hanging beside it on a cast-iron hook.

"Good Lord, that's a trek."

"You've been spending too much time sitting behind a desk," Jo pointed out mildly.

Elliot was too out of breath to argue.

She unlocked the door and was about to enter the room when a low growling sound came out of the darkness.

Elliot grabbed her arm. "I think somebody's in there."

Jo clucked her tongue and lifted the lantern. "Angus, that was naughty," she chided.

The raven stood on a perch beside the window. He clacked his beak and made a rusty laughing sound.

"Good God! He sounded just like some sort of jungle cat."

"He learned how to make that sound when Mungo and I briefly traveled with a menagerie in Prussia. They had a poor old tiger who barely had any teeth left. Talk like Teddy, Angus."

The raven roared loudly enough to rattle the room's only window.

Elliot snorted. "I'll bet your neighbors love that."

Jo tossed her reticule and shawl onto a small table. "Fortunately, the other side of the attic is only for storage, and nobody lives below me. It is leased by a group of solicitors who are only there during the day." She took his hat and set it next to her belongings.

When she unfastened her cloak, Elliot lifted it off her shoulders.

"Why, thank you," she murmured, taking it from him and hanging it on a coatrack that already held her plain gray wool cloak and the battered, old coat she'd worn all across France.

Elliot unbuttoned his coat, glancing around the room as Jo bustled about and tossed some coal into the tiny stove.

The apartment was a decent-sized room with a tiny box room that she must use as a necessary.

To say it was spartan was an understatement. There was a narrow bed, a small clothes cupboard, a writing desk, a bookshelf with a dozen or so books, a table with only one chair, and a large trunk at the foot of the bed.

"Would you like something to drink?" she asked.

"Whatever you are having."

Jo gestured to the chair. "Have a seat."

Elliot stared at the single chair.

"Go ahead," she urged, taking some cheese, bread, and a bottle of wine out of a cupboard above the counter.

Elliot sat and gorged on the sight of her. Even though she was dressed in a ball gown—no matter how simple—she somehow looked perfectly at home bustling about in the tiny kitchen.

"Did you enjoy your first ball?" he asked.

She shrugged as she brought a loaf of dark brown bread and a big wedge of Stilton to the table. "It's not a pastime I'm eager to engage in too often, but I enjoyed seeing where Marianne lives." She handed Elliot the bottle and opener and then returned to the cutting board to slice up an apple and a small piece of cured ham before taking a glass, plate, and knife from the same cupboard where she'd stored the food.

"I only have one of each, so we shall have to share our plate and glass," she said, setting everything down on the table.

Elliot pulled out the cork and then stood. "Here, you take the chair and—"

She ignored him and went to grab the trunk handle, dragging it across the room before he could even set down the bottle.

"There," she said, sitting on the trunk and then reaching for a piece of apple.

Elliot poured the wine and handed her the glass. They shared the simple meal she'd prepared, the food disappearing quickly.

"You were hungry," he said, refilling the glass. "We shouldn't have skipped supper. I'll wager Sin and Marianne had some delicious food for their guests."

"I enjoyed playing cards more than eating," she said, cutting the last piece of ham in half and pushing a piece toward him while popping the other bit into her mouth. "Who is Sir Stanley, and why was he looking at me so intently?"

Elliot shook his head. "I don't know why he was staring like that. He's one of my superiors at the Home Office. Not in the same department as I am, but high up in the hierarchy. To be honest, I'm surprised he even knew who I was."

She nodded, her expression pensive.

He loved watching her think. Her brain was wonderfully nimble, and he'd been awed by the speed and elegance of the plans she'd formulated during their time in France. But while he recognized her look as thoughtful, he had no idea what she was thinking.

He loved that, too.

In fact, he had to admit that he loved everything about her.

Except for her unwillingness to try to make their union a permanent one.

But he'd take impermanence for now. He'd take it and be bloody grateful.

Elliot stood and held out his hand, shaking her from her thoughts. "Come here," he said softly.

* * *

Jo shivered at the quiet command in Elliot's voice and what she heard beneath it: raw desire.

She held out her hand, and Elliot lifted her to her feet and tugged her toward him, his body lean and hard against hers. He cupped her jaw and claimed her mouth with a deep, thorough kiss—the sort they'd never had the time or leisure to enjoy in the past.

Jo gave in to temptation and explored his body, squeezing the corded muscles of his waist, her hands slipping around to his bottom.

He groaned when she dug her fingertips into the tightly packed muscle, using her thumbs to massage the dense sinews.

"Jo," he muttered as his hips jerked, thrusting his hard length against her belly. "You have too many clothes on." Elliot pulled away with a mutter of regret. "I want to see you in nothing but these." He ran a finger lightly over her pearls.

Jo's breathing roughened at the naked lust in his darkened gaze, and she nodded.

"Turn and I will unfasten your gown."

Either he'd had a great deal of experience getting women out of their clothing or he was naturally dexterous, because he had her standing in nothing but her stockings and garters in a fraction of the time it had taken the dresser at Cecile's house to get her into the gown earlier.

He took her by the shoulders and turned her slowly, until she was facing him.

She wasn't the only one struggling to breathe normally. His impassive expression had fled; in its place was frank desire, his eyes flicking up and down her body, landing on her breasts and fixing there.

Jo groaned and let her head fall back when his hot palms grazed her hard nipples, his warm hands caressing and teasing as her back arched, chasing his touch.

Elliot eased her backward, toward her narrow bed. "Lie down," he ordered, grunting with approval when she sprawled across the mattress and allowed her thighs to fall open.

He sank to his knees, his body shoving her legs wide, and lowered his mouth to one of her nipples. He sucked and nibbled until each breast was aching and heavy, and sharp bolts of desire were arrowing down to her sex. Jo lifted her hips and they both moaned when she ground her aching mound against his hard belly, her wet swollen folds sliding against the ridged flesh of his abdomen.

"Am I neglecting you?" he teased, the words hot puffs against the thin skin of her breast. "Do you need *this*?"

This turned out to be his hand, the slightly rough pads of his fingers parting her, one finger pushing inside her while he used the heel of his hand to massage the small bundle of nerves that was becoming increasingly demanding.

Jo's orgasm came at her fast, surprising her with its speed and ferocity.

She was still shuddering when he rose up between her splayed thighs, his cock hard, slick, and ruddy as he stroked himself. "I need to be inside you."

She shifted on the bed to accommodate him, and he lowered himself over her.

Jo wrapped her legs around his hips, earning a fierce look as he positioned himself and then entered her with a powerful thrust.

His eyelids fluttered as he held her full. "I can't seem to get inside you deeply enough, Jo."

She thrilled at the fervent need in his voice, pulling him tighter and offering herself up to him.

Elliot stared into her heavy-lidded gaze while he worked her with deep, measured thrusts.

Her lips curved ever so slightly as she stared up at him, her hands sliding up and down his hips, strong, rough fingers kneading and exploring him with arousing confidence.

Elliot pulled out until only his sensitive crown filled her, the tight muscles at her entrance squeezing him deliciously. He gently pulsed inside her, teasing them both for a moment before sheathing himself balls deep, touching something deep inside her that made her body shake and tighten around him.

"You feel like heaven," he whispered.

Control, he told himself. *You have all night*, he promised his body, thrilling at the realization that she'd agreed to take him—if not as her mate, at least as her lover.

As happy as he was at her decision, his joy was underlaid by a bone-deep regret that they could never be more to each other.

He banished his concerns for the future and concentrated on that moment, making tonight good for her, working her with deep strokes that made her body ripple and buck. Over and over and over, until she was whimpering with each stroke, her heels digging into his arse, demanding more, harder.

Elliot slid his hands beneath her thighs and then pushed her knees toward her pretty tits, folding her almost in half as he rose above her, angling her body so that the next thrust made them both gasp.

"Yes," she moaned. "Just like that."

"You want it hard, Jo?"

Her nostrils flared, and her inner muscles clenched around him.

Elliot laughed with pure joy. "I'll take that as a *yes*," he said, pulling out with agonizing slowness and then slamming into her.

The room filled with the sounds of slapping flesh and grunting, muttered curses.

"Touch yourself," he ordered roughly as his hips began to jerk less smoothly.

Her pale fingers slid down her belly, and the sight of her stroking her pretty pink bud was almost more than he could take. She must have been right on the edge, because her spine suddenly bowed, and she threw her head back, her body tensing and shaking with the force of her climax.

Elliot withdrew before he lost control, pumping himself three times with his fist before his lust boiled out of him and he covered her belly in hot streaks.

He struggled against the pull of sleep and blinked his eyes. The bed was so small that the only place to collapse was right on top of her, so he pushed himself to his feet, head spinning, and stumbled toward the small alcove off her room. As he'd suspected, there was a screened chamber pot along with a commode stand and a basin of cold water. He took a cloth from a small stack and wet it. Before he returned to the bed, he tossed the wet cloth onto the tiny stove. While it hissed and steamed, he turned to look at Jo. Unlike that time in France, she hadn't fallen asleep.

She was propped up on her side, her head on her hand and her eyes following him.

Elliot retrieved the cloth and went to her. "Here, let me clean you up," he murmured, using the tepid hand towel to wipe away the mess and then tossing it onto the floor.

She rolled to the side, yanked the blanket out from under her, then held it aloft. "Come in. There is room."

Elliot slid in alongside her, and she lowered her arm, covering them both. He turned onto his side so he wasn't hanging off the narrow bed.

"Cozy," he said, inching closer, until his spent cock was nuzzling against her private curls.

"I've never had two people in this bed before."

Elliot liked the sound of that. He liked the sound of her, full stop. Liked the needy, sensual, painfully erotic noises she made when she climaxed. It was the only time she lost complete control, not just of her voice, but of the tight grasp she always kept over her emotions. It was the real Jo, the one buried deeply beneath years of hiding.

"Boring."

He blinked away his thoughts and fixed his gaze on her. "Excuse me?"

"The ball—it was boring," she said, her pale gaze locking with his.

"Why, thank you, Jo. I don't recall a greater compliment."

Jo rolled her eyes and gestured between their close, naked bodies. "Clearly I didn't mean the part that involved *you*."

"Ah," he said, amused. "What did you mean?"

"I just meant all that . . . er, etiquette, I suppose it is called. Not asking somebody to dance until you are introduced. Only getting an introduction through *some* people, but not others." She shrugged her elegant shoulders. "The dresses and jewels were very pretty, and the duke's house is—well, it is outrageously luxurious." Something that looked a lot like shyness flickered across her face. "Other than the waltz with you, I found the dancing rather . . . flat."

"I actually happen to agree."

Her eyes widened in surprise.

"I do," he insisted, although she'd not argued. "I think it must have something to do with the way you and I live the rest of the time. It is difficult to find a ball invigorating when one has blazed through Europe in the midst of a war." Elliot slid a hand over her hip, the feel of warm satin skin sending a bolt of arousal to his slumbering, but greedy, cock. "Tell me about your life in Europe—when you worked alongside your father."

"What do you want to know?"

"Anything."

She shifted her jaw from side to side, considering his question, and then said, "He had a friend, a man he'd met during the fighting in America—a Hessian mercenary—who'd been working on the Continent for years. Evidently, he was the black sheep of a wealthy family and had many connections. He did any sort of work he could find. He offered protection, arranged for people to get their wives and daughters to safety, and also made a great deal of money just selling . . . things."

"Things?"

"Apparently rich people don't like to be seen visiting a pawnbroker."

Elliot snorted. "No, that's true."

"Sometimes they sold items of value because they were living beyond their means, but often because they were preparing to run and didn't want anyone to know." She cut him a meaningful look. "You know how it was over there."

Yes, he did. War was the great leveler in lots of ways. When two or more armies converged on an area, both the rich and poor were caught between them. Of course the rich, if they were smart, would leave before that could happen. But it was amazing how often people simply did not believe the worst could happen to *them*. And so they stayed, foolishly trying to appease one side or—even worse—believing they could play the warring factions against each other.

"When the Prussian began to gather intelligence for the various allied armies, we moved, and Mungo went out on his own. He didn't want to get involved working for the government—any government. By then he had enough of a reputation that people sought him out, so there was always plenty of work."

"Why do you call him by his first name?" Elliot asked.

She blinked, the slow, thoughtful blink that usually heralded a question in response to a question.

"I don't know. Why do you ask?"

"It's just unusual."

"What? You mean unlike the rest of my life?" she asked dryly.

Elliot chuckled. "Point taken."

She smoothed the edge of the blanket, her eyes distant. "It was just easier to call him by his name once I started working alongside him."

"And when was that, exactly?"

She looked up, a faint smile curving her lips. "Are you asking how old I was?"

"I suppose I am."

"I told you before that I started to follow him when I was twelve?"

"Yes." He cringed to think of a little girl wandering alone in Europe.

"We made an agreement. He would still work on his own, but starting then, he told me where he was going so I wouldn't wonder and worry. But he still refused to take me on jobs and made me wait until I was fourteen before I could actually work alongside him." Her smile grew into a smirk. "I can see by your horrified expression that you don't approve."

"No, but then it isn't my place to approve or disapprove."

"I think he chose his jobs carefully—with me in mind—so those first few years, he never took me along on any work that was especially dangerous. For example, the first job I ever joined him on was one where we were transporting a string of hunters for some nobleman who'd been too foolish—and optimistic—to sell or move them before he had a sizeable portion of the Russian army camping on his doorstep." She gave Elliot an almost impish look. "My job was to ride an expensive horse. I have to admit, those hunters were the finest mounts I've ever ridden."

He smiled. "Did it give you the urge to hunt?"

"Not hunt, but it did make me appreciate fine horseflesh."

He recalled that she'd always had quality, but not showy, mounts for herself and her people in France.

"He didn't take me with him on all his jobs until I turned fifteen, and even then, he tried to shelter me." Her expression hardened. "I put my foot down when he was almost killed—because he'd relied on a drunk to keep lookout—and after that, we always worked together."

Elliot burned to ask about the work they'd done that had drawn the attention of the Home Office, but he suspected she would kick him down the stairs if he mentioned it. He told himself that he would leave the matter alone, because she had already given her word that she had not engaged in treasonous behavior, but the truth wasn't so simple. He wanted to be with her as a man, not another spy. He wasn't sure what he'd do if he ever learned that she'd been engaged in activities that went against his own conscience. It was better not to ask than to be forced to forget.

"I want you again," he said.

Her eyes darkened even as he watched. "Then take me."

Elliot slid his hand around her waist and cupped the tight globe of one cheek, pulling her closer, until his erection prodded against her sex.

She took his shaft in her hand, lifted her thigh, and welcomed him inside her body.

He entered her slowly, hissing at the feel of her slick heat. Once he could go no farther, he held still, flexing his cock inside her.

Jo gave a low grunt of pleasure and tightened around him. "Will this bed be good enough for you?"

"I'm liking this bed more and more each minute."

She snorted.

"Will I cause you trouble visiting you here?" he asked.

"Nobody cares. In fact, the schedule I keep means that I rarely see any of the other occupants of the building." She slid her arms around his back, cupping his arse with her strong hands and pulling him toward her, massaging him with her inner muscles and almost destroying what remained of his wits.

"Are you sure?" he asked in a strained voice, his eyes crossing with the effort of trying to sound normal. "I am not a wealthy man, but I can hire a place where neither of us would be known. I don't want to—"

"Hush," she ordered, and then rolled her hips.

Elliot groaned, teetering on the brink of mindlessness.

But one thing still niggled.

He met her gaze and held it. "You meant what you said earlier—at Sin's? That you will never leave without telling me first?"

She hesitated for only a fraction of a second before nodding. "Yes, I meant what I said. I will tell you."

Elliot knew that something about her answer was . . . off, but this time, when she began to move, he didn't have the will to stop her.

Chapter 14

Jo had been worried about all the teasing she'd have to endure from Cecile and Guy about disappearing from the ball so early, but events conspired in such a fashion that hers and Elliot's absence from supper and the rest of the dance was completely eclipsed by other matters.

Indeed, their own little drama paled in comparison to what had transpired between their friends.

"Describe it again," Jo ordered.

Elliot grinned, the unadulterated joy on his face making him look boyish and far younger than his three and a half decades. "Again? I've already told you *three* times."

"I want to hear it again," she insisted.

They were naked and sweaty and lying on Jo's narrow bed. It was still light outside, and they were alone, Angus having flown off in disgust rather than listen to the sounds of their lovemaking. For all that the raven liked Elliot, he'd been acting a bit jealous.

"Alright, one more time," Elliot said, heaving a sigh, an action which made the chiseled muscles of his chest and abdomen tighten delightfully. Did it make her a shallow person that she enjoyed looking at his body so much?

If it did, Jo decided that she didn't care.

"I was having a drink at White's with a friend of mine from the Home Office—"

"Gossiping about the recent shake-up," she couldn't help interrupting.

He gave her a pursed-lip look, but his eyes were glinting with humor. "And how do you know about the *shake-up* at the Home Office?"

"I have my ways."

"Have you been poking that attractive nose around where you shouldn't be?"

"I'm not sure such a place exists."

Elliot laughed. "Just because you *can* do something doesn't mean you *should* do it."

It was Jo's turn to laugh. "Thank you, oh wise one. I shall keep that in mind. Go on with the story."

"I was having a drink with—"

"You already said that part."

He leaned forward and kissed her hard, his clever tongue probing and flicking and stroking her in such a way that she forgot everything else.

And then he pulled away.

Jo whimpered. "But—"

"Hmm, now where was I? Or yes, I was in White's, enjoying a drink, when rumor of a woman breeching the hallowed grounds of the club flew through the building on winged feet."

Jo rolled her eyes and mumbled *purple*.

Elliot grinned. "I stood up with everyone else and followed the source of the rumor," he went on. "And whom did I see but our very own Cecile Tremblay standing in the middle of one of the rooms facing down her cousin, that weasel Curtis Blanchard, who'd been happily stuffing himself and reading a newspaper."

"I still don't understand how she even got in the door?"

"Believe it or not, all she had to do was flick back her cloak. When the servant at the door got a look at her holster and pistols, he ran for the hills."

"That was probably a wise impulse," Jo said. She was a good shot herself, but Cecile was unearthly good.

"Indeed," Elliot agreed. "But back to my story. Blanchard leapt to his feet when he saw his cousin. *'Good God! What is the meaning of this, Cecile?'* Cecile took a step toward him and—like the cowardly cad he is—he stumbled back so violently that he fell over his own chair. You could have heard a pin drop as everyone shut up so they could hear what she said. *'I'm so glad you asked me that, Curtis.'*"

Jo could just imagine it—how magnificent Cecile must have looked!

"She looked magnificent," Elliot said, as if he'd read her mind. "And she was wearing the most *gothic* pair of gauntlets, complete with studded cuffs, which she removed with positively menacing slowness. Some brave and witless flunky dared to approach her and threaten to lead her from the club, but Cecile spun around, causing the room to erupt in gasps when the crowd saw her pistols."

Elliot said in a French-accented voice, "*Unhand me.*"

Jo couldn't help it; she laughed. "You sound *uncannily* like Cecile."

Elliot winked at her and continued. "The servant darted away, in fear for his life."

"And that is when *you* stepped in," Jo said.

Elliot puffed out his chest. "'*Leave her be,*' I thundered in a voice that caused everyone's knees to knock together in fear."

Jo slapped her hand over her mouth to trap the snort that threatened to sneak out at the image of soft-spoken Elliot *thundering*.

"'*Let her speak her piece,*' I added, and Cecile turned back to Blanchard, who'd collected himself enough to begin talking. *'You're making a terrible mistake, Cecile. You must come with me and—*' But Cecile had removed one glove, held it by the soft kid, and *thwack!* Right across the face with enough force that one of the studs cut Blanchard's cheek. *'I challenge you to a duel with pistols tomorrow at dawn,*' she announced in a ringing voice. Blanchard gave a piteous, disbelieving laugh and glanced around the room—which was filled with the most powerful men in Britain—as if hoping somebody would save him.

"When nobody spoke up, he squawked, '*Duel? What in the world are you talking about?*'

"Cecile sneered. '*Do you really want me to lay out my grievances in public?*' she asked. It was easy to see her question scared the hell out of Blanchard, because he threw up his hands and gasped, '*No! But you don't understand. You don't get to choose the weapon—that is—according to etiquette, you're the challenger and you can't—*'

"'*I don't follow your stupid rules, Curtis. Meet me at dawn with your pistols or be known to every man in this room for the gutless, puling coward you really are.*'"

"That's when you offered to stand second for her," Jo said, although she already knew the answer.

"It was, indeed."

"And then you served as her knight protector and escorted her from the club."

Elliot's eyes narrowed. "Why does it sound like you are mocking me?"

"I wouldn't do such a thing."

He stared at her for a long moment and then, moving with a suddenness that was always surprising, he rolled on top of her. "You are a very naughty girl to mock your knight protector."

Jo squirmed beneath him, but he had her trapped and immobile.

"I think you need to be punished for your insolence," he whispered, and then ran his fingers lightly down her side.

"No!" Jo shrieked, the word garbled with laughter. "Please! No tickling."

"Hmm," he said, his hands stilling. "I'm not sure you've learned your lesson."

"I have," she promised. "I've learned never, ever to tell you a dangerous secret like that again."

"You didn't actually *tell* me you were ticklish—I had to torture it out of you."

The torture in question had been Elliot making her climax repeatedly, until she'd had to offer him a secret to get him to stop. As far as tortures went, Jo was ready to endure it again tonight.

Unfortunately, Elliot had to leave in an hour, and Jo had to go to work later.

"Do you really think Blanchard will pay back the money he owes Cecile?" Jo asked.

He wrapped a strand of her hair around his finger, his expression thoughtful. "He'd be a fool if he didn't pay back what she is asking—which is a great deal less than he actually owes her—but the man is clearly a fool, not to mention a criminal, based on what he did to Cecile."

Curtis Blanchard had basically stolen Cecile's family gunsmithing company from her when she'd been young, poor, and afraid. It was Jo's investigation into Cecile's background—the job Guy had asked her to do—that had unearthed the depth of Blanchard's greed and criminality.

Jo couldn't blame Cecile for what she'd done, although she would have preferred that her friend had chosen a way of confronting her cousin that wouldn't risk life and limb. A man as crooked as Blanchard would react like a cornered animal: dangerously.

"Are you worried that he won't agree to pay?" Elliot asked, guessing Jo's thoughts in that terrifying way he had.

"If Blanchard shows up for the duel, you know how dangerous it will be—no matter how good a shot Cecile is."

"That's true," he conceded, "it isn't always the best shot who wins. But it won't come to that. Blanchard is terrified of her, and the amount she is asking for is almost laughably reasonable." Elliot sighed and picked up his watch, which he'd laid on the floor beside the bed. "Well, drat. I'd better get going if I want to be there on time."

There was Cecile's house, where he was needed in his capacity as second, even though there would hopefully be no shots fired.

Jo pulled the covers up to her chest and watched with interest as Elliot busied himself collecting scattered garments. This was the second time he'd come to her tiny garret in two days. She had to admit it was nice to have something to look forward to besides work and sleep.

Elliot sat on her only chair and pulled on his stockings. "What would you say to a short trip out of town?"

"What do you mean?"

"Nothing terribly exciting, just a few days at the seaside. I have a cottage—a *real* cottage, not what Sin or Guy would call a cottage, which would be a fifty-room mansion—that is just sitting empty. It's been a while since I checked in on it. It is secluded, and the only person you might see would be the old fellow who looks after it, although that is doubtful, as he is shy of strangers." He stood and pulled on his drawers and buckskins. "What do you say? A bit of a holiday?"

"I've never had a holiday," she admitted.

"Never?"

"Never."

"Now why doesn't that surprise me? You work all the time." He pulled his shirt over his head, unfortunately covering his delicious body.

"How long do you have in mind?" she asked.

"Half a day there, half back, and two nights at the cottage?"

Jo chewed her lip as he tucked in his shirt, slipped on his waistcoat, and then went to the tiny mirror beside the door and tied on his cravat.

She loved watching him dress almost as much as she loved watching him undress. He was so quick and efficient and did everything with a minimum of fuss.

"Well?" he said, turning to her as he buttoned his waistcoat. "Do you want to go?"

"I'll have to talk to Cecile first—to make sure she has somebody else to take my place. But it sounds lovely. But Angus comes, too," she quickly added.

Elliot laughed. "Of course, he does."

As things turned out, Jo didn't need to ask for days off, because two days later, Cecile gave the entire Fayre a month-long holiday.

Once again, it was Elliot who was the bearer of the news.

When Jo stared at him in shock, he laughed at her. "I'm beginning to question your spying abilities."

Jo had just been preparing to set out for the theater when Elliot had appeared at her door.

"What were you doing over at Cecile's house? Shouldn't you be at work at this time of day?" she asked.

"I was at work, but then I received a rather fascinating message from Guy."

Jo unwound her scarf and pulled off her mittens, tossing both onto the nearby table. "This sounds like something that will require some tea."

"Yes, a gallon at least."

Jo opened the room's only window and whistled. Angus, who'd been perched on a lamppost waiting for her to go to work, flew back up to the sill. Sometimes his expressions were so human, it amazed her. The big black bird took one look at Elliot and seemed to sigh and roll his eyes before flying over to his perch, a look of resignation on his face.

"Quit pouting," Jo chided. "This means biscuits."

"*Biscuits*," Angus croaked.

"And something else, old man," Elliot said, pulling a small bundle from his pocket and unwrapping a sizeable chunk of cheese.

Jo shook her head as Angus flew over and landed on Elliot's shoulder. "You are spoiling him," she said, but she was secretly pleased the two got on so well. Angus had never sat on anyone else, not even Mungo.

"Lord," Elliot grunted, handing over the cheese. "He weighs a stone. How do you bear it?"

"Practice," she said, putting the kettle on the tiny stove and adding a few pieces of coal. When she set out two cups—one brand new—Elliot chuckled. "Is that for me?"

Jo knew her face was red. She'd purchased the cup—and an extra spoon, fork, and plate—on her way to work yesterday.

"I don't want to share cups, because you like your tea too sweet," she muttered.

Elliot closed the distance between them and set his hands on her waist.

"What?" she demanded, looking everywhere but at his face.

He took her chin and made her look at him. "Thank you," he said simply, and then kissed her lightly on the lips.

Angus, the traitorous bastard, was watching the proceedings with a distinctly ravenish smirk on his face.

"Tell me what has happened *now*," she ordered, turning away to set the table with a clatter.

"I cannot believe this," Jo said.

Elliot knew he was grinning but couldn't help it. "You've said that four times."

Jo shook her head, her expression one of amazement. "How could I have failed to learn that Cecile is a duchess when I investigated her?" she demanded, not waiting for an answer before flinging up her hands. "Ugh. I cannot believe I neglected to find such information."

It was the most emotion Elliot had ever seen her show—other than when she was in bed. "You shouldn't feel bad, Jo—neither Guy nor I had any clue about it, either." The look of disdainful disbelief she gave him made him snort. "I can tell by your charming expression that doesn't surprise you—that you rank yourself far above the two of us."

"Ranking myself above Guy is no great stretch, I hope."

"No, that's true."

"As for you? Well, you must operate within the boundaries of the law." She smirked. "At least English law. I'll wager you did plenty of illegal things when you were in France."

Elliot didn't want to discuss that. Instead, he leaned his hip against the table and took her hand in his. "Now that Cecile has closed the circus for a month, you can come with me to Corton and stay a bit longer."

"That is the name of the town where your cottage is?"

"It's not a town—not even much of a village, really. I daresay it originally came into being to serve Somerleyton Hall, but that has been empty of residents for years, so the small population has become even smaller." Elliot squeezed her hand. "Well? Will you run away with me for a few days?"

She chewed her lip for a long moment and then met his gaze. "Let me talk to Cecile and make sure she doesn't need me. If she doesn't, I'll be ready to go when you are."

An hour later Jo, Cecile, and Helen sat in the cozy kitchen of Cecile's house.

"I'm pleased that you came," Cecile said, looking a bit frazzled. "I daresay you've heard some interesting . . . rumors and are wondering which ones are true?"

"You're a wealthy French duchess," Jo said, putting her out of her misery.

Cecile gave a startled laugh. "I should have known you'd have the real story. Who told you? Elliot?"

Why lie?

"Yes," Jo said.

Cecile heaved a sigh and glanced at Helen, who gave her a reassuring smile. Jo thought it was amusing that Helen, Guy's former betrothed, and Cecile, the love of Guy's life, had become not only roommates, but good friends.

Speaking of Guy . . .

"How is Guy taking all this?" Jo asked.

Cecile scowled. "Much as one would expect of a man: like a fool."

Jo cut Helen a quick look, disheartened when the other woman gave a slight shake of her head.

"But I did not want to speak to you about Guy," Cecile said, taking the matter off the table for discussion, which was probably just as well. Jo wasn't exactly skilled when it came to offering advice about men and the problems they caused.

"Cecile will be selling the Fayre," Helen said when Cecile appeared to sink into a fit of brooding, no doubt about Guy.

Jo wasn't surprised to hear it. "You wouldn't be the first duchess to sell the circus," she couldn't resist saying.

Cecile's eyes widened and then she laughed—a genuine laugh this time. "I never thought of that."

"Rather singular, isn't it?" Jo persisted. "Two women from a theatrical group becoming duchesses?" She cocked her head. "Except you've been a duchess all along."

Cecile had the decency to look a bit guilty. "Yes," she admitted. "Since I was fourteen."

Jo snorted and shook her head. "I'm not much of an investigator."

"You should not feel bad, Jo. Nobody in England knew the truth about that part of my past. Indeed, only a few knew about it anywhere."

"Why didn't you ever tell anyone?" Helen asked, putting Jo's thoughts into words.

Cecile shrugged. "I had no proof of my marriage because I lost everything in the crossing from France. Who would have believed me? Besides, you know how it is for French emigres here. We flooded this country for years. I once knew of a duke and duchess who operated a pawnbroker shop in Shoreditch, so I knew that having a title often makes no difference. It was just easier to keep it all to myself."

Jo could certainly understand her attitude. She'd never been accused of treason, but she could just imagine the way people would look at her if they ever found out who her father was. It was *definitely* better to keep that information to herself.

"In any case," Cecile said, "I wanted to talk to you both about the Fayre." She grimaced. "I don't want to close it permanently, but—"

"I will operate it for you."

Cecile and Jo both gawked at Helen.

She chuckled at whatever she saw on their faces. "I don't know why that surprises you both so much."

"But what about Cat?" Cecile asked. "You don't wish to be her governess any longer?"

"I love teaching Cat," Helen said, "but as a duchess, you will soon be moving among a different set people; people who would recognize me."

Cecile grimaced. "Ah, that is true." She glanced at Jo. "Would you want to stay, also? I know you mentioned moving."

"I've been considering staying in London," Jo said. Now more than ever since she'd finally put aside her reservations and taken Elliot as a lover.

"I would like to purchase the Fayre—and this house," Helen said. "I have a small sum of money set aside—it wouldn't be enough to pay for everything outright, but I could make payments to you."

"You must know that I've recently learned the duke left me a very wealthy woman. I could just give—"

"I don't want you to give it to me," Helen interrupted, "not that I don't appreciate the offer," she added hastily.

Cecile chuckled wryly. "I didn't want to just take it from Marianne, either, so I understand. You wish to stand on your own legs, as the saying goes."

Helen nodded.

"I have some money," Jo said.

The other two women couldn't have looked more surprised than Jo felt. She swallowed, her face suddenly hot. "Er, if you want a partner, that is."

Helen smiled, the expression transforming her rather plain features into something lovely. "Indeed, I would."

Cecile grinned at Jo. "I guess this means you definitely will not be moving."

No, it didn't look like she would.

Jo was excited by the prospect of putting down roots, but her excitement was leavened by a healthy dose of concern. Just how long would Elliot be satisfied with their relationship? And what would Jo do if he decided to push for changes?

Chapter 15

Elliot was bent low over the shadowbox table when the door opened behind him.

He straightened up and turned to find the new head of the Secret Office, Sir Stanley Gray, looking at him.

"I'm sorry to have kept you waiting, Wingate."

"I haven't been here long," Elliot said, returning the other man's surprisingly warm smile.

Gray gestured to the display Elliot had been studying. "I see you were looking at my American souvenirs."

"You have some fascinating things," Elliot said.

The older man strode over to join him, and they both stared down at the intricately beaded objects beneath the glass.

"That is a ceremonial breastplate for a Mohawk brave," Gray said, and then turned toward the wall-mounted shadowboxes. "Those are arrowheads, although of course most of the tribes use firearms now. But when I was there, many of the Indian fighters still carried bows."

"Brilliant workmanship," Elliot murmured, transfixed by the beauty of the item. "If I might ask, when were you in America, sir?"

Gray cut Elliot another of his charming smiles. "It's over thirty years ago, now."

Elliot knew that Gray had so distinguished himself during the colonial rebellion—or American War of Independence, depending on who you asked—that he'd been promoted up the ranks in a way that not many men of his background, the son of a butcher, could claim.

"Something to drink, Wingate?" Gray gestured to several decanters.

"Whatever you're having, sir."

"I'm having whiskey that a good friend sends me from the American state of Kentucky."

Elliot studied the older man as he poured two glasses of amber-colored spirits. He was perhaps an inch or two shorter than Elliot's own five-foot-ten and trim and fit. His once brown hair was now heavily salted with gray, and Elliot put him at somewhere between fifty-five and sixty-five. He'd heard nothing but good things about Sir Stanley during the decade he'd worked for the various intelligence gathering organs of His Majesty's government and had been pleased to learn he was taking the post.

Gray handed a glass to Elliot. "Have a seat," he said, lowering himself into his own chair behind the desk.

Elliot sat in one of the comfortable wing chairs and took a sip while Gray opened a file that had been lying on his desk. The whiskey was unusual—not like the Scotch he generally preferred—but quite delicious.

Gray looked up from whatever it was that he'd been staring at. "As I was bringing myself up to speed on the department, I came across a rather interesting—and disturbing—piece of information. I'll admit it was part of the reason I sought you out at Staunton's ball last week—I was curious about the man who'd soon be working for me. I've heard a great deal about you, Wingate, and all of it outstanding."

"Thank you, sir."

"Not until I was given the position was I privileged to view certain files, however."

Elliot waited patiently for whatever it was Gray wanted to say.

"It seems my predecessor kept some rather fascinating items secret from the Home Secretary." He slid a piece of paper across the desk to Elliot.

He leaned close enough to see what was on the sheet of parchment. While the few lines he read didn't surprise him, Elliot was disappointed all the same; he'd hoped—foolishly, it appeared—that Sir Humphrey Wardlow would have buried all evidence of Elliot's illicit adventure in France the year before.

Elliot sat back and took another, larger, mouthful of whiskey, enough to cause a slightly painful burn in his throat.

"You have nothing to say?" Gray asked.

"What could I possibly say that you don't already know? From the end of February 1815 until the middle of April last year, I engaged in an illegal mission into France during a period when our government was in the process of a peace negotiation. By all rights, I should have been not only sacked but thrown into the brig."

Gray sat back in his chair, picked up his glass, and took a drink, his expression unreadable.

Elliot was perfectly fine with silences, uncomfortable or otherwise, and in no hurry to either fill it or break it.

"Obviously the powers that be would not be happy if word of your *mission* were to come out," Gray finally said.

Elliot remained quiet, wondering where the hell this was going.

"Your account made no mention of an operative named Josephine 'Blade' Brown."

Seeing that Elliot had purposely left out Jo's involvement in all that business last year, he was more than a little bit startled at Gray's disclosure. "What makes you think it should have, sir?"

Gray smiled, but it wasn't the open, warm expression of only a few minutes earlier. "It is my business to know things, Wingate."

Before Elliot could come up with a response, the other man continued, "Is Josephine Brown the young woman I played cards with the other night?"

Elliot only hesitated for a moment, but Gray chuckled and said, "Thank you, that is enough of an answer. I want you to tell me how this woman was involved in your effort to rescue the Duke of Staunton's brother."

Elliot's first impulse was to tell the other man to go to hell—regardless of whether that meant the end of his job—or a trip to gaol.

Gray must have seen that, because he said, "We've been watching her lodgings for weeks now, Wingate. I know you have recently become a... er, visitor."

Elliot knew his face was hot; not with mortification, but with anger.

"You can tell me about Miss Brown, or I can bring her in and have some of our operatives question her."

That was a polite way of saying that Gray would torture whatever he wanted out of Jo.

Elliot forced down the fury he felt at the other man's threat and asked in a cool, well-modulated tone, "May I ask why you wish to know about her?"

"She is the only link to a case the War Department has been pursuing for decades."

"Decades? Josephine Brown is only twenty-nine years old."

"Actually, she is thirty-one, Wingate. But that is neither here nor there," he said with a dismissive wave. "Her connection to the case in question is tangential." He cocked his head. "Perhaps she told you the identity of her father?" He smirked at whatever he saw on Elliot's face. "Don't worry, I won't ask you to confirm that. I can see you would be less than cooperative, and it is not my aim to alienate you, Wingate."

"Threatening to bring Miss Brown in and torture her is an odd way of not attempting to alienate me, sir."

"Fair enough, that was ham-fisted of me." He cleared his throat. "Let me go back a little and give you some details that may make you more sympathetic to my questions."

Elliot seriously doubted that, but he nodded.

"In November of 1814, Callum Mungo Brown paid my predecessor a visit."

Elliot's eyebrows shot up.

"Yes, I can see that surprises you. I gather you're wondering why Wardlow didn't clamp the man in leg irons and throw him into the deepest, dankest cell we could find." Gray snorted suddenly. "If he had done so, Brown might be alive today," he added dryly. "But to answer your unspoken question, the fellow claimed he had information that would exonerate both himself and Major Lord John Townshend—also known as the Earl of Packenham—of any ill doing."

Elliot's jaw dropped. "Good Lord."

Gray nodded. "Indeed. Brown and Wardlow met that day, but my predecessor—for reasons unknown to anyone—left no record of what they discussed, other than to say he'd scheduled another meeting to examine the evidence Brown claimed to have. Unfortunately, before that second meeting could take place, Brown died in a freak accident. By the time Wardlow learned of the accident and sent agents to his lodgings to search his personal effects for whatever it was that he claimed to have, all Brown's possessions had been moved. The landlord was persuaded to admit that Brown hadn't lived alone, but with a young woman who was his daughter. Where the young woman went, the landlord couldn't say. The trail ended that day—abruptly."

Elliot held the other man's gaze but didn't speak.

"I'd believed that was the end of it all," Gray said, sitting back and turning his glass in his hands, his eyes on Elliot. "But there was a single, rather significant piece of information from the interview with the landlord—something everyone initially overlooked. You see, he mentioned that the daughter had a pet bird."

Elliot swallowed.

"Now, plenty of people have birds as pets, and nobody thought to ask the landlord anything more about it. Until I inherited Wardlow's files." He smiled at Elliot. "I'm sure you know what I learned when I sent a man back to talk to the landlord. Even more than a year later, he still recalled the woman's bird because it was unusual—a raven. Naturally I'd heard of a female knife thrower who performs with a raven. A few coins scattered liberally among the many employees at Farnham's yielded the information about the Fayre's trip to France last year. Putting it all together with you and the young woman from the ball the other night was simple after that. So, you now see why I'd like to talk to *Miss Brown*."

"Actually, sir, I don't. She has nothing to do with either Townshend, er, Packenham, or Brown, or what happened in the colonies before she was born. Only by an unfortunate accident of birth is she even connected to the case."

"That is true, and I must emphasize that she is in no trouble." An odd, almost pained look flickered across Gray's face. "There is something you should know, Wingate. John Townshend was once a close friend—a very *dear* friend of mine—and we were like brothers when we were lads."

Before Elliot could come up with a response, the other man chuckled. "I daresay you are wondering how a mere butcher's son came to be the friend of an earl?"

He'd been wondering exactly that, as a matter of fact, but it was hardly politic to admit it.

"I was a scholarship boy at Harrow." Gray grimaced. "I'm sure you remember those poor fellows from your school days?"

As a matter of fact, Elliot did. "Yes, sir. There were boys on scholarships at Eton."

"Either downtrodden or stiff necked, weren't they?" Elliot opened his mouth, but Gray beat him to it. "Oh, you can admit it. It was a dreadful position to be in, but a phenomenal opportunity for a boy who'd been born above a butcher's shop. I'll admit there were hard times and that I took my fair share of knocks. I probably would have taken more if not for John Townshend." He smiled fondly. "He was that rare man who didn't care what anyone else thought; he did whatever he felt was right." Gray's smile slid away, and he clucked his tongue. "I believe that characteristic eventually led to his downfall."

"You mean it was the reason he sold our nation's secrets to the enemy?"

Gray winced. "When stated so baldly, it's a harsh pronouncement. But the truth is that the colonial conflict divided this country unlike any other, aside from our Civil War, of course. Families split down the middle and fought each other."

"I am aware of the divisions the war caused, sir. But selling military secrets is not the same as openly choosing a side and taking a stand," Elliot said.

"No, it isn't," Gray admitted sadly. He shook himself. "In any case, I felt strongly about John's case back when it happened. I was especially concerned by his claim that he was innocent. You see, given what I knew about him, I believed he would have owned up to his behavior, no matter how it reflected on him. John was not a liar. I must admit I was more than a little relieved that he ran before the matter could come to trial. It would have been . . . agonizing. I thought the matter was over and done—a tragedy best forgotten—but now I find out that Brown had evidence that might clear my best friend's name. I'm sure you can imagine how I feel about what happened to the man."

"I do, sir. But I still don't understand what you think Miss Brown can do to help? Perhaps if her father were still alive, she might ask him what evidence he'd considered giving to Wardlow and convince him to—"

"It was Brown who had the evidence," Gray said.

"Yes, I know," Elliot said, confused by the interruption.

"But you said *her father.*"

"Yes, Callum Mungo Brown—Josephine Brown's father."

Gray's eyes widened. "She hasn't told you."

"She hasn't told me *what?*"

"The woman isn't Brown's daughter, Wingate. Her name is Elizabeth Josephine Townshend; she's the Earl of Packenham's daughter. And because the Townshend family's patent allows for female inheritance, she isn't just John's daughter—she's the current Countess of Packenham."

Chapter 16

Jo rinsed out her teacup and set it on the cloth before going to check her bag for the fifth time.

Quork, quork.

She looked up from her neatly packed valise to find Angus watching her, a strangely knowing expression on his corvine face. "I know I'm acting like an idiot, but this is the first holiday I've ever had, Angus. What if I forget something important?"

Angus merely stared.

Jo suddenly remembered she was supposed to be angry with the bird and scowled. "I was serious about your thieving, Angus. Don't you *dare* take anything from Elliot or his cottage or his servants or"— she flung up her hands—"just don't take *anything*. Understood?"

He snapped his beak at her, and Jo could only stare. Never had he behaved so . . . aggressively toward her. She was truly at wit's end. It was indeed fortunate that the Fayre was closing for the month and she could get away—or at least get Angus away—from some of her colleagues, especially the Fayre's magician, Francine. Or, to be more accurate, she needed to get Angus away from Henry, Francine's rabbit. For reasons unknown to her, Angus would not stop stealing the rabbit's toys. He was specifically fascinated by a carved wooden carrot that was Henry's favorite plaything.

Jo had done everything to stop him—she'd even carved him an almost identical carrot—but Angus had left the new toy untouched.

She stared at her bird—and her closest companion for years—and sighed. "Come here," she said.

Angus didn't hesitate to close the distance between them, landing on her shoulder with a gentle grace that never failed to astound her. She smiled up at him and scratched his ruff.

"I don't want to be angry with you."

He purred, which he knew she found adorable and impossible to resist.

"Why are you stealing things? Is this because we can't find your bone?"

The raven perked up at the word *bone*, which he recognized because it was the name of his favorite toy. A simple wooden carving that Mungo had made for him when the bird had still been a fledgling. Angus had loved his bone and hauled it with him everywhere for years. The blasted thing had got lost not long before Mungo's death, and her father had promised Angus that he would carve him another one, but he'd been killed before he could do so.

Jo had carved several since, but Angus had left them all untouched, even though they'd looked identical to the original. She could only assume that Angus liked the bone because Mungo had made it.

"I miss him, too, Angus," she murmured, smiling when the huge bird began to groom her, treating a lock of hair like a feather and preening it. If left unchecked, he would preen her entire head and leave her looking like a haycock. "Thank you," she murmured. "Do you want a treat?" It was the gentlest way she knew of to get him to stop preening her.

Angus hopped down to the back of the chair, and Jo took a dry piece of bread from the cloth bag of food she always kept for him. Once he was happily gnawing away on the crust, she turned back to her small pile of baggage.

She was considering re-checking the contents of her valise yet again when she heard Elliot's soft, familiar tread on the stairs.

Jo hastily checked her appearance in the mirror and settled the hair that Angus had ruffled. She'd left the door unlocked, so Elliot walked right in.

Jo turned toward him, already smiling like a fool. "I'm all packed and ready to—" She stopped in her tracks when she saw his face. "What happened, Elliot?"

Elliot held his gloves in one white-knuckled hand, his normally affectionate features stern and stiff. "I wish you would keep the door locked when you are here alone, Jo."

She blinked, both at his words and angry tone.

"This is my apartment, and I pay the rent," she retorted, her belly roiling with fear at his uncharacteristic behavior. "I can leave the door wide open if I choose."

Elliot filled his lungs until they looked ready to explode, and then let his breath out in a rush. "I'm sorry, you are right; I am in no position to tell you what to do." He pulled off his hat and tossed it carelessly onto the table.

"What is wrong?" she asked, even though she wasn't sure she wanted to know.

"I know the truth."

"What truth?" she asked, genuinely confused.

"That you are really Elizabeth Townshend."

Jo frowned. "*What?*"

Elliot's expression shifted rapidly from anger to disbelief. "You can't seriously expect me to believe you don't know who you really are."

Angus flew the short distance over to Jo's shoulder and hunkered close to her neck, clearly sensing Jo's distress. "I told you the truth about who I am." Something awful occurred to her. "Why are you asking me this? Have you been talking to somebody about me?" she demanded, her voice rising.

"Not by choice," he shot back, jamming his fingers through his brown curls and pulling hard enough that he winced.

"What does that mean?"

"You remember the man you met at Marianne's ball—Sir Stanley Gray?"

"Yes."

"He is my new superior."

"So?"

"He knows who you are, Jo—who you really are."

"You told him about me?" she shouted, closing the distance between them.

Elliot lifted both his hands and held them palms out. "Jo!"

Jo could barely make out his features through the haze of red. "You promised, Elliot! You gave me your word you'd—"

"*Jo!*"

She startled. "*What?*"

"Please put the knife away."

She followed his gaze to her hand; yes, she was holding a knife.

Jo blinked. Good Lord! How had that happened?

She looked up, and they locked eyes. "What?" she demanded. "Did you think I was going to stab you?" Before he could answer her, Jo shoved the blade into the sheath that was sewn into the pocket of her cloak. She lifted both hands to show they were empty. "There. Feel safer?"

His normally warm gaze was colder than the Atlantic Ocean in December. "As a matter of fact, I do."

Jo opened her mouth to retort—to say something hurtful—but then recognized another emotion in his familiar blue eyes: concern— not for his safety, but for hers.

Suddenly she thought how she must have appeared—armed with a knife and advancing on him, as if he were a stranger. Jo sighed. "I'm sorry, that was unnecessary." She strode to the window, opened it, and turned to her bird. "You can go, but come back soon."

Angus didn't hesitate; he escaped the room as if his tail feathers were on fire.

Jo wished she could do the same. Instead, she turned back to Elliot and said, "You should leave now."

"I'm not going anywhere until I get some answers."

She shrugged. "Fine. Stay as long as you like." She picked up her bag, glanced around the room one last time, and then strode toward the door.

"Where are you going?" Elliot asked.

"Somewhere else."

"There are men watching this building. If you go, you will be followed."

Jo dropped the valise on the floor. "You told your superior where I live? Who I am?"

"Gray already knew who you are, Jo, and he also knows where you live."

"If he thinks I'm Townshend's daughter, then he is wrong. I never even met the man. He died when I was only a baby. Mungo is my father."

"No, he isn't."

Elliot reached into his coat, and Jo stepped back.

Elliot gave a breathless laugh, his gaze going to her right hand; once again there was a knife there before she even realized she'd drawn one.

"Damn and blast," she muttered, shoving it back where it belonged.

"Good God, Jo," he said, his hand frozen inside his coat. "I'm not going to hold you at pistol point."

"I know," she admitted tightly. "It's just a habit, that is all." She jerked out a nod, and he slowly and deliberately extracted a slim package from his coat and held it out to her.

"This is for you."

Jo stared at it. "What is it?"

"It's easier if you look."

She chewed the inside of her mouth and snatched the package.

"Go ahead, open it," he said, crossing his arms and leaning back against the wall.

Jo scowled at him but tore off the heavy brown paper. Inside was a small leather book—no, not a book, she saw when she opened it, but a case for two small paintings. They were larger than traditional miniatures, perhaps the size of an illustration in a book.

She squinted at the young men in the pictures and strode over to the window for more light. The men were very similar. Indeed, they were almost identical but for the fact that one had blue eyes while the other had gray eyes—an unusual shade of gray that Jo had only ever seen when she looked in the mirror. Both men had blond hair, but the man with the blue eyes had hair the color of corn silk, the other man's hair slightly more golden.

And both men looked so much like her that it robbed her of breath.

"Jo?"

Elliot's low voice seemed to shatter the spell. Jo filled her lungs with much-needed air and looked up. "Is this—"

"John Townshend and his elder brother, Robert, who is also dead."

"Where did you get this?"

"Sir Stanley gave it to me."

Her eyes narrowed. "Why would he have such a thing?" she asked, her gaze once more turning to the images.

"He asked your father's cousin—the current Earl of Packenham, Richard Townshend—to send the portraits to him."

"Why would he do that?"

"Because Sir Stanley saw you at Sin's ball, and he was struck by your resemblance to John Townshend. He is the one with the gray eyes."

Yes, she recognized those eyes—not just the color, but the shape, too.

"Gray was great friends with your father—with John Townshend," he hastily corrected when she glared at him.

"Mungo is my father—the only one I've ever known."

"I understand what you are saying—that he is the father of your heart—but when it comes to legalities . . . well, you are undoubtedly John Townshend's daughter—his legitimate heir, in fact."

Jo swallowed down her angry denial; only a fool would not be-lieve she was related to both the men in the pictures. She'd never thought about her lack of resemblance to Mungo, assuming she'd taken after her mother, whom she could not remember. Mungo hadn't even possessed a portrait of her, so she had no idea what the woman had looked like.

Jo looked up. "If John Townshend is really my father, then who was my mother?"

"Dorothy Simms Townshend, who married your father shortly after he and Brown escaped British custody. It was Dorothy and her father—Jacob Simms—who helped Townshend and Brown with money and connections to people who would aid them while they were on the run. Simms arranged for the marriage of his daughter to Townshend and helped them disappear into the interior. Your mother was already pregnant at the time of the marriage, and she died in childbed. Both she and your father had contracted some sort of ill-ness. Brown lived with a woman—it appears they never married—and the two of them looked after you while your father was recovering. The illness left him weak, but he survived for two years after your birth. During that time, he apparently wrote letters and gathered what evidence he could while living on the outskirts of civ-ilization. He kept both his marriage and your birth a secret, never mentioning either in his letters. After his death, Brown and the woman took you to Europe and—well, you know the rest."

"Why would Mungo lie to me?"

"That part I don't understand. Perhaps he thought it was safer for you? Did he never hint that you might not be his daughter?"

"He loved me—he always treated me as if I was his child," she said, shame flooding her at her overly emotional tone. "I can't be-lieve this," she muttered, more to herself, staring once again at the portraits. "Why wouldn't Mungo tell me the truth?"

Elliot shook his head. "I don't know."

"If Townshend never told anyone, then how did Gray find out

all this?" she asked, closing the leather frame and covering up the unnerving paintings.

"Your father—er, Mungo—met with Gray's predecessor, claim-
ing to have evidence that would clear his and Townshend's names."

"*What*? When did that happen?"

"In November of 1814, evidently only a day or two before he
was killed."

Jo stared unseeingly at the opposite wall as she cast her mind back
to that dreadful time.

They'd moved to London only a few weeks before. Mungo had
already decided against the job with Helen's father, and they'd just
accepted the commission that would lead to her working at the Fayre
and eventually going to France.

Thinking back on the days before he died, Jo had to admit that
Mungo had seemed . . . distracted, but she'd believed that was because they were in England and he worried he might be recognized.

"I had no idea he was even pursuing the issue," Jo said. "He hadn't
mentioned it in years. And before you ask, I have no idea what *evidence* he might have been talking about. If he was hiding things, then
he hid them from me, too." Jo gestured to the trunk that she used as
a chair on occasion. "That is the sum total of his possessions. You are
more than welcome to look through them. There is nothing but a
few pieces of clothing, his favorite pistol, some books, and some
dreadful poetry written by John Townshend." Her lips twisted into a
bitter smile. "It all fits in a trunk with plenty of room left over. Not
much to show for a life, is it?"

"*You* are a monument to what sort of man he was, Jo. You are
educated, moral, kind, clever—"

"What else did Gray have to say about my father—Mungo and
Townshend?" she asked, not caring if it was rude to interrupt him.

When he didn't answer immediately, Jo sneered. "Or are you
not allowed to tell me, Elliot?"

"Of course I will tell you what I know, Jo. My first loyalty—I
know you don't believe me—is to *you*."

He was right; Jo *didn't* believe him. And if he ever got wind of the work she'd done in Paris a few years back—no matter that it had been at the behest of their own navy—he'd be running away from her as fast as he could.

"Gray said that nobody at the Home Office knew that Townshend and Brown didn't die until Jacob Simms, your maternal grandfather, contacted your cousin Richard—the current Earl of Packenham and your father's closest relative—about fifteen years ago and confessed what had really happened. Simms was dying and wanted somebody else to know the truth. He said he'd stopped receiving letters from Brown years before and feared something had befallen you. He sent along the marriage lines and some other personal effects of your father's that he'd been holding. After receiving the letter from Simms, your cousin Richard engaged a private inquiry agent to find you. They searched for ten years, following leads that went nowhere. They finally gave up five years ago. The assumption was that you and Brown must have both died, because people simply don't disappear as completely as you two did."

"So, there *were* people looking for us, then?"

Elliot nodded.

"I'm ashamed to admit that I always believed Mungo worried for no reason—that the government had long ago forgotten all about him and Townshend. What did you tell Gray about me?"

"I told him *nothing*," he said, his eyes fierce. "I give you my word, Jo. But that doesn't mean he's ignorant. He knows everything about you—*everything*. He knows about the journey through France last year, which was something I took great pains to hide in my reports to Wardlow—his predecessor."

"How did he learn all that?"

"He found a Fayre employee with loose lips."

Jo knew she shouldn't be surprised. After all, they'd traveled through France with Barnabas Farnham's lover Sonia informing on them the entire way. Why shouldn't there be others willing to sell them out?

Elliot took a step toward her and held out his hand. "I'm sorry I accused you of lying to me about who your father is."

Jo stared at him for a long moment and then placed her hand in his.

He squeezed her fingers gently. "You know what this means, don't you?"

"What *what* means?"

"You're not alone, Jo. You have family—cousins on your father's side, and family in America on your mother's side." He hesitated and then added, "And you're a countess in your own right." He smiled wryly. "You are Lady Packenham, one of the few titles that passes through the female line. You don't have to work at the Fayre, Jo. You don't have to work at all."

Jo stared down at their interlaced fingers, her head hot and spinning. She couldn't seem to follow any thought to a logical conclusion. Suddenly nothing in her life made any sense.

"Your cousins are desperate to meet you."

Jo shook her head as she looked up at him. "I can't."

"Why not?"

"Just—just because."

He gave her a quizzical look. "I don't understand?"

Neither did Jo. Why couldn't she meet her relatives? All her life she'd envied people with families, and now it appeared she had one. And yet the thought of meeting them made her stomach roll and pitch as if she were on the deck of a ship.

"They are nice people," Elliot said, rubbing the top of her hand with his thumb. "My mother was friends with Lady Packenham"— he broke off and pulled a face. "Well, I suppose she is plain Mrs. Townshend, now."

"I've taken away their titles," Jo said.

"You can't take away something that never belonged to them. You've been the heir since birth. That is the way these things are. Your father was the third son, so nobody would have expected him to inherit, but his two elder brothers died, the second one while your father was in America. He'd planned to leave the Home Office and take up his duties as head of the family. But then—well, you know what happened."

"How is it that you know so much about my family? Or is this all from Gray?"

"Some is from Gray, but the aristocratic families of England are a small group." He smiled. "You and I are cousins—many times re-moved—on my mother's side." He lifted her hand to his mouth and kissed her palm. "Don't you know what this means, Jo? You don't have to keep running. Your cousins are both accepted in society—nobody blames them for your father's behavior. In fact, they are in town right now, staying at the family house on Berkeley Square." He smiled. "Your ancestral house is not far from Sin and Marianne; you will be neighbors."

Jo snatched her hand away and stood, shoving past him. "No, we won't. Because I won't be living in that house." She glared out the window, her eyes flickering over the steady foot traffic below. Who was it that was watching her? The big man in the green coat scraping mud off his boot and leaning against the alley wall across the street? Or perhaps it was somebody in the building across from her. There was a bank full of clerks; she saw them filing in and out of the drab building day after day. Maybe it—

The floor squeaked, and she felt Elliot behind her. "I know this must be upsetting—especially about Mungo—but—"

"But I need to stop acting like a child and behave like a rational adult and accept what has happened."

He chuckled softly, and a hand came to rest on her hip. "I wouldn't have put it quite so bluntly, but . . . yes."

Jo sighed and leaned back against his already familiar and beloved body.

Elliot's arms slid around her and kissed her temple. He was the perfect height—five feet and ten and a half inches—and didn't tower over her. He was just tall enough for her to rest her head on his shoul-der. Who knew that she could become so enamored of such a small thing?

It's not his shoulder you want, hen. It's the man.

You! You have no right to come into my head after lying to me.

Mungo's laughter was the only response she had.

"I suppose this means I shan't be able to partner with Helen and buy into the Fayre."

Elliot's arms tightened. "I'm afraid not, my love."

"They'll expect me to behave like a lady and go to balls and— ugh!" She twisted in his arms and glared up at him. "I won't live that way, Elliot. One night at Marianne's ball was more than enough."

He smoothed a stray hair off her brow and cupped her face, stroking her lower lip with his thumb, his pupils expanding even as she watched. "One night?" he teased. "That was more like one-quarter of a night." His expression turned serious. "You shan't have to dance until dawn and attend three different balls every night—or become a fixture of the gossip columns like Guy—but there are duties you won't be able to ignore."

Jo groaned. "Oh, I can imagine. But I don't want to talk about any of this now. I don't suppose we are still taking our holiday?"

He hesitated, but then shook his head. "It would not be wise to leave London now, darling."

She didn't bother arguing. "Just give me tonight. Tomorrow I'll face up to my responsibilities and meet my cousins and behave like an adult. But please, Elliot, just take me to bed and make me forget about all this for tonight."

He held her face and kissed her, slowly and deeply. "I think that is an excellent idea," he said, and then he took her hand and led her to a bed that—just like her life—wouldn't belong to her for much longer, either.

Chapter 17

It was the light that woke Elliot. Or, to be more precise, turning to avoid the sunbeam shining through the window and realizing he could turn.

Something that shouldn't be possible in Jo's narrow bed.

Unless Jo wasn't in it.

He pushed up on his hands and glanced around the small room. "Jo?"

But there was no answer from the screened area in the tiny box room.

And Angus's perch was empty.

"Jo," he called out more loudly, which was foolish because the place was so small you could hear another person breathing.

Heart pounding, Elliot pushed himself from the bed and opened the tiny cupboard that held her few garments.

The relief he felt when he saw the clothing was so strong, it almost drove him to his knees. But then a nasty thought struck him and he squinted at the contents; there was the ball gown and a rather ugly brown and yellow dress, but none of the gray ones she favored.

He spun around and stared at the trunk. She'd said it held Mungo's things. If it was empty . . .

Elliot dropped into a crouch and unbuckled the leather straps with shaking hands. When he lifted the lid, there was nothing inside.

Elliot slammed the trunk so hard, he heard the cracking of wood. "Goddammit, Jo! You *lied* to me," he shouted.

He hastily yanked on his clothes, his mind racing. How in the world had she packed all her things and left without his hearing her? How long had she been gone? Where would she go?

"You bloody promised me," he accused the empty room like a madman.

Elliot pulled on his boots, stuffed his cravat into his coat pocket, and strode toward the door.

Just as he closed his hand on the knob, it turned, and the door opened.

Jo flinched when she saw him standing there, her expression as guilty as hell.

In her hand was the same valise she'd packed for their brief holiday, and it was stuffed full.

"Ah," she said, dropping the bag with a loud thump. "I was hoping you might still be sleeping."

Elliot crossed his arms, not trusting himself to speak. When had he been this angry? Not for years, that was certain.

"I'm sorry," she said.

He lifted an eyebrow.

"I'm very sorry."

He opened his mouth to say something—he hadn't yet decided what—but there was a *tap tap* on the window.

Jo glanced over Elliot's shoulder at the window and grimaced. "Er, just a moment while I let him in."

He fumed in silence while she opened the window and the bird hopped inside. Angus gave Elliot an especially speaking look—as if to say: *You owe me.*

Jo pulled off her bonnet and tossed it onto the rumpled bed.

"Did I mention that I was sorry?" she said, giving him one of her extremely rare smiles, a very sheepish one. "How about some tea?"

The fear that had savaged him hadn't yet fled, and Elliot felt vaguely ill, but tea would give them both something else to focus on.

While she bustled around in the makeshift kitchen, Elliot made the bed, hung up her hat, and carried her bag away from the front door.

He also washed his face in cool water, finger-combed his unruly hair—to little effect—and tied on his battered cravat.

By the time he was finished, she was placing a plate of bread, ham, and cheese, and what appeared to be a glass container full of something . . . brown.

"What is that?" Elliot asked, pointing to the unappetizing-looking jar.

She perked up at the question. "Oh, it is the new method of preserving foods," Jo said, setting out the milk and sugar she kept just for him.

"Ah, I read something about that—a Frenchman, Apert his name is, I think?"

"Yes, he started it, but now there is somebody here in London doing it. I was most excited when I saw some of it for sale. It was quite dear, but I thought it worth trying." She fixed him with a charmingly eager look. Elliot had noticed that she was adventurous on her trips to the market, frequently bringing back foods that neither of them had tried before. It was a little quirk—in an otherwise practical and serious woman—that he found adorable.

But it still didn't make him forget that she'd almost left him.

She handed Angus a lump of cheese, which the big bird took with his usual gentleness.

Elliot pulled the trunk over to the table so he'd have a seat. He had planned to buy a second chair this week, but now that would not be necessary.

"Here, take the chair," he said when she would have sat on the trunk.

She sat and poured their tea.

Elliot sniffed the mystery substance in the jar.

"It is beef. Don't you want to try it?" she asked, leaning forward eagerly.

It didn't smell like any beef he'd ever smelled before. "Er—"

"Just a little on some bread."

The meat looked gray and was about as appetizing as—well, he had nothing to compare it to. It was perhaps the least appetizing food he'd ever seen.

But she looked so excited that he couldn't bear to disappoint her. "Yes, I will try some. Thank you," he said when she handed him a piece of bread with a lump of gray-brown beef.

And then she sat and watched him.

Elliot said a prayer and took a bite. He wanted to spit it out immediately, but she looked so . . . hopeful. He chewed as little as possible and then swallowed.

Her face fell. "You don't like it."

"Well, it's probably an acquired taste." And one he had no intention of acquiring any time soon. He set down the bread and took a gulp of scalding tea, hoping to burn the ghastly flavor out of his taste buds.

"Why did you leave, Jo?" he asked when it was clear she had no interest in raising the subject.

"I'm used to moving to avoid trouble," she said, crumbling her bread rather than eating it, her distant gaze that of a person who was mulling over the past. "It became a habit. I even moved once here in London after Mungo died, when there really wasn't any reason to do so." She looked up, her normally opaque eyes showing emotion for a change: anxiety.

Elliot reached across the table, and she met him halfway. "I'm glad you came back."

"I'm glad, too."

She didn't look glad. She looked like a woman facing a long, solitary march to the gallows.

"I don't know if I can do this, Elliot."

"Do what? Meet your family?"

"That and go to balls or parties and act . . . normal."

"Of course you can do it. You are the most competent person—man or woman—I've ever met, Jo."

"Competent, yes. But being a l–lady isn't about handling knives or meting out justice to criminals or—or anything else that I know how to do." She gave him a pleading look. "You know me better than anyone else, Elliot. I hate talking to most people, and I go out of my way to avoid situations where conversation is necessary. For the past eight years, my best friend has been a bird. Can you see me engaging in idle chatter or flirtation night after night?"

An odd mixture of sadness, jealousy, and empathy swirled in his chest. Sadness because she thought he knew her best and yet he felt that he hardly knew her at all. Jealousy at the image of her flirting or chatting with other men, and empathy because he didn't care for the London social whirl, either.

"You can approach this as slowly as you need to. There are a great many other things that are more important than immediately launching you into society and engaging in the social whirl, Jo."

"*The social whirl.*" She groaned. "I loathe even the sound of that. I've seen what Marianne has had to do, and I'm telling you right now that I simply cannot do it. Organizing dinners and balls? Being presented at one of those dreadful Drawing Rooms and having to wear one of those ridiculous gowns?" She shivered, and it didn't look like an exaggeration.

Attending one of the Queen's Drawing Rooms was the least of it. As a member of the House of Lords, although she would never actually take her seat, and a peeress who also controlled several seats in Commons, Jo would need to be received by the king. Elliot decided it would be better to keep that information to himself for the moment.

Instead, he said, "It is likely that most of those things would not need to take place right away." That was a bit of a fib, but the wild look in her eyes convinced him it was a necessary lie. Elliot had never seen her so blue-deviled before, and it unnerved him.

Nor had he heard her speak as much as she had last night and that

morning. She was skittish and frightened and required careful handling. He hated that he had to *handle* her at all, but running was not
an option for her; she could not delegate away her title and responsibilities, and now that Sir Stanley knew about her, her cousin would
hear about her, too—if he had not already. Even if she ran away,
Richard Townshend could not simply resume the title and position
as head of their family. Her succession was, as the French would say,
a *fait accompli*.

There was also the matter of the reception she would face. He'd
not been entirely honest about that. There were still many people
who'd not forgotten nor forgiven the Townshend family, but that
notoriety was something that she could not change and would need
to bear.

"Will you help me?"

Elliot turned away from his thoughts at her question and smiled
at her. "Yes, of course. In any way you ask—but what do you mean?"

She made a vague, encompassing gesture with one hand and
shrugged. "With all of it."

Elliot hesitated.

Jo sat back in her chair, her expression shuttering.

When she tried to pull away her hand, he tightened his grip.
"Steady on," he murmured. "I wasn't hesitating because I don't want
to help you. I was hesitating because I will hardly be in the position
to do so."

"What do you mean?"

"I mean that unmarried aristocratic men and women must abide
by a great many social strictures." He gave her a look of genuine regret. "We can no longer continue the arrangement we have enjoyed, Jo."

Was it bad of him to enjoy her look of unhappiness at those particular words? Probably. But the truth made him more than unhappy.
It made him reckless.

"Unless . . ." He stopped and held her gaze.

"Unless we were more to each other."

It wasn't a question, but he nodded.

This time, her expression—one of genuine alarm—made him feel like a bully. Elliot opened his mouth to reassure her, to promise that he would assist her in every way possible, and then some, regardless of whether she wanted to be with him, but she wasn't finished speaking.

"Do you still wish to marry me, Elliot?"

Jo couldn't seem to stop behaving like somebody else. She'd never once acted so willfully or childishly. Judging by the way Elliot's eyebrows almost touched his hairline, he concurred.

"Forget I just said that," she said.

Elliot gave her a look she could not decipher and shook his head. "Once again, you have leapt to the wrong conclusion."

"Oh?" she said stiffly.

"Have you forgotten that I love you?"

As if she could forget such a thing.

"Or perhaps you think I did not really mean what I said?" He squeezed her hand painfully hard. "I am not so fickle as to have fallen out of love with you since I made that declaration. But things have changed dramatically between us—I don't think you know just how much. You are a wealthy woman, Jo. The Packenham fortune is substantial."

Jo struggled to absorb that information. She was rich?

"I am the youngest son who works for his crust. Not only does that disparity exist between us," Elliot continued, "but you are hardly in any frame of mind to make such a serious decision right now."

Jo knew everything he said was true—and also honorable—but it irritated her nonetheless.

"Are you saying you will not marry me now because I'm *too* good for you?"

He gave her an exasperated look. "I believe it was you who dictated this arrangement, Jo. I would have joyfully married you when you were Mungo Brown's daughter. I would joyfully marry you now that you are a wealthy, titled heiress. But I can't help feeling that marriage—to me or anyone else—is not what *you* want."

Did she want to marry Elliot? Did she love him? She loved *being* with him, but was that the same thing? He was right that she simply could not seem to think straight.

He squeezed her hand, gently this time. "Don't look so . . . *hunted*," he said, his expression so gentle and loving that she had a sudden, terrifying, urge to throw her arms around his neck and weep all over his chest. "I will not abandon you to the wolves of the *ton*."

She smiled weakly at his jest. Elliot meant well, but he'd not heard Marianne talk about her foray into society. Jo knew her every movement would be scrutinized. No doubt her cousin's wife—or somebody with similar credentials—would attach themselves to her and guard her like a mythical dragon protecting its hoard.

It would be stifling, demoralizing, and she'd never get to spend more than two dances' worth of time with Elliot.

Jo would bloody bolt before she allowed that to happen. She could endure a great deal of physical pain, but when it came to tolerating vapid, hollow, pointless social engagements?

This time it was Jo who squeezed Elliot's hand. "I need to ask a—a favor."

"Anything for you."

She chewed the inside of her cheek ragged. "If we were betrothed, then I could see you more often?"

"We just discussed that, Jo. I'm—"

"No, you don't understand. I don't mean a *real* engagement, just something . . . temporary."

"Temporary," he repeated. His expression went blank—utterly and completely. She'd seen him do that with other people—close himself off—but he'd not done so with her. At least not since they'd become lovers.

"I'm sorry," she blurted. "I shouldn't have—"

"How temporary?"

She swallowed down the surge of pain she felt at his question. Of course, he wanted to know how long he'd have to pretend. It was her idea, so why did the fact that he might have time limits hurt her feelings?

"Do you think I will have to assume these . . . duties you mentioned this Season?"

He hesitated, and then nodded. "It's a bit of a sticky situation for your cousins. If they were discovered to have known about you and not said or done anything about it, then it would look as if they were trying to continue in a position that was no longer theirs."

"I understand. So, then I will be able to get most of it over with these next few weeks?"

He had the nerve to grin. "By *get over with*, I assume you mean address all the critical duties?"

She nodded.

"Well, there are seven or eight weeks before the *haute ton* abandon London for their country houses, so that will give you ample time to do quite a bit—certainly those responsibilities associated with your investiture. Once the Season is over, you will be able to rest." He pulled a face. "At least until hunting starts. Your cousin is quite mad for it," he said at her querying look. "Your county seat is just north of Oakham, right in the heart of hunt country. Your Cousin Richard hosts some of the best-attended hunts in the nation. Even Prinny joined back in the days when he was a bit more active."

Jo's eyes widened. "The Regent socializes with my family? Despite everything?"

Elliot nodded. "He did what he could to ease the shame of your family—as did many others. As bad as the *ton* can be at times, they can close ranks around their own when necessary, regardless of party or position."

"Do you hunt?" she asked hopefully.

"I enjoy it a great deal, but I'm afraid I'm not downy enough to keep a string of hunters. I'm fortunate in that Sin keeps me mounted from his stud, insisting that I'm showing off his stock when I hunt his horses."

Jo had ridden across half of France with Elliot and knew the Duke of Staunton would benefit plenty having Elliot ride his horses. Like most men of aristocratic birth, he rode as if he and his horse were a single being.

She met his gaze, unable to read what he was thinking. "I would be much happier agreeing to all this if I knew you would be part of it. Can—would—"

Elliot smiled, took her hand, and bowed over it. "Yes, I will be honored to be your betrothed through the end of the Season."

Chapter 18

Think what you are doing, Elliot!

The same phrase had been echoing in his head ever since he'd left Jo's apartment yesterday morning. A full twenty-four hours later, one would have thought he'd have come to terms with what he'd committed to, but he was more concerned than ever after talking to Sin last night.

Elliot and Jo had agreed that she would tell the truth of her identity to Marianne, Cecile, and Helen—her closest friends, in effect—and he would tell Guy and Sin.

Unfortunately, Guy and Cecile were—yet again—at loggerheads.

Yesterday afternoon—after leaving Jo's—he'd gone to Cecile's house to speak to Guy, only to learn he'd essentially moved out and was visiting his mother and sisters before he sailed for Boston.

Cecile had been seething beneath a tense, brittle veneer of civility.

Jo, who'd gone to Cecile's house for the same reason as Elliot, had pulled him aside. "This is not a good time for me to talk to her." she'd whispered.

"No," he agreed, stealing a quick kiss and smirking at her look of surprise. "I gathered that. What are you going to do?"

"Helen and I have come up with a plan," Jo said.

"What sort of plan?" he asked, kissing her again.

"A plan to get Cecile and Guy to work out their difficulties."

Elliot had laughed. "That must be quite a plan."

"Trust me," Jo said, and then *she'd* kissed him, not nearly so briefly.

In fact, matters had been heating up quite nicely, and Elliot was about to try to persuade her to go back to her lodgings and put off the rest of their errands until tomorrow—when a clearing throat made them both spring apart.

"I'm sorry to interrupt," Helen said, amusement glinting in her eyes. "But Cecile wants to talk to the two of us about the contract."

Elliot gave Jo a pointed look, and she gave him a slight shrug. So, she'd not yet told Helen about her new situation, either.

"*Coward,*" he'd mouthed, and then left her to her meeting and the unhappy chore of having to confess to her friend that she'd no longer be able to operate the Fayre with her.

That had been yesterday afternoon, the last time he'd seen her. He'd wanted to go to her last night, but he'd been called into work on unexpected business and hadn't got free until nearly midnight.

Only one night without her, and already he was edgy and cranky. Lord. What would it be like when they weren't able to touch each other at all?

Elliot grimaced just thinking the miserable thought.

He was on his way to see Sir Stanley and let him know Jo had agreed to meet her cousins.

"I'm only doing this so quickly because Sir Stanley already contacted them," Jo had warned him. "But I don't want him—or them—to think this means that I'm going to immediately move into their house—"

"*Your* house," Elliot had muttered.

She'd given a dismissive flick of her hand. "You know what I mean."

"But, Jo, you know you'll need to move out of your garret and in with your family eventually."

"Eventually, but not right away." She'd given him a piteous look. "Can't I at least have a month to become adjusted to the notion?"

"A month? Probably not. Perhaps a week. Certainly no more than ten days."

She'd grimaced. "I'll give it some thought, but no decisions just yet."

And then she had truly shocked him.

"I will talk to Sir Stanley about Mungo and answer his questions. Not that I know anything," she'd assured him. "I was serious when I offered you the chance to look in Mungo's trunk, Elliot. There is nothing of any importance, I give you my word."

Elliot had burned with curiosity to take her up on the offer, but it had seemed like a caddish, overeager maneuver, so he'd told her he'd look at Mungo's meager possessions when he next visited. And there would be a *next time*—they'd both agreed on that.

Unfortunately, Elliot knew it was his duty to convince her to move into her family house on Berkeley Square sooner rather than later. Putting off the inevitable would be impossible now that her cousins knew she was alive. They would face shame and ridicule if word ever got out that they'd known the true heir was living in poverty while they occupied her house.

They weren't the only ones who'd face ridicule if the truth got out. Elliot would look like an opportunistic cad if people discovered that he'd been treating Jo like a mistress. Worse than a mistress, actually. If she'd been a mistress, he would have at least provided her with a decent place to live and showered her with luxuries. Instead, he'd camped out in her tiny flat and eaten the food and wine she'd purchased without contributing more than a few meals here and there.

And then there was the damned sham betrothal that he'd agreed to, which was a bloody disaster in the making.

But they had no choice, at least not if Elliot wanted to spend any time with her at all.

He'd already examined the question from all sides, and Jo was right; if they weren't betrothed, he'd only see her briefly at *ton* functions. She might not realize it, but that would mean that he'd have no chance with her. Because regardless of what Jo thought now, she would find things to enjoy about her new life. She was an heiress and countess, but she would be sought after for more than money or a title. She was a fascinating woman and so different from most of the milk-and-water misses who made their come out every year that she'd draw men like bees to honey—powerful men who could give her much more than Elliot could.

When he had expressed those thoughts—in far more circumspect terms—to Sin last night, the other man had scoffed.

"Jo will want to make your betrothal *real*, Elliot. She probably already does—she's just got too much on her plate right now to think straight."

Sin's confidence on the matter had made him feel slightly better. But then, Sin didn't know Jo. Hell, even *Elliot* didn't know her. At least not well. Who knew what the woman would do?

He had smiled at his friend and ignored his prognostication. Instead saying, "She's going to need all the help she can get."

"That's true—for some things. But she's well-mannered, well-spoken, and attractive, so she's got that going for her."

Coming from a man who'd married a woman who worked in a circus, Sin's confidence had meant something.

"Yes," Elliot had agreed. "But she's also stubborn, pathologically reserved, and more dangerous than a barrel full of vipers. Can you imagine her in a ball, knives magically appearing in her hands while she faces off against some spotty-faced young fool who tries to steal a kiss?"

Sin had laughed at the image, and Elliot had joined him. But he hadn't laughed for long. His friend still didn't know what Jo had done to Broussard and his men in France—or the way she'd reacted with *him* when she believed he'd told Gray about her—and Elliot wasn't about to tell him. It wasn't that he thought she was out of control, but she did not operate by *ton* rules—that much was certain.

"Are you sure I can't tell Marianne about all this?" Sin had begged, right before Elliot had parted ways with him last night.

"If it were up to me, I'd say tell her. But it's not, so you'd better let Jo handle it in her own fashion."

Although Elliot wondered what the woman was planning. He lived with the constant, nagging worry that she would simply disappear rather than face her new life. He'd never admit it to Jo, but he was grateful that Gray had men stationed outside her apartment. Not that he had much faith in anyone following her if she didn't want to be followed.

Elliot pushed aside his concerns as he approached Whitehall, nodding to the two soldiers stationed outside the entrance.

Once inside, he headed in the opposite direction from the more ostentatious offices occupied by senior Home Office officials.

The corridors became narrower and less luxurious the longer he walked, until he opened an innocuous door on the back side of the staircase—a servant entrance—and descended one level, entering the modest anteroom to Sir Stanley's office.

During Wardlow's tenure, the room had contained a desk that was always occupied by a long-suffering secretary who'd answered to the name of Ogden.

Sir Stanley had eliminated both the desk and Ogden, instead filling the small space with two leather settees, a chair, and a stack of sporting and hunting periodicals, making it resemble the waiting room of a Harley Street physician rather than the lair of a spy master.

Elliot glanced at his watch, saw it was only a few moments until his appointment, and knocked on the door to Sir Stanley's windowless room.

"Come in!"

Unlike last time, Sir Stanley's desk was now piled high with parchment.

He smiled up at Elliot. "Why don't you pour us a drink before you take a seat." He gestured to the piles of paper. "I think I've earned it today."

"Any preference?" Elliot asked.

"Whiskey—always."

Elliot poured two and handed one to the older man, who took a sizeable swallow and then gave a sigh of contentment. "Better already. So," he said, setting down his glass. "You wanted to speak to me—I hope this is about Lady Packenham?"

Elliot wanted to laugh at the other man's form of address but knew it would not go over well. But if Sir Stanley tried to call Jo that . . . well, that wouldn't go well, either.

"She is adjusting to the news, but very slowly, sir."

Gray's eyebrows shot up. "You're saying she didn't know who her father was?"

Elliot bristled at the disbelief, but he kept his own voice cool. "She did not know."

Gray looked as if he wanted to say something about that, but then shrugged. "Well, it doesn't really matter either way, I suppose."

Elliot thought it mattered a great deal, but he kept that opinion to himself.

"I daresay she is thrilled to discover she's not only a countess but also a very wealthy young lady."

"She is adjusting to the idea," Elliot repeated.

Gray snorted. "Only a young man could ever believe a woman would want anything more than money and the respect of her peers."

Again, the other man's words rankled. He opened his mouth to say something that would likely end his career, but Gray surprised him.

"I'm sorry. That was ill done of me, Wingate. You know her better than I do; if you say she isn't champing at the bit for a life of luxury and ease, pretty gowns, and expensive baubles, then that is no doubt the truth."

His apology startled Elliot, but he was grateful for it. He liked his job and would not want to find another. But it was best that Gray knew he'd tolerate no disrespect toward Jo. Based on his apology, the man had discovered that without matters becoming unpleasant.

"I do hope she is prepared to leave her life as a circus performer behind her and assume her duties."

"She is." Elliot didn't tell him how grudgingly and slowly she'd make that transition. Gray would discover that soon enough.

"Good, good. So, then, Packenham"—Gray broke off with a grimace—"Damn, but that will be difficult to remember! I mean Richard Townshend and Mrs. Townshend, are most eager to meet her, as I'm sure you can imagine. I assured them she was only in need of minor polish to make her debut." He smiled at Elliot, as if waiting for him to thank him or agree with the assessment. He would be waiting a very long time.

He must have realized he'd misstepped yet again, because he stopped waiting and said, "They are already making plans for her presentation—both to the Queen and the Regent—as well as organizing a ball to take place in the last week of the Season." He cleared his throat and leaned on his desk. "Naturally I did not inform them of your recent nighttime visits to Lady Packenham's lodgings."

"We are betrothed, sir. Although of course I shall wait to call on Mr. Townshend for his blessing before we make any announcement."

Sir Stanley's expression was that of a man who'd just put a bad oyster into his mouth and was unsure how to get rid of it.

After a look at Elliot's face, he must have decided to swallow the unappetizing morsel. "Ah, I see. Well, she is well above the age of consent, so I wish you very happy."

"Thank you, sir."

"Now then, when can we arrange for them to meet."

"Miss Brown has agreed to present herself at Townshend House two days hence, sir." It was Elliot's turn to clear his throat. "She has asked that I accompany her."

Sir Stanley did not look pleased by that information, but he nodded. "Very good. And as for moving in—"

"That has not yet been decided, sir."

The older man gave him a hard look. "I trust you've communicated the delicacy of this situation to her, Wingate."

"Yes, sir."

Sir Stanley heaved an exasperated sigh. "Very well, very well. So, when will she speak to me?"

"Tomorrow evening at nine o'clock, if it suits you."

"Yes, that suits me well enough. The building will be empty at that time and—"

"Er, not here, sir. She's asked that you meet her at The Greedy Vicar. If you don't know of it, it is a pub in—"

"You will attend that meeting, as well?"

"Er, yes, sir. She has asked me to do so."

Gray grunted. "Now, where is this place—what did you call it?"

"The Greedy Vicar. I take it you've not heard of it?"

"No." The older man's expression was getting sourer by the minute.

"It is a public house, sir—a place where theatrical folk congregate. Her appearance at such a place will draw no attention, as she's been there many times before, and there are always women present."

"Indeed?" Sir Stanley sniffed. "Well, how . . . *bohemian* that sounds." To Elliot's surprise, he cracked a grin. "It has been many years since I loitered at theater doors with flowers and sparkly trifles hoping to catch the eye of a pretty piece of muslin."

Elliot dearly hoped he kept that sort of comment to himself tomorrow night, or he might find himself becoming acquainted with Jo's knives.

"So be it," Gray said, his tone that of a man finished with the conversation. "I look forward to hearing all she has to say on the subject of Brown and her father."

So did Elliot.

* * *

Jo studied her reflection in the mirror and briefly considered changing out of her gray work dress to go to the meeting with Elliot's superior.

"What do you think, Angus? This old gray or my ball gown?"

Angus ignored her, too involved with the rat he'd managed to capture on their way home from the theater.

She scowled at the mess he was making on the newspaper she'd set out for him. "You'd better be finished with that by the time Elliot arrives," she said, squinting at her hair. Should she re-plait it?

"Oh, stop," she muttered to herself, turning away from the mirror altogether. "Did you hear me?" she asked the bird. "Outside," she added, which was her way of telling Angus he'd have to take his messy meal up to the roof. She slid open the window, and he scooped up what was left of the large rat and hopped onto the wide sill. "Back by dark, Angus."

It was May, and the sun didn't set until almost eight-thirty, so he would have plenty of time to eat and return home before she left. When they'd been in the country, she'd never worried about him staying out overnight, but London was full of danger.

She'd just turned from the window when she heard familiar footfalls.

Elliot opened the unlocked door and gave her a pained look.

"I locked it," she lied.

"Oh, really? And who unlocked it, then?"

"Probably Angus."

Elliot paused in pulling off his gloves, his forehead furrowed. "Does he really know how to do that?"

Jo couldn't help laughing. "I would have thought *you* were too smart to believe such lies."

He tossed his gloves into his hat and then strode toward her. "I'm horribly gullible where you are concerned," he said, wrapping his arms around her and giving her one of the thorough kissings she was starting to need.

Jo closed her eyes and allowed her hands to wander his hard, muscular body, briefly wondering if they had enough time for her to at least strip off his coats and shirt and gaze upon his chest. But when she began to pull his shirttails from his pantaloons, he pulled away.

"No time for that, darling," he murmured, sounding as breathless as she felt.

Jo groaned but released him.

"How are things over at the Fayre?" he asked, tucking some stray hairs back behind her ear.

"Cecile and Guy are still fighting with each other, so Helen and I will have to implement our plan tomorrow morning." It had been Helen's idea to lock the feuding lovers in a room with food, wine, and a chaise longue and not let them out until they mended their ways. Jo wasn't sure the plan would work, but she agreed with the other woman that something drastic needed to happen before Cecile left for the Continent next week.

Elliot tucked his shirt back into his pantaloons and adjusted himself in a way that made Jo smirk.

"Yes, proud of yourself, aren't you?" Elliot said, shaking his head. "I shall look a right tosser if I stride into The Greedy Vicar with a cockstand."

Jo grinned and closed her eyes. "Give me a moment to picture that."

"I'm pleased to amuse you, my dear."

She opened her eyes and found him giving her a look of fond exasperation. "Are you sure you're ready to talk to Gray?"

"Oh, yes."

He didn't look entirely convinced but nodded. "Well, do remember you have a rather important meeting tomorrow at four o'clock."

"As if I could forget," she retorted, no longer amused. "Do you think I can wear this tonight?" she held out her arms.

"Yes," he said without hesitation. "You should dress normally.

As for tomorrow," he said, relentlessly dragging the subject in the direction he wanted. "Gray told me your cousins have given most of the servants the afternoon off. Only the butler will be there to greet us, and he knows about you." He smiled. "Apparently he worked there when your father was alive and is most eager to make your acquaintance."

Jo knew his words were meant as a comfort, but the knowledge that some servant was looking forward to meeting her because she was the daughter of a man she'd never met—well, it was just one more confusing piece of a rapidly growing puzzle.

Elliot took her chin, tilted her to face him, forcing her to meet his gaze. "Everything will be fine, I promise."

She heaved a sigh and nodded, feeling like a weakling and fool for being so anxious. Why was it easier to confront an armed encampment of hostile French mercenaries than two middle-aged people who were her blood kin?

She turned away from him and gestured to the bed. "I set out all that Mungo left behind when he died." Jo could see by the way Elliot's expression fell that he'd been hoping for more.

"I told you there wasn't much. Go ahead and look," she said when he hesitated.

"You're sure you don't mind? I feel like a bit of a beast pawing through his things."

"There is nothing he wouldn't have wanted anyone to see."

Jo set the kettle to boil while Elliot sat on the bed and carefully went through each item. Only when he got to the three small leather-bound books did he ask any questions. "You say these poems were written by John Townshend?"

"Yes," she said, measuring out six spoons of tea and one for the pot. "Mungo said there were more books but that they'd left them behind when they fled."

Elliot paged through each of the books, pausing when he reached the end of one. "The handwriting is different in this one."

Jo put the lid on the pot of tea and went to look. "That's

Mungo's handwriting." She pointed to the last dozen or so sections of the poem.

> *The lights are more vivid, the nights are more cool,*
> *One life can be lived, one heart can be true.*

Jo snorted and shook her head. "This really is dreadful. No wonder Mungo never told me he'd taken up writing poetry, too. *More cool?* Is that even grammatically correct?"

"Poets have dramatic license," Elliot murmured, his eyes still riveted to the page.

"If you say so."

There was a tap on the window, and she saw Angus had returned. It was also considerably darker outside.

Jo opened the window, glad to see there was no sign of rat when Angus hopped inside and flew the short distance to his perch. A quick glance at the clock told her it was almost time to leave.

"We'd better have our tea and then go, Elliot." When he didn't answer, she turned to him. "Elliot?"

He looked up at her slowly, his eyes widening with wonder. "This isn't just bad poetry, Jo."

"No?" she asked, adding the ridiculous amounts of milk and sugar he liked to his tea.

"It's a code of some sort."

Jo's head whipped up. "What?"

"I'm sure of it." He lifted the book he'd been studying. "I have no proof, but I'd stake my life on this being the evidence Mungo was going to give to Wardlow."

"How can you know that?" Jo demanded.

"Why else would Mungo finish another man's poem, Jo?"

That stopped her.

"Besides, there is just something in the structure that smacks of basic code."

"What do you mean?"

It was difficult for Elliot to justify his gut feeling because it was just that: instinct. "I don't know how to explain it," he finally admitted. "But I'm willing to bet this is written using a replacement code. Unfortunately, you need to know the source of the letters replaced in order to read it."

"What would be a *source*?"

"A book, a letter—anything with words on it, really. And you'd need to know the formula that was used in order to decode it." He glanced around at the few items on the bed. There were six books, all inscribed with Packenham's name. "It could be one of these books, but without the key—which would tell us what letters on what line or in what word on what pages, for example—there is no way of knowing."

"Could you figure it out?"

"If I had more time with the books, perhaps. But it is doubtful. I am no code breaker, Jo."

She chewed on that for a moment and then said, "I don't want to tell any of this to anyone yet."

"You mean you don't want to mention it to Sir Stanley?"

"Him or anyone else. After all, what do you really know?"

"Nothing," he admitted, "but—"

"But?"

"You don't want to tell anyone, but I do happen to know a rather brilliant cryptologist."

"A what?"

"A master of code. He no longer works for the Home Office because he was injured badly during the war. If anyone could do it, Daniel Morrison could."

"You want to give him these books?"

"If you want to know what they really say," he said.

"I want to think about this first."

Elliot met her gaze and saw this was not a subject she was willing to negotiate.

The fact that they would soon be facing Sir Stanley with this knowledge weighing on him was not . . . ideal.

But he loved her, and this is what she wanted, so he nodded. "Very well," he said, "take all the time you need."

Her grateful smile and obvious relief were his rewards. "Thank you." She sighed and glanced at the clock. "Well, I suppose it is time to face the music."

Chapter 19

Sir Stanley Gray looked almost comically uncomfortable in his corner seat when Jo and Elliot entered The Greedy Vicar a short time later.

The relief the man felt at their arrival was palpable. He stood as they approached the table, his gaze fixed on Jo. "Thank you so much for coming, my dear. And Wingate," he added absently, staring at Jo.

Jo's expression was the impassive, cool, controlled exterior she always showed the world—to everyone but Elliot.

"Ah, my dear," the older man said, risking life and limb to take Jo's hands in his. "You are the very image of your father." Gray smiled tremulously, his gaze misty and fond.

Jo shuffled her feet uncomfortably at his obviously emotional state.

"But I'm keeping you standing," Gray added, clearing his throat, releasing her hands, and gesturing to the table. "Please, both of you, sit."

Once they'd all sat, Gray raised a hand to call Dora, the serving girl, over.

"Hallo, Jo, Smithy," she said when she approached their table. "The usual for you both?"

Jo and Elliot nodded.

Once she'd gone, Gray smiled, although Elliot couldn't help

noticing it was strained. "You must come here a great deal if the wench knows your preferences," he said to Jo, mild disapproval coloring his words.

Jo bristled—although probably only somebody who knew her well would notice—not appreciating any chiding, no matter how mild, from this stranger.

"Elliot said you wanted to talk to me about my father and Mungo."

Gray flinched slightly at her sharp tone but recovered quickly. "And I greatly wanted to see you, of course. But you are right, my dear, I do have some questions."

Elliot could see the endearment rankled and couldn't help wishing that Gray was a bit more . . . professional and less emotional.

"I know very little," Jo said. "Elliot said he told you that."

"He did tell me. But what I'd like to talk to you about isn't so much what you might think you know, but what you noticed and don't realize you know."

Jo shrugged. "Go ahead and ask."

Gray reached into his coat, and Elliot felt, rather than saw, Jo stiffen. A quick glance at her side showed a blade in her hand.

The older man didn't seem to notice and drew a slim book from his coat. "Do you mind if I jot a few things down?"

"No."

Gray looked nonplussed by her abrupt answer, and Elliot could see the other man mentally reevaluating how much work it would take to *polish* Jo for her new position.

"Now then, I thought we might work backward from the last, er, *job* you and Brown worked together before his death."

"I won't talk about past clients."

Gray's mouth hung open for a moment, but then he smiled, the expression forced. "Ah, that's very commendable."

Jo just stared.

Gray sighed, set down his pencil, and clasped his hands on the table. "My lady—"

"Please don't call me that."

"That is who you *are*," Gray persisted.

"I hardly want the fact noised about in a pub in Whitechapel," Jo retorted.

An angry flush crept up Gray's throat at her not-so-subtle reproof, but he nodded and said, "Very well, *Miss Brown*. What I wanted to say is that you don't appear very eager to help me clear your father and Callum Brown's names."

"I'm *very* eager to do that," Jo said. "But I don't see how disclosing information about prior employers will aid you."

Neither did Elliot.

"It's possible that some of the people Brown worked for might know something. After all, how did he come to be acquainted with all these people if not because of some link to his past?"

Before Jo could speak, Dora interrupted, setting down two pints of the house brew. "Here you are."

"Thank you, Dora," Elliot said, reaching for his coin purse.

Gray shook his head. "I will pay," he said, digging around in his pocket.

"I hear the Fayre is taking an early break this year," Dora said to Jo while Gray counted out the correct change.

"Yes, a few months early."

"Strange time to be breaking, isn't?" Dora persisted. "I heard Cecile is—"

"Thank you, miss," Gray said pointedly as he slid his coins across the table.

Dora gave him a startled look, shrugged, and picked up her coins. "I'll see you after a while, ducks," she said to Jo, giving Gray a pointed look of her own.

Once she'd gone, Gray said to Jo, "You really must depress that sort of pretension, my dear. You are a wealthy, powerful peeress of the realm and—"

"The only connection Mungo had to the past—that I know of— was with a Prussian mercenary named Strauss. He was the man who hired him initially. But Mungo and he went their separate ways when

I was twelve. After that, he received more offers of work than he could accept, thanks to years of building his own reputation for effectiveness and discretion."

Gray hesitated, and then turned to his book and jotted something down—the Prussian's name, probably. "What about a diary, correspondence—things of that nature?"

Jo didn't even blink before lying, "Nothing that I've found."

"Is it possible he kept anything of value in a bank? They will often store important documents for their depositors."

"I never knew him to use a bank."

Elliot wondered where she kept her money—because he knew she had enough to invest in the purchase of the Fayre, which was no small amount—and nightmarish visions of her keeping it inside her mattress flickered through his head. He could just imagine her curious, thieving raven finding such a bonanza and hiding it away somewhere, never to be found again.

"Although your maternal grandfather sent back most of your father's possessions—books, a few letters between your parents, and several volumes of his poetry"—he paused and smiled at Jo—"were you aware he was an aspiring poet?"

"No, I didn't know that."

Elliot was astounded—and more than a little uneasy—by how convincingly she lied. He'd questioned many, many prisoners over the years, and never had he seen such a smooth liar. Which begged the question: had she lied to him about anything?

Although he was doing an excellent job of concealing it, Jo knew Elliot was uneasy about her lying. Well, Gray *was* his superior, so she was sorry to put him in this position, but something about the man rubbed her the wrong way.

Yer nose has been bent outta joint since learning I'm not yer da, hen.

Jo pursed her lips at the sound of phantom Mungo and ignored him, too angry at the dead man to even talk to his shade.

"Was he any good?" she asked Gray, preferring to talk to him rather than listen to a ghost nattering in her head.

"I beg your pardon?"

"The poems? Was he a good poet?"

Gray's face creased into a genuinely fond smile. "Just between the three of us, he was dreadful." The old man laughed at his own words, and Elliot smiled.

When Gray saw she wasn't amused, his humor dimmed. "He was not a good poet, but writing poetry was good for him, as it gave him an outlet for those parts of himself that his father had always sought to suppress."

"What parts?"

Gray paused, obviously considering his next words. "John had an artist's soul, not a warrior's—not that he wasn't a damned fine soldier." He coughed. "Er, beg your pardon."

Jo felt her first glimmer of amusement at his apology. If he thought he was soiling her delicate ears with vulgar language, he was several decades too late.

"While his poetry was, er, *bad,* his skill at the piano was awe-inspiring. If he'd been born to another life, he could have become a concert pianist."

"His father wouldn't allow that?"

Gray smiled sadly. "No, I'm afraid the old earl was cut from traditional cloth. No son of his was going to pursue such a namby-pamby endeavor. It was the military for his third son, just as it had always been." Gray shrugged. "I think John never touched another piano after his father forbade his studies. He took up writing poetry not long afterward. He wrote for himself, not for others, and had no intention of ever seeking publication for his work."

For the first time since she'd learned John Townshend was her real father, Jo felt a glimmer of interest in the man.

"Your grandfather also sent a crate full of your mother's things. Simms had no other children and believed—if you'd survived—the best chance of your receiving your parents' effects would be through your family here. Shall I have them delivered to you?"

"You have them?" she asked, confused.

His pale, papery skin colored slightly. "Er, your cousin Richard immediately brought the items to the Home Office when he received them."

"To inspect them for possible clues as to what my father had done?" she guessed.

"Yes. Nothing was ever found, but I'm afraid the items merely sat in storage afterward—our fault, entirely—so the boxes are in London. Would you like them?"

Jo felt an odd sense of unease—almost nausea—at the thought of pawing through the personal effects of two strangers, but there was no point in being missish about it.

"Yes, please have them sent to me." She smiled faintly. "Mr. Wingate tells me you already know my address."

Gray's cheeks darkened still further. "Er, yes, of course—I shall send them immediately. Some of the items of jewelry from your mother's family are probably quite valuable."

Jo had given very little thought to the woman who'd borne her and knew that probably made her an unnatural child. She supposed, now, that the pearls she wore were from her real mother. She'd never thought to have them valued, but she'd been naïve to believe Mungo could have afforded such jewelry on a sergeant's salary.

She had asked Mungo about her mother a few times when she'd been younger, but he'd become teary-eyed and his answers had been choked and vague, so she'd simply stopped asking. She wondered now if he'd been sad because of the lies he'd told her? Or had he been thinking of his own lover? A woman he'd never married and who'd given him no children.

Well, what did any of that matter now?

When Jo didn't reply, Gray went on. "Is there anything at all you can think of—no matter how small or insignificant seeming—that might give me some clue as to what Brown was going to bring to Wardlow when he agreed to meet him? Can you think of where he might have kept such . . . evidence? Perhaps a friend who might be keeping it for him? Or was there some place he might have hidden it? I can't tell you how thrilled I was to learn he had some way to clear

John's name. It is beyond frustrating to know that evidence is out there—somewhere—but hidden."

Jo looked into the man's eyes and saw genuine interest and compassion in his gaze; suddenly she felt bad that she was being so intractable. He was trying to clear Mungo's—and her real father's—names. Just because she'd lived her life running because of their alleged treachery didn't mean Gray was at fault.

"I'm afraid I don't have anything for you right now," she said, her tone gentler than it had been all night. "But I will put some effort into trying to remember."

Gray's face creased into a smile at her words. Then he ruined all the goodwill he'd just accumulated by saying, "Good girl. No doubt it will be easier for you to relax and comb your memory once you are no longer living in such squalor and working to survive."

Jo scowled and opened her mouth to correct him, but Elliot beat her to the punch.

"Thank you, Sir Stanley. We appreciate your taking the time and making the effort to come and meet with Miss Brown here tonight," he said hastily, surreptitiously laying his hand over hers—and her knife—under the table.

The older man looked pleased by Elliot's words, and Jo realized she should probably learn a few of her lover's tactics when it came to communication.

Unfortunately, she had one more thing to say, and there was no way to phrase it prettily. "I would appreciate it if you called off the two men watching my lodgings."

Gray blinked, and his eyes widened in surprise before sliding to Elliot.

"He didn't tell me," Jo lied smoothly. "I saw the men ages ago, and once I knew you wanted to speak to me, I simply put the two things together."

"The men aren't there to spy on you, but to ensure your safety, my, er, Miss Brown."

Jo had to smile at that, and Gray looked stunned—as if he'd not believed her capable of it.

Once again, Elliot stepped in before she could say anything offensive or outrageous. "I will see to Miss Brown's safety, sir, but we are grateful for your efforts on her behalf."

Gray snorted softly and said, "Very well, I will remove your protection detail." His tolerant expression hardened. "But I will only do so if you give me your word that you will move into your *real* house and be done with this farce in no more than a week."

Jo briefly met Elliot's gaze. He'd not wanted to pressure her about the move, but she knew he believed it was something she could not avoid for long. She had already decided on a week—why put off the inevitable?—but her contrary streak, a characteristic that was usually slumberous but truculent once roused, reared its head.

"Two weeks," she countered.

"Ten days," Gray said.

Jo met Elliot's gaze, and she nodded. "Ten days it is."

Chapter 20

The first thing Jo noticed about her cousin and his wife was their age and seeming fragility. For some reason, she'd expected them to be in their fifties or sixties, but they were clearly much older.

Indeed, the handsome couple who warmly and enthusiastically greeted her at the foyer of Townshend House had to be nearing eighty.

Mrs. Edith Townshend lifted a hand to her mouth, her eyes glassy with unshed tears. "Oh, my dear! You are the very image of your father. Isn't she, Richard."

Jo's cousin Richard, just as emotional as his wife, nodded and sniffed, his eyes shimmering dangerously. "Indeed, she is, my dear. Indeed, she is."

"It's a pleasure to meet you," Jo muttered, her heart racing, skin clammy, and breathing ragged. The urge to turn and run was almost unbearable.

But then Elliot set a hand on her elbow. "It's a pleasure to see you both again—it has been many years, not since my brother Nigel's wedding," he murmured, breaking the awkward silence that had speedily developed.

Richard Townshend visibly wrenched his gaze away from Jo and smiled at Elliot, his expression chilling several degrees. "Ah, yes,

Winstead—Norriton's youngest, of course I remember you. Yes, the last time we saw you was at your brother's wedding. Do you recall, Edi?"

Mrs. Townshend nodded and surreptitiously wiped away a tear with a lacy handkerchief. "Yes, indeed. It's a pleasure to see you again. I was terribly sorry to hear about your dear mother."

"Thank you," Elliot said.

"But what are we doing standing about in the foyer?" she suddenly asked, her cheeks flushing. "Come—let us retire to the sitting room, where Wilmot will bring us tea." She hesitated and then said, "Unless you would like to see your house and—"

"Tea sounds lovely," Jo said, absolutely not interested in touring a house that looked bigger than the theater the Fayre operated in.

There was a flurry of hat and cloak and glove removal, and then all four of them trooped up the stairs and her cousin Richard opened the door to a sitting room that could have fit ten of her apartments inside it.

"Do have a seat," Mrs. Townshend said, gesturing to a cluster of chairs and settees in front of a fireplace that had a fire burning, even though it was warm today.

Jo sat on the edge of an exquisite silk settee and was embarrassingly relieved when Elliot settled beside her.

Richard and Edith Townshend took the sofa across from them, and another uncomfortable silence descended.

And then three of them—everyone but Jo—started talking at once:

"I understand you—"

"Sir Stanley tells us—"

"Thank you for allowing me to accompany—"

They all broke off, and everyone chuckled.

"Let's try that again," Mr. Townshend said. "Thank you for accompanying our cousin here today, Wingate."

"It is my pleasure, sir."

"We understand from Sir Stanley that the two of you have an, er, understanding?" the older man persisted.

"Yes, we do. No disrespect to you, sir, but we formed our attachment before Jo—er, Lady Packenham—knew the truth about her identity."

Mrs. Townshend leaned forward, her expression intent. "So it's true you only learned who your father was a few days ago, my lady?"

"Please, call me Jo," Jo insisted, her voice sharper than she would have liked, but it also gave her the woolies to be addressed as *lady* anything.

"You use your middle name, then," Richard said. "That was your grandmother's name."

Jo nodded. She hadn't known that Josephine was actually her real name. She'd used male names while growing up—both she and Mungo had changed names often—but she'd always felt a special affection for Jo.

The room became quiet again, and Jo felt an unaccountable wave of restlessness. Was this how her life would be from now on? A series of vapid conversations bookended by uncomfortable silences?

Rather than run from the room as fast as her legs would carry her—which was what she *wanted* to do—she tucked a stray lock of hair behind her ear and scratched her head, vaguely amused when Edith winced; apparently ladies were not supposed to have itches.

The door opened, and a stately looking man who could only be the butler entered. His eyes immediately went to Jo, his gaze rapt.

Honestly, she'd had more interest shown in her in the last ten minutes than when she performed on stage.

Jo cleared her throat. "Er, hallo," she said, smiling at the servant and nodding a greeting.

Judging by her relatives' startled glances, countesses weren't supposed to greet butlers.

"This is Wilmot," Richard said. "He knew your father and has worked for our family since he was just a boy himself. Wilmot, this is Lady Packenham."

"It is such a pleasure to meet you, my lady." The old servant's eyes were as dewy as her cousins' had been. If Jo managed to escape the room without anyone weeping today, she'd count that a victory.

"Thank you," she said awkwardly.

Once the servant was gone, Edith gestured to the tray. "It is your house; would you like—"

Jo stood up before she realized what she was doing. Naturally, her uncle and Elliot stood up along with her.

"This isn't what I pictured for myself, Mr. and Mrs. Townshend. I've not been raised for any of *this*"—she gestured at the house around them—"but Elliot has conveyed to me the importance of assuming my position—my duty. That said, I would be grateful if both of you wouldn't mind going on as you've been doing. At least for a while."

The older woman's hands fluttered nervously, like butterflies. "But of course, my dear. I really wish you'd call me Edith."

Jo nodded. "Edith."

Edith smiled. "Please sit and let us have some tea."

Jo sat, and so did her two shadows.

"How do you like your tea?"

"Black for me," Jo said.

"Milk and three sugars," Elliot admitted, the slight flush on his sharp cheekbones—a sign of his embarrassment at preferring such a sweet, milky brew—made Jo want to laugh. Fortunately she didn't, because she wasn't sure she'd be able to stop once she started.

"Sir Stanley has told us a little about your life," Richard said while his wife made tea. "It sounds as if you have had an interesting time of it."

"And difficult, too, I'd imagine," Edith interjected.

Had her life been difficult? Jo didn't feel as if it had. "Mungo took excellent care of me when I was little, and he taught me how to protect myself and earn a living," she said when she saw the others were waiting.

"But you won't have to do that any longer," Richard said. "You are a very wealthy young woman."

"Not so young," she couldn't help correcting. "I'll be thirty-two next year." The fact that she was older than she'd always believed had not surprised Jo as much as everything else she'd learned in the last few days.

"That is young to us, my dear." Edith held out a cup and saucer, and Jo rose to take it.

"Edith and I have not been blessed with any children," Richard said, his tone apologetic—as if he owed Jo cousins—and the pain that flashed across Edith's face told Jo their lives hadn't been without pain, despite their wealth.

"So," Edith said, forcibly brightening, "you have been working in the same circus where Staunton's wife once worked."

Jo sipped her tea and nodded. "Yes."

Her cousins both blinked at her brevity, but what else could she say?

"Jo and I recently attended the Staunton ball," Elliot smoothly added, nodding his thanks at her cousin for his cup of tea.

"Indeed?" Edith asked, perking up. "That is—well, that is a most fortunate connection to have. The duchess has become quite the rage this year. Her aunt Julia and I were schoolmates several centuries ago."

Jo smiled at the little jest; it touched her deeply how much this pair of strangers wanted her to like them.

"I've met Her Grace several times; she is lovely and unaffected." Edith delicately cleared her throat. "I take it that she is aware of your change in status?"

"Not yet," Jo admitted, ignoring Elliot's disapproving look. "But I will tell her soon."

"You are just becoming accustomed to the fact yourself, of course," Richard said. "It isn't a wonder that you need a bit of time. That said, we were hoping you would make your home with us sooner rather than later."

Jo was surprised that Sir Stanley hadn't shared the deal he'd ne-

gotiated. She was tempted to lie and say she'd planned to move in
after the Season was over, but Elliot was giving her that eagle-eyed
look, so she nodded and said, "I need a little more time to resolve
several matters." Especially with Helen, who was still expecting Jo to
be one of the leading acts in the Fayre when it reopened less than a
month from now. "Will next Friday be convenient?"

Edith nodded. "Nine days will be plenty of time to have everything prepared for you." Her eyes flickered over Jo's serviceable but
plain gray gown. "It would be best if you arrived garbed, er—" She
floundered for the correct, inoffensive words.

"I have proper clothing," Jo lied again. But that was a lie she
could rectify over the next nine days.

Jo glanced at Elliot; some of the other lies would not be so simple to fix.

Jo was exhausted and confused after her meeting with her cousins. The hackney ride back to her lodgings took place in silence.

"Shall I stay tonight?" Elliot asked, once he'd walked her to her
front door and unlocked it for her.

Jo needed time to think—and to absorb all the changes that had
happened and the others that were about to happen—but she also did
not want to be alone, which was a strange feeling for her.

When she met his concerned gaze, she knew that she wanted
him there more than she wanted privacy. "Please stay."

He nodded and followed her into her tiny room. Not for the first
time did she wonder what he thought of the way she lived. Was he
like Sir Stanley or her cousins, all three of whom clearly believed she
was suffering in squalor?

Jo shrugged the thought away and made a soft clucking sound to
Angus, who opened his eye just long enough to give her a look before tucking his beak back beneath his wing and resuming his late-
afternoon nap. Even though the circus was closed down, and they no
longer needed to work at night, he'd not yet got into the habit of
being awake all day.

Jo saw Elliot looking at the two crates that were sitting outside the box room. "Oh, those came today—from Sir Stanley," she said. "I've not looked inside. Do you want to have some tea and we can see what there is?"

"You don't want to go through them alone the first time?" Elliot asked.

She smiled and slid her arms around his waist. "You are crediting me with more sensibility than I possess, Elliot. I knew neither of these people, even though they apparently created me. If those were two boxes of Mungo's things, I would feel differently. But these things belonged to strangers. Besides," she said, lightly kissing his elegant, high-bridged nose, "you are my lover. I don't mind sharing with you." Jo could see her uncharacteristically sweet words touched him. "Go ahead and drag it all out while I start the tea."

Jo had no expectations of what her maternal grandfather had deemed worth sending all the way from the wilds of America to London more than a decade ago, but—aside from a lovely diamond pendant, a gold ring, and a bracelet set with stones that were probably garnets, the only other items of any interest were three love letters from her mother to her father, which Jo had not wanted to read other than to glance at them and learn what they were—there was very little in the two crates.

Elliot had laid everything out on the bed, and they'd gone through it methodically, looking for anything that might be considered a clue. There was a dress that must have belonged to her mother, the gown in a style that was popular thirty-odd years ago, the heavy brocade creased with age.

There was a family bible from her mother's side and some pressed flowers and other trinkets whose meaning would only have been clear to her mother or father.

"Except for these"—Elliot held up the three leather-bound books of poems that had been in her father's box—"nothing in either of these boxes seems like anything that might hold the information we are looking for."

Jo lifted the teapot inquiringly, and Elliot shook his head. "If I have another cup of tea, I'll float away." They'd already had two cups each as they'd gone through the boxes.

Jo gestured to the meager contents. "Not much to show for two lives, is it?" But then, what would she leave behind her if she were to die tomorrow? Angus was the only *thing* of value she had, and it terrified her to think of dying before her bird did.

Elliot set the books aside and met her gaze. "What did you think of your relatives?"

Jo pushed aside the detritus on the bed and flopped down beside him. "They seem genuinely happy to see me—if a bit befuddled as to what they will *do* with me."

"You just need some time to get to know each other."

Jo feared that she'd have that in great abundance. She closed her eyes and took a deep breath, telling herself to be calm.

"My grandmother has written, asking me to come see her," Elliot said.

Jo opened her eyes. "When will you go?"

"Tomorrow. If you have no objection, I thought to bring some of the poems to the man I mentioned—Daniel Morrison. It will only be a short jaunt out of my way to stop at his cottage en route to my grandmother's."

"Yes, please do bring them to him," Jo said, trying not to get her hopes up that the code breaker would find something to exculpate both her fathers. "Do you want them all?"

"I'll just take the three books that came in the box right now."

Jo knew what he meant: he'd take the ones that Sir Stanley already knew about. So, Elliot expected the older man to be watching them, did he?

"How long will you be gone?" she asked, suddenly not wanting him to go at all.

"Three days at most." He rolled onto his side and cupped her cheek with his warm palm, his lips curving into a faint smile. "You are probably getting sick of me and want your house and bed back."

Jo shoved everything off the bed, letting it all fall to the floor with a clatter.

Elliot laughed. "Hmm, somebody is . . . eager," he teased, as her hands went to the placket of his pantaloons. His eyebrows arched, and his smile pulled up on the right side, exposing the dimple that somehow managed to change his face entirely—from a handsome but stern man past his first youth to a mischievous boy. "Does this sudden burst of affection mean you might miss me?"

Jo just snorted, shoved him onto his back, and then wrenched down his skin-tight pantaloons.

He groaned when her hand closed around his hot length. "Jo," he muttered, his eyelids drooping.

She gorged on the sight of his long, thick shaft while pumping him from root to tip.

Elliot's hips rolled, thrusting his cock into the tight tunnel of her fist, his nostrils flaring as he regarded her through slitted eyes. "I want your mouth."

Jo smirked and sank to her knees, holding his gaze while she slowly and deliberately swallowed him inch by inch.

"Oh, God," he gasped.

His body was tense, but his hand was light when it settled on her head. She could feel the struggle raging inside him—his desire to use her for his pleasure warring with his ingrained courtesy. The gentleman in him won the battle, and he allowed her to work him at her own pace.

Rather than reward his chivalrous impulse, Jo teased him cruelly, bringing him to the edge of his climax not once but three times, until he growled, his nostrils flaring as he glared down at her, his nobility falling away in tatters to reveal the untamed man beneath.

His long, elegant fingers closed around her head, and he took what he wanted.

Jo opened herself to him, taking him as deeply as he needed, reveling in her own power as he called out her name, his climax all the more explosive for being denied so long.

Only when he began to soften did she release him, dragging her tongue along the ridged muscles of his belly until a happy rumbling sound emanated from his chest.

"So good," he muttered thickly, giving her a sleepy, sated smile. "Thank you, Jo." He began to push up onto his elbows. "Let me—"

"Shh," she whispered, pushing him back down. "Rest—I'll want you wide awake and vigorous. We've got all night, Elliot."

"Mmm, we do." He slid his arms around her, his body warm and heavy as he let her bear his weight. "That was lovely," he murmured in her hair, his embrace tightening.

It had been. She adored pleasing him, knowing that she—plain, odd Jo Brown—could make such a clever, reserved, and formidable man come apart. At least for a little while, he belonged to her.

Jo burrowed her face into his neck, inhaling his masculine scent and holding it in her lungs for a long moment before expelling it and finally answering the question he'd asked earlier. "Yes, I will miss you."

Chapter 21

Jo and Angus entered Cecile's—now Helen's—house a few days later to find the normally boisterous and noisy kitchen strangely quiet without Cecile, Guy, Cat, and her dog George.

Thanks to Helen's plan to lock Cecile and Guy up together in a room, the stubborn lovers had thrashed out their differences and made up.

Jo had worried that forcing two people to spend time together would actually do more harm than good, but Cecile and Guy had emerged from the room after six hours like a pair of lovebirds.

They had left for France several days before and would be gone at least a few months on an extended visit to Cecile's long-lost family.

Rather than the usual collection of employees lingering around the scarred kitchen table, there was only Helen.

She looked up from a thick ledger and smiled when Jo entered the room. "Hello, you two."

Jo nodded, and Angus *quork*ed and immediately flew over to the perch Cecile had long ago set up for him, complete with a bowl of water and another bowl that usually held kitchen scraps Cook collected for him.

"I just made a fresh pot of tea," Helen said.

Jo poured herself a cup and then sat down across from Helen, loathe to begin her confession.

Helen cocked her head. "What is it, Jo? You look like you have something you need to say. Have you changed your mind about owning a circus? Don't worry if you have. You needn't—"

"My name's not really Jo Brown. It's Elizabeth Josephine Townshend." She cleared her throat. "And I'm the Countess of Packenham."

Helen stared, her lips parted.

Jo took a too-large gulp of tea, scalded the roof of her mouth, and mentally cursed her stupidity.

The only sound in the kitchen was the *tap tap tap* of Angus's beak against his food bowl as he rooted through the scraps.

Finally, just when Jo was wondering if she should get up and leave, Helen smirked. "What? Not a duchess? That brings down the tone of the place, doesn't it?"

Jo choked on a laugh.

"Sorry," Helen said, not sounding sorry at all. In fact, she looked quite gleeful. "I couldn't resist."

"It is rather comical, isn't it?"

"*Comical* isn't the word I'd have used—*amazing* was more what I was thinking. Not to mention coincidental—or did you know about your illustrious connections for years, as Cecile did?"

"No, this came as quite a surprise."

"Ah, I see. So then you are not a widow?"

Jo frowned, needing a moment to understand what Helen was asking. She chuckled. "No, I inherited the title thanks to a rare royal patent that allows the earldom to pass through a female of the line if there is no male heir."

"Well, it is quite amazing that this has happened so quickly after Cecile's discovery."

Jo smiled at her. "Perhaps lightning will strike a fourth time?"

"Ha! I hope not," Helen said.

"You don't want to be a duchess—or a countess?"

"No!" Helen shot back, and then she looked sheepish at her emphatic response. "I'm sorry, that probably didn't sound very nice. But what I meant to say is that I like my new life of relative anonymity."

"Yes," Jo admitted. "That is something I have enjoyed and will miss." She was glad when Helen didn't try to convince her it would be otherwise; as a former heiress who'd been betrothed to not one, but two, dukes, Helen was well aware of the cost associated with joining the ranks of the *haute ton*.

"Don't feel bad that you can't invest in the Fayre and—"

"I still want to invest—if you'll have me," Jo interrupted.

"Are you sure?" Helen asked. "You needn't do so just because you worry about me. Cecile has been embarrassingly generous with her terms. I can shoulder the purchase by myself."

"If you'll have me, I'd love to be your partner—albeit a silent one."

Helen smiled, the expression transforming her rather average features into something lovely. "Thank you. That would actually make the purchase much less . . . stressful, as I will then have some operating money, should there be any unexpected expenses, which I have no doubt there will be."

Jo nodded, relieved that she could help the other woman. She hated giving her word and then not living up to it. Mungo had said once, if he'd said it a hundred times, that a person's most valuable possession was their word.

"So," Helen said briskly. "When will you be stepping into your new life? Will you have time to interview new acts with me? I'd planned to seek a replacement for Cecile, of course, but now I shall need two."

Jo grimaced. "I'm sor—"

"Oh, hush, I am just teasing you. I shall miss you, and so will the punters, but the Fayre will prosper—I will make sure of it." She hesitated and then said, "I trust you didn't say anything to Cecile about this before you left?"

"No, I wanted to wait until she had time to settle."

"So, Guy doesn't know either, then?"

Jo shook her head.

"I'm glad I asked. I'll make sure I don't slip and let anything out in my letters to her."

"Thank you," Jo said.

Helen smiled. "Of course. Now, how long do I have you, and when can you watch some auditions with me?"

Because Jo's next meeting took place somewhere far more formal than Helen's kitchen, she was forced to garb herself in one of her three *non-work* outfits the following day. She'd ordered the two walking costumes when she'd gone to select a ball gown with Cecile. It had taken several weeks for them to be finished—she wasn't one of the modiste's more important clients—and the first outfit had only been delivered a few days before.

Both the gown and matching spencer were a beautiful shade somewhere between gold and mustard. The design was simple in the extreme, but Jo thought the ensemble made her look quite elegant, if not in the highest kick of fashion. Cecile had tried to convince her to add some contrasting turquoise trim and a hat with feathers dyed to match, but Jo had wisely declined, taking instead the advice of the woman who owned the dress shop.

"You are that rare blond who looks best in white," the intimidating modiste had told her. "With your pale coloring, it is easy to be cast into insignificance by too much color. But you can wear pastels, yellows, and pinks if you stay with simple embellishments."

That was fine by Jo, who despised frills, lace, and too much ribbon.

"Well, what do you think, Angus?"

The raven, who'd been dozing, looked over at the sound of his name. Jo would have sworn he was smirking.

She picked up the gold-beaded reticule that Cecile had made her purchase, put some money and an extra knife inside, and was ready to go.

Angus perked up when he saw her heading for the door.

"Oh, *now* you're interested," she teased. "Yes, you can come along."

At least as far as the fancy clothing store where she'd be meeting the Duchess of Staunton. It had actually been Jo's idea to do some of the dreaded clothing shopping while telling Marianne the truth.

With Angus on her shoulder, she made her way down to the ground floor and out to the street. She'd just raised her arm to hail one of the hackney cabs that clustered near the corner when a slight movement caught her eye across the street. A man—in drab, plain clothing—hailed a hackney just a half a tick after Jo.

It was the same man she'd seen loitering around the area since Elliot had told her that she was being watched. It didn't surprise her that Sir Stanley had lied about calling off his men, but it annoyed her. She knew he wasn't watching her because he feared she was hiding anything; he was having her watched in case she decided to bolt.

She was about to climb into the hackney that rolled to a stop when the driver leaned down and said, "Oy, you can't bring that bird inside me cab."

"*Oy!*" Angus shouted back at the cabbie.

"Bloody 'ell! It talks," the driver gasped, goggling.

"*Bloody 'ell!*" Angus shot back.

Jo turned her back on the driver without commenting and waved down another hackney, one whose driver she recognized. She might have argued with the first man, but she was curious to see what her watcher did.

When he, too, waved off his driver, she smirked.

"'Ello, Miss Brown," the new cabbie said, tipping his battered hat. "'Ello, Angus."

"'*Ello, moi friend,*" Angus called back, sending the old man into whoops, just as he did every time Angus said it.

"Hello, Mr. Prichard. Bond Street today, a place called Madam Silvia's."

The driver whistled through a gap in his teeth. "Posh, that. And might I say you look fine as a fivepence?"

"Thank you." Jo climbed inside, not bothering with the steps, something she wouldn't be allowed to do for much longer.

* * *

Elliot watched the bespectacled man across from him as he flipped through the handwritten books of poetry, but his mind was elsewhere—on his grandmother, who'd been frailer than ever and who'd looked so enlivened by his visit that he'd extended it until almost seven days had passed. His thoughts also kept wandering to Jo, whom he missed with a ferocity that worried him.

Once he'd seen the way things were going with the dowager, he'd written a brief note to Jo, telling her of his delay in returning, which now meant he'd only have one night with her before she moved into her new home. It might very well be the last night they shared together if she eventually decided to end their mock betrothal.

Of course, she couldn't write back to him—how would he explain such a letter to his grandmother when he could say nothing about his impending faux betrothal? He'd not yet decided how to deliver that news to her. She was an old lady and very set in her proper ways; it was doubtful she'd understand a *temporary* betrothal, especially when Elliot didn't understand it himself.

He knew Jo had feelings for him, but he could scarcely press her on the issue when her entire life was being turned on its head.

"Mr. Wingate?"

Elliot realized Daniel Morrison was staring at him. "I beg your pardon?"

"I said there is clearly something to these poems."

"You mean you believe they are a code?"

"They might be. I hope they are, because otherwise, they're the worst poetry I've ever read."

Elliot couldn't help smiling. "Yes, they are quite bad."

Morrison flipped through several pages until he found what he was looking for. "You see here—where the handwriting changes?"

Elliot looked at the page where Brown's writing began. "Yes, that's where Packenham's writing ends and Brown's begins."

Jo had agreed that he should tell the cryptologist the truth of what he was working on.

"Anything to break this code, if it is one," she'd said.

Morrison clucked his tongue. "Well, it's very strange. In fact, it is what persuades me this might indeed be some coded message."

"Why? Perhaps Brown suddenly wanted to take up poetry?"

"In the middle of another man's *poem*?"

"Oh, is it in the middle?" Elliot looked at the page again, stomached a few lines, and then realized the other man was right. "Hmm, I suppose that is odd."

"Very. At least if either Packenham or Brown were truly interested in poetry."

"Well, can you do anything with it?" Elliot asked.

"I'll be honest, Mr. Wingate. Without knowing the source of the code, there is very little chance I can be of help. But if you don't need the books back immediately, I can give it some thought."

Jo hadn't said one way or the other, but Morrison was less than half a day's ride from London, so Elliot could fetch the books for her if she decided she wanted them.

"Go ahead and keep them."

Morrison nodded. "You say that both of these men are dead?"

"Yes."

"Did they have large libraries or access to large libraries?"

"They were both on the run for years, so I doubt it."

"That is fortunate, because the code would be impossible to decipher if they had access to many books. It will be nearly impossible even if they only had a handful of books."

"I will see if there is anything in their personal effects."

"If this is indeed coded, the book would be well-thumbed."

Elliot nodded. "Could it be two books?"

"If it is, then our chances are nil. To be honest, I'm not optimistic. However"—he lifted his leg, the one that was missing a foot—"since this happened, I have nothing but time, so I will be glad to have something to keep my mind occupied."

Elliot felt a pang of pity for the other man, whose injury appeared to have reduced his once-active, exciting life to a stagnant existence. "Thank you so much for undertaking this challenge for me," he said.

Morrison waved away his thanks. "I'm sorry I wasn't here when you called last week. It was the only day of the month I leave the property—to visit my physician."

"I'm just grateful you can look at the books—and if you think there is any chance of deciphering them, well, no harm done with an extra week. The matter has already waited more than three decades, after all."

"Do you really believe Townshend was innocent?" he asked, walking Elliot toward the door to his cottage, deftly using one crutch.

"Apparently he and Brown claimed to their dying days that he was a double agent and that they were laying a trap to catch whoever was really selling information."

Morrison paused, his hand on the doorknob. "If that is true, then the person responsible was never caught."

"Yes."

"They might still be alive."

"Yes, they might. It is possible this could be very dangerous if word was to get out. Does that change your mind about helping?"

Morrison grinned; the first truly happy expression he'd worn since Elliot had stepped into his house. "Indeed, no. In fact, it makes this job all the more appealing."

Tonight would be Jo's last night in the little garret, and she was surprised by how much that thought saddened her. She spent the evening packing up her few possessions and cleaning. Just when she'd begun to believe that Elliot would not be back in time to share the evening with her she heard his light, familiar tread on the stairs some-time after midnight.

For some odd reason, Jo's heart pounded, and her skin was sud-denly clammy, as if she were *nervous*.

"You're a fool, Josephine," she muttered beneath her breath as she paused in front of the mirror and grimaced at her dusty, frazzled appearance. But other than wiping a smut of dirt from her nose, she didn't have time for anything else.

Jo opened the door when she heard the jingle of keys on the landing.

Elliot smiled, his expression weary but eager as his dark blue gaze flickered over her. "You're a sight for sore eyes, darling. I thought you might be sleeping," he said when she stepped back and gestured him inside.

Jo removed his valise from his grip, tossed it aside, and then wrapped her body around his, kissing him before he could even take off his hat.

"Mmmm," he moaned against her, his arms so tight around her that her ribs creaked.

When he finally pulled away, they were both breathing hard.

"I missed you," he said, staring into her eyes with a warmth that filled her with both joy and shame.

Joy, because she felt the same way.

Shame because she couldn't seem to make herself say the words.

Instead, she kissed him again, gave him another crushing embrace, and then stepped back and asked, "Tea?"

"Ah. That would be lovely."

"Take off your coat and gloves and sit," she ordered.

"With pleasure," he said. "How are you, Angus?"

Angus woke long enough to *quork* softly, and then tucked his head under his wing and ignored them.

"I think he likes sleeping at night, the way nature intended for ravens," Jo said.

"What about you? Do you miss performing and staying out late?"

"A little. It was exciting and I liked using those skills. I also think I'm more of a night owl."

"Well, you will get plenty of late nights once you begin attending *ton* affairs."

Jo didn't want to think about that, so she ignored it.

"Did you carve him a new toy?" Elliot asked a moment later, gesturing to the brightly colored wooden bone sticking out of Angus's food cup.

Jo laughed softly as she filled the kettle. "Not a new toy, a *lost* toy. It's the one that Mungo carved for him. It's been lost for ages, and I found it again while I was packing up. I hope it will stop Angus's thieving, which seemed to develop right around the time his favorite toy went missing."

"Where did you find it?"

"It was in Mungo's shaving kit, of all places."

Elliot frowned. "I thought we'd gone through everything."

"It was sitting in the box room, mixed in with my things, so that is why you wouldn't have seen it. Don't get too excited," she said with a wry look. "That was the only item of interest in the small bag, unless you think some soap, a razor, and a comb might hold the clue to those poems?"

He chuckled. "Probably not."

"So," she said, changing the subject to something more interesting, "how was your grandmother?"

"She is old and fading fast," he said, the sorrow in his voice caused Jo's own chest to ache in sympathy. "I would not have stayed as long as I did if I'd not believed my visit was so beneficial to her health."

"I'm sure it cheered her greatly to see you." Jo knew that *she* loved having him around. "It is good that you stayed, Elliot," she said, taking out the bread, cheese, and ham she'd planned to eat for breakfast and cutting it up for him.

"Yes, I'm glad I did." He pulled a face. "Even so, I could have wished the visit had taken place even two weeks later so I wouldn't have had to miss your last days of liberty."

"There hasn't been much liberty. Between Helen and Marianne, I've been run ragged."

"Ah, you finally told them."

Jo grunted.

Elliot chuckled at her crotchety scowl. "I'm sorry for laughing, but you should be grateful that Guy and Cecile are not here to help them torture you."

"Yes, there is that," she admitted. She set the food down in front of him and then said, "Give me your foot."

Elliot hesitated only a moment before complying. "It's a measure of my exhaustion that I am willing to use you as my bootjack, darling."

Jo waited to grin like a smitten fool until she'd turned her back and straddled his leg; she loved it when he called her *darling*.

After a bit of a struggle, she had both boots off him. "Your feet are swollen," she said, setting the second exquisitely made boot down by its partner. "Would you like some hot water to soak them?"

Elliot's hand froze with a piece of cheese midway to his mouth, and then he threw back his head and laughed.

"What is so amusing?"

"I am not an invalid, Jo."

"One does not need to be an invalid to enjoy soaking one's feet."

He tossed the cheese onto the plate and then grasped her by the waist and pulled her onto his lap. "The prospect of soaking my feet isn't what made me ride through the night directly to your door," he murmured against her throat, his mouth hot as he covered the sensitive skin with kisses.

"Oh?" Her pulse sped as she felt his hardness pressing against her bottom.

"Unbutton my breeches, Jo."

"So bossy," she said, her hands nonetheless doing his bidding.

"Mmm-hmm," he murmured, resuming his kissing and throwing in some nibbling while lifting his hips so she could push down his drawers and breeches.

When she would have sunk to her knees and taken him in her mouth, he held her where she was. "No. I am too horsey and sweaty. Take me inside your body and ride me."

"Ah, I see how it is," she said in a breathless voice as she lifted her skirts and straddled his thighs. "You are lazy and wish me to do all the work."

"You have discovered my evil plan." He smiled sleepily and unbuttoned her plain, serviceable dressing gown, hissing when she grasped his cock with her cool, rough hand and slicked his shaft with a few firm, efficient strokes. "Mmm. I love it when you touch me, Jo."

She stood on her toes and positioned him at her entrance, sliding down his hard length slowly.

They both groaned, and Elliot's eyelids flickered. "I have missed you," he said, pushing down the neckline of her oldest nightgown to bare her breasts and sucking a taut nipple between his lips.

Jo let her head fall back as she posted him slowly, reveling in the hot suction of his mouth on her aching breast. She was vaguely aware that steam was blasting from the spout of the kettle but couldn't bring herself to care.

Elliot switched breasts, tormenting the new nipple more vigorously than the first, nipping and sucking as his hands gripped her waist to bring her down hard, meeting her with a powerful upward thrust.

Once he'd established a rhythm, he lowered a hand to the apex of her sex and pressed his thumb against her engorged nub. "Come with me, Jo," he murmured, lifting them both up with the force of his bucking.

Jo's crisis built quickly, the exquisite tension inside her threatening to explode at any moment. Beneath her spiraling bliss was the vague awareness that his shaft had thickened even more, and his thrusting had become jerky.

"Now, Jo," he hissed in her ear, his thumb stroking her over the edge while his hips pumped savagely several more times before he froze, buried deep inside her.

Climaxing together was a wonderful experience; sharing the ultimate pleasure with a person she truly cared for was more intimate than anything else in her experience.

Jo had loved Elliot for what felt like a long time, maybe even before she'd rescued him from Broussard. Maybe since the first time he'd stood on stage and faced her knives without flinching, his cool blue gaze looking deep inside her even back then, noticing something special about her that nobody else seemed to see.

"I love you, Elliot."

His body, which had just sagged with relief, instantly stiffened, and he held her at arm's length to study her face, his own flushed and wondering.

Jo smiled down at him and brushed a curl back from his brow.

His surprised expression shifted into a smile. "Does this mean we have a real betrothal?"

The hopefulness in his gaze was like a fist around her heart, and she hesitated—not long, but long enough.

He grimaced. "I'm sorry, I said I wouldn't push—"

"It is not that I don't want—"

"Hush," he murmured, kissing her lightly and stroking her shoulders. "Now that I know you love me, I can wait as long as it takes. Let us stay with our arrangement. We can decide the matter once things have settled, once you are certain."

Jo nodded and embraced him, nuzzling her face in his neck. She was afraid that he'd see the truth if he looked too deeply. As much as she loved him—and she did—it still might not be enough for her to marry him and accept this new life.

If she ended up needing to run, the last thing Jo wanted to do was break her vow to him.

Chapter 22

Jo's cousins were transfixed as they looked at Angus, and the expressions on their faces were not ones of joy.

"He is a raven, then," Edith finally said, breaking the awkward silence that had reigned ever since Jo had entered Townshend House half an hour before, garbed in her yellow-gold walking costume, with Angus on her shoulder.

"Yes, ma'am."

"Please, call me Edi," her cousin said.

"Thank you, Edi. You both must call me Jo."

She'd had no idea the Townshends were going to have every servant, from grand to humble, lined up to meet her.

The reaction to Angus—with the exception of two scullery maids and a bootblack who couldn't have been more than eight or nine—had been wide-eyed shock.

The children had been delighted with the giant bird, who'd eyed them with fascination. Angus had never spent much time around little people and Jo could see that he was as curious about them as they were about him.

Her cousins, unfortunately, had looked horrified, rather than merely shocked.

Jo had greeted each and every servant before following Edi and

Richard up the stairs to a different sitting room from the one she and Elliot had visited the last time. Just how many sitting rooms did the house have?

Wilmot and the housekeeper, Mrs. Wilmot, had been the only two servants who hadn't appeared to notice the two-foot bird on her shoulder. They appeared to be the consummate servants, not lifting so much as an eyebrow, behaving as if peers of the realm often arrived at the house with a wild animal in tow.

For his part, Angus had been on his best behavior. Other than a few *quorks*, there had been no colorful language, whistling, or other mimicry—which was his specialty. His uncanny ability to copy human voices even surprised Jo sometimes. He'd greatly expanded his vocabulary during the year and more they'd worked at the Fayre. He also had a propensity to pick up the most inappropriate words and sayings. Jo sincerely hoped he wouldn't let any of those slip out today.

Wilmot had brought in the tea tray, and the big raven sat up and peered at the contents. Jo knew he would be expecting a reward for his excellent behavior.

Everyone watched silently as Wilmot laid down the tray.

"*Biscuit*," Angus muttered.

"Oh, my goodness!" Edi shrieked, a hand on her chest as if she were suffering some sort of attack. "It *talks*!"

"He."

"I beg your pardon?" the older woman asked, her gaze still on Angus, as if she were unsure what to expect next.

Jo could hardly wait until Angus started stealing her things.

"He is a male and his name is Angus," she explained patiently.

"Oh."

Richard gave a forced, jovial laugh. "Oh, my great aunt Bathsheba—your great-great aunt—used to have a parrot. A huge blue and gold brute who had the most *vulgar* vocabulary." His eyes slid to Angus, apprehension coloring his pale features. "Er, does he—"

"Not usually," Jo lied. She turned to Wilmot, who'd stopped to watch the show. "Could I have one of those biscuits, please? The one with currants—he's partial to those." She forced a smile for her cousins. "It's a reward for his being such a good boy down below with all the servants."

"*Good boy,*" Angus echoed, his voice a slightly froggier version than Jo's, but still astoundingly similar.

Wilmot handed her a plate with one biscuit in the middle.

Jo took only the biscuit and handed it up to Angus, who grasped it with a gentleness she always found endearing.

"What do you say, Angus?"

"*Cheerio!*"

Her cousins laughed, and even Wilmot's staid features shifted into something that looked like a smile.

"Thank you, Wilmot," Richard said, cutting the show short.

Once the butler had gone, Edi busied herself with the tea tray.

"Where does, er, Angus live?" Richard asked.

"With me."

Edi's head whipped up, her jaw sagged, and she shot her husband a desperate look.

"Wouldn't he be happier outside? In a tree?" Richard asked.

"He goes out during the day, but he's never lived in the wild, so he knows to come home before it gets dark."

Richard filled his lungs, held the breath, and then expelled it slowly and nodded.

Edi handed her a cup of black tea and then looked anxiously at Angus.

"He likes milk and two sugars in his," Jo said, and then smiled when the older woman's eyes bulged.

"Ah, you are jesting," Edi said, looking more than a little relieved.

"Yes. Angus doesn't fancy tea. Whiskey is his drink."

"*Whiskey,*" Angus repeated, carefully nibbling his biscuit.

Again, Jo smiled. "That is another jest."

Her cousins chuckled nervously.

It was going to be a long, long, long day.

"My God, I've missed you, Jo," Elliot muttered beneath his breath, somehow managing not to move his lips at all. His handsome face flexed into a cool, aristocratic smile. "Ah, good to see you again, Mrs. Townshend, Mr. Townshend," he said when Jo's cousins bore down on him like a pair of frigates with all guns blazing.

"Josephine did not mention you would be among the guests tonight," Edi said, regarding Elliot as if he were something stuck to her shoe.

Jo hated how dismissive the older couple was to Elliot, but she could hardly chastise them.

The Duke of Staunton drifted up beside them. And *he* could and did chastise in his own cold way. "Wingate and I were both at Eton, and we roomed together at Oxford. I count him as one of my dearest friends." Sin stared coldly down his perfect, aquiline nose at the Townshends in a way that would melt iron.

Jo's cousins were not immune to Sin's aristocratic hauteur, and both assumed less adversarial expressions.

"Is that so?" Richard asked. "I'm a Harrovian, myself." He winked at Jo. "Never had your father's brains, so I didn't go to university."

Jo smiled, the others chuckled, the conversation moved on. People spoke of other people they knew, a play was discussed, somebody else mentioned a recent junket to Richmond.

Inside her head, Jo was screaming.

Marianne appeared beside them and edged close to her and Elliot. "Jo hasn't seen the portrait gallery, Elliot," she lied, since she'd shown it to Jo herself. "We've still time before dinner. Why don't you show her?"

Jo gave her friend a look of gratitude, and Elliot held out his arm. "May I?"

Her cousins watched like raptors eying an escaping meal as Elliot and Jo left the cavernous drawing room.

"To the right," Elliot murmured, leading her in that direction. "You look positively edible in that gown, Jo."

"You've developed a taste for muslin, have you?" she asked, arching an eyebrow at him.

Elliot laughed, and the warm, intoxicating sound heated her veins like Mungo's beloved Scottish whiskey. "These have been ten of the longest days of my life, Jo."

She snorted bitterly—an unfeminine sound which Edi was attempting to break her of. "Has it only been ten? I was sure it was at least a hundred. You, at least, have been at liberty."

He leaned close and whispered. "I'm not free since you captured my heart."

Jo laughed. "Perhaps you should take up writing poetry? You could pick up where Mungo left off."

"Cruel, cold woman," he teased, nodding at a footman who leapt forward to open one of a double set of doors.

The door had barely shut when Elliot spun her around and lowered his hot mouth over hers, pushing her up against the wall.

A picture frame dug into her shoulder, but Jo didn't care. They kissed as though they could consume each other, savoring taste, touch, and smell.

Jo dug her fingers into the hard muscles of his shoulders so fiercely they ached, and still she could not get close enough.

It was Elliot who finally pulled away, the long corridor echoing with the sounds of their raspy breathing. He rolled his hips, thrusting his erection against her belly. "See what you've done to me?"

Pride and desire mingled inside her.

He snorted. "Proud of yourself?"

Jo didn't deny it.

He adjusted himself with a pained wince. "Do we have to go another ten days before we can see each other?"

She shook her head, running one hand through his curls—which seemed to have grown even longer in barely a week and a half—and stroking her other hand over the hot bulge in his black satin breeches.

"*Jo,*" he hissed, his hips thrusting against her hand, grinding his hard cock against her palm. "You're going to make me embarrass myself."

"Then let me take it out," she urged, her fingers going to the catches.

He made a sound that was half gasp, half laugh. "*No,*" he said, taking her wrists in his hands and holding her trapped. "Somebody could come strolling through that door at any moment. Now, behave yourself. Isn't that what you've been learning? How to behave like a lady?"

"Is that what you want? For me to behave like a lady?"

He gave an exasperated sigh. "You know I like you just as you are."

"Never mind," she muttered, and then kissed him hard. She kissed until his body started to respond and then pulled away.

"Where are you going?" he demanded, reaching for her.

"I'm behaving like a lady."

"Like a temptress, more like." Elliot gave a frustrated laugh.

"That's one of the few lessons I've not yet had."

"Trust me, you don't need any training in that area. Come, tell me how things have been progressing with your new family. We've only got a few minutes alone before we'll need to return."

"Or we could just use that panel right there"—she gestured down the corridor—"which I know for a fact leads to the servant stairs, and then we could run off to the Continent together."

"Jo."

She groaned. "What do you want me to tell you? That I've enjoyed myself? It's torture, Elliot, pure and simple."

"Haven't you enjoyed any of it?"

"No."

"Not even shopping with Marianne?"

"If it were only Marianne, that would be bearable. And if we were shopping for something of interest—like new knives or a mount—that would be enjoyable. But it's my cousin and Marianne's aunt and some bossy, annoying modiste incessantly pecking away at me. And it's constantly trying on clothing and hats and sipping gallons of tea and talking about things that don't matter and—*urgh!*"

Elliot claimed her mouth again, and this time, his kiss was thorough and languid and sensual. While it didn't calm her pulse, it did steady her nerves.

And then he pulled away just when the temperature in the chilly gallery began to spike.

Jo scowled up at him. "What's the word for a *male* temptress?"

"As far as that sort of thing goes, the only word you need to know is *Elliot.*"

Jo rolled her eyes.

"I see your cousins have not warmed to me yet."

"They believe I should meet other eligible men." She snorted. "Eligible. What a loathsome word. I would rather eat a block of wood than meet men—eligible or otherwise."

"Maybe you should. Not eat a block of wood," he clarified at her disbelieving look. "But maybe you should meet some other men."

Her jaw dropped. "Are you trying to rid yourself of me?"

He grabbed her upper arms roughly and yanked her against his body. "Don't be a fool." He claimed her mouth with a kiss that was as hot and brutal as a brand, and it served to make her already aching sex throb even harder.

Jo sucked his tongue when he crudely pantomimed his desire for her. She pushed closer, sliding her hands over his tight, hard buttocks, which felt sinfully good sheathed in satin. She insinuated her fingers beneath his tailcoat and under the waistband of his breeches, grazing the even smoother satin of his flesh.

Naturally, he chose that moment to pull away.

Again.

"*Tsk, tsk,*" he chided in a gratifyingly breathless voice.

Jo groaned. "Can't we do as we did at Sin and Marianne's ball and sneak out early?"

He smirked at her frustration. "Speaking of balls, when will you attend your first one?"

"Thankfully, not for several more weeks as I'm not yet polished enough or civilized enough to be released into the *ton* quite yet. My first ball is an annual squeeze given by somebody named Castleton, or Castleby, or—"

Elliot laughed. "You mean the Duchess of *Castleford's* annual ball, to which marriage-mad mamas have been known to joust to the death to acquire an invitation. *That* squeeze?"

Jo gave him a sour look. "I'm so pleased you find all this amusing."

"So am I."

She snorted and shook her head, but she couldn't be angry with him. It *was* rather funny—even though it was miserable, too.

"So, what will you be doing until Castleford's ball?"

"More dancing lessons, how to hold a teacup, walk like a lady, talk like a lady, how to pretend to find boring conversations interesting, flatter boring men and pretend they are fascinating rather than hold them at knifepoint—" She broke off when she saw he was choking back his amusement. "You are getting your revenge for all the times Angus humiliated you on stage, aren't you?"

"Perhaps," he admitted, grinning unabashedly. "How is the old boy?"

"He's started stealing again."

"I didn't know that he'd ever *stopped* stealing."

"He was better after finding his bone, but moving into the new house has been . . . well, unpleasant. Angus has always been light-fingered, or light-beaked, rather, but lately he's become even worse than when we worked at the Fayre. He doesn't even bother hiding the things he steals—he just throws it all over the floor in my chambers. Oh, you can laugh," she said when he did exactly that. "But you don't have to live in a room that looks like a dragon's lair with stolen booty lying around."

"What do you think is wrong?"

"Lord knows. He doesn't seem to like *anything,* not even his precious bone. He's been positively fiendish. He has taken a dislike to Edi, and she reciprocates the feeling. He hates not having the run of the house—especially during mealtimes—and becomes surly whenever I go down to a meal. I thought a solution would be to take him down to the kitchen and have a light snack with him before breakfast and dinner—that way I could please Angus *and* Edi. But when I took him down to the kitchen, you would have thought I'd run amok with a cleaver. The servants stood about like wooden totems, and somebody sent word to Edi, who"—Jo saw that Elliot was trying not to laugh and shook her head. "It's not funny."

"It really is."

Jo snorted.

He took her hands and drew her closer. "It is *your* house, sweetheart. They are *your* servants. If you wish to bring your bird to the dining room or the kitchen, nobody can make you do otherwise."

"You don't know Edi. She gives me such mournful looks—as if I'm the biggest disappointment of her life. And Angus has taken to echoing her—you know how he does?"

Elliot laughed.

"He has an unerring ability to echo the most ridiculous words." She laughed, despite her frustration. "It's not his fault that Edi says such vapid things. But he does like to needle her and has latched onto the word *vulgar* and hurls it at her whenever she is around."

Tears were running down Elliot's cheeks.

"Yes, well, I hope you are enjoying yourself," she said unnecessarily, as it was patently obvious that he was. "Ugh. Do I have to remain at the house until the end of the blasted Season, Elliot?"

"It would be best."

"But do I *have* to?"

"When is your presentation? I should think that is the only function you *really* must attend. But your cousin would know better than I do."

"Thankfully, I don't have to attend any of the wretched Drawing Rooms in one of those ridiculous gowns. I'm apparently going to be honored by a meeting with the Regent." She gave a bitter laugh. "I can't even imagine how that conversation will go."

"Don't worry about conversation, Jo—Prinny would rather hear himself talk than anyone else. He will like you just fine."

"Why he bothers, I don't know, when I have no actual right to sit in Lords."

"Would you want to?"

She shuddered. "*No.*"

Elliot laughed. "I'm sorry, I know it's cruel to laugh. But it will soon be over. And you've suffered so many worse hardships in your life."

"It's funny how I can't seem to remember any of them," she muttered. "What have *you* been up to?" she asked, not wanting to dwell on her own life. Or lack thereof.

"I paid another visit to my grandmother."

"How is she?"

"She seems better than the last time." He smiled. "She was very much heartened to learn that I only have to return to the Continent once more—the last visit for a while, I've been promised—and then I shall be available to dance until dawn for the weeks that remain this Season."

Jo's heart sank at his words. "I thought you didn't have to go back to Paris." She gave him a wry smile and said, before he could answer, "I'm sorry, that was rather plaintive and . . . whiny."

"I think I liked it—it means you will miss me, doesn't it?"

"Of course, I'll miss you—how could you doubt that?"

He gave her a tender look. "It is still nice to hear it."

Jo's face heated at the affection—no, the *love*—she saw in his gaze. "When are you going, and how long will you be away?"

"I am leaving in a few days. I've been told the visit will be brief—no more than a week."

"I thought Sir Stanley promised to keep you close to home for the rest of the year."

"He did, and he apologized. I don't know why he is sending me," he added before Jo could ask.

"And you couldn't or wouldn't tell me if you did, would you?"

He just gave her that mysterious smile that made her want to kiss him. "You will be so busy that you won't even notice I'm gone."

Jo knew that was the opposite of the truth and didn't want to think about the next ten days without him—she'd have plenty of time to dwell on his absence when he was actually gone.

"Oh, I wanted to tell you that I also visited Morrison again and brought him the books you gave me."

"What did he say?"

"He said it was more books than he'd been hoping for, especially when all six of them appear to have been heavily thumbed and used."

"He's not optimistic, then?"

"Well, let's just say it didn't help him much. But the man has a nose for breaking codes and has solved far more obscure ciphers than this one. He just needs some time."

"I'm starting to think that proving my father's innocence isn't as critical as I'd believed," Jo sighed, trying not to feel hopeless but failing. "My cousins seem to have recovered their social standing well enough, regardless of the scandal my father caused." Although she had learned that there were still people who cut them—Jo knew that from Marianne, who was her best source of information these days.

"Clearing their names—and making the truth known—is what Mungo and your father wanted. It's what both of them lived for, wasn't it?"

"Yes, that is true," she admitted. "I don't remember my father, but pursuing the truth never made Mungo a happy person. I don't want it to consume my life, too." Jo met his gaze. "Does it matter to you if my name remains tainted?"

"You know it doesn't," Elliot said without hesitation. "But, at the same time, if what they claimed is true, not only was there a grave miscarriage of justice, but a traitor might still be at large in our government."

"That was something that always bothered Mungo, as well." She hesitated and then asked the question that had been niggling at the back of her mind: "Do you think that person—if they are still alive and active in the government—will be concerned about their safety?"

"That has been a worry of mine. I must admit I am relieved that you are no longer living alone. Not that you aren't perfectly capable of protecting yourself," he hastened to add. "I wouldn't have pursued this matter if I felt you were in any danger. But you know nothing and have made that quite clear to Sir Stanley, so if this traitor still has access to information at the Home Office, then at least they will know you can't hurt them."

"What about the poetry books?"

"The only people who know about those are you, me, and Morrison."

"You don't think Sir Stanley suspected anything?"

"It seems odd that he'd just hand them over if he did."

Jo agreed. "You trust Morrison?"

"Completely. We've worked together many times in the past. Although I don't know much about his personal life, I've been impressed by his loyalty and ethics time and again."

"Why doesn't he work for the Home Office anymore?"

"He was caught in an ambush last year—at the same time you and I were in France—and he was tortured. His foot was—well, he had to have it amputated when he came home. I think he could still find fulfilling work, but he is a little bitter that he would be deskbound."

"I can imagine."

The low dinner gong sounded, and Jo groaned.

Elliot pulled her close and kissed her thoroughly. "We have to go in," he murmured when he finally released her.

"I know."

"It's only for a little while, Jo," he said, running his knuckles over her jaw. "Once the Season is over, you will find life in the country far less . . . structured. Your family's property, Briarly, is among the most beautiful in England. You will love it there."

Jo nodded and forced a smile. She could well believe that, but she also knew that their false betrothal agreement would end when the Season was over. Her home in the country might be lovely, but Elliot would not be there with her.

Chapter 23

Three interminable, Elliot-less weeks later Jo was lying in her enormous four-poster bed staring at the early morning sunlight glinting through a gap in the drapes, trying to drum up the energy to get up and go about her day. Thanks to a late night at one of the dullest dinner and card parties in the history of Britain, she hadn't returned home until almost two in the morning. It was already six-thirty—a good hour and a half past the time she usually woke up—and her head was heavy and fuzzy after less than four hours sleep.

Rather than leap out of bed, which was normally her way, Jo took a few extra minutes to laze in the warm, soft sheets. The Castleford ball was tonight, which would make today a very, very long day. It would be the only ball that she would attend this Season, as she'd denied Edi the right to throw a welcoming ball for her.

"Next year, Cousin Edi," she'd said—more than a few times—needing to dig deep to keep her tone pleasant.

Edi had finally accepted her decree, but Jo knew the older woman would try to force her to attend more than one function per day for the remaining weeks of the Season.

The only good thing about the ball tonight was that Elliot was *finally* returning today, and would meet her there.

Jo had hoped that life would slow down after her wretched dinner with the Prince of Wales—and forty of his closest cronies, but her cousin Edith was determined to squeeze every drop out of the Season—and Jo in the process.

Meeting the Regent hadn't been as awful as she'd feared. Elliot had been right when he'd said that Jo wouldn't be expected to speak much. There had been so many other people in attendance—all of them clamoring for the prince's attention—that all she'd had to do was nod, smile, and try not to eat with the wrong fork or inadvertently insult anyone.

"Just ask your dinner companions about themselves," Elliot had advised. "If there is one thing you can be certain of, it's that people adore talking about their favorite subject."

Those had been his words of wisdom the last time they'd had a chance to talk—which had been almost three weeks ago, thanks to the extension of his trip to Paris.

Three. Long. Weeks.

Life had lost its luster without the prospect of seeing Elliot regularly—even if it was only getting to look at him across a dinner table. Thankfully, they'd at least been able to exchange letters.

As much as it had horrified her cousin Edi, Elliot had shattered the prohibition that prevented men and women who were not married—or at least publicly betrothed—from sending letters when he'd addressed one to *Angus Brown*.

Amused and relieved, Jo had written back under the same name. She'd challenged her cousin to find an etiquette rule that forbade a person writing to somebody else's pet bird.

His letter had sounded so much like him that it had made her love him even more. Indeed, she'd longed for him with a physical yearning, and that soul-deep ache—as if she were missing a limb—had forced Jo to accept the truth: she did not want to live without him. Even spending part of the year enduring a Season would be bearable if she could have Elliot beside her in bed every night.

Jo had toyed with the idea of writing him and telling him that she'd accepted his *real* offer of marriage. After all, she was a coward when it came to emotional declarations, and that would have spared her an uncomfortable time. But even Jo knew that to admit her love and desire for him via letter would be ill done of her. Elliot deserved a face-to-face declaration of love and acceptance of his suit.

Just settling the matter in her mind had made the last week easier to bear.

As far as Jo was concerned, the sooner she and Elliot married, the sooner she could end the farcical thinking her cousin Edith clung to: that Jo would meet and marry some titled, wealthy scion and cast Elliot aside to climb the social ladder.

Tolerating *ton* society would be far less stressful with Elliot at her side. She'd acquitted herself with the Regent, and her political responsibilities had been taken care of, so she could leave London and spend the rest of the year at Briarly with a clear conscience, no matter how much Edi might want her to accept house party invitations or go to Brighton.

Tap, tap, tap. Quork, quork.

Jo smiled at the familiar morning sound, already pushing back the covers and swinging her legs to the floor. "I'm coming, Angus."

Quork, quork.

"I know, I know," she muttered, shoving her feet into her slippers before heading toward the window, where she'd set up his perch. It looked over the square, which her cousin Edi hated because people could see the raven come and go, but Angus enjoyed watching the activity.

Jo gave him a quick pet and a kiss on the head and then lifted the sash. She watched him for a moment, and smiled when she saw that he was headed in the direction of Hyde Park. She shut the window most of the way, leaving it open enough that he could come inside if he returned while she wasn't in the room.

Jo yawned and considered her options. She could get dressed and try to sneak in an early morning walk without a servant, or she could go back to bed and sleep for a few more hours.

The bed beckoned.

She took a step and then almost turned her ankle on something that made a loud *crunch* beneath her slipper. Jo squinted down at what she'd crushed.

"Oh, no," she murmured, dropping to her haunches to pick up Angus's bone, which now had a long crack down the length of it.

Jo carried the bone to the window and held it up to the light to inspect the damage. That's when she saw the carving was hollow. She peeled back a long splinter of wood and exposed something that looked like parchment.

Heart suddenly pounding, Jo fetched one of her smaller knives from the reticule she'd been carrying last night and used it to carefully spread the cracked wood and remove the parchment.

What came out were seven sheets of almost translucent paper filled with row after row of numbers, separated by commas.

Jo swallowed, her hands shaking as she spread the delicate pages out on the secretaire. She was no code expert, but it didn't take a lot of knowledge to guess what these sheets were: here was the key to the poetry books Mungo had toted about with him for decades.

She released the breath she'd not been aware she was holding and stared at the pages, some of which looked older than others, more yellowed. If this was what Mungo had been about to take to the Home Office, then why had he waited so long? He'd carved this bone while they were still in France—perhaps as much as a year before they'd returned to England. He would have sealed the papers inside it then, wouldn't he?

He must have learned something that day when he'd spoken to Elliot's former boss—or, more likely, he'd learned something *before* their meeting, which had convinced him to seek the man out.

That had been the most surprising discovery: that Mungo would have voluntarily approached any government official when he'd spent so much of his life avoiding such contact.

Jo picked up the bone and examined it more closely. That's when she saw the wood hadn't been glued together lengthwise, as she'd originally believed; the joint was in the middle. Despite the damage, it took only a little fiddling to open the carving as it was meant to open. Mungo had carved a set of grooves into each side that formed a lock when they were pushed together and turned in opposite directions. It hadn't been sealed at all; he could have opened it at any time and inserted the papers. Or made changes or added new papers.

She sat back in her chair, her mind racing. What in the world had he discovered to make him approach Elliot's old boss, Wardlow?

Her lips curved into a smile when she imagined Elliot's reaction to her discovery.

Jo turned over the papers consideringly. By themselves, they told her nothing. It would be much better to present him with some actual information.

An idea formed in her head—an *exciting* idea.

Elliot had said Daniel Morrison lived just off the North Road in a cottage not far from the Three Brothers posting inn.

That was before Edgware, so less than ten miles from London.

Jo glanced at the clock. It wasn't yet seven; she had plenty of time to go and come back, but not in a carriage. She'd need to rent a hack, and she'd need to dress in breeches, neither of which she could do from home—at least not without drawing attention from Edi and creating a fuss.

She'd go to the Fayre and leave from there. That way, she could tell Helen where she was going, as well.

After a little bit of trickery with her maid—whom Jo refused to take with her to visit the Fayre on the grounds that she would be there all day long, packing up the belongings she'd left with her ex-employer—Jo was mounted on a decent hack from the livery down the street and already riding through Clerkenwell by ten o'clock.

Angus was delighted to be on the road again and was dipping and diving and generally behaving like a newly fledged raven on his first flight. It had rained last night, but it mustn't have been much, because while the dust had been dampened, the road wasn't miserable and mucky. It was, in short, a lovely day for a ride in the country.

Jo felt a little bit like a new fledgling, herself. It had been ages—

not since last year in France—since she'd worn her ratty old clothing. She would have been on the road earlier if she'd not enlisted Helen's help and copied the contents of the six sheets of paper onto other pieces of parchment as a precaution.

The other woman had helped her with the transcription process without asking even one question. Perhaps the saddest part of Jo's new life was the fact that she would not get to operate the Fayre with her new friend. Helen Carter was an interesting woman who'd left behind her life as one of the wealthiest heiresses in Britain to work as a governess-cum-circus-manager, and she seemed to love her new existence, even though she had a great many concerns and responsibilities.

Jo had told Helen that she was going to visit a mutual acquaintance of hers and Elliot's but hadn't mentioned Morrison by name.

Although she knew she was probably being unduly cautious, she didn't want to give the other woman any information that might put her in danger. Jo tried to behave the way Mungo would have done. She didn't really believe that anyone was following her—other than Sir Stanley's pitiful spies, whom she'd easily lost that morning by leaving through the Fayre's alley door rather than through Helen's house—or that she was in danger.

If there really had been a traitor in the Home Office during the Colonial War, that had been over three decades ago. Her father was dead; Mungo was dead; it was just as likely that this spy—whoever he was—was dead, also.

But she had exercised caution, regardless of her skepticism. If anything were to happen to her today, Elliot would have the information from Angus's toy bone and he would also know where she was going and why.

The lightness in her chest slowly turned into excitement the closer she got to Daniel Morrison's house. If he could decode those books, and if the truth was somewhere in them, that would mean her father and Mungo weren't only innocent, but they'd been heroes for trying to catch the traitor who'd sold Britain's secrets. She could marry Elliot guilt-free. Because even though Jo was now wealthy and titled, she'd spent enough time among the *ton* to know that the taint of her father's past was certainly still tarnishing her family name. She'd received the cut direct from a surprising number of people, considering all the invitations she and her cousins received.

Jo could scarcely believe it when she saw the Three Brothers Inn sign just ahead.

"The hour and a half fled far too quickly, didn't it, Angus?"

The raven, who'd looped back when she'd slowed her horse, *quork*ed his agreement.

She turned onto the first road after the busy posting house and rode for perhaps half a mile before she encountered a small cottage with an uninteresting, but meticulously maintained front yard. Although the curtains in the front of the cottage were all drawn, there was smoke coming from the chimney.

Jo guided her horse around a sizeable mud puddle before dismounting. She tethered her mount at the decorative cast-iron post and made her way down the narrow gravel path that led to the front door.

She knocked on the handsome, freshly painted front door and waited. And then knocked again after a few minutes.

When nobody answered, she pushed her way between the huge box hedge that fronted the cottage and peered through a narrow gap between the curtains. The house was tiny—probably no more than two rooms—and with the curtains closed, it was as dark as a cave inside.

Jo squinted through the gloom, which was lit only by the glow of the hearth in the larger room, which served as a combination living room and kitchen.

Something caught her attention—something on the floor not far from what must be the back door.

Jo pressed her face against the glass; were those . . . legs?

She pounded on the window, but nothing moved.

Jo struggled out of the box hedge and hurried around the side of the house. The garden in back was as neat and tidy as the front and showed signs of recent tending; a small three-legged stool, bucket of weeds, and leather work gloves were scattered at the end of a row of healthy-looking vegetable marrows.

Somebody was obviously inside. She knew the man had been badly wounded—he'd lost a foot or part of one leg—was he lying in there hurt?

Angus landed on her shoulder.

"What say you? Shall I bull my way inside?" she muttered to the raven as she strode toward the door. "I want you to stay outside, boy. Wait for me."

Angus understood the word *wait* and he flew off and perched on the eave over the door. There were no windows on the back of the house, and Jo stood to the side as she tried the handle; having shot somebody through a door once in the past, she knew better than to take any risks.

The door wasn't locked and swung in with an unnerving creaking sound.

"Mr. Morrison?" Jo called out, peering around the frame. The first thing she saw was his head and torso. Despite the urge to rush in, she entered the house carefully, examining the few places a person might hide. After assuring herself that there were no cupboards big enough to conceal a human in any of the rooms, Jo went to the prone body and dropped to her haunches. The man was youngish—in his mid-thirties—and had short blond hair that was matted with blood at the temple, his fair skin already bruising.

Jo felt for a pulse and let out a sigh of relief. He was alive, and his heartbeat was steady and strong. She pushed up to her feet and quickly investigated the three rooms that comprised the small house more closely. The narrow bed had been turned over, the mattress torn open; drawers had been pulled out, their contents scattered.

A low whistling sound grew louder, and Jo turned, dread heavy in her belly. The kettle that was hanging from the tripod in the hearth was boiling, steam jetting from the spout.

It hadn't been doing that when she entered.

Which meant whoever had clubbed Morrison must still be—

Kraa! Kraa!

A shadow fell over the room even as Jo spun toward the back door. A huge man stood in the opening, the sun behind him throwing his face into darkness. He held a truncheon in one massive paw and a coil of rope in the other.

"Come nice like, missy, and you won't get 'urt," he said. "I'm just to take you to talk to—"

Her first knife hit him in the thigh, and Jo knew immediately that she should have aimed for his head, because he merely glanced down at the two-inch blade in his leg as if it were an annoying insect.

He shook his head and pulled out the knife, chuckling. "Now what did you 'ave to do that for?" He dropped the knife with a clatter and lumbered toward her.

Outside, Angus's cries increased in frequency and volume, and Jo didn't hesitate to draw her largest blade, the four-incher, which she aimed for his throat.

The man might be huge, but he was sluggish and slow to duck; the knife struck its target dead on, and the giant made a choking sound and reached for the knife handle.

"You'll live longer if you leave it in," Jo advised.

Not a lot longer, but at this point in his life, she imagined every second was precious.

He ignored her advice and yanked the blade out. Blood spurted from the artery like a geyser. "Bloody 'ell," he croaked, reaching up to his throat and then examining the blood that covered his hand. "I'm dyin'!" He staggered to the side, and the sun illuminated his face for the first time. His small dark eyes were wide with wonder, his heavy jaw sagging open. "I fink—I fink—" He stumbled toward her, and Jo embedded two more knives in his massive form as he came at her, remembering at the last minute that Morrison's body was on the floor behind her as she moved to evade the monster.

Her last two knives were little better than toothpicks and certainly wouldn't stop him if all the others had failed to do so, but Jo threw them anyhow—not that the behemoth noticed.

He backed her up against the front door and lifted his truncheon, his breathing labored and thick. But the club slipped from his big hand and clattered to the floor, and he looked down, perplexed.

Jo took the opportunity to kick him in the knee as hard as she could.

He gave a gurgling scream and tipped to the side like a felled tree. Jo didn't wait to see if he was still alive; instead, she ran for the back door and the sight beyond it: Angus dipping and attacking while a man swung his pistol from side to side, trying to take aim at the flapping bird.

"Angus! Go!" she yelled, but her words were cut off by the deafening *crack* of a pistol and an agonized *kraa!*

"No!" Jo screamed as the raven's large black form fell from the sky in a clumsy tangle of wings, a cloud of feathers raining down after him as his body plummeted into Morrison's vegetable garden.

Fury crackled in her brain, and Jo turned to the man still holding the smoking pistol.

"You *bastard!*" she shouted, her voice breaking with a sob. She'd thrown the last of her knives in the house and hadn't stopped to retrieve them, so she took a running jump and landed on the stunned man— who was far smaller than the giant in the cottage, but still bigger than Jo—and brought them both to the ground with a bone-jarring *thud*.

"You *killed* him! You *killed* him," she shrieked, punching any part of the man she could reach.

Once again, a human shadow fell over them, but this time Jo's head exploded with a blinding flash of light and pain before she could turn.

"Angus," she whispered.

And then darkness claimed her.

Chapter 24

The last nine days were among the most unpleasant in Elliot's memory—today's journey from Dover being the worst of them. As if spending almost three pointless weeks in France wasn't bad enough, the mail coach from Dover had been held up while he'd been fitfully dozing.

It had only been thanks to Elliot and another passenger—both of whom had been armed and had assisted the mail coach outriders—that he'd made it home with his valuables intact. The highwaymen had not been so lucky, and the last he'd seen of the three men was their bodies stretched out beside the road, a silent, gruesome warning to anyone who saw them before the mail coachmen notified the authorities when they reached their destination.

Thanks to their timely, accurate pistol work, the coach was scarcely an hour late.

But it was an hour that he didn't have to waste, and Crisp had to barber Elliot while he bathed to make up for lost time.

The work he'd been sent to do in Paris—interrogate an agent detained by the small, unofficial British delegation in the city—had proved fruitless. He should have been home at least a week ago, but Sir Stanley had sent a messenger asking him to investigate several other matters.

Elliot was beginning to wonder if his new division chief was up to the challenge of running the Secret Office. All three of the matters he'd spent his time on in Paris could have been better handled through official channels. Especially the *agent* he'd questioned, who should have been turned over to the French authorities.

Perhaps there had always been a part of his job that had been frustrating and bureaucratic and he'd only noticed now because he'd missed Jo with a ferocity that left him restless and irritable.

Or maybe he'd just lost his taste for the work, a great deal of which felt more than a little unsavory.

In addition to his pointless tasks, Paris had been bloody chaotic and dangerous. Despite the return of the Bourbon monarch, the capital was suffering badly, still reeling from the effects of Napoleon's return the year before. People were hungry and suffering and crime was rife; Elliot had been held up at knifepoint not once, but twice, during his stay.

Thanks to the fracas on the journey from Dover, he'd arrived too late today to call at Townshend house and knew the ball tonight—surrounded by hundreds of revelers—would not be a place where he and Jo could converse privately.

Quite honestly, Elliot was bloody well on the verge of putting a betrothal announcement in one of the newspapers—staking his claim in a most obnoxious, public way—just so he could *officially* visit Jo at her house without her cousin Edi giving him the evil eye. At least he'd had the foresight to ask Jo to save the supper waltz and a later waltz for him, although he'd not received a response to his second letter. Hopefully, she'd received it, and her reply was just slow in making its way to Paris. He dearly hoped he'd be ensured of a few minutes of her company tonight.

"If I don't, I shall have to kidnap her," he muttered as he finished tying his neckcloth.

"I beg your pardon, sir?" Crisp asked as he returned with Elliot's coat.

"Nothing, I was"—a loud rap on the door interrupted him, and he frowned at his valet. "Am I expecting anyone?"

"No, sir."

"Help me into that and then go see who it is."

After a brief struggle with his tightly tailored tailcoat, Crisp left the room.

Elliot had just slipped on his grandfather's ring—a gift that his grandmother had given twice: once to her beloved husband many decades ago, and then to Elliot upon the old earl's death—and was choosing a cravat pin when Crisp popped back into the room.

"I think you should come right away, sir," his valet said, visibly agitated.

"Who is it?"

"It is Mr. and Mrs. Richard Townshend, sir. And they've come to talk to you about their cousin, Lady Packenham."

"Nothing?" Elliot asked for the third time, even though he knew he was being more than a little obnoxious.

Edith Townshend wrung her hands in a way that he might have found affecting if she'd not snubbed him at every turn for the past weeks. "She left nothing—no message or note. Her maid attempted to accompany her to that place where she used to work, but Josephine dismissed her and said she'd be spending the afternoon packing. When she didn't show up in time to dress for dinner, we sent a footman to inquire after her."

"Whom did he speak to?"

Edith and Richard looked at each other and shrugged. "I'm afraid we don't know," Richard Townshend admitted. "But our servant said the person he spoke to told him that she hadn't been there all day long. That he'd only seen her briefly this morning."

"Is Angus at home?" he asked, without much hope.

"No," Richard said. "That is what made us start to worry. Usually the creature is in and out of her room—via a window—several times a day."

"People have begun to *notice*," Edi added in a censuring tone that made Elliot grit his teeth with annoyance.

"But nobody has seen the animal today—not her maid, who was occupied in Lady Packenham's dressing room, or even down in the kitchen, where she sometimes brings the bird to eat."

If Angus was missing, that meant they'd both gone somewhere.

"Is any of her clothing gone? Her valise?"

Edith shook her head. "No, we thought about that." She pulled a face. "I know she has not been . . . content these past weeks, but surely she'd not simply run off, would she?"

Elliot ignored the question—not because he wanted to punish the worried woman, but because he couldn't bear to consider that possibility himself.

"What should we do?" Richard asked. "We'd hate to go to the authorities. Do you think we should say something to Sir Stanley? He is quite taken with Josephine—perhaps he might help?"

"Here is what we should do," Elliot said. "You and Mrs. Town-shend should attend the ball and make Jo's apologies for missing the affair—say she is home, in bed, sick with an influenza."

The older couple nodded uncertainly.

"I will go to the Fayre and talk to the owner. If Jo went there today, Helen will know about her visit. If I don't get any information there, I will go see Sir Stanley and ask for his help—he will know how critical it is to keep any inquiries discreet."

"And will you let us know what you find?" Richard asked.

"I will send word as soon as I learn anything." Elliot gave them as much reassurance as he could spare and then said, "Now, the sooner I am on my way, the sooner I will have information."

Elliot didn't have to wait long at the ticket box before one of the Fayre employees, a lad-of-all-work named Richie, came to fetch him back to see Helen.

"Did something happen to Jo?" the newest owner of Farnham's

Fantastical Female Fayre demanded the second the boy left them alone in her small business office.

"I don't know," Elliot admitted. He'd thought about how to approach Helen the entire way over. He didn't know the woman very well—she'd come along after Elliot's brief stint as a Fayre employee last year—but he did know that she was calm, level-headed, and practical.

"She was here this morning briefly," Helen said, not needing Elliot to explain—yet another point in her favor. "She gave me a message for you if something should happen."

Elliot's heart leapt—partly in joy, partly with fear. "Yes?"

"She said she was going to see a mutual acquaintance today—that it required her renting a hack so she could be back in time for a ball tonight. I take it she didn't return?"

"No. If she rented a horse, she probably rode astride?"

Helen nodded. "She changed into her disguise while she was here." She gave him a worried smile. "I'll be honest; I didn't even recognize her by the time she was finished."

"Gray hair, clothing that made her look blocky, and thick spectacles?"

"That sums it up."

"And that's all she said—a mutual acquaintance?"

"Yes. She said you'd know whom she meant."

"Did she bring anything with her? A satchel, perhaps?"

"Not that I saw. She told me her entire trip was only about twenty miles and that she should be back by five o'clock at the latest."

The only *mutual acquaintance* they had who lived within that range was Daniel Morrison. Everyone else they knew lived in London right now. Well, except for Guy and Cecile, but they were in France, not on the outskirts of the city.

If she'd gone to see Morrison, that could only mean she'd discovered something new.

Oh, God, Jo. What have you learned?

Helen cleared her throat, and he looked up from his anxious musing. "Yes?"

"She gave me something before she left." Helen found a key on the chatelain she wore and opened a drawer in the desk. She glanced up at him and pulled the drawer all the way out. "It's got a false side," she explained, pushing the side of the drawer to expose a narrow hiding spot. She pulled out several tightly folded sheets of paper and handed them to him. "Perhaps this might explain what she was doing?"

His fingers trembled as he unfolded the sheets.

Elliot recognized what this must be immediately. "Good God," he muttered, looking up. "Did she say where she found these?"

Helen shook her head. "She just asked me to copy them while she got ready to leave. She took the originals with her."

Where the devil had she found them?

"Is she in danger, Mr. Wingate?"

Elliot shook himself and met the woman's concerned gaze. "I don't know," he answered honestly. "But I'm going to find out."

"Is there anything I can do?"

Elliot smiled. "Actually, there are several favors I must ask."

"Please, I'd love to help."

"Could I trouble you for a piece of paper and something to write with? I need to send two messages before I leave."

Elliot knew he was riding recklessly, and on a night when there was scarcely a quarter of a moon, but it was either risk his neck riding *ventre à terre* or lose his mind riding slowly.

By the time he reached Daniel Morrison's secluded cottage, it was just past eleven o'clock. Rather than go racing in, he left his mount at The Three Brothers and jogged the half mile to Morrison's.

There was a light burning inside the cottage but no horses tethered at the hitching post, indicating the man didn't have any visitors.

Elliot had asked at the inn if a man wearing Jo's disguise had left a mount earlier in the day, but the stable lad and ostlers hadn't seen anyone matching her description.

Elliot had his miniature lantern with him, a device that had multiple shields of varying opacity. He allowed himself just enough light to confirm that Jo had been there—he recognized her boot tread as the same pair she'd worn in France. There were other prints, as well—both human and horse—and it looked as if at least two other people had been there at some point since the last rain. He didn't see any sign of a scuffle in the prints, but that didn't mean there hadn't been one.

He lowered the shields on the lamp and made his way around back. There was only one outbuilding, and it wasn't large enough to hold a horse. A quick check inside the shack exposed nothing sinister, just a rake, shovel, and some other gardening tools. There were no windows on the back of the cottage, so he raised a single shield to allow for a bit more light. He wasn't sure what he hoped to find, but something inside him cried out against simply marching directly up to the house.

A rustling off to his right drew his attention and he turned toward the garden. The last time he'd visited Morrison, the man had been outside tending his vegetables when he'd arrived. Elliot blinked as he recognized the Morrison's garden stool sitting at the end of a row. There were also gloves and hand tools—scattered about in the dirt.

Daniel Morrison was a meticulously tidy man, and the last thing he would do was leave expensive work gloves and tools lying about in the mud and dirt.

Elliot had just turned toward the house again when he heard another rustling noise come from out in the garden. Casting caution aside, he lifted two more shades on the light. "Who's there," he hissed, his pistol in his other hand.

"Elliot!"

He gasped. "Jo!" he shouted, swinging the lamp from side to side and squinting into the darkness.

"Elliot!"

Something rustled among the foliage, and Elliot lowered the light, gaping when he saw a familiar glossy black shape.

"Bloody hell, Angus!" He hastily dimmed the light to its lowest and rushed toward the bird. Even in the near darkness, he saw that there was something wrong with the raven's wing.

Quork, quork.

The bird hopped toward him, dragging the injured wing behind him.

"What happened?" Elliot asked stupidly.

"Elliot!" the bird said in a voice so like Jo's, it made him shiver.

"Shh," he whispered, dropping to his haunches. "Quiet time," he said in a low voice, using the phrase he'd heard Jo use before. He clucked his tongue. "Come here and let me look at you, old chap."

The raven hopped closer, and Elliot lowered the light. "I'm going to look at your wing," he said, feeling like an idiot for speaking to an animal, but Jo always told the raven what she was doing, and the bird seemed to find the sound of his voice soothing. And, thankfully, he didn't snap his beak at Elliot when he reached out and opened his wing.

Elliot sucked in a breath when he saw the ragged feathers. "Well, this must have smarted like the dickens," he murmured. "But it's not as bad as it looks, is it?"

The raven's silence spoke volumes.

The injury was small, at least when it came to the bird's actual flesh, but something had torn out several of the big feathers that were probably necessary for flight, which would explain why the raven was hiding on the ground.

Elliot quickly checked over the rest of the bird, relieved when he didn't find any other injuries. "Alright, old fellow, I guess you can't tell me what I'll find inside that cottage, can you?"

The raven remained silent, and Elliot pushed down the nausea that rose inside him. Jo would never have left her bird injured and alone. A grounded bird was an easy target for predators like stray dogs, and even a house cat could be a menace to Angus in his current state.

"Don't borrow trouble, Elliot," he whispered, and then extended his arm. "Up on my shoulder, boy. Let's find somewhere safe for you to wait."

The raven obligingly climbed up his arm to his shoulder.

Elliot grunted; the bloody bird weighed at least two pounds. How in the world did Jo tolerate such a weight? "I guess she must love you, eh?" he murmured once he'd stood.

Angus gave him a gentle nip on the ear.

"I'll find her," Elliot promised. "Let's get you in a tree to wait."

Once the raven was safe on one of the lower branches of a big yew tree, Elliot extinguished the lamp and set it near the trunk. The last thing he needed to do was rush into the house, drop the lantern, and set the cottage on fire.

"You wait here, Angus. *Stay*," he added.

The raven *quork*ed softly and began to preen himself. Elliot thought that was an excellent sign; if the bird was interested in personal hygiene, how injured could he be?

He'd taken a few steps toward the house when the back door opened, the light from inside spilling out and illuminating the environs enough that if anyone were to look in his direction, they would easily see Elliot standing like a post in the middle of the yard. Fearing that movement might draw their attention more quickly he froze rather than dropping to his knees or stepping back.

"—won't be coming tonight," one of the men said as he stepped outside. "But you'd better wait here in any case, and I'll go back and see what 'is nibs wants us to do next."

"You goin' to that theater?" the man inside asked, his voice clear but his person hidden from Elliot's view. "I reckon one of those circus bitches 'elped her escape us this morning. We ought to go and teach 'em a lesson."

The other man laughed in a way that made the hairs on Elliot's neck stand up. "Yeah, we'll do that—teach 'em some manners. But not until we've got Wingate."

He jolted at the sound of his own name, and something—a

twig—snapped beneath his boot. The man who was outside spun around on his heel, his expression shifting to one of comic surprise when he realized who was standing right in front of him.

"Well, I'll be! Look 'oo we 'ave 'ere!" he said, fumbling for a pistol tucked in his breeches.

Elliot didn't hesitate. He drew his pistol, aimed for the torso, and pulled the trigger.

Chapter 25

Jo woke up with a pounding headache, and it took her a few moments to recall why.

And then her memories flooded back to her: the cottage, an unconscious Daniel Morrison, the two men who'd obviously attacked—

She gasped. "Angus!" The word came out harsh and raspy, as if she'd not spoken for years.

Jo struggled to her feet—or at least she tried to, because she realized that she was tied to the chair where she'd been sleeping.

She blinked to clear her fuzzy vision and glanced around the room. It was a plain bedchamber, something that you might find at a convent—which she'd hidden in once during her years in France.

There was a hearth on one wall, but it was empty and cold, no fireplace tools conveniently hanging on the metal hook that was set in the wall with four nails.

She looked around for something that she might use as a weapon, tugging on the rough rope that bound her wrists and checking for slack.

But whoever had tied her had done a thorough job. And there was nothing but a bed, a second wooden chair—like the one she was sitting in—and a screen that she assumed hid a chamber pot.

Right now the hook—a rough-hewn, cast-iron thing—was

looking like her best option. If it didn't work, then she'd go see if there was a chamber pot and hope it was ceramic so that she could smash it on . . . Jo glanced around for something that would break thick ceramic. Other than the iron hook, there was only the stone hearth, but that would make a great deal of noise.

Well, she could figure that out if and when the time came.

But first things first.

Jo inhaled deeply and exhaled slowly several times, until her head felt clearer. Her feet were tied together, but not to the chair. She smiled and pushed up carefully, then took tiny, shuffling steps toward the hearth. She had to stop twice to rest her shaky legs, but she made it without causing a lot of racket and carefully turned her chair until her back was to the hook.

She bit back a whimper of pain when she raised her arms and realized that somebody must have wrenched her shoulder at some point.

After a few moments of contortion, she had the rope against the metal and began to saw her hands back and forth.

Some rough part of the cast iron was catching on the sisal rope, but the process would be a long one. She was just about to take a rest when she heard heavy footsteps beyond the door.

She only had enough time to lower her hands and push a foot away from the hook before closing her eyes and letting her face go slack.

"Oi! Whatcher doin' over there?" a voice she didn't recognize muttered. Heavy footsteps thumped toward her, and a hand bit into her shoulder and shook her. "Wake up, girlie!"

It was easy for her to play a rudely awakened person with a head injury.

"Wha—" she blurted, blinking and staring up at a wiry, dark-haired man she'd seen several times before—one of the men Sir Stanley had sent to watch her lodgings.

Jo almost laughed as everything became painfully clear.

Instead, she drew her knees up as hard as she could and punched

them into the man's groin as he reached behind her to either check
the rope or do something with her bound hands.

His yelp was loud but muffled by the fact he fell forward into her
lap, his mouth landing on one of her thighs.

Jo scooted the chair back. When the man fell to the floor, moan-
ing and clutching his jewels, she used the rope that held her ankles
together to pin his neck to the floor.

He gagged and choked and thrashed, making so much bloody
noise that if there were anyone else in the—

Jo heard the door open and bang loudly against the wall behind
her. "Here then, what is all this racket?" a familiar, patrician voice
demanded.

Before she could turn around, she heard the sound of a hammer
being cocked and then a low, rumbling chuckle.

"By God, you're a treat, my lady. But why don't you step off
poor Wilmer's neck before he passes out?"

Fifteen minutes later Jo was tied to a different chair, in a different
room.

This time, Sir Stanley had directed his minion to attach her feet
and hands to the wooden arms and legs.

"That should hold you, I hope." The older man didn't put away
his gun or come all the way into the room and sit down until Jo was
fully bound.

Gray smiled at her, his expression avuncular. "You are a great
deal like your father, my dear."

Jo just stared, visualizing what she'd do to him once her hands
were free. Even one hand would be enough to wreak the damage she
had in mind.

He chuckled. "Oh, if looks could kill, I suspect I'd be a bloody
stain on the floor." He cut an unpleasant, condescending smirk at his
associate, who was lingering near the door, red-faced and unhappy
looking. "Much like poor Wilmer was almost a stain. I understand
you even brought down big Jack with your knives." He shook his

head, a marveling expression on his face. "That man once fought off *five* assailants at the same time, and yet he was killed by a mere slip of a girl."

"What do you want from me?"

"What makes you think I want anything?" A smug smile spread across his face. "You've already delivered the keys to the castle to me, so to speak."

Jo ground her teeth, furious that the man was right about her idiocy. "Then why am I here? Why haven't you just killed me?"

His fluffy white eyebrows shot up, his expression that of an amused, indulgent grandpapa. "Are you in such a hurry to die?"

"If it means I won't have to listen to you blather on."

His smile hardened, as did his pale blue eyes. "I'm afraid you'll have to listen to a bit more *blathering*, my dear. Mr. Morrison is busily transcribing the books I have, but I know he doesn't have all of them. It is a shame you didn't bring the other book with you."

"Book?"

Sir Stanley heaved an exasperated sigh. "The other book of *poems.*"

Jo frowned. "What other book? If you've got the volumes that were in Morrison's possession, then you've seen everything I have," she lied.

Gray pinned her with a skeptical glare, as if he could stare the truth out of her. "Do you know what I did for His Majesty's government for eleven of the last forty years, my dear Josephine?"

"You mean other than selling Britain's secrets to her enemies?"

This time there was no mistaking the rancor in his gaze. "I was an interrogator for more than a decade." He smiled thinly. "Trust me when I tell you that I could get answers from a stone. It has been some years, but I daresay it is a skill I could pick up again if need be."

Jo ignored his unsubtle threat. "I hope you were paid well for betraying not only your country, but also your friend."

Gray leaned forward, his hands clenching into fists on his thighs. "You have the hubris of the very young—one would think you would have grown out of it by now, my dear."

"I didn't realize that believing in loyalty to one's country and friends was hubristic."

Gray sneered. "You speak of matters you can never, ever understand. You weren't even born when the Colonists rebelled; you can't have any notion of how that conflict almost tore this country in half. It was father against son and brother against brother. There were tens of thousands who believed as I did: that the colonials were our family, not our serfs. To go to war with them was an atrocity against our very own people."

"Ah, so it was pure altruism, then. You took no money for the information you sold? You betrayed your government for free?"

The ugly red flush that stained his cheeks told her that she'd delivered a hit.

"Some of us were not born with a silver spoon. I grew to boyhood above a butcher's shop, *my lady*, not into the lap of luxury like your father. John could always champion whatever cause he chose because there was a fortune waiting for him to fall back on. Honor is *easy* when that is the case."

"You speak of him with such scorn, Gray, and yet my cousin Richard told me that my father was the reason you went to Harrow and the reason that you moved up so rapidly in the government hierarchy of the country you chose to betray. Without him, you'd *still* be living above that butcher shop."

"And do you think I've been allowed to forget that for more than a minute?" he retorted with more heat than he'd shown before.

"Are you saying my father advocated for you and then held your origins over your head?"

"Not him," Gray admitted, "but everyone else at that bloody school and then afterward in London. Not for one second was I allowed to forget who I was or where I came from. Not once was I allowed inside the inner circle."

"Perhaps they smelled the stench of treason on you, Sir Stanley. Did that ever occur to you?"

He pushed to his feet and stalked toward her. "Long before I chose to pursue my ideals, I was treated like an interloper. I have never married, because the women of my class would be miserable in my world, and yet the women I now associate with have never given me so much as a second look. I will die without issue, without anyone to leave my legacy to."

"Why don't you look on the brighter side of things, Sir Stanley?"

His eyes narrowed suspiciously. "What is that?"

"At least there will be nobody left behind to suffer the ignominy of your name once the truth of your treachery becomes known."

Gray was an old man, and he moved like one. Jo saw his hand coming and could have lessened the impact of the blow, but she relished the pain almost as much as she relished the look of horror that spasmed across his face at his brutal response.

"Good God! I—I cannot believe I did that. I am sorry," he said dazedly, staring at his hand as if he had never seen it before. "Never in my life have I struck a woman."

"I'm sure that *killing* a woman is much more honorable."

His head whipped up, and he stared at her with loathing and disbelief. "You have a viper's tongue for a woman bound to a chair. A *smart* woman would be trying to appease and please her captor."

"Why? Are you saying that you aren't going to kill me? That you will let me go free if I speak the right words?"

"It was actually my plan to send you somewhere nobody would listen to anything you said, my lady."

Jo snorted. "Oh, transportation. And that's not as good as a death sentence for a woman?"

"I'm sure somebody with your skills would always end up surviving."

"My skills will hardly save me from starvation or disease in the hold of a transport ship."

He smirked. "Into every life a little rain must fall, my dear."

"You think my life has been luxurious and easy, *Sir* Stanley? Thanks to your treasonous actions, both my parents' deaths were likely hastened by running from persecution in the wilds of America. My only caretaker for most of my life had to move from place to place like a hunted animal, always looking over his shoulder—running until the very last day of his life for a crime he did. Not. Commit." Jo was so furious she could barely force the last words out. She jerked her arms against her bindings hard enough to make the wooden chair creak, and Gray flinched back and then flushed at his fearful reaction.

"You had better kill me now, Sir Stanley, because if you don't, it will be my life's goal to hunt you down and slowly carve you into small pieces."

His eyes narrowed, and he smiled in a way that chilled her. "You obviously care nothing for your own life, but perhaps you might try cooperating to save your lover's?"

His threat caused a sickening lurch in her belly.

Gray smiled and nodded at whatever he saw on her face. "Yes, I can see you take my meaning. I'd hoped to take the last book without any of this . . . nastiness, but wherever you've hidden it, not even my best men have been able to locate it."

"There is no book. You saw the ones my grandfather sent, and I gave the others that Mungo had to Morrison."

"You are a liar. But I suspect Mr. Wingate will be more cooperative."

As if to punctuate his words, a door slammed, and there was the sound of more than one pair of feet outside the room.

Gray cocked his head. "Ah, here is the gentleman I speak of even now."

The door opened, and Elliot stood in the doorway, his face bruised and bleeding. A hulking man lurked behind him.

Jo wanted to weep.

Instead, she met Elliot's cool gaze and gave him a cocky grin she was not feeling. "Fancy seeing you here."

Elliot smiled back, but his eyes were pure ice. "Did he hurt you, Jo?"

"No. But his minion killed Angus." Jo shot a venomous gaze at Wilmer, who was currently trying to blend into the drapes.

"Angus is fine—he just hurt the tip of—"

"Oh, this is touching," Sir Stanley snapped. "Did he tell you where the book is?" he asked Elliot's captor.

The big man, who was shifting about as nervously as a cat in the rain, nodded. "Aye, I've got the book."

"Well, what are you waiting for, you oaf? Bring him in here and shut the—"

The man shoved Elliot so hard that he came stumbling across the room. Only when he slammed into Sir Stanley and grabbed both the older man's arms did Jo realize Elliot wasn't bound.

"*That* would be a terrible idea," a familiar voice said from the doorway.

The Duke of Staunton stood where Elliot and the huge man had been just seconds before, and he held a pistol aimed at Wilmer, who'd been sidling toward the gun that Sir Stanley had set on the table.

"Hands up," the duke ordered, as he stepped into the room and four extremely large men and one slender man using a crutch filed in behind him.

The last man to enter was one Jo had only seen unconscious. She smiled at Mr. Daniel Morrison. "I'm glad to see you up and about, sir."

Morrison smiled shyly back. "The same for you, my lady. You looked rather the worse for wear on our carriage ride here." He scowled at Sir Stanley. "I'm sorry I couldn't help you then, but I'm afraid my hands were tied until we arrived here, where I've been forced to work at gunpoint by my former employer."

"Just what do you think you are doing?" Sir Stanley protested as Elliot lifted him to his feet and one of the big men—Jo thought they might be some of the duke's footmen—grabbed the older man's arms and pinned them behind his body, holding him easily.

Elliot ignored Gray's question. "Please search him before you tie him up, Phillip," Elliot said to one of the other servants before turning to Jo.

He dropped to his haunches in front of her, shaking his head and making a distinct *tsk, tsk*ing sound. "Couldn't even wait a few hours for me to get home, could you? Had to go rushing headlong into danger all by yourself, didn't you?"

She gave him a sheepish smile. "I wanted to have a nice surprise for you when you returned."

He snorted and tossed aside the rope, massaging her booted ankles. "Oh, I was surprised, alright."

"You've got nothing! No proof," Sir Stanley snarled as Elliot stood and went behind her to untie her wrists.

Morrison smirked and held up the last book of poetry, the one Mungo had written in shortly before his death. "I've only had a chance to glance at the last few pages, but I think there is ample evidence in this volume, sir."

"You said there was nothing!"

Morrison grinned. "I lied. Mungo Brown paid a visit to your predecessor's office, and Wardlow was willing to listen. He was also willing to provide Brown with a list of agents and their various postings during—"

"It's treason to share such information," Sir Stanley shouted.

The room was utterly silent before at least four of the people crowding around Sir Stanley burst out laughing.

"Treason? That's rich coming from you," Elliot said once everyone had stopped. He rubbed Jo's freed wrists and squeezed her hand before coming to stand beside her.

"None of that can be substantiated," Gray insisted. "Most of those people are long dead. Besides, it's all utter drivel. I demand you release me. You have no authority to apprehend me."

"Maybe we won't take you in," Elliot said in a musing tone. "Maybe we'll save His Majesty the cost of housing and prosecuting and executing you." A nasty grin spread across his face as he turned to Jo. "What do you think, my dear?"

"Sounds like an excellent idea to me," Jo said.

Gray sputtered and turned to Staunton. "You're a duke, for God's sake! Are you just going to stand by and let these two lunatics behave like vigilantes?"

Sin ignored him and crossed the room to Jo, holding out his hand. "I thought you might want these."

Jo gasped. "My knives. I'd thought I'd lost them. Wherever did you find them?"

"One of Sir Stanley's men had them." Sin chuckled. "I've had them thrown at my head far too often not to recognize them as belonging to you, Jo."

She slid four of the blades into their various sheathes but kept out the two longest knives, spinning them in her palms, almost laughably relieved to have them back in her possession.

"Thank you." Jo sheathed the knife in her left hand and then closed the distance between herself and Sir Stanley. She flicked the tip at his face, the razor-sharp steel leaving a cut so thin that the beads of blood that appeared were mere specks.

Gray yelped, although Jo knew he would hardly have felt the cut.

"That's for slapping me," she said.

Sir Stanley cringed against the man who was restraining him, his eyes darting between the duke and Elliot. "Good God! You're not going to allow her to—"

A familiar, beloved *kaa! kaa!* came from out in the corridor, and a liveried servant entered the room holding a flapping, squawking raven at arm's length.

"Angus!" Jo sheathed her knife, pushed past Gray, and grabbed her bird, hugging him so tightly he squawked, "*Elliot!*"

Jo laughed. "That's right—you know which side your bread is buttered on, don't you, lad?" She released the raven, who scrambled onto her shoulder and then she turned to the man who'd rescued not only her, but her beloved pet. "Thank you," she said, quietly.

Elliot smiled, his love for her shining in his dark blue gaze. "It was my privilege, Jo."

She blinked rapidly and quickly turned away before she started blubbering. Instead, she faced her erstwhile tormentor, her knife seeming to have a mind of its own as it leapt from its sheath into her palm.

Sir Stanley's pale blue eyes flickered from the blade to her face. He sneered. "You might as well kill me now, because nothing in those books will hold up in a court of law."

"Perhaps you are correct," she agreed, an unpleasant smile curving her lips as she dragged the tip of the blade lightly down his jaw.

Jo saw calculation in Gray's eyes and knew it wasn't death he feared the most, but the exposure of his treachery and the public shame.

"But then, perhaps you are wrong." She slid her blade back into her breeches and took a step back. "I'm not going to kill you, Sir Stanley. I suspect it will be much more painful for you to go on living."

Chapter 26

Having the Duke of Staunton in the house meant that the local magistrate couldn't get there quickly enough. The man was also eager to do anything that Sin asked and speedily took Sir Stanley and his henchmen into custody.

"One of the perks of being a duke," Elliot teased a few hours later, as the three of them stood outside and watched the cavalcade of constables and prisoners rumble away down the pitted drive.

As they walked to the house which had been Jo's prison only a few hours before, she said to the duke, "Thank you for sending your man Justin with Sir Stanley. It would be a shame if the old crook managed to take his life and cheat justice."

Sin nodded. "I agree with you when it comes to Sir Stanley requiring close observation. He will not want to face the shame of exposure and will need close watching."

It had taken almost four hours to explain who everyone was and why they were there and to give all the relevant statements to the magistrate. They could have waited for that last part, but Jo had been insistent that the story of Gray's treachery be heard by as many witnesses as possible, just in case he somehow *did* find a way to take his life.

As a result of all their work, the day was rapidly dwindling. "I take it the two of you will ride back with me?" Sin asked as he dropped into a chair in the small sitting room they'd moved to after Gray had been seized. The house was actually quite nice, although the furnishings were on the sparse side.

Jo groaned, and Elliot turned to her. "What is it?"

"I'm not up to facing Edi and Richard right now."

They'd already sent a messenger to assure her cousins that she'd been located and wasn't in any danger. No doubt the older couple would be expecting her to come home soon.

Jo gestured to the house around them. "Can't we just stay here for the rest of the day—and tonight—and go home in the morning? I know there are bedrooms here because the room I woke up in had a bed."

Elliot laughed and then saw she was serious. He glanced around at the clean but spartan parlor and then exchanged glances with Sin, who was watching their interaction with a glint of humor in his gaze.

"What is this place?" Sin asked before Elliot could answer. "It doesn't look like anyone lives here."

"My guess is it is one of the houses the government keeps to, er, question people sometimes."

Sin's lips twisted. "Ah."

"Gray admitted he'd started off as a torturer," Jo said, absently scratching Angus beneath his chin.

Elliot winced. "The correct term is interrogator."

Jo snorted.

Elliot turned to Sin. "If we stayed, would you mind—"

"Making up a believable lie for Jo's cousins?" Sin guessed.

Elliot's face heated. "Er, yes, something like that."

"Of course, I can do that." He looked at Jo. "I'll leave Marcus and Neil with you—just in case there are any unexpected . . . visitors."

"Thank you," Elliot said, pleased the other man had offered the use of his brawny, armed footmen before he had to ask. Elliot didn't think that Sir Stanley was acting in concert with anyone else, but it would be better to be prudent than sorry.

"Shall I have fresh clothing brought to you along with your coach tomorrow?" Sin asked, looking at Jo.

"I suppose I can't wear this home," Jo said, looking down at her grimy breeches. She cut Sin a faint smile. "Yes, I'd like some fresh clothing, please. It's just like old times, with you fetching and carrying for me, Your Grace."

Sin's pale cheeks flushed at Jo's teasing. "Yes, well, as my wife likes to say, even a duke should be of some use."

Elliot laughed. He could just hear Marianne saying that in her tart, deadpan way.

Sin pushed to his feet, hesitated, and then said, "Would it be alright with you if I shared the news with her—that you have proof of your father's innocence?"

"Yes, please do," Jo said.

Once Sin had shut the door behind him, the two of them were alone.

"Don't scold, Elliot," Jo begged as he opened his mouth. "I already know I should have waited for you to return home before riding off to see Morrison, but all is well that ends well, isn't it?"

Elliot fixed her with a stern look but couldn't maintain it for long. "I *should* scold, but if you promise never to fling yourself into danger again?"

"Done," she said with far too cavalier an attitude to be serious. "And thank you for finding Angus for me," she said softly, no longer teasing. "If you hadn't done so, I hate to think of what might have happened to him."

"Well, you don't need to think about that. Did you look at his wing?"

She nodded. "Wilmer shot off his flight feathers, and he's got some bruising in the empty quill sockets, but I don't think it's serious."

"How long will it take for them to grow back?"

"A while," she admitted. "He won't be happy, but he's been flightless before. One year he molted and lost all his flight feathers. Haven't you, boy?" she asked the big raven, who inched closer to her neck and tried to look wounded and pitiful. She chuckled. "He's very good at playing up his injury." Jo stood and walked across the room to the window. "Down, Angus," she said, bending low enough for the bird to hop onto the sill. "You're too heavy today."

The raven made a pathetic *quork*ing sound, and Jo chuckled and opened the window. "No going out. I'll take you in a little while."

Amazingly, the raven seemed content to sit and look out into the fading afternoon.

Jo returned to her chair and sat with a sigh, absently rubbing the shoulder where the bird had been sitting.

Elliot leaned close enough to take her other hand. "You *are* hurt. How did it happen?"

She shrugged, winced, and then said, "I really don't remember. Things happened rather . . . quickly."

"What *did* happen?"

But before she could answer, there was a light tap on the door. "Come in," Elliot called.

Crisp entered, bearing a large tea tray, his sharp gaze already fixed on Jo.

"Oh," Jo said, "I didn't know there was anyone else here. Did you come with His Grace?"

Elliot coughed. "Er, he actually came with me—or *after* me, to be precise. This is Bevil Crisp, who has been with me for years. Crisp, this is the Countess of Packenham."

Crisp laid the tray down without making a sound and then bowed with enough grace to impress a court functionary. "It is a pleasure to meet you, my lady."

Jo smiled and nodded.

"It was Lady Packenham who rescued me in France last year," Elliot explained.

One of the valet's eyebrows rose a fraction of an inch, which was the equivalent of raucous cheering from Crisp. "I am most grateful to you, my lady. Mr. Wingate is an exemplary employer, and I would have hated to lose him."

Jo laughed, and Elliot couldn't help smiling at the other man's dry wit.

"*Elliot.*"

Crisp's head whipped around, and Elliot had the singular pleasure of seeing his unflappable servant flapped for the first time in all the years he'd known the man.

"He seems to be saying your name a lot," Jo observed.

"It's how I knew he was out in Morrison's garden," Elliot said. "I think he now views my name as a magical talisman for getting what he wants." Elliot stood and took a piece of buttered bread from the tray Crisp had brought and offered it to Angus.

As usual, the raven was gentle when he took the food.

"This is Lady Packenham's associate—his name is Angus," Elliot said, smirking at his still-startled servant. "He is quite fond of cheese and apples, if there are any to be had."

"Ah. I was just going to ask what your plans might be, sir. I'm afraid the larder is quite bare. But if we are staying, I passed an inn on the way here. I can procure food for you and—how many others will there be, sir?"

"That would be five of us, including yourself, Crisp. And yes, we'll be staying the rest of the day and leaving tomorrow morning."

"Very good, sir. I shall see to the food and also to the rooms. I took the liberty of exploring the top floor and discovered four chambers, sir. They are modest but surprisingly clean."

"I don't suppose you saw a bathtub in your explorations?" Elliot asked, amused by how Jo perked up at his question.

"Actually, sir, there is a hipbath in the kitchen. I shall ask the two gentlemen His Grace left to help carry it up to the largest chamber."

"Thank you, Crisp."

Once his valet had gone, Elliot gestured to the tea tray. "Shall I?"

"Thank you, I would love some."

"Are you quite alright, Jo? You look wan."

"Just hungry."

"You took a knock on the head; you should probably rest."

"I'll rest after tea," she promised. "And after I've heard your story."

"I thought I was getting yours first."

"Mine is boring. I want to hear yours."

He laughed. "I sincerely doubt that *boring* is the right word for what you've gone through, but your wish is my command," he said, rinsing the pot out with hot water as he collected his thoughts. "I went to see Helen—"

"I knew you would."

He smiled at her smug look. "She told me where you'd gone, and I imposed on her to send messages to Sin and Crisp, telling both of them where I was going and asking Sin to bring reinforcements—"

"Wasn't he at the Castleford ball?"

"He was. I daresay I owe Marianne an apology for stealing her husband for the evening."

"She'll probably be furious that he didn't ask her along."

"Probably. In any event, when I reached Morrison's cottage, I did a bit of sneaking and snooping and knew that you'd been there, as I saw tracks from those"—he pointed at her boots—"all over the place. . . ."

She lifted a foot and glanced fondly at the hideous, rope-bottomed boot. "Rather distinctive. I suppose I shouldn't commit any crimes wearing them."

"No, that's probably not a good idea for several reasons," he agreed wryly, filling a plate with buttered bread and bringing it to her.

"Ah, thank you." She consumed a slice in three bites and then cut him an embarrassed look. "I'm sorry," she said thickly, "but I've not eaten anything since yesterday morning."

Elliot brought another piece to her raven, who was also looking rather, er, ravenous, and then resumed his seat and his story.

"Angus and I had just enjoyed a joyful reunion in Morrison's garden when the back door to the cottage opened and two ruffians came out. I immediately recognized one of them as one of the fellows who'd watched your apartment."

"Had you suspected Gray before then?" she asked.

"No," he admitted. "And I feel like an idiot that it didn't even cross my mind."

"I didn't suspect him, either," she said. "Why would we? The man was supposedly my father's best friend. But do go on with your story."

Elliot swallowed before admitting this next part. "I shot the man, er, fatally," he added, just in case she was in any doubt.

Jo lowered the piece of bread she was holding without taking a bite. "I'm sorry, Elliot. I know you'd managed to avoid that all these years on the Continent."

"Yes, it's a bit ironic that I killed somebody the same day I resigned my position."

"*What?*"

He nodded. "If you were in danger, I knew I'd not be able to adhere to the law, so I scribbled out a rather hasty letter of resignation when I was sending all my other messages in Helen's office." He pulled a face. "It is doubly ironic that the man I sent the letter to ended up being the villain of the piece." He sighed and squarely met her pale gaze. "I'm so sorry that I am the one who brought Gray into your life, Jo. If I'd refused to—"

"He would have found a way to get to me no matter what, Elliot. You know that."

"Still, I hate that I didn't see through him sooner."

"I didn't know either, until I recognized one of his henchman just like you. Gray had us both fooled." Jo shook her head. "What sort of life must he have had with this secret hanging over his head all these years?"

"A miserable one. He never married or had children and has given his entire life to his job." He paused and then added, "Although I have no proof, I'd wager that he's been fairly honorable in just about every other way."

"He thinks selling those secrets to the rebels *was honorable*—or at least that is what he claims—and has no remorse for pinning the blame on my father."

"That is hard to believe—especially after all your father did for him. As for believing that what he did was just, well, he wouldn't have been the only one in the government or military to have felt that way at the time. But the fact that he could sacrifice two men to pay for his own sins is unforgivable."

"Do you think there is enough evidence to convict him?"

"Morrison certainly looked convinced by what he had already and he'd barely started decoding the one book."

"Gray sounded just as convinced that there *wasn't* enough," she pointed out.

"I'm not sure how much of that was genuine and how much was bluster." He gave her a smile he hoped was reassuring. "Let's wait until Morrison has finished all the transcription before we jump to any conclusions."

Jo nodded, but he could see she was impatient and couldn't blame her. She had waited decades for evidence of Mungo's innocence.

They'd sent the code breaker back home with the magistrate, who'd agreed to post several guards outside his cottage while he finished his work. Sir Stanley might be in custody, but they couldn't be sure whether he'd worked alone all those years ago or how long his reach might be.

"Go on with your story," Jo said.

Elliot poured out their tea and said, "After I shot the man, the second one, Mick—despite being large and intimidating-looking—surrendered himself and seemed to collapse. He confessed to me that he'd been charged with desertion and Gray had pulled him out of the brig and offered him a way out of jail. He was supposed to leave England and disappear after he'd completed this job, but Mick isn't a complete idiot and had begun to realize—after seeing how several other people had *disappeared*—that the only place he'd be *disappearing* was in a shallow grave."

Elliot handed Jo her cup of black tea and doctored his own cup with sugar, but no milk, as there wasn't any.

He took a sip of the scalding liquid and sighed happily. "Mick was more than willing to tell me what his orders were and give me the location of where Gray was holding you. Sin, along with Crisp, his servant cavalcade, and the last of Mungo's notebooks, arrived shortly after my confrontation with Gray's men. We decided to be cautious when we approached the house to free you, because we didn't know how many other men Gray might have." He stopped and shrugged. "And the rest you already know. Now it's your turn; tell me your story."

It took far less time to tell Jo's tale.

"Was the man I killed still in Morrison's house when you arrived?" she asked Elliot once she'd finished.

"No, the men had done a half-hearted cleaning job, and I didn't ask where they'd put the dead man. Apparently, they'd removed your knives from the corpse and divided them up between them."

Jo scowled. "Vultures."

"Can't blame them for recognizing quality."

Jo snorted. "I suppose not." She finished the rest of her tea, set down her cup and saucer, and then stretched and yawned, wincing at the various aches and pains.

"What you need," Elliot said, "is a hot bath and some rest."

"Yes, please."

"What order would you like them?"

She would have liked to bathe first, but Crisp had scarcely been gone three-quarters of an hour. And also, there was Angus, who doubtless wanted to go outside for a bit.

"Angus needs to—"

"Hush," Elliot murmured. "I'll take Angus out for some exercise—you just concentrate on yourself. Bath or rest?"

"I'll take a nap first."

Elliot came to her and offered his hand.

Jo took it and stood with a groan.

"Poor darling," he murmured, slipping his hands around her waist. "Did you get roughed up?"

"I was unconscious, but I suspect they weren't exactly gentle transporting me here." Not to mention she'd wrestled around with Wilmer before being conked on the head. But the last thing she wanted was Elliot fussing over her injuries. They only had tonight together before she'd be back in the house on Berkeley Square and under strict surveillance. Jo intended to make excellent use of their limited time.

"Before I let you go rest, I wanted to tell you how much I missed you." Elliot kissed the tip of her nose. "A great deal."

"I missed you, too," she said, wondering why it was so difficult to speak the affectionate words when her heart was full of love for him.

But he seemed pleased by that tepid declaration and, after giving her another entirely too chaste kiss, he took her hand and led her to the door. "You go up and settle, and I'll find Crisp and arrange for your bath. How about three hours?"

"I think that will be plenty of time to rest."

He turned to go, and Jo caught his arm. "Yes?" he asked, his eyebrows raised.

"I meant what I said earlier—about rescuing me. Thank you."

He looked surprised. "Of course, Jo." He gave a slightly self-conscious laugh. "Besides, I think I'm still a rescue or two in your debt after France."

Jo shook her head, holding his gaze and willing him to see what was in her heart—to know the truth of what she felt but could not find the words to say. "Not just for saving me from Gray, but for . . . changing my life. For believing I was worth the effort of persevering. I—I love you, Elliot. A great deal."

His lips parted, and she heard him draw in a breath, but he didn't speak.

She clumsily kissed him and opened the door before he could do

it for her, her vision becoming blurry as she glanced to and fro, looking for the stairs Crisp had mentioned.

As she hurried to her room, Jo cursed her unusually emotional
state, and dashed the tears from her cheeks with the back of her hand.
No doubt she'd feel much calmer after some rest.

Yes, that was all she needed: rest.

Chapter 27

Thanks to the inestimable Crisp and Sin's strapping footmen, Elliot was reclining in steamy luxury beside the kitchen hearth a few hours after Jo had gone up to rest.

He had not been idle while he waited.

In addition to taking Angus out for an airing, he'd composed several urgent messages that he'd sent to his former employer in the Secret Office, Sir Wardlow; an extended message to his eldest brother, the earl; and a far briefer, and more circumspect, letter to his grandmother, assuring her that he'd be visiting her within the next few days.

Crisp had been busy, as well. Savory smells drifted from the hearth, and two fresh loaves of bread were cooling on the kitchen table. Elliot was sipping a delightful claret, and there were two other bottles to accompany dinner, not to mention fresh flowers miraculously appearing here and there.

Sin had sent one of his servants haring back from London with a large valise of clothing for Jo, and a bottle of his prized whiskey.

Indeed, he'd sent so much clothing that one would have thought he and Jo were spending a week at the former interrogation house, rather than one brief night.

Elliot soaped up the cloth, washed his feet, and contemplated the evening ahead.

Tonight wasn't the right time to press his suit with her. Now that her family's reputation wasn't just likely to be cleared, but her father declared a national hero for all that he had suffered, she would have an entirely different perspective on life among the *ton*. Elliot had seen the way some people had held her and her cousins at arm's length now and knew how much of a toll it had taken to be thought of as a traitor's daughter. Now that she no longer had such opprobrium hanging over her head, she would be mobbed by prospective suitors.

It wouldn't be fair of him to pressure her. Especially as he wasn't even employed any longer. Not that his modest income would mean anything to a woman as wealthy as Jo.

"More hot water, sir?"

He looked up from his foot to see Crisp waiting with a large can of steaming water.

When he hesitated, Crisp pointed to a narrow groove that ran down the center of the kitchen floor. "If you are worried about making a mess for me to clean up, you needn't. The excess water will drain."

The door to the kitchen opened, and Jo—wearing only her breeches, stockings, and a loose linen shirt—stood in the doorway.

Elliot hastily sat up, sloshing water over the side. "You're up," he said stupidly.

She gave him a slow, sensual smile, her lids lowering over her eyes. "I am. I came to see if you were . . . up, as well."

He gave a choked laugh and immediately glanced at Crisp. His proper valet had twin red flags flying over his narrow cheeks and was staring at the far wall, clearly wondering what his next move should be.

He needn't have bothered.

Jo strode toward him, her hand out. "I'll finish bathing Mr. Wingate."

Crisp cleared his throat, cut a desperate glance at Elliot—who nodded—and then handed Jo the can. "There is more heating on the hearth," he murmured. "If you will excuse me, my lady, sir."

"I think you've shocked my valet," Elliot said when the other man fled.

"Was that bad of me?" she asked, not looking too concerned.

"Probably, but I'd much rather you bathe me than Crisp."

Her eyebrows shot up. "You require assistance, do you?"

"I'm quite . . . dirty. Filthy, actually." Elliot set his hands—which he'd laid over his rapidly swelling cock—on the edge of the tub.

Jo's gaze dropped immediately to his bobbing prick, and the heat that flared in her darkening gaze caused his bollocks to turn to stone. "What's that you have there?" she taunted, pouring the contents of her canister into the tub, taking care not to scald him.

Elliot looked down at his rigid shaft. "What? This old thing?" he asked, sliding a hand around it.

Jo grunted, the low, animal sound making him even harder. "Just how old is your . . . thing?" She gave a surprised snort of laughter and lifted her gaze from his cock to meet his eyes. "How is it that I don't know how old you are?"

"Perhaps because you never asked?" He gave her an arch look. "I will be five-and-thirty on my next birthday."

"And when is that?"

"February twenty-second."

"Hmm," she said, her gaze once again lowering to where his hand was lightly stroking. Her pupils flared, black swallowing gray. "That is lovely," she said in a hoarse voice. "Will you make yourself come for me, Elliot?"

Elliot swore the room tilted and spun at her erotic request. "You—" His voice broke, he cleared his throat, and tried again, "You want me to, erm, pleasure myself?"

She nodded slowly, her eyes locking with his as she hooked her foot around the leg of the milking stool he'd been using to hold his towel, and dragged it closer. She tossed the towel aside and plopped down. "Yes, please."

He knew his face would be flaming. Although he'd had numerous lovers, not one of them had ever asked to view such a private, shameful act.

"Please," she repeated when he hesitated.

Elliot nodded. "As you wish." He spread his thighs and slid a bit lower, an action that exposed more of his legs above the water. "Touch me, Jo."

She slid a hand into the water without hesitation, her expression rapt as she gazed from his cock to his face and back, her rough, strong hands rubbing up one thigh, the tips of her fingers brushing his tight sac.

He groaned, and his eyelids fluttered at the rare sensual pleasure of feeling another's touch on such a private part of his body. "Yes . . . just like that." Elliot's initial reticence drained away with each slow pump of his fist and the heat in Jo's hungry gaze.

If Jo had ever seen a more erotic sight than her normally reserved lover shedding his inhibitions and performing for her pleasure, she could not recall it.

He was not only a beautiful man, but he possessed the sorts of skills she respected and admired: toughness, resilience, and a quick, clever mind.

Not to mention a taut, fit body that was hard-muscled in all the right places.

"Make it last," Jo ordered when his hand began to move faster on his shaft—a sight that she was burning into her mind's eye.

He groaned and gave her a pleading look. "It's been weeks since we've been together, darling. I'm lucky I lasted this long. Please, Jo . . ." He pushed out his lower lip in a pouting way that was so adorable she wanted to bite it. "Please," he begged in a voice that was raw with need. "I need release so badly."

His words detonated an explosion of desire in her body, and it took all her self-control not to scramble into the tub, climb on top of him, and ride him until he screamed her name.

Instead, Jo settled for reaching high up his thigh and curling her fingers around the furry pouch pressed tightly against his body. "Come for me, Elliot."

The words weren't even out of her mouth before his back arched and his hips jerked out of the tub. "Jo!" he shouted, pumping himself hard twice more and then spilling over his slick abdomen in thick ribbons, his entire body flexing with the force of his orgasm, until he laughed weakly and sank into the tub.

"Well," he said in a breathless voice, smiling up at her, "there's an activity that has never been so enjoyable before."

Jo sat back from the table and gave a pleasurable sigh. "That was absolutely delicious, Crisp. Thank you so much," she said when the valet came to ask if either of them wanted anything else.

Elliot could tell by the faint tightening around his servant's eyes that he was pleased by Jo's compliment. The man loved to cook and would probably be a chef if he hadn't been so loyal to Elliot all these years.

"It was my pleasure, my lady." He turned to Elliot. "I delivered the bottle from His Grace to the small sitting room off your bed-chamber as you've requested, sir." He hesitated and then added, "I took the liberty of starting a fire, as there is a bit of damp in the room."

"That sounds perfect, Crisp. I shan't need you again tonight."

"Very good, sir. My lady." He bowed and left.

Elliot stood and offered his arm. "I think my valet is already halfway to being in love with you."

"Only halfway?"

He laughed. "You must be losing your touch. Although I don't see how. Did I mention how stunning you look tonight?"

It was Jo's turn to laugh. "Several times, but thank you again." She gestured to the aqua blue ensemble. "I can't believe my maid packed this gown. I somehow suspect Marianne's hand in this choice."

"I suspect *both* Sin and Marianne are engaging in a bit of match-making. And Crisp, as well."

"Hmm," she said, cutting him an arch look. "Do you think their efforts will be successful?"

"The evening has been a delight, thus far."

She blushed faintly at his heated look, the slight pinkness in her cheeks making her even lovelier. He'd not been hyperbolic in his praise; the celestial blue gown made her look like an angel. Somehow, he thought she'd roll her eyes if he told her so.

Elliot opened the door to his chambers and escorted her to the sitting room, where Crisp hadn't just built a fire, but also placed flowers and a colorful throw rug he appeared to have found somewhere. Elliot was both amused by and grateful for the man's blatant attempt to set a scene for seduction.

"How many of these sorts of places are there around London?" Jo asked, settling onto the small love seat in front of the fire.

"You mean houses owned by the government?"

She nodded.

"I don't really know. Dozens? Hundreds, maybe."

"I gather the government seizes properties used in criminal enterprises?"

"For the most part. There are also estates that go to the crown, of course—when a line is extinct." Elliot poured them both a glass and then settled onto the sofa beside her.

"Thank you," she said, and then took a sip and gave him an appreciative look. "This is very good."

"Sin sent it," Elliot pointed out. "He has excellent taste and the funds to indulge it."

She cocked her head at him, her playful expression turning serious. "Are you really finished working for the government?"

He swirled the rich liquid around in his glass. "I am. It was not an impulsive gesture."

"Oh?"

"My grandmother has asked me to come and manage her property. She is fading far too quickly and wishes to leave the estate to me upon her death."

"Ah. You will need to be there a great deal, then?"

"She has an able steward but wishes me to come to know the property as my own."

She nodded, staring pensively at the glass in her hand. "There are some things I need to tell you, Elliot. Things that I feel better about sharing now that you are no longer obliged to report what I say to your superiors."

"I wouldn't have done so, Jo."

"Oh, I know that, but I didn't want to put you in that position. But now . . . well, it is important that you hear them."

Elliot couldn't help feeling a certain amount of dread—especially given what he'd seen in her Home Office file—but she was right: he was no longer required to report anything she told him, at least not by virtue of his employment. Of course, he would always be duty bound to report certain matters as an Englishman, but she didn't need him to tell her that.

"What do you want to tell me?"

"It's about when the Home Office brought me in for questioning back in '14."

"You don't need to tell me anything, Jo. You said you'd not been disloyal to Britain, and I believe you."

"I am grateful for your trust. I would have put your questions to rest sooner, but much of the work Mungo and I did was actually *for* the British government. We were working for Admiral Hastings during the time period your superiors were so curious about. Hastings had told us that he'd disavow that if we ever were questioned."

Elliot couldn't help feeling a bit of relief at her confession. "I can't say I'm surprised," he said, pulling a wry face. "There are those in our government who take almost as much pleasure in hiding secrets from other departments as keeping them from our enemies. Thank you for telling me, Jo. But what I really want to talk about is us. What made you decide to accept me—not that I am not over-bloody-joyed by the news." He kissed her hard, without finesse, a brand more than an act of intimacy. "I was going to kidnap you and carry you off to my cottage if you didn't agree to marry me. I'd made the decision in Paris when I realized I'd go bloody mad if I had to run your cousins' damned gauntlet every time I wanted to see you." He gave her a stern, possessive look that was unfeigned. "And it made me sick with jealousy to think of you driving in the park, walking, picnicking, and waltzing with every eligible male in London."

Jo snorted, rolled her eyes, and kissed him.

It was a slow, sensual, consuming exploration that left him hard and hungry for her.

"You foolish man—don't you know there is nobody I've ever met who can even hold a candle to you?"

Elliot turned his eyes ceilingward and said, "Thank you, Lord. I shall be a better, more virtuous man, henceforth."

"Not *too* virtuous, I hope?"

"When will you marry me?" he demanded, hiking up her skirt and then pulling her over until she straddled his thighs.

"I'm sure Edi will be able to have something planned in three months—four at the—*mmmph!*" She melted in his arms, her mouth opening to his savage, needy tonguing.

Elliot didn't let her come up for air until he was getting a bit dizzy. "You provoking, teasing creature. You will marry me immediately."

"Oh, but I *so* hoped for a large wedding at St. George's with every single last member of the *ton* in atten—*mmph.*"

This time, she laughed when he finally allowed her to breathe. "If that is meant to be a deterrent to willful behavior, I must tell you that it is having the opposite effect." Her expression turned serious. "How soon can we do it—and with as little fuss as possible?"

"I could send a message to Sin tonight, and he can terrify a special license out of his cousin tomorrow and meet us at the church of your choosing."

"Who is Sin's cousin?" she asked in between kisses.

"The Archbishop of Canterbury."

"Hmm," she murmured, nibbling on his jaw and doing disreputable things to his trapped erection with her delightfully fleshy bottom. "He sounds like an important man."

Elliot laughed at her wide-eyed, vapid, ingénue look. "Not really, only the head of the Anglican Church." He caught her plush lower lip between his teeth. "Well, will you marry me tomorrow?"

"Can we do it without telling Edi?"

Elliot snorted. "You are truly a wretch. The poor woman has no children, and if you rob her of this, she will never forgive you."

Jo grumbled and hemmed and hawed, but he could see she would capitulate.

"Fine," she said, pulling off the cravat he'd carefully tied for her only a few hours earlier. "But if she says one thing about Angus acting as my attendant . . ."

Epilogue

Unfortunately, Elliot and Jo did *not* marry the next day.

As eager as the Archbishop of Canterbury was to please his far wealthier cousin, even he could not be induced to issue a special license on the Sabbath.

Being left with no choice but to wait another day, Elliot had pled his case with his wife-to-be.

"Much as I deeply desire to grant your wish for a speedy London wedding with only Sin, Marianne, and Angus in attendance, I know for a fact that my grandmother—of whose eye I am the apple— would never speak to me again if she was not invited to bear witness."

"I take it she cannot be in London in two days?" Jo had asked, without much hope.

"I'm afraid not. I feel I should also mention that I have a rather large family, love."

After a great deal more discussion, Jo was slowly brought to agree that they could not possibly marry any sooner than ten days later. Nor could they marry in London, due to the Dowager Countess of Norriton's inability to travel.

And so they married almost exactly two weeks to the day at the church in the village of Spire, which was the town nearest his grand-mother's house, Foxglove.

After all those concessions, Jo had hoped for one of her own.

But, despite her begging and pleading, Elliot refused to give in.

"I'm sorry, darling, we can't spend the entire two weeks before the wedding at the 'Torture Cottage,' he'd argued, using the name they'd affectionately dubbed their brief hideaway.

Jo had managed to keep him to herself at the Torture Cottage for three days before Elliot had brought in heavy artillery in the form of Marianne, Helen, and yes—even Cecile, who'd returned home early, along with Guy, thanks to a message Elliot had sent to the couple.

"How is it that you always manage to get your way?" Jo had asked at one point.

Elliot had prudently left that question unanswered.

In addition to the dowager Countess of Norriton, all Elliot's brothers and their wives and children, a dozen other relations, Helen, a handful of Fayre employees, Sin, Marianne, Sin's Aunt Julia, Ce-cile, Guy, and their adopted daughter Cat, and—yes, even Richard and Edi—had attended the wedding.

And, of course, Angus—no matter how much her cousin Edi had tried to persuade her otherwise—had joined the festivities, if not as an actual attendant, because that honor had gone to Helen, then as an honored participant.

The raven wasn't yet flying, and so he'd stood on the shoulder of Elliot's best man—Guy—and had provided a moment of comic relief when he'd nipped Guy's ear while he fumbled for the ring.

"It was a good day, wasn't it?" Elliot asked his wife of barely seven hours as they relaxed in the master suite at Foxglove, which Elliot's grandmother had insisted on vacating for Elliot and Jo, no matter how much they'd tried to talk her out of it.

Jo yawned and sprawled on the settee—which probably hadn't been reupholstered since the reign of the first Hanoverian king—looking strangely at home in the old-fashioned chamber.

"It was a wonderful day," she agreed. "And Sir Stanley's confession was the perfect wedding gift."

They'd received word from the Home Office only the day before that the old traitor had agreed to the charges against him to avoid a protracted and very public treason trial.

"He did the wise thing. No doubt he knew the way the wind was blowing from the stories already circulating in the newspapers," Elliot said, handing Jo a glass of wine before settling down beside her. "Will you want to be there for his punishment?"

Jo pulled a face of disgust. "No, watching a public execution holds no allure for me. It is enough that my father and Mungo will be cleared."

Elliot thought there would be a great deal more than that—perhaps even an elevation of her rank, and certainly some monetary compensation—but that was a matter for some other day.

"I couldn't help noticing that Helen and Mr. Morrison have been enjoying each other's company these past few days," Jo said, cutting Elliot a sly smirk.

He chuckled. "Now that you are married, you are going to join the matchmakers?"

"Helen is a lovely person, and while I think she is content as she is, I don't believe she is happy."

"But if she were to marry Morrison, she'd break the tradition."

"What tradition?"

"That of the owners of Farnham's Fantastical Female Fayre discovering that they are peeresses."

Jo laughed. "I've already had this talk with Helen. She is adamant that is the *last* thing she wants. I told her a person doesn't always get a choice."

"Is being a countess really so awful?"

She pursed her lips and then sighed. "It is better with you beside me."

Elliot wondered if he'd ever stop feeling the sudden rush of emotion that struck him when Jo said something like that—something so . . . affectionate. He hoped he never became accustomed to it.

Jo set down her glass and took his free hand in hers. "Your grandmother told me something interesting today at our wedding breakfast."

"Oh?" Elliot was delighted that the two women seemed to get along so well for all that they were so different—or at least, they valued things that were very different.

"She said that she'd given you a list of potential wives—women she'd approved—earlier in the year."

Elliot groaned, that horrid period in his life the last thing he wanted to think about or talk about on his wedding night.

"No—wait," Jo said, squeezing his hand. "I'm only bringing this up because my name wasn't on that list, at least not at the time," she chuckled. "Your grandmother said it would be on there *now*. But what I'm trying to say is that you asked me to marry you knowing that our marriage would be a bar to inheriting Foxglove."

Elliot shrugged. "So?"

"*So*? So you would have given up this delightful estate and would have disappointed your beloved grandmother to marry me! And I didn't even appreciate how much of a sacrifice you were making."

Elliot made an exasperated noise, set his own glass down, and grabbed his brand-new wife by the shoulders. "You don't understand, do you? Not even now. Giving up Foxglove if I could have you wouldn't have been any sort of sacrifice, Jo. If you had married me, we could have gone to live on the Continent and earned our way doing what you and Mungo did, or we could have bought a caravan and started our own circus with just one spectacular knife-throwing act. There are many places to live, and many ways to earn one's crust, darling, but there is only one woman in my three and a half decades whom I've fallen deeply, hopelessly in love with."

"Oh, Elliot." And then his even-keeled, self-possessed lover threw her arms around him and choked back a sob. "That is the nicest thing anyone has ever said to me."

Elliot chuckled, touched by her uncharacteristically emotional reaction. "Well, darling, I hope you like that sort of thing, because I'm going to be saying some variation of it every day for the rest of our—hopefully very long—lives."

Author's Note

I always have a lot of fun researching my books, but this one was extra special because of Angus.

As I sit here writing this note there is a mated pair of ravens strutting around in the yard just outside my office window. Every year a pair arrives in late winter and takes up residence in the three-story tall evergreen in our front yard. In a month there will be one or two huge fledglings tripping over their big feet, taunting my dogs and chickens, and generally learning how to be big ravens. The adolescents will remain until late fall, flying farther and farther afield, until one day they won't return.

The cycle will, hopefully, start again next year, when I will be working on some other book.

Ravens are smart, loyal, and they remember those who do them a kindness. A recent study found they also hold grudges against people or animals who do them wrong. So be good to ravens!

Humans really did almost drive ravens to near extinction during the eighteenth and early nineteenth centuries. England's most famous ravens—those who live at the Tower of London—are late comers and are thought to have been imported during the Victorian Era, although their origin is a matter for debate.

So, where did I come up with the idea for Jo? She is a conflation of two real-life spies, both of whom mainly appear in footnotes in academic works looking at the various intelligence gathering networks during the Napoleonic Era.

The first is a woman named Rose Williams who was an agent for the abbé Ratel, a man who oversaw one network of pro-royalist spies. Ratel provided information to both French royalists and the British government. There are few official references to Rose other than the fact that she sometimes disguised herself as a cabin boy, transported both information and money, and offered her Paris residence as a safe house for other agents.

The second inspiration is Nymphe Roussel de Préville, the twenty-year-old mistress of intelligence agent Pierre Marie Poix. There is even less in the record about Nymphe, only that she was reputed to accompany him on "his adventures" (see https://www.napoleon-eries.org where you can peruse some interesting articles that have distilled much of the scholarly work on the period).

It's a tragedy that so many stories like Rose's have gone untold. I like to think that my character Jo, with her badass self-defense skills and dangerous, nomadic lifestyle does a good job of depicting the bravery of these forgotten women.

One of the fun parts about writing all three books in this series is that the heroines were commoners (or at least they start out that way) which meant they had a degree of freedom that upper class women could never have dreamed of.

Jo has her own apartment and is the mistress of her life, deciding what jobs to take and where to live. I suspect there were women like her—who could find employment based on skills, regardless of any sort of personal recommendations—but I'm guessing there were not many.

Major Townshend and the spy ring in the story are a product of my imagination. That doesn't mean there weren't people whose loyalties were either fluid or suspect. Just consider the tale of Benedict Arnold, whose very name has become synonymous with treason and treachery.

Acknowledgments

Thanks so much to Vanessa Kelly for helping me out when I write myself into a corner. And thanks to Jeffe Kennedy for listening to my whining. Actually, thanks to Vanessa for that, too—not to mention Brantly, George, Linda, and Shirley, all of whom listen to me complaining about plot problems often, and never tell me to shut up, but do their patient best to help me figure things out.

Thanks to my editor, Alicia, for her gentle and kind editing. Thanks also for this awesome title! I beat my brains out for weeks trying to come up with an alliterative title that fit and she scooped me with a single effort.

Thank you, Alicia, for not strangling me when I completely change the story on you. And then do it again. And again. I blame a lot of that on the characters, themselves, but—strangely—nobody ever believes me.

A *huge* thanks, as always, goes to my best friend and heart's companion, Brantly. He listens to me agonize (and yes, whine) suggests plot changes (that I almost always reject) and brings me food when the muse *finally* decides to show up—and then the wretched cow cracks the whip and makes me write late into the night—and he supports me in all these ways with awe-inspiring grace.

Last, but certainly not least, I want to thank those readers who've taken the time and made the effort to reach out to me and tell me how my stories have moved them. Many of the emails I've received have come when I believed *the well was dry*. It's amazing—and heartening—how a kind letter from a stranger can sometimes fill that well until it overflows.

Don't miss any of Minerva Spencer's
Wicked Women of Whitechapel!

Who says a woman can't win in a man's world?

THE BOXING BARONESS

Minerva Spencer

"Spencer gives you all the feels!"
—Sabrina Jeffries

**Of questionable birth, but made for greatness, the Regency-era heroines in Minerva Spencer's thrilling new historical romance series possess both clever minds and unusual skills that enable them to go
head-to-head—and heart to heart—with the best of men, including those of the *ton* . . .**

Magnetic and educated, Marianne Simpson has the manner of a lady and the looks of a lover, not a fighter. Neither of which explains her occupation as a boxer in her uncle's circus, Farnham's Fantastical Female Fayre. Nonetheless, when St. John Powell, the exquisitely handsome Duke of Staunton, begins turning up at her shows, she finds herself dangerously distracted by the powerful peer's mysterious presence. With her safety at stake, Marianne's days in the ring are numbered. But how long can she fight her attraction to the man the *ton* calls Lord Flawless?

St. John Powell doesn't just want Marianne Simpson, he *needs* her . . . to rescue his brother, who is being held for ransom by a treasonous English baron—the man all of Britain knows as the Rake of Rakes. No matter how little Marianne wants to see her duplicitous ex-lover, the man responsible for the humiliating nickname the Boxing Baroness, St. John must convince her. Even if it means climbing into the ring with the beautiful boxer and taking everything she's got . . .

In a man's world, she's a lady boss . . .

THE DUELING DUCHESS
Wicked Women of Whitechapel

Minerva Spencer

"Spencer gives you all the feels!"
—Sabrina Jeffries

Regency-era England may be a man's world, but a lady boss is about to show them how it's done . . .

When Cecile Tremblay lost everyone and everything in the French Revolution, she never imagined that she'd earn her living as a markswoman in a London circus. But Farnham's Fantastical Female Fayre has become her home, her family, and her future. Another thing Cecile never imagined was becoming entangled with the man gossip columns call the Darling of the *Ton*. But mere weeks after her rejection of his insulting carte blanche—and his infuriating engagement to an heiress—Darlington is back, this time to beg Cecile for help. And help him she will, by teaching him about honest work—and the right way to treat a woman.

Gaius Darlington has always led a charmed life. Until now. Suddenly, a long-lost heir has appeared to claim his title, possessions, and property, Not only that, but Guy's fiancée has jilted him to marry the usurper! Yet there is a silver lining: it's no longer Guy's duty to marry an heiress to save the dukedom. He's free to wed the woman he loves—if only he can earn her forgiveness.

They say hell hath no fury like a woman scorned. But fury is just a step away from passion, and Guy knows just how to arouse Cecile's . . .